C000318805

Carol Marinelli recently [...]
for her job title. Thrilled to [...]
her answer, she put 'writer [...]
Carol did for relaxation, and she put down the
truth—'writing'. The third question asked for her
hobbies. Well, not wanting to look obsessed, she
crossed her fingers and answered 'swimming'—
but, given that the chlorine in the pool does
terrible things to her highlights, I'm sure you can
guess the real answer!

USA TODAY bestselling, RITA®-nominated
and critically acclaimed author **Caitlin Crews**
has written more than one hundred books and
counting. She has a Master's and a PhD in English
Literature, thinks everyone should read more
category romance, and is always available to
discuss her beloved alpha heroes. Just ask! She
lives in the Pacific Northwest with her comic
book artist husband, she is always planning her
next trip, and she will never, ever, read all the
books in her 'to-be-read' pile. Thank goodness.

SECRETLY BOUND

CAROL MARINELLI

CAITLIN CREWS

MILLS & BOON

First published in Great Britain 2024
by Mills & Boon, an imprint of HarperCollins*Publishers* Ltd,
1 London Bridge Street, London, SE1 9GF

www.harpercollins.co.uk

HarperCollins*Publishers*, Macken House, 39/40 Mayor Street Upper, Dublin 1, D01 C9W8, Ireland

Secretly Bound © 2024 Harlequin Enterprises ULC.

Bride Under Contract © 2024 Carol Marinelli

Forbidden Royal Vows © 2024 Caitlin Crews

ISBN: 978-0-263-32020-6

08/24

This book contains FSC™ certified paper and other controlled sources to ensure responsible forest management.

For more information visit www.harpercollins.co.uk/green.

Printed and Bound in the UK using 100% Renewable Electricity at CPI Group (UK) Ltd, Croydon, CR0 4YY

BRIDE UNDER CONTRACT

CAROL MARINELLI

MILLS & BOON

PROLOGUE

'I DON'T THINK this is going to work...' Grace Andrews was *not* talking about the faded crimson shorts she held in her hand, nor the washed-out tops that lay spread on her bed.

'They're all going to get ruined anyway.' Her friend and flat-mate Violet peered at the 'essential items' list. 'You can buy new stuff after the jungle...' She paused then, and must have seen the anxiety darting in friend's green eyes. 'You're not talking about the clothes, though, are you?'

As tatty as they were, no.

Grace stood in her dressing gown, her long brown curls wrapped in a towel, her flight just a matter of hours away. There was every reason not to go.

'I should be looking for a new job. It's hardly fair on you, me working from home.'

'It makes no difference to me.' Violet shrugged. 'I'm at the library all day...' She glanced up. 'Though you are working ri-diculous hours.'

'I'm used to working at night,' Grace said.

It wasn't a lie. Data entry might not sound exciting, but it had proved to be a lifeline and meant she'd been able to arrange her hours to suit as her mother's health deteriorated. But, yes, it wasn't the best pay, and certainly it wasn't going to be enough to support her mother long-term.

Grace picked up the backpack she'd been half-heartedly pack-ing and, clearing a space on the bed, took a seat. 'It's not just that.'

Two years ago Grace had booked and paid for a month's vaca-tion to Malaysia, starting with a five-day river trip through the Borneo jungle. It was the most unlikely of locations for Grace, who'd never been further than a school trip to France. Only it wasn't just the sale price that had caught her attention. The stun-ning wildlife, as well as the luxurious river-edge villas, had enticed, but the remoteness of the jungle, along with being off-grid for a little while, had truly appealed.

The purchase had been made prior to her mum's dementia diagnosis. At the time Grace hadn't known what was wrong—just that things had changed with her mother around the time she'd turned nineteen. Eventually things had become so dire that she'd given up teacher training college and moved back home from the flat she had shared with Violet.

The holiday had been something to cling to…

She'd been purchasing hope, Grace now realised. Some sort of assurance that things would surely get better…

Only they hadn't.

Violet had been with her throughout.

They had been friends since infant school. Grace, the new girl at school after her parents' break-up, had hidden shyly behind long dark curls. She'd been in awe of the popular Violet, with her bright sunny nature that matched her golden hair. But one playtime she'd seen Violet being teased about her father being in prison.

Grace had pushed her own awkwardness aside and stepped in. 'Leave her alone!'

'What's it to you?' The lead bully had sneered.

'She's my friend,' Grace had said, taking Violet's hand.

And, apart from one regrettable incident just before her mum had been diagnosed, friends they had remained.

It had been Violet who had held Grace's hand when she'd made the heartbreaking decision to sell the family house and place her mother in a care home. And it was Violet she now shared a flat with once more, and who sat beside her on the bed and did her best to reassure Grace.

'You need this holiday—you've been dealing with this for…'

'Years,' Grace nodded.

She'd never really had time to look back and examine it.

The diagnosis had been hard, but the years prior had been their own separate version of hell.

'Maggie thinks it's a good idea if you don't visit for a while…'

Maggie, the care home's manager, had been firm, telling Grace her month's absence would give her mother the best chance to settle in.

There was a sick feeling in Grace's stomach when she thought of her mother sitting alone in the care home, waiting for her to come.

'I just don't want Mum to think she's been forgotten.'

Grace knew that feeling rather too well.

Looking out of the window…waiting for her dad's car. Running for the post on her birthday… Sometimes there *had* been a car, and he'd taken her to the fair, or to a park, but more often than not he'd failed to show up.

Finally, and without explanation, he'd stopped all contact.

'Look, I know I can't visit her…' Violet's voice trailed off.

Neither she nor Grace wanted to raise the incident that had caused their friendship to waver, when—before her diagnosis—Grace's mum had accused Violet of theft.

To this day Grace regretted her response. For a short while it had been easier to doubt her friend than accept how unwell her mother was.

'Violet…' Grace wanted to apologise properly, but Violet perhaps sensed it, because she hurriedly spoke over her.

'I promise to keep an eye. The care home's just opposite the library… I can check in with the staff… Anyway,' Violet persisted, 'you have to go. There might be some gorgeous…' She paused and gave a little grimace. 'Well, perhaps not a wildlife nerd, but once the jungle part's over and you hit the islands…'

'Believe me, romance isn't on my mind.'

'Who said anything about romance?' Violet nudged her. 'One hot night would do me. It might give me something to dream about while I'm filing the late returns.'

Though Grace laughed, she knew that for all Violet's teasing it was a bit of a front.

They were both wary of men…albeit for different reasons.

Still, lately Violet seemed more ready to shake all that off, whereas Grace felt…

She took a moment, trying to work out how she felt.

Stuck?

No, that didn't quite fit—after all she was going on holiday and her world was opening up again. The years between nineteen and twenty-five had vanished in a blur of struggling to work and care for her mum…

Lost.

It was more than that…

Grace might be sharing a flat with Violet again, but she felt so very different now than she had before.

Adrift.

Yes, that was more how she felt—adrift. As if she'd lost sight of the person she'd once been, while conversely being anchored.

She hadn't told Violet everything—possibly because she didn't want to burden her, or because she just wasn't ready for another person to know the truth. Violet thought things were fine now, but Grace knew the money wasn't going to last and could practically see the overwhelming responsibility to provide looming. Her mother was only in her fifties.

'Don't throw this holiday away,' Violet said gently.

Grace nodded, knowing better than her friend that she might never get another chance—at least not for a very long time.

A little serenity might be required!

For now, her mother was safe.

Violet's pep talk had worked and, with her mind *almost* made up, Grace glanced at the time. 'I'm going to take her in a cake and say goodbye…'

'Are you sure?'

The doubt in her friend's voice told Grace that Violet didn't think it was such a good idea.

'Won't that just confuse her even more?'

'I honestly don't know,' Grace admitted.

What she did know was that even if her mum didn't always understand, for Grace it felt important to tell her mother she loved her and to say goodbye properly.

Her father had never afforded her the same courtesy.

CHAPTER ONE

'THERE'S NOTHING FURTHER to discuss.'

Carter Bennett ended his latest brief relationship in much the same way he would abruptly terminate an unproductive meeting, or simply withdraw from what he considered a stalemate negotiation.

While he might currently be in Manhattan, the laws of the jungle had been coded into his psyche long ago.

Carter knew from bitter experience that in the jungle there were no laws—you made your own.

And now Carter had but one.

He allowed no person or place to get close.

A billionaire nomad, he had offices, properties and investments in several international locations that he moved between. As for friends—while he wouldn't describe them as such—he had a few trusted acquaintances dotted around the globe.

But not women.

There was no proverbial little black book.

Carter never left an ex on tap or on call. Be it a casual fling or a burgeoning relationship, he always severed ties completely and did so now.

'We're done.'

'You're a cold-hearted bastard, Carter.'

'Absolutely, I am,' he willingly responded. 'And that is why I made it exceptionally clear from the start that we were going nowhere.'

He glanced at the glossy magazine on his desk that had a photo of the two of them on the cover.

He couldn't even remember the occasion.

His black hair was freshly cut, but that afforded no clue, given he had it trimmed every couple of weeks. The scar on his fore-head was always visible…the suit was from his preferred London tailor… They were coming out of a theatre—but, again, that was nothing unusual. It was his preferred place to take dates.

Carter was considered a theatre buff. In truth he simply liked taking his dates there, or perhaps to the ballet or the opera. Drinks first, or a pre-performance dinner, then hours—apart from the pesky interval—without conversation.

Followed by sex.

Ironic, really, that the only photo the paparazzi had been able to find to announce their so-called engagement had Carter practically scowling. It was a stretch to say they'd even been dating, let alone about to get engaged.

'From the word go I told you I don't do relationships!' Carter tersely reminded her. 'You were the one who chose to do an interview suggesting otherwise.'

Terminating the call, he tossed the magazine into the trash.

The press on both sides of the Atlantic were having a field-day with the rumours this rather elusive bachelor was *finally* about to settle down.

Never.

Carter knew he was dead on the inside. There was a black void in his soul—one he knew could never be filled. Money, women, a new car, a night at the casino, a new abode…they brought a fleeting reprieve but, like a temporary crown, they were soon tarnished. As for settling down—Carter didn't even know what those words meant. The only thing he settled were deals. The only thing he was married to was his work as an architect.

There was nothing temporary or fleeting about the structures he helped create. They were tangible, permanent…

Lasting.

That the press was circling was nothing new—he'd lived with it all his life. Carter Bennett had been making headlines before he'd even been born into his wealthy and somewhat infamous family.

Gordon Bennett, his English father, had caused a stir in the upper echelons of society when he had called off a very suitable engagement to hurriedly marry a gorgeous and equally well-connected American socialite, Sophie Flores.

Carter being the reason!

The couple had gone on to live a bohemian life—sometimes

bringing Carter along, but more often leaving him with nannies, or his eccentric grandfather in Borneo, until he'd been old enough for boarding school, where he'd thrived. He'd liked the routine, along with the education, and had shared a room with a boy called Sahir, a young prince, whose protection officer had sat outside as the young boys built ever more intricate towers and bridges.

When Carter had turned eight he'd become a big brother. It hadn't curtailed his parents' thirst for adventure and the unconventional. This time around, though, his parents had decided to 'explore as a family', and had pulled Carter from school to join them on their adventures in the jungle surrounding his grandfather's property.

Tragically, he had again become something of a sensation when he'd 'miraculously' survived an incident that had claimed Carter's parents and his baby brother.

Crocodile Attack! That had made for an excellent headline— especially when attached to the Bennett and Flores names!

Only Gordon Bennett's body had been found, and for a full week it had been assumed Sophie and her two children had perished. But just as the story had started to fade from the front pages and screens, Carter had been back in the headlines again.

Carter Bennett Found Alive—more to come!

Details had proved sparse, though, and confusing. Somehow he'd got through infested waters and been found by local Iban people in dense jungle, some considerable distance from the river, barely clinging to life. Help was on its way, reports had said.

For Carter, help had already arrived.

He could recall opening his eyes to see his friend, Arif's father.

'Selamat...' Bashim had said, and gently told him he was safe. He had been able to tell in an instant that the young boy hadn't been attacked by a crocodile—his injuries had occurred in the long, lonely days after.

'Were you trying to find help?' he'd enquired gently.

But Carter had had no energy to answer.

He had a vague recollection of the motion of being carried back to Bashim's longhouse on the river's edge, and the cry of delight from Bashim's son Arif when they'd arrived. Though he'd lain there almost catatonic he had glimpses of that time—the skill and care they'd taken as they tended to his wounds, the love they'd shown to his devastated grandfather. His friend Arif, just eight himself, had held Carter's hands when the dressings on his head and back were being changed or helped him sip water.

'What did you see?' the little boy had asked, but Carter had not answered. 'Why won't he speak?' Arif had asked his papa. 'Why can't he tell us what happened?'

'Give him time,' Bashim would respond. 'He's not ready.'

To this day, those questions remained unanswered.

The empathy shown to him by Arif's family and all the locals had been in stark contrast to what lay ahead—doctors, psychologists, investigators and his remaining family...

The press, curiously deflated that the child's injuries weren't from a crocodile, had turned its focus on what would become of the tragically orphaned boy.

For a while he'd stayed with his late father's British lawyer and his wife.

His English uncle had been in rehab and on his third marriage by then, so not really an option. And Carter's paternal grandfather refused to leave his sprawling property deep in the Borneo jungle—the same untamed land that had claimed Carter's family...

The spotlight had turned to Carter's aunt on his mother's side—a famous New York philanthropist. In truth, she'd spent far more than she'd donated, though she had clearly felt she had to be *seen* to be doing the right thing and had taken him in.

For Carter it had meant yet more nannies, but even that had proved too much for his glitterati aunt. Especially as he'd been a child who suffered with night terrors and on occasion startled the Fifth Avenue household awake!

After a couple of years appearing with her nephew on suitable occasions, with her interest waning, his aunt had shipped Carter off to England, to 'connect' with the other side of his family...

More accurately, he'd been sent back to boarding school.

A few nights of alarming his old friend Sahir's protection officer with his night terrors had quickly forced Carter to become disciplined, even in sleep, and he'd trained himself to wake up until they'd finally faded.

Most of his summers had still been taken in Borneo, though, and he'd come to dread them.

His friendship with Arif had changed. Carter had no longer wanted to go exploring with him. Arif had tried to be patient, but he'd get bored with hanging around his grandfather's luxury property. It was the rest of Wilbur Bennett's land that enthralled Arif—tens of thousands of hectares of undisturbed rainforest, not some manicured gardens and a pool.

As an adult, Carter had continued to visit.

His grandfather, always passionate about the land, had worked with the locals to preserve and monitor the rare wildlife there. Though there were still private wings to the residence, the rest of the property provided a temporary home to visiting animal scientists and researchers, as well as offices. As his grandfather had aged, Arif had increasingly taken over the running of the estate, although Carter had never had any real desire to get involved, and there had frequently been tension between the two men.

Carter had changed at a visceral level, and while Arif seemed to understand that, he refused to accept that Carter no longer wanted his friendship.

He didn't.

Carter did not want to think about losing another person he cared about to the jungle. Arif still took himself out there—not just as a guide, but to head search teams when some tourist got lost or a group went missing…

In truth, on his grandfather's death a year ago, Carter's hope had been to sever all ties to the place that had taken so much from him and still had the ability to take more.

But Wilbur Bennett's last will and testament had attempted to put paid to that.

Carter returned to his drafting desk. These days he used a lot of computer-aided design, but that wasn't going to cut it for this particular client. Crown Prince Sahir of Janana was battling with his father and elders to approve the rebuilding of a destroyed wing of the Janana Palace and had brought Carter on board. The last couple of years had been spent travelling to and from Janana. The work was intricate, even by Carter's exacting standards. Aside from that it was being challenged at every stage by the king and elders who would prefer the ruins were left undisturbed.

He couldn't quite summon his usual focus and paused for a break. Even gazing out at the Chrysler Building or the Empire State Building and admiring their architectural feats didn't work its usual magic.

It wasn't the demise of his latest relationship that was proving a distraction, his mind kept flicking to the Petronas Towers in Kuala Lumpur, and how they'd been the impetus for his chosen career.

Restless, he got up and stood gazing down on Central Park, enjoying the lush green in the middle of Manhattan where he often went for a run.

Perhaps that would clear his head?

But instead, he paced the luxurious penthouse, taking full advantage of the panoramic views. It felt more like a cage than premium office space. He looked towards the Hudson River, noting that it was sparkling and blue today. Unlike many, Carter actually preferred the days when it was brown… Though never as brown as those rivers that split the island as it meandered through the jungle… And the green of Central Park was never quite…

Well, he tried not to compare.

He chose not to compare.

Carter had done all he could to move on with his life.

But then, out of the blue, Arif had called and told him what was occurring.

'*If* you care, then you cannot turn your back.'

Carter had heard the emphasis on *if* and chosen not to address it.

He didn't want to care.

'Mr Bennett?' His PA, Ms Hill, buzzed, reminding him that

Jonathon Holmes, the British lawyer who dealt with Carter's private legal affairs, was scheduled to arrive.

'Let me know when he's here,' Carter said. 'What do I have on after that?'

'An online meeting with Prince Sahir. Do you want me to set things up in the boardroom?'

'No.' Carter glanced at the plans he was working on. 'I'll take it in here.'

Glancing down, he saw that his once crisp white shirt had been marred by a couple of hours at the drawing board, so he went to the private shower and dressing room in his office to change his shirt before the meeting. Stripping off his shirt and washing his inky hands, he paused when he caught sight of his reflection. The scar that ran straight from his hairline was pale now, but it still sliced the jet-black arch of his right eyebrow in two.

Women actually liked it.

'How did that happen?' any date would inevitably ask.

But Carter would brush both the question and the enquiring hand away.

He preferred not to recall that time—and there were only small glimpses—of falling from on high, the metallic taste of iron filling his mouth, how he'd known he had to stem the bleeding...

Carter turned around and, rarely for him, craned his neck to view his back in the mirror. Possibly a little pale from way too many hours spent at the drafting desk by day, though more likely way too many late nights.

There were scars there too—although nothing like the neat gash on his face. On his shoulder and down his back the flesh was pitted, as if hot oil had been poured there. It looked as if he had gone into battle.

With barely a memory of doing it, though.

'Kalajengking,' Bashim had told him—scorpion bites.

As well as that, he'd been found unconscious on a nest of fire ants.

In regard to that fateful day he had no memory of the gory details, and in truth preferred it that way. As for his time spent alone in the jungle…it didn't matter that he could barely recall it. The fact he'd survived should surely be enough.

Women didn't like the scars on his back quite so much, and if they inadvertently touched the scar tissue during sex he'd feel them hastily recoil.

Carter wrapped a long arm around his chest, to his back, and felt the waxy, cold flesh for himself.

No wonder they pulled away.

'Mr Bennett…?' He heard the tap on the bathroom door and Ms Hill calling his name. Thank God for their polite boundaries.

He was dressed in a matter of moments and back to his measured self.

Jonathon Holmes was as stern-faced as ever, and Carter greeted him with a handshake. 'Thanks for coming at short notice.'

'Of course.'

'How's Ruth?'

The usual pleasantries were exchanged, but the moment Carter's PA had closed the office doors he was hit with a question.

'So, are the rumours true?'

'What do you think?' Carter responded drily. 'Of course not.'

'And here I was thinking you were asking me here to draft a water-tight prenup. I'm ready for her…'

'Who?' Carter frowned.

'Whomever Mrs Bennett turns out to be.'

'Never going to happen.' Carter gave a firm shake of his head. 'I am not getting married to appease my late grandfather. What the hell was he thinking?'

His grandfather had done the unthinkable.

Ignoring Carter's cautionary words—that his cousin Benedict could not be trusted—he'd left the house and land to both his grandsons. With one proviso. If Carter married in Sabah, and remained married for a full year, he would have the option to buy his cousin out.

He seemed to have forgotten that Carter did not do sentiment in any way, shape or form, and would not be coerced into marriage.

'I warned him repeatedly that he was making a mistake…'

Carter sighed. He didn't doubt that the cutthroat Jonathon would have wanted every loose end neatly tied.

'Yet he went ahead?'

'He was always his own person.'

'True.'

While for Carter marriage was not an option, neither was he any good at fifty-fifty—especially when it came to his cousin Benedict. He'd offered to buy him out, in order to void the will, yet Benedict had not only declined, he'd put in a counter offer.

'Are you considering accepting?' Jonathon asked. 'It would be one less thing to worry about. You've got enough real estate of your own to deal with. You certainly don't need the headache of this...'

'I've heard from Arif.' He saw Jonathon's slight frown and explained. 'He co-ordinates all the research and rehabilitation projects from the property.'

'Was his father the man who rescued you?'

'Bashim.' Carter nodded, although he did not want to get into all that. 'Arif told me there's been a lot of activity around the property. There are drones going up, aerial shots—'

Jonathon interrupted him. 'Benedict can't sell the property without your consent.'

'Can he lease it out, though?' Carter asked.

'There it starts to get messy, but the short answer is no.'

Carter chose not to wait for the long answer.

'Arif has heard some talk. Apparently, there are discussions underway for the location to be used as a base for a television reality show. There's also talk of a movie...'

Jonathon shook his head. 'Not without your say-so. As well as that, they'd never get permission.'

Jonathon started to launch into how tightly controlled the land was, but Carter was already ahead of him.

'Given my grandfather's standing, the officials might trust that Benedict is doing the right thing.' He told Jonathon what he knew. 'There are location scouts and television executives staying at some of the resorts.' Then Carter told him what he thought. 'I doubt they'd bother going if they didn't think there was a chance...'

'Benedict's probably relying on you backing down. He must know you can't bear—' Jonathon halted. 'Well, that you haven't been back once since the funeral.'

Carter pulled the stopper from a decanter and when Jonathon nodded poured them both a drink. But unlike Jonathon, Carter couldn't sit. He walked across his lavish office and leant his tall frame against the thick glass of the floor-to-ceiling windows, looking towards the East River now.

'If you don't want to spend the next few years fighting through the courts, then maybe it's time to let the place go,' Jonathon suggested. He didn't do sentiment either. 'It's always been a headache...you lost your parents there...'

'And my brother,' Carter reminded him, because in all this the real innocent party tended to be forgotten. 'He should never have been there in the first place.'

'No.'

It was a rare admission from Jonathon, who had handled his parents' affairs before they'd been transferred to Carter. No one had dared to speak out against the Bennetts at the time—it had been far easier to let that little detail slip from the articles.

Slip from people's minds....

His brother's name had been Hugo, though he'd been affectionally known as Ulat. It meant worm, and was a sweet term the locals gave their newborns who, for superstitious reasons weren't named for many months. Carter, when he had been born, had been known as Ulat too.

Still, the hungry international press hadn't bothered to find out about the local ways. It had been easier to file a piece citing his father as a hero for trying to save his gorgeous wife and infant...more lucrative to focus on the miracle of Carter's survival after he'd spent a week alone in the jungle rather than query their questionable parenting choices...

Carter sorely wanted an end to his own private torture, but neither could he turn his back completely. 'Tell Benedict I'm willing to negotiate.'

'You're sure?'

Finally, with a last warning that he was being too generous, Jonathon shook Carter's hand. 'Leave it with me.'

Carter couldn't, though.

It gnawed at Carter's guts. It crept under his skin and interrupted his mind.

His gaze moved down to the busy Manhattan streets below. Yet his mind was still drifting back to Borneo. To the wild untamed rainforests...the hot, humid air that could make New York seem positively mild by comparison. He thought of the Iban people, their longhouses along big stretches of river... And then he thought of production companies, carving up the quiet waters. Sure, there were tourists, but rules were strict and the locals were both protected and protective.

'Ms Hill...' Carter buzzed his PA. 'Can you please reschedule Prince Sahir?'

Carter paused. This change of plan was something he truly didn't want.

'And if you could also clear my schedule for the week and arrange transport to Sabah.'

'When would you—?'

'Now,' Carter interrupted, rolling up the blueprints, deciding he would work on them there.

It had to be now, or very possibly he'd change his mind.

Eighteen flying hours later, Carter was at Kuala Lumpur airport.

He still wore the business suit he'd had on for a brief meeting with a financier in KL, and his tie was still immaculately knotted—albeit a little tight around his tense neck. When he was midway along the roped-off section for first-class passengers, about to board the flight that would take him to Sabah, the sight of a passport on the floor caught his attention.

Carter's first thought was that it was not his problem.

Then his eyes lifted to the potential owner, who lay dozing on an airport bench.

His second thought...

Sleeping Beauty.

No, he mentally corrected, because in the books he had long-ago read to Hugo she'd had raven-black hair and dark red lips. This woman's hair was more a glossy chestnut and her long curls tumbled off the chair...her slender hand was almost touching the floor where the passport lay.

She was, though, deeply asleep.

He went to turn to his security guard, or to Ms Hill, who usually accompanied him on business trips. But very deliberately Carter had left his entourage behind, as he always did when he reluctantly returned to the place where his demons resided. Certainly he did not bring lovers, though God knows at times he would prefer the distraction.

He walked on, saw the air stewards smiling to welcome him. And yet, glancing back, Carter saw that no one had woken her and her passport still lay there.

With an almost irritated hiss at his inability to let it go, he turned around, walked back along the roped-off section and over to the bench where the sleeping woman lay. She wore a dusky pink top and black cargo pants rather well, her slim legs were knees up, her white sneakers resting on a bag.

And, yes, she was beautiful.

Stooping his tall frame, he picked up the dark document and, meticulous by nature, checked she was the owner.

Grace Andrews was twenty-five, had been born in London, and, yes, a brief glance at the photo told Carter that indeed the document belonged to her.

He did not linger on the image long enough to take in the colour of her eyes, instead he snapped it closed.

'Madam.'

She really was deeply asleep.

'Madam,' he repeated.

He was about to move his hand to her shoulder, to rouse her, but her top had slipped, revealing a dark bra strap, and he pulled back, not wanting to alarm her.

'Ms Andrews...'

Still no reaction, so he resorted to her first name. Loudly.

'Grace!'

Green.

As her eyes slowly opened Carter found the unnecessary answer—her eyes were green.

Watching a woman awaken was a rarity for Carter.

Given his decadent history, that might appear to be a contradiction, but usually by the time morning came around Carter was turned the other way, wishing the woman away...

On occasion he was aware of lovers quietly climbing from his bed and slipping into the bathroom for a quick freshen-up. Certainly they weren't in there for extended periods. None of his lovers would do anything so crass! Instead, they quietly returned to his bed, freshly brushed and scented, eyedrops in, seemingly flawless, perfectly fake, and before he'd even opened his eyes Carter would know he'd been lied to.

Watching Ms Andrews was different.

Her beauty was unmanufactured—his experienced eyes could tell that at a glance—from the natural brows and lashes, right down to her soft, plump lips. Her face was untouched by needles or God knows what else, and her pale skin wore not a scrap of make-up. For a brief moment, as she woke, two utterly perfect crystals met his, her pupils constricting in the light, revealing ever more of verdant mossy green, and if eyes really were the windows to the soul he could have sworn she was smiling at him.

But then the real world impinged.

He watched confusion start to flicker in her eyes, followed by a flutter of panic. Like a kaleidoscope twisting in reverse, the prisms shattered as she took her gaze from him and glanced at her surroundings, a frown appearing, the clear green fracturing, her soft smile fading as she abruptly sat up, her top slipping down further, her hair a chaotic tumble...

'It's fine,' Carter reassured her.

* * *

Grace didn't hear him, though.

She'd woken to find a stranger standing over her.

A black-haired stranger, with a clean-shaven strong jaw, a straight Roman nose. But what drew her attention was the perfect separation of his left eyebrow—a thick white scar cut through the gorgeous jet arch and into his hairline. His eyes were as grey as sleet on a cold winter's day, and he had a stern, grim, yet somehow plump and completely kissable mouth. His stance might be construed as forbidding, yet there was no sense of threat. The citrussy, spicy scent of his cologne and its smoky undertone was so delectable, so real, it took away from the hard bench beneath her body and the harsh lights behind him...

In truth, for a moment, when their eyes had first met, she'd *welcomed* him to step into her dream.

Then it had dawned on her that this was no dream! The stranger her eyes had beckoned to join her was real...

The sounds of the airport seemed muffled and lost to her senses as she first took in his features, then looked to his proffered hand and saw she must have dropped her passport.

'Gosh!' Grace hauled herself to sit up and glanced around. The departure lounge that had been nearly empty when she'd given in to exhaustion and closed her eyes to doze was now full. She glanced at the screen and saw that first-class passengers had already been invited to board.

'I must have...'

He proffered the passport again and, orientated now, she reached to take it. Grace saw the glint of an expensive watch and crisp white cuffs beneath the sleeve of a dark grey suit, and even his hands were immaculate, right down to his manicured nails.

'Goodness...' she said, closing her hand around the passport that must have slipped from her pocket. 'Thank you.'

He said something, but his voice was barely audible, his words just a deep, indecipherable burr.

'Sorry?'

She asked him to repeat. His voice did not match his impact.

His words were so faint that she was forced to look at his mouth to make out what was being said.

God, those lips, she thought. For even if he appeared to be forming stern words they remained full and plump.

But now, when he pointed his index finger in slight rebuke, she caught what he said.

'You should be more careful.'

Grace was about to tell him that usually she was…boringly careful. But Mr Stern was already walking on.

Coming to fully, she thought of his wagging finger and felt both foolish for dropping her passport and also a bit cross.

To his departing back, and under her breath, she muttered a quiet, 'Yes, sir!'

Or rather, Grace *thought* she had muttered—but, watching his shoulders stiffen before he abruptly turned around, she realised he'd somehow heard.

He shot her such a look that Grace swallowed hard. So hard it caused a sudden popping noise in her ears, followed by a voice over the Tannoy calling for *'passengers requiring assistance'* to board.

The world instantly got louder.

There were people all around, talking, babies were crying, and Grace realised that the aeroplane ear she hadn't known she had must have suddenly rectified.

And it dawned on her that very possibly she'd been shouting!

'My ears…' She pointed her fingers to the problem. 'I couldn't hear myself…'

He must think her mad, Grace decided. Soon he would walk over and tell her that next time she could take care of her passport herself…

It came as a ridiculously nice surprise when his sulky mouth moved into a slight smile. A smile that told her she was forgiven. Better still, this austere man seemed vaguely amused.

'Thank you,' she said again, hopefully a little less loudly than last time, and he gave her a brief, polite nod before moving on.

He was carrying a long leather cylinder and a laptop bag, and she watched as he walked along the VIP section towards the smiling flight attendants. And then her moment with the beautiful stranger was gone for ever.

Gosh, Grace thought, her heart hammering—not just at the near miss with her passport, but more at the impact of him.

She tried to shrug the brief encounter from her mind and looked around at her fellow passengers, who barely deigned to give her a glance.

She checked her phone messages and listened to Violet wishing her a safe trip. Then she felt the familiar knot of anxiety tighten as she opened her emails. It was merited, because there was the July invoice for her mother's first two weeks in the nursing home.

It would already have been debited, so she could easily ignore it, and there was a part of her that wanted to wait until after her holiday. To simply escape the issue for a while...

Hairdresser...

Manicure...

Group Trip...

Gardening Club...

Grace closed her eyes.

Those were the exact things she wanted for her mother, but the top-up fees were beyond anything she'd remotely envisaged.

Her mind was still on the blasted account as she boarded, but as she waited for the flight attendant to check her boarding pass Grace let her gaze drift to the left, possibly hoping to see the delectable stranger. She peered at the business class cabin and saw the champagne being taken around, though there was no sign of him.

A curtain was pulled back and she glanced beyond and briefly glimpsed a flash of a white shirt and a glint of a gold watch, then a jacket being handed over, before the curtain was abruptly closed.

He was beyond business class, and somehow she'd already known that.

That stunning, prepossessing man was beyond anything she'd ever seen.

He was simply *beyond*.

CHAPTER TWO

SERENITY?

Not quite…

Even so, sitting in the boat with her fellow travellers, Grace had certainly caught a few glimpses of it. In witnessing Mother Nature at her finest, there were times she had to pinch herself to believe she was really here.

It had been the most incredible few days. Sunrise boat trips followed by a gorgeous breakfast with her group, then a day to explore the boardwalk around the gorgeous resort. Or simply to rest on a lounger and watch the gentle activity on the river. Or relax in her suite.

After several turbulent years, finally there had been time to reflect and think—about her mother, her future, how wonderful Violet had been.

And there had been time to daydream…to lie in a hammock and think about gorgeous strangers who stared right into your eyes. How he'd smiled…

Today, before dusk, the ten in her party had set out again, to watch the animals and birds prepare for the night ahead. While she still hadn't seen orangutans, tonight had been a highlight—on their way back they'd had to stop the narrow open boat as pygmy elephants crossed the river.

They were not so small…

Night was closing in as the exhilarated group made their way back, the lights of the villa twinkling invitingly ahead.

'We're rather late,' Felicity, their extremely efficient guide for the evening, reminded them. 'So get changed for dinner as quickly as possible.'

Guests were expected to dress for dinner, and on the day Grace had arrived a red sarong shot with silver had been waiting on her bed. At first it had felt strange to dress up, but Grace had started to enjoy how seriously meals were taken here. A gong would summon the guests to a stunning alfresco dining area set high over the river. There the guests would sit in their allocated groups and share in a sumptuous buffet dinner.

Mindful that they were running late, Grace had a very quick shower, then ran a comb through her newly wild hair—the humidity hadn't been kind. Her long curls seemed to have doubled in volume and her comb kept snapping off teeth. Giving up on taming it, she tied it up in a messy bun—and then it was time to tackle the sarong.

Grace headed out, walking through the softly lit grounds to the gorgeous alfresco area, slipping off her shoes before entering.

'Hey, Grace…'

One of the group, Randy, greeted her, as did everyone else, but then they all got back to their conversations.

Selecting a fragrant dish, Grace took a seat at the table. As much as she was loving her time here, she did feel like the odd one out. She knew she was out of practice socially, and her attempts at conversation and even her little jokes all seemed to fall on deaf or bemused ears.

Most in the group were considerably older—retired or semi-retired couples—and were well travelled. There were a few younger ones—a couple on their honeymoon and Corrin, who was German and a keen photographer. The only thing Grace had to take pictures with was her rather basic phone…

'Wow!' Randy was looking at some stunning footage Corrin had taken, and they were speaking about apertures and such.

Possibly, Grace thought as she selected dessert, she'd put herself a little on the outside right from the start. When they'd first introduced themselves she hadn't really wanted to admit how worried she was about her mum, so had been vague with her responses, and had perhaps sounded standoffish—which hadn't been her intention.

Grace was eating some fruit, the meal almost over, when Randy glanced towards the entrance and rolled his eyes.

'Late as always…'

She knew who he was referring to—a loud group who neither changed for dinner nor removed their shoes.

'I swear they're developers,' Randy said, standing up, as did his wife. 'Enjoy the peace here while you can—it won't last long if they get their hands on it...'

He wished everyone goodnight and left.

'Do you think they are developers?' Grace asked Corrin.

'They are not interested in much.' Corrin shrugged and, collecting her camera, told Grace she was going to bed. *'Ich geh ins bett.'*

'Sleep well.' Grace smiled.

Given the early-morning starts, they all seemed to drift off to bed about nine. Well, except for the newlyweds, who played Uno every night! For Grace, having spent the past couple of years working late into the night, as well as keeping an ear out for her mother, it felt a little early for the day to be over.

She wandered from the dining area, happy to be away from the obnoxious group that had just arrived. Not quite ready for bed, she took a chair beside a low table close to the walkway. There was no internet or phone signal, but Grace scrolled through her phone, trying to find the footage she'd taken tonight.

'Watch out for the monkeys!' Felicity warned as she passed. 'I'll see you bright and early...'

It was dark and late as Carter approached the resort.

He slowed the speedboat as he passed the longhouses, so as not to disturb the Iban people, as was the custom here.

Usually he arrived at his grandfather's by helicopter, but he had arranged for his speedboat to be waiting and had travelled by river. He'd made several stops along the way, both at the resorts and sharing meals with the locals, finding out all he could before meeting with Arif. After this he would travel on to his late grandfather's, but soon, Carter hoped, he could head back to the States—or Janana, given the last-minute cancellation of his meeting with Sahir.

Pulling in to the jetty, he stared at the dark stretch of river beyond, thinking of the turn-off a few miles ahead and the network of tributaries to negotiate before he came to the part of the world he hated the most.

'Carter!'

As he secured his boat Jamal, Arif's wife, came down the stairs to greet him.

'Welcome…we heard you were back.'

'Word travels,' Carter agreed.

'I haven't seen you for so long. Not since the funeral.' Jamal met his eyes then. 'I can't even remember the last time you visited us here at the resort.'

She pushed out a smile, but he could see the worry behind it.

'A suite is ready for you, of course, though Arif is not here right now. He's taking a night group out, but he'll be back by morning.'

'That's fine.'

He was actually relieved to avoid heavy topics tonight, as well as the ongoing tension between himself and Arif. Instead, he asked about the couple's young children, and found out the eldest was out in the jungle with his father tonight.

'Already?' Carter frowned, appalled at the thought of a child out there. 'Reheeq's only four…'

'He's six—and you went out long before then.' Jamal laughed. 'Here…' She gave him a key. 'Do you want dinner while your luggage is unloaded?'

'I'm fine,' Carter declined. 'I've had a lot of stops along the way.'

'Then I'll show you to your suite…'

'No need.' Carter knew the place like the back of his hand.

'It's good you're here,' Jamal said, then glanced up from the little jetty to the softly lit dining area above. 'I had better go… there are still guests dining…'

She dashed off, which in itself was unusual for Jamal, but walking down the walkway he heard rather raucous laughter from the dining area and knew she must be busy.

For most the resort was a tranquil paradise, with trailing flowers, the sound of cicadas… But for Carter, being back was his own version of hell. The dense jungle was not just close, it shrouded the resort and—call it denial—he would by far prefer not to have known that Arif and his young son were out there tonight.

But then from dark thoughts there was a sudden and very unexpected distraction.

It would appear that Grace Andrews, the woman from the airport, was staying here at the resort.

Carter recognised her immediately—recalled her name instantly. He'd even thought about her on the flight. Flying at altitude, cabin lights dimmed, he'd found that he'd smiled when recalling their brief interaction, and how she'd blushed when he'd overheard her calling him 'sir'.

Now her beauty, even in the dim lighting, was almost luminescent, and his eyes were instantly drawn to where she sat on a large chair, with her legs tucked under her, looking through her phone. She was wearing a red sarong, revealing slender arms and shoulders, and her hair was tied high in a loose knot. She was alone.

'How are the ears?' he asked, and watched her jolt.

'Oh!' she said as she looked up. 'It's you.'

Then she smiled, her full lips spreading, as did the pink tinge to her creamy complexion. She smiled not just with her eyes, as she had so briefly at the airport, and not just with her lush lips, but with her whole self.

Putting down her phone and uncurling her legs, she sat up.

For Carter the initial impact he'd felt on sighting her was followed by two counter punches—one to his groin, as his body reacted to her effortless beauty in a familiar way, and also a rare hit to his chest, a surge of pleasure simply to see her warm smile. Though he doubted Grace could begin to comprehend just how welcome her greeting was at this intolerable time.

'My ears are much better, thank you.'

He watched as she tucked loose tendrils of hair behind little pixie-looking ears. After a difficult few days Grace really was a sight for sore eyes. Oh, there had been no hostility on his journey—the locals were too kind and welcoming for that. It was more that he'd been able to feel their concern, and a slight air of suspicion also—which, given it was his cousin who posed the danger, he knew was merited.

Yes, Grace Andrews was a pleasant surprise indeed.

'Your voice is a lot…' He paused before selecting his word, thinking how loud it had been when he'd woken her. It was gentler now, as well as a little throaty and… 'A lot softer than I recall.'

* * *

And all the huskier for seeing you! Grace thought, clearing her throat, while wondering what on earth had happened to her vocal cords.

He was as stunning as she'd remembered him to be. And, yes, when recalling their first meeting she'd wondered if she'd somehow exaggerated his beauty. But if anything she'd underplayed it. He wore a dark, untucked yet fitted shirt, with the sleeves pushed up, and grey linen trousers. He was unshaven and sporting several days' worth of dark stubble. But even casually dressed, even with that black hair a touch dishevelled, he cut an expensive dash.

'All alone?' he asked, glancing down at the single iced tea on her table.

'Yes. Well, except for the newlyweds and…' She gestured with her head to the noisy group in the dining area behind.

'Are they in your tour group?'

'No, thank goodness.' Grace shook her head. 'They got here before us. I think they're…' She halted, certain he didn't want to hear her musings, but it would seem she was wrong.

'Mind if I join you?' he said, gesturing to the empty seat opposite.

'Of course not.'

'Do you want a drink?' he offered. 'I'm going to find some wine.'

'I'd love one—though I doubt you'll have much luck. I think there's only beer.'

'I'll see what I can do.'

As he sauntered off she briefly closed her eyes, warning herself not to read too much into him joining her. It wasn't as if he could be spoiled for company! She had to somehow ignore just how gorgeous he was and her almost violent attraction to him.

She took a deep breath, deciding to examine this moment later.

This moment when her heart felt like a trapped butterfly in her throat.

This moment when she was still fighting the surge of adrenaline that had made her want to leap from her seat the second she saw him—like some overgrown puppy.

She opened her eyes to the sight of him returning with a bottle of wine and two glasses. He gave a slow smile of triumph as he held up the bottle, and it felt as if she was the only woman here.

Well, she *was* the only woman sitting alone here, Grace reminded herself.

Yet somehow, holding her in his gaze, he made her feel a little as if she was the only woman in the world.

Oh, yes, it would be far wiser to dwell on his impact later. These feelings he evoked were unfamiliar.

Tantalisingly so…

Carter pulled out the cushioned chair opposite Grace, ensuring a clear view of his target—the group of men in the dining area didn't look like regular tourists.

'I feel at a bit of a disadvantage,' Grace admitted as he sat.

'How so?'

'Well, you saw my passport, so you know my name, my age, where I'm from…'

'Ah, but I have a terrible memory,' he teasingly lied. Then, while opening the bottle, told her all he had gleaned. 'Grace Andrews, twenty-five, born in London, though I didn't get your date of birth.'

She laughed lightly, though her green eyes waited and if he wanted to observe these men, then he'd have to give up more.

'Carter,' he offered, 'Carter Bennett.' He briefly glanced over to the group as he poured the wine. He was excellent at mining information and decided to utilise that skill now. 'God, they're loud,' he commented, leading the conversation back to where she'd left it a short while ago. 'Usually everyone's in bed by now, or winding down—they seem to be just getting started…'

'Mmm…' She shrugged creamy shoulders, then, rather than elaborating on the group, asked about him. 'You didn't say how old you were.'

'Thirty-five.' He chose to be more direct. 'So, who are they?'

'I've no idea.' She shook her head. 'Randy, one of the guys in our group, heard them discussing building an airstrip. He thinks they might be developers, or something.'

Carter at first made no comment, but he was rather sure he knew who they were now—they weren't developers, they were television or movie executives wanting easier access to the residence and land. He needed to observe them some more to be certain. While inviting a tourist to regale their adventures was something he'd usually avoid, he was rather brilliant at feigning interest when it was to his advantage. 'How are you enjoying your trip...?' he enquired politely.

'Very much.' She nodded. 'It's gone by too fast...just a couple more days here...'

'Then what?'

'I still haven't made up my mind,' Grace told him as, rather than sliding it across the table, Carter handed her a drink.

Grace took it a little tentatively, hoping her hands weren't too slippery from a mixture of both the humidity and her own jangled nerves, but he held the glass securely until she had a firm hold.

It was the tiniest thing, really, but she was grateful that he at least was entirely in control. Or perhaps it was just that the brief touch of their fingers and fleeting contact hadn't affected him in the slightest.

Of course not.

'Really, I'd be happy to stay on a little longer,' Grace admitted. 'I'd love to see orangutans.'

'You haven't yet?'

'A nest, and one from a distance, though I'm dreadful with binoculars.' She gave him a smile. 'Seeing orangutans has been on my bucket list since before I even knew what bucket lists were...'

'How come?'

She blushed, and it was something she tended not to do. Or maybe she did—she'd just never been so conscious of it until she met him.

'It's silly...' she dismissed her reasoning. 'My father got me a baby one for Christmas when I was little. Not a real one...'

'I would hope not! I've heard they do terrible damage to curtains.'

She smiled at his subtle humour, and then it turned into a

laugh, and his company was so pleasant, even if there was still heat in her cheeks.

'You can send him a photo of a real one soon.'

'I don't think so...'

'You'll see plenty if you go to one of the rehabilitation centres—'

'I meant, we're not in contact.' She gave a tight smile and got back to talking about the orangutans. 'They've always fascinated me. I'd just love to see one in the wild.' Before he could say it, she put up her hand. 'I know. Felicity has already reminded me it's not a zoo.'

'Felicity?'

'One of the guides,' she explained. 'I believe she's here doing research. Ornithology,' Grace added. 'Anyway, seeing orangutans in the wild is probably not all I've built it up to be...'

He opened his mouth, as if about to say something, then must have changed his mind and closed it. But as she went to take a sip of her wine perhaps he changed his mind again. 'Grace, it's even better.'

'Oh...'

Her surprise wasn't at his comment, more at the slight husk to his voice, the note of pensiveness, even. But then he gave a casual shrug, as if it might reduce the sentiment of his words.

She narrowed her eyes as she looked at him. 'You're not here on a tour...'

'Is it that obvious?'

She shrugged. 'You just seem...' Her head moved to one side in slight assessment. 'Well, you arrived alone, *and* you know where the wine's kept.'

He gave a half-laugh. 'My grandfather has—or rather he *had* a place a few miles from here.'

She blinked, and he knew she had noticed the change of tense when he'd mentioned his grandfather.

Please don't offer condolences, he thought, but she just briefly met his eyes and a gave him a pinched, regretful smile that said enough.

Actually, it said more—it told him that she'd heard, or rather understood, he'd rather not go there.

'So,' Grace summed up, 'not a tourist, but not a local either?'

'Correct.'

He was grateful she'd changed the topic, and he rested his eyes upon her as she told him they'd all seen the pygmy elephants tonight.

'Just incredible...'

There was a tremor of excitement in her voice, and he found his focus honing in on her, the men in the dining area forgotten as her delicate hands reached for her phone.

'I took some photos, and I think I got a couple of videos. I was about to look when you...' She paused, and then got back to searching on her phone.

Carter was not one for tourist photos—or any photos. Usually someone reaching for their phone would have him reaching for his wine, or the exit—and yet as she held up a grainy image on an utterly basic phone Carter found out something.

It wasn't just elephants that didn't forget.

There was a twist inside him, a whisper of long-ago carefree days spent tracking them with Arif. How everything would halt when they chose to appear by the river—even seasoned locals could not but stop and smile at their majesty.

His father had been in constant awe of them too.

'Carter, look!'

It had been more than half a century since he'd recalled his father's voice with such clarity.

Not that Grace could know that, of course.

'It really was the most incredible thing I've ever...' she started but then halted, perhaps changed her mind, because she went to place her phone back down on the table. 'You must have seen them a thousand times.'

He was about to nod, even if only to halt the memories raining in, yet he didn't want to crush her fervour nor shut it down. Also, for the first time, there was no pain in recall.

'Not for a long while,' Carter admitted, standing to move his

seat around to be by her side. The men he'd intended to watch—
the very reason he was here—were forgotten.

'This was earlier...' Grace told him, and he tried to look down
at the phone rather than notice the dash of coral polish on her toenails. 'We first saw them by the river.'

His gaze left her pretty feet to look at the images, and there
was something about the photos lack of polish that made there
really rather special.

'That's quite a herd,' he commented.

'Eleven...maybe twelve.' She nodded, and he caught the scent
of fragrant hair and warm skin. 'And there was a calf,' she added.
'Well, two. But one was just so tiny. This was taken at the start.'

She showed him a very shaky video, and he looked at the elephants at the riverside, their silvery ears flapping as if waving,
carrying on eating and bathing, oblivious to their audience.

God, but he remembered this.

Carter was certainly not one for poring over holiday images,
and such, yet he patiently watched her slender finger as she swiped
through more photos, the sky darkening with each image.

'We were heading back to the resort when they appeared again.
I don't think Felicity was expecting it at all! We had to stop to
let them cross.'

He could hear the tremor of excitement in her voice.

'It was getting dark, so you can't see much...'

'May I?'

He took the phone and watched the footage, heard her laughter in the short video. It moved him. Her slight gasp as another
elephant appeared, followed by her cry of delight as a small calf
disappeared beneath the water.

The dulcet notes of her pure pleasure were captivating.

'I didn't even know they could swim,' she admitted, her head
moving closer to his, a curl just dusting his cheek. 'And then...'

Together they watched as one of the mothers pushed her little
one up onto the muddy bank and the elders stood patiently, waiting for all to gather.

'They really take care of each other.'

'They do.' Carter said. 'Once, I thought...'

He halted—not just his voice, but his thoughts—as he always did when his mind drifted back. Yet as he stared at the images on the phone her silence was patient enough to allow him a small recollection of happier times.

'Once, I thought I'd found an abandoned calf.'

'Oh, my goodness. What did you do?'

'Nothing—luckily. Arif intervened, told me the herd were close. It could have turned nasty—they weigh in the tons.'

'Arif?' Grace checked. 'The guide here?'

He nodded.

'Thank goodness for friends.' She laughed, but then it trailed off. 'I almost didn't come... I cancelled this trip a few times. But my friend Violet practically marched me to the airport.'

She didn't elaborate, and Carter found he wanted her to.

Grace had found out something too—the inescapability of desire.

They were both looking down at her now blank phone, and she was suddenly utterly aware that he sat close to her. She could see his long, lean thigh next to hers, and his beautiful fingers holding her phone, the sorts of things she'd never really noticed in a man before...

Since that first meeting at airport she'd been doing her level best to get him out of her mind, and now he'd arrived at the resort she was trying to treat him just as she would any of her fellow travellers.

Yet for all her denial, for all her bravado, her heart—which had barely slowed since his arrival—picked up pace again. And when their fingers brushed as he handed her back the phone, the butterfly in her throat felt like a trapped, panicking moth.

'Thanks,' Grace said, placing it on the table and wondering if he'd move his chair back now. But he remained by her side, which meant they had to turn a little to face each other. 'It's nice to show someone.'

'Aren't you all swapping photos at dinner?'

He clearly knew the resort well. 'I don't really...' She didn't know how to say that she didn't quite fit in—it wasn't a flattering thing to admit. 'They're mainly couples.'

'Yes?'

'And I'm not the best photographer...'

'I liked your pictures.'

'Thank you.' She rolled her eyes, but then her gaze went straight back to his. 'They don't get my jokes either. Mind you, they're pretty dreadful.'

'I'll try and remember to laugh.'

Carter didn't look like a man who laughed very often, and yet he made her smile with rare ease. More, there was a gentle yet particular attention he gave.

As if he even registered her blink.

Certainly she noticed when he did—the bat of his spiky black lashes and then the captivating return of a slate-grey that seemed to set the world into slow motion.

Her reaction was heightening—more now than just a faint blush or a fluttering heart. There was a pleasurable air of light tension. Her breasts, her stomach, and even lower felt subtly...provoked. Stirring, stretching, tuning up like the orchestra at the start of a concert...or rather tuning in to new sensations. She had never felt such attraction, and most bewildering of all, for Grace it felt reciprocated.

As if Carter felt it too.

Of course not, she told herself, reaching for her wine, determined to appear unaffected. It wasn't just that he was out of her league, or that he was out of her realm, it was the fear of misreading him. The fear that it was woeful inexperience that had her misinterpreting the static air between them.

He took a drink, drained his glass, and her eyes flicked to his mouth as his pink tongue lightly licked his bottom lip.

Such a simple motion, yet Grace found herself, both entranced and determined to act as if she hadn't noticed.

Grace tried to deny she was, for the first time, on fire.

CHAPTER THREE

'SO…' CARTER NOTICED Grace pushing out a smile and retreating from their silent flirt. 'You're visiting your grandfather's home?' she asked.

For a moment there he'd thought they might kiss, pick up his key and head to bed…

It was that easy for him.

Yet, as pleasurable as an escape would be, he wasn't here for that.

And also he was enjoying their conversation.

Unexpectedly so.

'Yes.' Carter nodded.

He rarely discussed personal matters, yet here he was, sitting above the river, dragged back to a world he'd hoped to avoid. And he'd never see her again.

'He left his estate to both my cousin and I.' He gave a small grimace and she must have noted it.

'You don't get on?'

'We don't,' he agreed, topping up their glasses. 'I have no idea what my grandfather was thinking. He must have been losing his mind.'

'Please don't—'

She put up a hand, her voice still soft, but passionate and urgent. Enough so that he put down the bottle.

'Sorry…' She seemed embarrassed to have halted him. 'I just hate that turn of phrase. My mother actually *is* losing her mind.'

'Then I apologise for my careless words.'

'It's fine.' She shrugged tense shoulders, took a breath, and he watched her force them to relax. 'I shouldn't have said anything.'

Grace didn't really know why she had.

For days she'd actively avoided the topic, and though she'd started to regret holding back from the group it felt too late now to amend that. But with Carter there was a certain allure in his grey eyes. Or perhaps, sitting there on a sultry night, surrounded by a sky hung with stars, it was easier, just for a short while, to let down her perpetual guard.

'When you say she's losing her mind…?'

Grace would never get used to saying it, and her lips were tight around her words. 'She has dementia.'

'She must be young?'

'Yes. She's just gone into a nursing home. A nice one,' she added, deciding she'd said enough—it was hardly gentle conversation.

'How long has she been unwell?'

Grace hadn't expected the question. She looked at eyes that, colour-wise, remained as cold and grey as a winter's day, yet she felt as if she sat by a fire, the world outside a window, all the warmth and comfort here.

'A few years…'

She'd been thinking back on it earlier, as she'd lain on the hammock. 'I never even considered it at first.' She saw…not a frown, more his eyes narrowing in a kind of interest. And maybe it was the wine, or maybe this week had given her space, because for the first time she felt able to examine those bewildering times.

'She became…' How best to put it? 'Tricky.'

'I am guessing that's an understatement?'

'Not at first.' Grace shook her head. 'It was hard to pinpoint, I just knew something was wrong. I tried to rationalise it…' She gave a pale smile. 'Ignore it.'

'Did the rest of your family notice?'

'It's mainly just us. There's an aunt and cousin, but they didn't think anything was amiss…' Grace said. 'I was sharing a flat with my friend Violet, and I moved back home. I didn't tell her why.'

'How come?'

'There are some things that you just don't share.' Grace thought back. 'Things you don't want others to see. Well, that's how it felt for me.' She looked at him. 'I felt disloyal, maybe?'

He frowned, as if deeply considering her words. For a moment she thought he had a question, or was about to say something, but he stayed silent.

'Then she accused Violet of stealing a necklace.'

'That was the tipping point?'

'No.' Grace swallowed before adding. 'Unfortunately not.'

She'd stopped crying a very long time ago, but this memory was one of the few things that could almost reduce her to tears.

'I didn't accuse her…but I didn't defend her as I should have.'

The cicadas were silent, as if they too were listening, but then a loud burst of laughter from the group of men snapped her back to the present.

'It was the impetus to talk to our family doctor.' She met Carter's very accommodating gaze. 'When I was first told all I worried about was that it might be hereditary.' She was past putting herself in a flattering light. 'How selfish is that?'

'Practical, maybe?' Carter suggested. 'I'd want to know.'

'Well, her type of dementia isn't, as it turned out.' She thought for a moment. 'It's just a cruel disease…'

'Was her illness the reason you cancelled your trip?'

Grace nodded. 'I was her carer—and working too, of course. But I was lucky enough to be able to do my job from home… data entry…'

'So, you were doing two jobs?'

'I'm not sure taking care of my mother counted as a *job*.' She frowned at his rather direct summing up. 'And as well as that I would never have…' She paused, that disloyal feeling revisiting her. No, she would not be discussing her mother's finances. 'Well, if I'd known all that was coming, I wouldn't have planned a month away.'

'But now she's being taken care of?'

'Yes…' She wavered, knowing he couldn't possibly get the pain behind her choice. But neither did he *need* to know, so she forced a smile. 'There's a choir group, gardening…she's got a better social life than I have!'

He didn't return her smile. Only it didn't feel as if another of her little jokes had fallen flat—instead, it was as if he was giving her a pause before elaborating.

But she was already a little stunned that she'd told him so much.

This stranger.

Who magnetised her...who'd drawn thoughts out of her like iron filings...

She felt embarrassed by how much she'd said. 'Sorry for over-sharing.' She grimaced. 'I haven't told anyone here. This place, though...' She looked out to the river and the sky above. 'It makes you slow down.'

'And, of course, there's no internet,' he pointed out.

'True!' She glanced up as the newlyweds passed and said good-night. 'Sleep well.' Grace said.

'Newlyweds?' he checked.

She nodded.

He frowned. 'Playing cards?'

I know! Grace wanted to say, because she'd thought exactly the same.

She didn't go there, though—after all, she had no sex life to compare.

However, if she were on her honeymoon...with someone as...

'I ought to get to bed.' She put down her glass. 'We're meeting at dawn. Last chance to see the orangutans!'

'Good luck,' Carter said, and put down his glass too. 'I'll walk you back to your villa.'

'There's really no need—it's just there.'

It was literally ten or so steps away, but he looked at her as if there were things she did not know.

'There's every need,' he responded. 'We have company.'

He nodded towards the fence that lined the route to her door and she jumped a little when she saw a group of macaque mon-keys, sitting happily observing them.

'I didn't even notice.' She gave a nervous laugh and watched as he picked up their glasses and bottle.

'They can cause a lot of havoc in one night,' he explained, then left her to return the bottle and glasses to wherever he'd lo-cated them.

So could he, Grace thought, popping her phone into her bag as she awaited his return.

An hour in his company, immersed in those grey eyes, and her head was in disorder, thrown completely off balance by her own reaction to this intriguing man.

And, while she'd terminated their night, it had nothing to do with not enjoying his company. And certainly it wasn't because of her early start in the morning.

Quite simply, she was desperate for order to be restored.

For the fire he seemed to have lit inside her to be doused.

'It's that one,' she said, pointing to her villa, and he walked her the short distance, the curious monkeys observing them as they arrived at her door.

'It was nice seeing you again, Grace.'

'And you.' Grace nodded and went for her key.

Then she looked up at him.

More than nice.

And despite her previous need to conclude things, now that the moment was here she was suddenly desperate for more of this disorder, desperate to explore these new sensations, to know his kiss.

Possibly her eyes revealed some of her thoughts, for his fingers took a stray strand of her hair and tucked it behind her ear. His direct touch came as a relief rather than a shock. It felt like tangible proof that the attraction was mutual—that she wasn't imagining that someone so suave and gorgeous might be desirous too. His palm remained, and rather than brush his hand away, she lingered in the bliss of the slight, lightly provocative touch, wanting to arch her neck to rest into it.

'Unexpected,' she added.

'Nicely so,' he agreed.

Her nerves felt as if they were wound tight enough to snap, yet there was also a low beat of excitement…like distant drums. Did he know this was her most thrilling moment? That standing here, miles from anywhere, bathed in stars and touched by him, she was feeling the most peace, the most excitement she'd ever known? And it wasn't the cruel shelter her mother's disease had caused that had kept sensation at bay. Nothing had ever come close to the thrill of his company, his touch. And if she knew how, she would step into his kiss, or lift her face…

Carter was sorely tempted to lower his head and taste that ripe mouth. More than tempted. He wanted to gather that slender body and hold it against his, to sink into familiar escape with this captivating beauty…

She wasn't used to this, though—he was experienced enough to tell that.

There had been two chances to move their conversation to bed and she'd refused them both.

Now, though, he felt her warm cheek, saw that full, waiting mouth, and he knew where it would surely lead.

And she'd regret it.

Not the night, but his cold departure in the morning.

Silence thrummed. Her lips were slightly parted and her eyes were on his. And he was so close to succumbing… But then he heard a low gecker from their audience on the fence, followed by a small coo. He glanced over her shoulder as three possibly wise monkeys brought him sharply to reason, and instead of kissing her and doing more, so much more, Carter used his mouth for good.

'Goodnight, Grace.'

He saw the dart of confusion in her eyes, the warmth of her cheek flaring to heat his palm as he denied them.

But surely it was better this way?

He was here to gather information and then get the hell out. He knew, too, that being here always put him in a dark place.

As well as that, she hadn't been versed in his cold and soulless heart—those gorgeous green eyes were unaware that he had nothing, *nothing* other than sex to give.

'You should go in,' he said, dropping his hand and then watching as she fumbled in her small bag for her key.

Grace took two attempts to get the blasted key in the lock. Humiliated and embarrassed as the sexiest man she'd ever encountered sent her off to bed without so much as a kiss when she'd been so sure.

With her back turned she bit her lip at the sting of his rejection. But, used to hiding her true feelings, she managed an over-the-shoulder smile.

'Goodnight.'

'Sleep well.'

She closed the door between them and felt the breeze from the fan, but it neither cooled nor composed her.

She felt awkward and upset that she'd so spectacularly misread things. But as she stripped off her sarong and put out her clothes for the morning Grace groaned in embarrassment when she thought about how she'd shown him the elephant videos, then droned on about her mother.

God, no wonder she hadn't been on a date in for ever, or been kissed in…

Grace honestly couldn't remember.

Actually, she could. That guy at teaching college. But as she stepped into the shower his name remained elusive.

Carter wouldn't kiss like he had.

That much she knew.

Even the shower did little to smother the orchestra trapped in her frustrated body, for it played on tunelessly. Only now it played into a void. She shaved her legs—just because—and she shaved under her arms, conditioned her hair… But it was her centre that ached for attention. Her small breasts felt too big, and between her thighs she ached, even as she wrapped herself in a towel.

Of course he didn't want her in that way, Grace reprimanded her reflection in the mirror over the sink. He'd merely been passing the time.

Her cheeks were still flushed as she brushed her teeth—and, no, it wasn't from the wind on the boat or the sun. Replacing her toothbrush, she stared at her reflection in the dim low-wattage light and wished that Carter stood behind her and touched her cheek where he just had. Wished the night had ended differently.

As she lay in bed the monkeys scampered across the roof for

a while, but soon even they gave in and she was left with a heavy regret.

She wished she'd known Carter Bennett's kiss.

Then, just on the edge of sleep, when her defences slipped a fraction, allowing her to wander the unguarded corridors in her mind, she dared admit to more.

She wished she'd known far more than just his kiss…

CHAPTER FOUR

THE NIGHTMARES WERE BACK.

Carter had considered them long since gone, but after more than two decades' absence they'd returned.

As always, they started benignly. He was casually strolling through Kuala Lumpur Airport, pulling up his boarding pass on his phone, when he heard his father's voice.

'Carter, look!'

Nonplussed, he turned and saw Grace, saw her passport lying on the floor.

Just like last time, he decided it wasn't his problem.

Damn.

There was a feeling of obligation he could not ignore.

'Grace!' he called out. 'Grace!' he said again, and then remembered she couldn't hear him.

Grace really *was* Sleeping Beauty now.

Instead of an airport bench she lay on a glass altar. There was no velvet rope parting them, nor a carpeted floor to cross, just dense jungle between them, and her passport was sinking into the swamp that surrounded her.

'Grace!'

He tried to call out to her again. Warn her that she'd never get home if she lost it. That she shouldn't be heading into the jungle in the first place. If she did…

Even in sleep, Carter did not allow himself to complete the thought.

Even in sleep, he refused to remember.

Instead he shot awake, as he'd trained himself to do decades ago, and snapped his eyes open.

Thankfully it took him less than a second to orientate himself—the dark wood, the high beams, and the background noise of a jungle that was never truly silent.

'Damn!'

He sat up and hauled himself out of bed, ruing his decision to return—especially by river.

Washing his face, he saw the shadows beneath his eyes and blamed them on the lack of sleep.

For once, it wasn't because of sex.

He'd wanted her badly, but he was a cold bastard at best.

And here he was at his worst.

So instead of bedding the gorgeous Grace he'd put that restless energy into something a little less destructive.

He'd told Jamal to go to bed and then had a few choice words with those movie executives…

He thought a swim might clear his head, so he went through his luggage and found running shorts his assistant would have packed and, having pulled them on, he grabbed a sarong and tied it on his hips.

His head was pounding, and not eased by the humid air as he stepped outside. Even the water was too warm as he dived in.

Morning hadn't even broken, yet the day already felt far too long.

Grace wasn't faring much better.

She was still cringing, of course, but Carter had told her he was leaving today, so hopefully she wouldn't have to face the man she'd…

She'd what? she challenged herself as she walked towards the jetty.

She hadn't dived into his arms or moved towards his mouth.

She'd just…

Hoped…

Thought that maybe…

'Morning!' Arif greeted her with a smile. 'Felicity will be with you soon. Oh, and there's a treat tonight,' he told her, and pointed to the sky. 'We'll be meeting a bit later. Felicity will give you the details.'

'Thanks.'

Then she saw Arif look over her shoulder.

'Hey,' he said, and a very fond smile lit his face. 'Finally!'

Grace knew that the person behind her had to be Carter.

'Arif,' he said.

And she stood there as he joined them, braced herself to come face to face with him, but was woefully unprepared. As he came into view the sight of him, dripping wet and wearing only a sarong tied low on his hips, was a lot to deal with at this hour.

She had to fight not to look at his body, to ignore the long, yet muscular arms and the fan of black hair on his chest.

'Morning.' Grace forced a pleasant smile, only it wavered when she saw his pallor and the dark rings under his eyes.

He looked grey compared to the way he'd looked last night. So much so that had Arif not been standing there she might even have forced her own awkwardness aside and asked if he was feeling all right. Then again, she doubted he'd have appreciated her concern, for her smile wasn't returned.

He just gave a vague nod, then addressed Arif. 'I'll get us both coffee...'

Grace felt her teeth grit at his cool dismissal and headed to the jetty.

'Here she is!' Felicity was clearly raring to go. 'Okay, that's everyone.'

As the boat pulled out she saw Carter and Arif were sitting opposite each other in the dining area, but quickly she looked away. It was their last morning boat trip. Tomorrow they were going on a jungle walk. And Grace didn't want to waste this gorgeous day... didn't want the highlight of her time here to be him.

As the boat made its lazy way along the river, the beauty of the new day greeted her. Herons skimmed the water, and the trees teemed with life, which at times they stopped to observe.

Watching the little silver leaf monkeys happily play—swinging, running along the branches and jumping—should make last night a little easier to forget.

And yet she kept remembering.

Little things...

The littlest of things…

How he'd looked—really looked—at her little video of the elephants. Told her how he'd once found a calf…

It hadn't seemed as if she was boring him then.

And he was the first person she'd ever told about her mother.

Well, aside from Violet, her awful cousin, Tanya, as well as the doctors, nurses and…

Carter was the first person she'd told not because it was necessary to do so, but because it was a huge part of her life…

'No luck!'

Felicity brought her back to the present. It would seem there would be no wild orangutans either.

'Just a nest,' Felicity added, putting down her binoculars and smiling at Grace. 'I know you've been itching to see one.'

'Not just one! I'd love to see a family,' Grace admitted.

'Oh, the males don't hang around after mating.' Felicity shook her head, and then punched her hand with her fist. 'Hit and run.'

Grace blinked. She'd heard the blunt terminology from Arif, but it sounded rather more shocking when delivered in Felicity's well-spoken voice. Then again, Felicity was a vet, and very earthy, and happily pointed out mating wildlife and so on. All the stuff that made Grace blush from her hair roots to her toenails when she thought about it…

It hadn't last night.

Grace screwed her eyes closed, determined not to be so pathetic. Only as they headed back for breakfast, instead of scanning the trees for signs of life, she was back to dreaming about Carter, barely noticing that the boat had slowed, as it often did when they passed longhouses.

'He's very well camouflaged…' Felicity told them, and Grace realised she must have spotted something as they drifted.

Hoping, *hoping*, that she was finally going to see an orangutan in the wild, she was about to look up when she saw that Felicity was pointing downwards.

'How old…?' Randy asked as Corrin focussed her camera.

'Perhaps six months…less than a year…'

It was then that Grace saw the tiny crocodile, possibly the length of her forearm, his shiny skin yellow and brown, much like the muddy river bank, his little jaw wide open as he bathed in the morning sun.

He was cute, Grace thought, and attempted a joke. 'You know what *not* to do,' she said.

'What's that?' Felicity asked.

'Smile...'

Nobody got Grace's little joke about the old song warning people never to smile at crocodiles, so she sat there blushing as Felicity first of all blinked in bemusement and then addressed the group.

'Saltwater crocodiles are a huge problem for the locals. Their dogs and chickens are easy prey, but also small children, fishermen...'

'The Bennett family...' Randy drawled. 'Three killed...'

'Well, we don't think the crocodile directly killed all three,' Felicity said, in rapid defence of nature. 'It's believed that the father drowned trying to save his wife and baby boy...' She spoke on about the new hunting rules that were meant to deal with the threat. Then, 'That little fellow might look sweet, but he can grow to more than six feet in length and has a life-span of seventy years.'

'Bennett?' Grace checked—because wasn't that Carter's surname?

'Probably happened before your time,' Randy said, then looked to their guide. 'Is the Bennett place where you're based?'

'It is.' Felicity nodded.

Grace was trying to listen as Felicity explained about her grant, and her research, and how she was based at Wilbur Bennett's home, yet try as she might to concentrate, her mind kept drifting.

Was it Carter's family that had been killed?

Randy confirmed that it was. 'Saw him at the pool this morning—you should see the mess of his back.'

'That wasn't from the crocodile attack,' Felicity intervened, but to no avail.

'Shame he's going to turn it into a film set,' Randy said.

'Though you can't blame the guy for wanting nothing to do with the place.'

Felicity looked flustered, clearly trying to dampen the conversation down. 'That's just rumour and speculation...'

Things had moved *way* beyond rumour and speculation!

Arif had brought him up to speed.

'I didn't know whether to call,' Arif admitted. *Again.*

Carter didn't respond to those words, just poured another coffee as Arif spoke on.

'I wasn't sure you'd even want to know.'

'Well, I know now,' Carter retorted briskly. 'And I'm on to it.'

They had discussed the issue for a good couple of hours, and Arif seemed less than reassured by Carter's solutions.

'Barristers, lawyers, attorneys...' Arif gave a tight smile, clearly frustrated by the lack of direction and nervous about the path ahead. 'The damage is happening *now*. We've even got some of the executives staying here at the resort, although they didn't introduce themselves as such.'

'I saw.'

'They leave this morning, thank goodness. Though they prefer not to travel by river.' He stared back at Carter. 'They're flying in and out from *your* helipad.'

'Not this morning.'

'There's a boat booked to take them there; they have Benedict's permission.'

'Well, they don't have mine.' He told Arif what he'd done. 'I had words with them last night—told them in no uncertain terms that I was in residence and denied them all access.'

God, but he loathed this joint ownership. Carter abhorred anyone encroaching on his space at the best of times.

'I also made it clear that, whatever Benedict might have told them, I would not be selling.'

'Good.' Arif nodded, a touch mollified now.

Carter saw that the groups were starting to return from their trips and knew he and Arif were about to head to the office.

Or they should have been.

'Are you okay, Carter?' Arif checked.

'Of course.' He nodded, realising Arif had noticed his distraction.

He'd caught sight of Grace helping herself to breakfast.

She poured juice and selected fruit, and as she turned she looked over, just for a second, her lips parted as if she had a question. But then her mouth snapped closed and she turned her back.

Good, Carter thought. *Turn away now.*

He was leaving for his grandfather's residence after this day with Arif, and anyway she was by far too sweet for a jaded cynic like him…

Even though things between him and Arif were tense there was a moment of relief as they moved to the office. He heard Arif let out a soft laugh at the sight of the executives mopping their brows as they climbed onto a boat to commence their long journey to the airport.

Carter barely noticed them. He could feel Grace's gaze on his back, on his scars, and though he was more than used to it, he felt an aching need to turn around.

Instead, he headed into the office with Arif and there stared at maps of the river he'd rather avoid. Heard about the programmes being run, and the disruption his cousin and his contacts were causing…

'Bornean banded pitta.' Arif tapped at the map for perhaps the fiftieth time, this time mentioning a rare bird. 'Abandoned three eggs…' he told Carter. 'And Felicity has data on the helmeted hornbill—so rare, but starting to return until the drones went up.' Arif spoke with both knowledge and passion. 'It's a declining species.'

It was late in the afternoon when Arif suggested that they walk.

Carter, though still only in his sarong, nodded. There needed to be no delay for getting changed—it made no difference here.

The grounds were extensive, with a boardwalk that skirted the jungle. And beyond were tens of thousands of hectares—a relative drop in the ocean, and yet untouched and vital and so full of life. And what he was here to discuss.

'How come you're still working as a guide?' Carter asked. 'I thought you'd be too busy co-ordinating all the projects.'

'I try to let the scientists do their work.' Arif shrugged. 'They don't need me looking over their shoulders. Anyway, I already know there are two new baby orangutans this month alone on your land.'

Carter thought of Grace and how she ached to see them in the wild—and, while this Felicity might be right about the jungle not being a zoo, he wished Grace could have seen them.

'Look...' Arif said, and lithely leapt over the wooden fencing. He glanced back, as if expecting Carter to follow, though he made no comment when he didn't.

Watching Arif disappear into the thick foliage, Carter felt a curl of dread, though he did his level best to ignore it. He stood scanning the trees, noting the freshly broken branches that had caught Arif's attention, and then exhaled in relief when Arif reappeared.

'Anything?' he asked.

'Pygmy elephant tracks. The groups saw them last night—that's why they were late back...'

'I heard.'

As they walked in silence, Carter again thought of Grace, and how last night he'd seen them through her eyes, as if for the first time. Her laughter and excitement, her sheer wonder, had brought some of the allure and the magic back.

If he could have made the journey here with his eyes closed he would have, or even kept them fixed ahead. Yet somehow Grace had forced them open, reminding him of better times...

'Do you remember when I thought I'd found that calf?' he said suddenly. 'I was so sure it was lost.'

Arif laughed. 'The herd was watching. The mother would not have been pleased if you'd approached him. She'd have attacked.'

It was the first real conversation they'd had about times prior to the incident...a time where they'd been just kids and friends... and Carter quickly regretted it—because Arif pounced.

'Do you ever think of going back into the jungle—to where it happened, to where you were found?' Arif asked, as he always did. 'My father is too old now, but I would come with you, of course. It's the anniversary soon—it might help you...'

'With what?' Carter challenged. 'I survived and I'm grateful. I've moved on with my life. I don't see the point of going there.'

As well as that, he did not need any reminder of the looming date.

They arrived back at the resort as dusk was falling. 'Stay for dinner,' Arif invited. 'It's the new moon, so we'll eat a bit later tonight, but we'd love you to join us.'

'I think it better that I head for the property,' Carter declined. 'I'll get straight on to Jonathon and tell him to progress things.'

He glanced around the resort and knew that his restless eyes were looking for Grace. Yes, it would be better by far to get the hell away.

'We'll catch up soon. I'll keep you informed.'

'I'll have your things moved to your boat...' Arif said, but then hesitated. 'First, though...' he nodded in the direction of his office '... I have something that is yours.'

Carter frowned.

'Give me a moment,' Arif said. 'I'll just ask Jamal to excuse us.'

Carter was not used to waiting outside anyone's office, but he stood there, no doubt about to be delivered another lecture and to be told he wasn't doing enough.

'Hey...'

He looked up and there was Grace, her hair wild and curly, her lemon top bright. Her face, which had been pale at the airport, now had a light dusting of freckles across her nose. Compared to last night, her eyes seemed a bit guarded, but her soft voice told him she was pleased that he was still here.

Walk away now, he wanted to warn her, because his black heart would soon darken those clear green eyes.

But instead of walking she stood there. 'I thought you'd gone,' she said.

'I'm about to.'

'Oh.'

She was waiting for him to elaborate, but deliberately he did not. His eyes had left her face, trying to ignore the soft curves of her slender body, how her yellow top, damp from the humid air, clung to her small breasts and narrow waist and skimmed her flat stomach. Despite the warmth her nipples were hard—not obviously so, unless you ached to know them, touch them, taste them…

Even looking down at her sneakers did not ease his sensual thoughts, for her legs were smooth and beneath those sneakers he knew there were coral-painted nails. It was her voice, though, the slight uncertainty to her tone that he deeply ached to address. Yes, he wanted to admit to her, she was right…this attraction was real.

His words might be curt, but physically he was lying. His body was beckoning hers, his arms were aching to draw her in. His stomach was tight, aching to fight arousal, yet his nonchalant stance, leaning on the wall, denied the untapped passion that thrummed between them.

'Well…' Grace said into the long silence. 'It was nice meeting you.'

He nodded.

'I'd better go and get ready for dinner…'

Carter frowned, looked at the darkening sky. He knew the routines here, and that a new moon meant dinner would be served later, but he did not want to get into conversation.

'Yep.'

He was abrupt in his dismissal, but better that she walked off a bit hurt and confused than that he take her by the hand and get her the hell out of here as he so badly wanted to.

'Arif is ready for you.' Jamal came then, and gave him a small, almost sympathetic smile. 'It's been nice seeing you, Carter.'

'Thank you.' He pulled himself away from the wall, barely glancing at Grace as he stepped into Arif's office, with no idea what was to come.

It was just a small workstation, really. A desk with pictures of the various guides on the walls, along with their beloved wildlife, as well as the usual office equipment.

Arif was standing behind his desk and he asked Carter to close the door, then addressed him. 'You asked the point of going back to where it happened?'

'No,' Carter corrected. 'I said I see no purpose in *me* going back.'

'You anger is misdirected.'

'No.'

'Yes,' Arif insisted. 'How can you fight for something you don't love? You blame the land.'

'I don't.' Carter closed his eyes. He did not want a lecture, and while he admired Arif, while they might have once been close friends, Arif did not have any deep knowledge of him.

'You blame your parents, then?'

Carter stared ahead.

'Yourself?' Arif pushed, and their eyes met.

Carter's flashed a warning for Arif to leave things.

'I found this.'

Carter frowned when he saw Arif's eyes fill with tears.

'It is not mine to keep…'

He pushed a silk pouch forward on the desk and Carter glanced down. When he made no move to touch it, Arif opened the cord and slid a heavy band of solid silver onto the desk.

The walls seemed to fall, and the floor must have dissolved, for everything disappeared. And even though Carter didn't touch it, in one blinding flash he saw perhaps a hundred occasions when he'd picked up this silver teething ring and handed it to Hugo. Seen his brother's wide pink smile and that one tiny tooth, his little fat hand reaching out, clasping the ring and biting down on it.

His voice, when finally it came, was a raw husk. 'Where did you find this?'

'Close to where it happened.'

'But every inch was searched…' Carter argued the facts, but then halted, because that made him sound naive. Of course the jungle was not a neat field. 'When?'

'A year ago,' Arif said. 'Almost. I went back on the anniversary, I was placing offerings on behalf of your grandfather when I saw something glinting…'

Carter stared ahead rather than look down at the familiar silver as Arif spoke on.

'I remember you once asking your mother if it would break his teeth.'

Now he looked down at the teething ring…so familiar. It had first been his grandfather's, his father's, his, and then Hugo's. Polished to perfection for each new child.

The same had been done now. He could see Arif or Jamal must have spent hours lovingly making sure it gleamed.

And even though he still didn't touch it, there was no damage that he could see. Apart from a few tiny scratches, it might be sparkling in the finest antique jeweller's.

He wished he could pick it up, hold it, trace the little scratches on the silver that Hugo's one little tooth had made. But he would not stand in an office and weep as expected. He did not know how to summon emotion on demand—for he'd rather have none.

'I know you must—' Arif started, but Carter stopped him right there.

'You have no idea how I feel.'

'That's just it—you refuse to feel!' Arif said.

He was perhaps the only person on the planet who would speak so bluntly to Carter, but they had known each other since they were both still called Ulat. They had spent summers together before tragedy had struck as well as after.

Arif picked up the teething ring and held it out to him. 'You won't even touch it?'

'You should have left it there…'

'Why?'

'Because that's where it belongs. With him. Undisturbed.' Carter was not a suspicious person, but in this he was certain. 'I think it should be returned.'

'That is for you to decide.'

'On the anniversary,' Carter nodded, relieved it was about to be sorted, but Arif had misunderstood what he meant.

'I have a conference on the exact date, but if you want me to take you in, then I shall cancel it.'

'I meant for you to return it.'

'No.' Arif shook his head. 'It is your property.'

Carter watched as he returned the teething ring to the pouch.

'I shall have it packed along with your things.'

'Fine.' Carter refused to plead, and just stared at Arif. 'I'll be in touch.'

He walked out, refusing to look back, ready to board his boat and get away. But he had to wait for his things, and as well as that he needed to breathe before facing that journey.

Damn you, Arif...

He strode past the deserted dining room and out to the board-walk, then leant against the wooden rail and stared up at the dark near-moonless sky. He did not want to be here. God knew if Bene-dict turned up now then he'd be tempted to just sign over the place if it meant he could get the hell out...

Then he heard a sharp, panicked intake of breath and, turn-ing around, realised it was Grace walking towards him and that he'd scared her.

'It's just me.'

Grace put her hand to her chest and exhaled in relief, but her heart was still hammering.

'What are you doing out here?' he asked.

She shrugged and went to walk on, still hurt by his dismissal, but she didn't want to look churlish. 'I messed up with the tour,' Grace admitted. 'I knew the times had changed tonight, but I thought dinner was before we went out.'

'It's a new moon,' he explained.

She frowned, not understanding.

'Didn't Felicity tell you?'

'Probably,' Grace said. 'I wasn't really listening.'

She certainly wasn't about to admit she'd spent most of today trying not to think about him.

Now, standing in the oppressive, humid air, she saw the tension on his features.

Heard his silence.

'I'll leave you in peace.' She started to walk off.

'There's no peace to be had here.'

Grace paused and, given what she'd found out today, she understood why he felt that way.

'Someone on the tour said something about...' She took a breath and made herself ask. 'Was it your family who were attacked?'

'Yes.'

'I'm so sorry.'

'It was a very long time ago.'

'Even so...' It was too dark to read his features, but he must have seen her eyes move to his scar. 'Felicity said...'

'There are a lot of rumours. None of them true. I was there, and even I don't know what happened.'

She waited, but he didn't elaborate or tell her what that meant.

Even the thought of him having been there made her shiver. She doubted he'd appreciate knowing that, so she quickly blamed her shudder on the dark night.

'I feel as if a hundred pairs of eyes are watching me.'

'Thousands,' he corrected.

'Don't.' She gave a nervous laugh. 'Really?'

'Of course.'

There was the sudden hoot of an owl and a rustle of the low bushes nearby and she moved a little closer to the other human present. Only the other human present startled her more than the jungle at night, because he placed a hand on her bare arm and the contact was electric.

'It's fine,' he told her, when there was a loud crash in the trees behind them. 'It's just your friends the elephants.'

'How do you know?'

'I used to...' He halted. 'I used to know these things.'

They looked out into the night and listened for several moments. The silence between them was far gentler now, and his eyes were narrow, yet alert, as the noise faded into the distance.

'Aren't they too close?' Grace asked. 'I mean…' She looked at the wooden fence that lined the boardwalk.

'It's their land,' Carter said, and they both turned to lean on the fence. 'The staff are all aware. If they get too close they'll try to move them back. They're quite a way away.'

He looked at her properly then. She was wearing her sarong, and it was the first time he'd seen her with her hair down. He knew he'd hurt her, and it pricked his conscience.

'I was short with you before,' he said. 'I apologise.'

'It's fine.'

'No.' He shook his head. 'You didn't deserve it.'

Now it was Grace who turned and looked at him.

'I can see why you don't care what happens to your grandfather's home, but…' She swallowed. 'It's just sad to think of it changing.'

'What did you hear?' he asked, then guided her so that she stood in front of him.

He moved her so easily, Grace thought, and she went so easily. It was as if the wooden floor beneath her feet was air, or she was skating on ice.

Not that she'd ever skated. But even so the thought made her smile as she faced him—or was it the simple relief that they were talking again and alone? His scent cut through the dank humid air, and they were staring at each other as intently as they had the moment they met.

'What's everyone saying?' he asked.

'That you're going to have a film crew come here.' She looked for a reaction but got none. 'It would be a shame to spoil it.'

'Arif would concur.'

She must have heard the edge to his voice. 'Did you two just have an argument?'

'I guess you could call it that.'

Carter didn't tell her what it had been about, though, and nor did he tell her the plans were his cousin's, deciding that in this case perhaps it was better the devil she *didn't* know. A sell-out and a power-hungry rat she would possibly be able to fathom more easily than a man whose heart had turned to stone at the age of eight. A man who was a cold, empty shell, who could crush a pretty soul like Grace's in the palm of his hand.

Yet she stood as if undaunted—in fact she disputed the supposed evidence.

'It's just rumours,' she added.

And in her sarong her shoulders were near naked, her dark curls were still wet from the shower, and he didn't care about the rules tonight.

'I missed you last night,' he told her.

She let out a short, incredulous breath, minty and fresh, and he looked down at the mouth he had forced himself to deny.

He could deny it no more.

Grace found out not only what she'd missed last night, but all she'd been missing. For when his mouth lightly grazed hers, she almost folded inside at the slow, sensual contact.

He could have kissed her the moment she met him, Grace now knew, as her lips brushed his, parting a little. It might have been described as a light kiss, but it was potent, for no contact was broken and she closed her eyes to the heady bliss.

As his hand slid to her waist he pulled her into him. The slip of his tongue, her involuntary moan, seemed to inflame him, as if he'd been waiting for this kiss for a very long time.

So, too, had she.

His kiss was masterful, honed to perfection, and when she closed her eyes, when she sank into sheer bliss, Grace didn't even care how those skills had been acquired, she just relished their application.

He tasted her, curled her tongue, sucked the tip, so slow and thorough. And that combined with the expensive scent of him, and the heat from his naked torso, had her coveting more of him. She pressed her hands on his bare chest—not to push him away, just to feel beneath, to touch him and feel the fan of hair—then moved them up to his hair, simply to feel more of him.

There was no comparison to the teenage kisses she'd known. It felt like a discovery as she simply allowed the passion in. His hands were more specific—one came to her breast and felt it through the flimsy fabric. She should remove his hand, Grace knew, tell him it was too much, too soon. Only it wasn't enough, and it was by far too late, for she'd ached for this since last night.

She felt her stomach tense low down as he lifted her hair and kissed her neck with the same deep attention he had given her mouth. His hand left her breast and pulled her closer in, and possibly he lifted her a little, for her bare feet felt as if there was no ground beneath them.

Her eyes were closed, her mouth frantic. 'Why didn't you kiss me last night?' she breathed.

'Shh…' he said, kissing down her neck towards her shoulder. 'I'm kissing you now…'

'Why?' she asked again, still bemused, only more so now. A night and a day of frustration had her demanding answers and she moved her neck so they faced each other, breathless, mid-kiss, suspended in want. She could feel where his mouth had been, and watched as he pondered her question.

'Because you don't know me.'

'You don't know me either, Carter,' she responded. Because if he knew she had never been touched, or the true chaos of her life back home, then she was certain he'd be gone.

'If you did know me, you'd know we can go nowhere. I don't do relationships.'

'So, you think with one kiss I'd assume we were in a relationship?'

'Grace, I think we both want more than one kiss.'

She swallowed, more than aware of her own desire. Certainly she could feel his, wedged against her stomach, beguiling and tempting.

'As I said, you don't know me. I don't get involved.'

But, again, Carter didn't know her either.

They really were going nowhere.

In a few weeks she'd be back home, facing the problems she'd left behind, and right now she felt this rare liberty—as if this was the only real chance she had to be free, to know herself, to be with another person as the woman she wanted to be.

She knew, too, as she had on sight, that she did not belong in Carter's world, and nor did he belong in hers.

They met tonight, in this rare, sultry place, and for the first time in so many years she wasn't scared about tomorrow.

'Yes.' Grace nodded. 'I do want more than a kiss.'

He slid his hands down her hips, held her bottom, while his eyes never left her face.

'We can go back to my grandfather's place,' Carter said, then added, 'Take my boat.'

She pulled her head back. 'I thought…' She swallowed. 'Can't we go to your suite?'

'Here?' He frowned taking her face in his hands, looking right into her eyes.

'Please.'

'Are you a quiet lover?' he asked, and she felt her cheeks burn beneath his palms.

'I don't know,' Grace responded. 'Maybe?'

It was the closest she could come to telling him she'd never made love.

CHAPTER FIVE

CARTER STEPPED INTO a speedboat and then offered her his hand.

Grace took it gladly.

She knew there was no future, no romance. Just this night…

And she knew she might never again get the chance to be wild and free and with someone so beautiful.

After six missing years Carter made her brave enough to discover this side of herself.

His speedboat was beautiful, with a small cabin and plush, comfortable seats, and instead of releasing her after she'd boarded he pulled her in and kissed her again. A soft, slow kiss that told her this was all okay.

'It's an hour or so, with a stop on the way—and, yes,' he said, as he started the engine. 'I'll get you back for your dawn—'

'Actually,' Grace cut in, 'there's no dawn tour. Tomorrow it's a jungle walk…'

Carter felt his chin rise, his shoulders and neck tightening—though it was not echoes of the past that had tension ripping through him, but thoughts of her in the jungle tomorrow.

'Who's…?' Even his vocal cords had tightened, and he cleared his throat as the boat moved off. 'Is Arif taking the group out?'

'No, I think it's Felicity.'

He said nothing, his eyes fixed ahead. He'd barely heard of Felicity, let alone seen her, but knew she wasn't a local and was here doing research. He reminded himself that Arif wouldn't let her take a group out if she wasn't skilled, but hadn't Felicity been here mere months?

It was dark, with no glint of moon, and even the stars were hidden behind low black clouds as they put-putted past the longhouses. But when they turned off the main river…when the last of the light was gone…he heard her deep intake of breath…

'You're fine,' he said, drawing her close so she stood by him.

'Will we see other boats?'

'Most can't get down here,' Carter said, and steered them into a small tributary, then another, where the branches were hanging low, the banks closer, forming a natural tunnel. He guided them down, then they came to some mangroves and he turned the engine off.

'What are you doing?' she whispered as he turned the lights off and they were plunged into darkness.

He turned her around and wrapped his arms over her shoulders. 'Look,' he told her.

'I can't see anyth—'

For a second she thought she had something in her eye. Little lights were darting across her vision. But then she gasped as she saw the river trees as if draped in fairy lights, flickering on and off, dots of yellow and cool icy green.

'Fireflies,' she gasped.

'And a new moon,' he said. 'Which makes them especially bright. Now do you get why the group went out later tonight?'

Grace started to laugh—a giddy laugh, a carefree laugh—and she spun around, stunned by the tiny lights, the sheer volume of them.

'It looks as if they've been strung on the branches…as if…' She had never seen anything so beautiful, so pretty, so wondrous. Some of the lights darted, and some of them seemed to flash in unison, as if synchronised. 'This is so precious!'

'Yes.' He turned her to face him. 'And so are you,' he stated, for he needed her so badly tonight.

Beyond the display in the lush trees where the fireflies gathered were the bare, silvery mangroves where his family had been lost. Where not only his heart had been carved out but his spirt, too, leaving him a stranger to those who had once known him.

'Take another look,' he said. 'They disappear once the lights come on.'

For Grace, they would never disappear.

Even before they'd made love the night was perfect. As if Carter himself had been standing on ladders and arranging the lights just to give her this sight.

'Thank you,' she said as he started up the boat. The light show was over but her heart was soaring even as they were plunged back into the night. Bolder now, she moved behind him as he took the wheel. Wrapping her arms around his waist she leant her head on his strong back and gazed out to the darkness. 'For bringing me here.'

Carter loathed the rare times he was here. It was like sailing through hell. But tonight he felt the low grip of her arms around his waist as he stared ahead. Feeling her warmth, he carefully guided the boat through the winding, narrow stretch. The dense vegetation was gone; the river here was lined on either side with bare silvery mangroves.

Grace's touch, the heat from her body and the promise of bed was everything he needed to get through this stretch of river he particularly loathed.

'Was it here?' she asked, and he assumed she must have felt the tension zip through his shoulders.

Usually he'd ignore such a question, but then, there was nothing usual about this situation. He'd avoided being here, and certainly had never brought a woman. There was no demand for him to answer...just a calm, patient presence...and they were, after all, just together for one night.

'Just there,' he finally answered, pointing to the exact spot. 'That was where my father tied the boat off. A local fisherman saw it empty.'

He turned the boat's flashlight on and aimed it towards the riverbank, but there were no predatory glinting eyes, just the pale mangroves and the still, dark water. He thought of his mother, impatient when they couldn't get the small boat close enough...

'Sophie!'

He could almost hear his father warning her...see Hugo smiling over her shoulder, looking at him.

Moving the flashlight, he shone it into the mangroves, almost expecting to see Hugo's innocent smile.

That damn teething ring.

Arif should have left it there, undisturbed.

* * *

Carter turned off the flashlight, and Grace knew he was shutting down any further discussion about it. She didn't blame him.

It was eerie to be on the river now, a relief to leave that stretch behind.

More so for Carter.

'Not long,' he said, as they turned down another waterway and finally she glimpsed lights.

'Are there people at home?' she asked as he tied the boat.

'There are some residences and offices, but their jetty is further along.' She saw him look at her taut features. 'Don't worry, Felicity won't see us. The banyan tree is a great divider.'

She laughed. 'Why am I so scared of her?'

'I don't know.' He pointed to his laptop and she passed it out to him. 'That too,' he said, and she handed him the leather cylinder he'd been carrying at the airport.

'So much for spontaneous,' she quipped.

'When it rains in Borneo…' he said, offering his hand and pulling her out. 'I am not risking them.'

The lawn was so unlike the jungle, trimmed and cold beneath her feet, and then they came to a stone path and walked up some steps.

'Wait here…' he told her, and she watched as he opened up some French doors.

She gasped as he turned on lights. 'A ballroom?'

'It was,' he said. 'Now it's a conference room, but there used to be parties held here. Arif and I would watch.'

He didn't elaborate, just deposited his luggage by the doors and then his attention was fully upon her.

She felt shy, and just a touch awkward—possibly because of her inexperience, or just because she was here, in this stunning, opulent home, where apparently you entered via a ballroom.

But then she met his eyes and any gathering doubts flew away. For there was nothing in her head other than his male beauty. Not a thought save for one—that it *had* to be him. This night could only happen with him. On this hot, sultry island, all her secrets would be held in the jungle...a place she was never going to return.

'Can we dance?' she asked.

'I don't dance.'

'One dance,' she said, and draped her arms around his neck.

They swayed to no music and she inhaled the scent of his chest and then kissed his salty skin. Breathing him, licking him, tasting him... And not caring, barely noticing, when he unknotted her sarong and it fell to the polished wooden floor.

Oh, the feel of her breasts against his chest, his hands easing her knickers past her thighs. She pushed them down and stepped out of them.

'One more dance,' said the man who never danced as he discarded his clothing.

And she thought there might just be music, because they moved slowly as if to a rhythm.

His breathing was ragged in her ear, and then he took her hand and slipped it between them, and she held him, stroked him. Then they separated and he toyed with her breasts, lowering his head and tasting them one by one.

'Please...' she said when he stopped his attention there.

But he desisted, and neither did he pull her back into his embrace. The sight of the silver he'd left on her stomach was the most erotic thing she'd ever seen. His erection was alive between them, as if searching for where Grace ached the most.

'Take me to bed,' she pleaded, and he did.

But first—hopelessly unromantic—he took condoms from his luggage.

'I don't bring anyone here,' he told her.

She liked that. Knew this was a rarity for them both.

As he picked her up she coiled her legs around his waist. He took the long, winding grand stairs and kissed her at the top, then carried her down a corridor, then another...

She clung on to his neck, kissing his face, his mouth, his neck, feeling the passion she hadn't known she was capable of, or had simply not allowed to emerge.

* * *

Carter loathed coming here.

Past the photos…up the stairs.

The bombardment of memories felt too much at times, but tonight all he had to deal with was her body, coiled around him, and the kisses she rained on his face. Transported by desire, he opened the door to his wing and kissed her hard against the wall. His hand reached down. He was desperate to have her…the bedroom was by far too far away…

'Bed,' she insisted.

He kissed her all the way there then dropped her onto the bed, put the condoms aside, wanting first to taste her, and for her to put her mouth on him. He looked at her glittering eyes, her pale body, and then to her lips, wet from his kisses. He slid a hand between her thighs and felt her, warm and slick. He touched her tender spot and watched her bite her lip. He stroked her with light beats of pressure, watching her twitch, her knees lifting and her hand coming over his.

'Oh, God…' she gasped, and he forgot about mouths…forgot everything… For even though he wanted so badly to watch her come, he needed her more.

His kiss was fierce and consuming as he settled his thighs between her own, and he lifted and held himself, guided himself to her entrance.

He could feel her, slick and warm, and he heard her soft moans. She was so oiled he was tempted to simply slip in, to lose himself, but he hauled himself back from the edge and reached to the bedside.

Grace breathed in relief. The slight nudge of him had hurt and she wanted to regroup, to tell herself that it was done, he'd broken her, and he never had to know.

Her hand slid from his shoulder as he moved to get protection, and then she felt the waxy skin, the pitted cool flesh, and the thought of her own imminent pain receded.

She felt him still…felt as if she was touching something forbidden—as if beneath her fingers was a secret. She felt a crevice, felt the thick scar tissue beneath. She almost expected him to object by moving away, but he was still. She would never know him after this night, and she wanted to know what she could. So she continued to touch him, to feel the cool, tough flesh and the dints. She knew from his breathing that he was more than aware of her perusal, more intimate than her touch in the ballroom.

He was so aware. He felt her exploration. The skin on his back was usually dull to sensation, but always he was aware of a lover's recoil—as if they could not stand the imperfection, the truth that their polished lover was flawed.

Yet Grace's fingers felt like a gentle enquiry, and he closed his eyes at the tenderness of her touch, grateful for her lack of questions, her quiet acceptance.

Protection forgotten, he moved to enter her.

His kiss was deep and wet—a hungry kiss, a devouring kiss. His hand was on her cheek and there was an unvoiced concurrence as still she explored his naked back, moving down past his shoulders, low on his ribcage.

This was no accidental graze of her fingers. They stroked the damaged flesh and he did not know why he allowed it—just knew that here, in this hellhole he'd returned to, it helped.

He guided himself to ease inside her, and there was that resistance again—not her…he could feel her wanting and her softly parted thighs, the ache of desire cording them.

Then he met her eyes, like that very first time, and they were as clear and as perfect as they'd been when they'd first looked into his.

She confirmed what he'd just found out.

'I've never made love…'

'I don't do love,' he responded.

'I've never had sex.'

He stared down at her, wondering why a beautiful twenty-five-year-old might avoid such a vital pleasure?

They both had scars, Carter realised, and neither of them was denying them tonight.

'Do you want…?'

His voice was a low burr. He was trying to get his head around what he was being told, trying to claw for his usual logic, but she was almost sobbing, pleading…

'You know that I do.'

He had never made love to a virgin. There was no place in his bed for tender hearts. And yet those rules seemed to have vanished, and raw desire, older than the land that surrounded them, was calling. More than that, he wanted her untutored, untouched body, and as she closed her eyes he held his unsheathed, thick length and watched the grit of her teeth as he nudged in. He heard her moan and watched a tear squeeze from her closed eyes, and then he felt the tightness, and had to stop himself from sinking too fast into her exquisite pleasure.

'Look at me…' he told her.

She didn't know how to. But the searing agony was fading, and it was the most deeply intimate moment of her life—not just in the physical sense. His warm breath and his mouth were still above her, and his precision hadn't wavered when she'd revealed her truth.

So she looked at him, and for a moment there wasn't a single lie, nothing between them—just this night.

Then he closed his eyes and drove deeply in.

It hurt, but he pushed fully in, and although it hurt some more there was a giddy rush, a sense of liberty, a pure and intense pleasure, and she opened her eyes and stared back at him. She felt as if something had just been put right…as if this very moment was the reason she was here.

'No one ever has to know,' she whispered, liking the secret between them that here, for tonight, she could find herself.

She shuddered with pain and pleasure as he moved. The rawness and the sensations were too much, while conversely not enough, and when he drove in again she moaned, not wholly in pleasure.

He pushed her damp hair from her face and the slightly sick feeling receded. She had nothing with which to compare—just this deep sense that it could only ever have been him, because her body was coming alive, thrumming beneath him.

She had never locked eyes so intensely with another.

'Move with me,' he encouraged her, putting a hand on her bottom and lifting her as he drove more deeply in, then moving it to the small of her back as she moved of her own will to meet him.

'I'm going to come...'

'No,' he told her, because she wasn't lost yet.

He was deep in her tight space, so close to coming himself, and yet prolonging the intense pleasure by moving slower than his urgent desire.

He felt her holding on, hot and crying, watched her biting her lip. And he adored her internal fight, and the little pulses when she gave in. How she closed her eyes as she gripped him intimately.

He moved up onto his forearms and he took her, each thrust a little closer to the tempo he wanted to be met. He watched her eyes widen, felt her calves wrap around him, and there was something a little selfish about the way he took her, and something a little greedy about how she begged him.

Grace was sobbing and moaning in pleasure, her fingers digging into his taut buttocks, jolting with the raw power of him. She'd thought tonight she'd know pleasure—she'd never thought it would be so raw and pure.

Then he stilled and she felt a final swell. His shout was silent, and she felt as if her heart had been rapidly drained...as if every drop of life force had flooded her sex. And, no, she wasn't a noisy lover. She was almost as silent as him as the world went black and he spilled inside her. She felt tender, raw and exquisite with the depth of her orgasm and the intensity of his.

She knew she was crying...knew he was watching her fall

apart beneath him, witnessing her unravel as she had never felt able to before.

She wanted to roll over, to curl up and hold her aching self, will herself back to calm. But she was on her elbows, watching his taut, flat stomach as he slowly slid out. And it was his hand that calmed her, grounded her as she tried to catch her breath.

When she rolled over it was not to turn away, but to turn in to him, her leg over his, his hand on her hip, her face, now burning from exertion and crying tears on his chest.

Then she watched a little fascinated as he positioned himself so that what had been hard inside her now lay long on his thigh. She could hear the hammer of his heart slowing, and guessed there were questions ahead, but then he kissed the top of her head, as if in a little sign of no regret.

And, for now, tomorrow just didn't matter.

CHAPTER SIX

CARTER BENNETT HAD been completely certain it would never happen to him.

So certain that he would only ever practise safe sex that he'd never got around to having the vasectomy he'd intended to.

He'd definitely never brought a woman back here—and nor did he generally lie in bed holding her after. But they were both silent, as if processing what had taken place, with Grace's head on his chest as he stared at the ceiling.

It was she who spoke first.

'You think I should have told you?'

He shook his head, but she was staring out of the French windows to the black moonless night so probably didn't see. 'You did tell me.'

'I meant earlier…' she amended. 'If I'd told you I was a virgin you'd have turned that speedboat around.'

Carter thought of how badly he'd needed her and wasn't so certain he would have.

'I didn't want your judgement,' Grace told him.

'What does that mean?'

'For you to assume I couldn't handle a one-night stand.' Her voice was defiant as she pulled away from his embrace and rolled onto her back, then pulled the sheet up to cover her. 'I put my life on hold for a long time. I'll no doubt be doing the same again in the near future.' She let out a shaky breath. 'I wanted a night like this before I went back to reality.'

'The reality is, we didn't use anything.'

The defiance left Grace. 'No…'

'You're not on the pill?'

'I'm not.'

She closed her eyes, knew that in that part she'd been way more reckless than planned.

'There's a pill for the morning after...' Even as she said it her voice trailed off. She was not sure if she wanted that option...

'I'll go to the pharmacy at nine,' he said.

Grace said nothing.

'That was a joke,' Carter said. 'Albeit a bad one...'

She turned, and was surprised to see that his rather haughty face wasn't accusatory—in fact his features were softened by the slightest smile.

'Grace, we are in the middle of nowhere.'

'True...' She found herself able to stay facing him. 'I wasn't thinking.'

'Neither of us were,' Carter agreed. 'And you're wrong. Had you told me back on the boat, I don't think I'd have turned around.' He paused, as if surprised by his own admission, but then he was frank. 'I would, however, have made it far clearer that we had no future. I don't get involved—'

Grace interrupted him. 'Carter, we have no future.' She looked him right in the eyes as she continued. 'That was the best part about it.'

She had no real future.

Not one that involved dating and romance. Instead she had a sick mother to support—what guy would understand that?

And until tonight she'd had no real past—not when it came to men.

Or dating.

No social life or adventures to count.

For years she'd lived in some sort of vacuum, focussing on taking care of her mother, working while she could, losing herself a little more each day. If it hadn't been for Violet, she'd barely have glimpsed the outside world.

'It was just tonight—and, believe me, that's all I wanted.'

'Why wait, though?' He frowned.

'I've had a lot going on. It kind of killed any chance of romance.'

'Well, if that's what you feel you've missed out on, then we are certainly missuited—because I don't do romance in any way shape or form.'

'I know,' Grace said, though she didn't necessarily agree.

She thought about the fireflies, the way he had held her, the dancing in the ballroom. Not to mention the fact that they were still in his gorgeous bed, talking. This felt more romantic than she'd ever hoped.

Still, rather than admit that, she tried to make a joke. 'At least I know now that I'm quiet in bed.'

He said nothing to that—didn't even smile.

Oh, why did her jokes always fall flat? Grace thought.

But then she felt a shift, so subtle it was nothing she could define…just a light tension between them.

And she knew it was the stir of arousal.

How, when she was still coming down from her first time?

She took a breath, trying to ignore his naked body lying beside her, trying to ignore the thrum in hers. Forcing herself to consider the ramifications of that one, heady indulgence.

'What if I am…?' She could barely say the word, the thought too daunting to contemplate.

'It will be dealt with.'

'Hmm…' Grace wasn't sure she wanted to know what his method of *dealing* with things might be.

'When are you due?'

When she didn't answer, he persisted.

'Grace, when was your last period?'

'I'm not sure…' She sat up, tried to get her head around dates, but it was hard to get her thoughts out of this night, let alone cast her mind back. 'Just before I came away.'

'It will most likely be okay.'

'Yep.' She took a breath and looked around the vast room. She knew he was trying to reassure her, but she didn't feel reassured. She'd always wondered how people lost their heads and took risks…in truth she'd privately been a bit dismissive…

Now she knew better.

'I ought to get back.'

'Already?'

She nodded, and went to get up, but he reached for her shoulder to halt her.

'Why are you being so brittle?'

'Because I feel stupid,' she admitted. 'Because I wanted everything that happened tonight, except for the part where we didn't
use protection.' She ran a hand through her wild hair and refused
to let him see how panicked she felt. 'Can I use your shower?'

'Of course.'

She glanced around the room for her clothes...

'They're in the ballroom,' he said.

'God, so they are.' She closed her eyes, a little mortified by
the rather loose behaviour he seemed to have unearthed, but then
opened them to his lazy smile.

'I'll find you a sarong.'

'Thank you.'

'I don't have any female underwear, though.'

'No hidden stash?' she teased, and instantly regretted it.

Except he laughed, and she could, right there, have gone over
and kissed him. Finally, someone who got her stupid jokes.

She looked at him, lying with the sheet barely covering that
gorgeous body that had been over hers, and deep inside.

'Shower?' Grace said.

'Just through there.' Carter pointed, watching as she climbed
out of bed, seeing a little of the evidence on her thigh and her gorgeous bottom and hardening again.

'Can I use...?' she began.

She was as turned on as he, he could see the glitter in her eyes,
the way she bit her lip, her thighs poised as if she might dive back
into bed.

'Shampoo?'

'Sure.'

He was still pointing as she disappeared into the bathroom and
Carter stared at his own finger and knew he'd been tempted to
crook it...to beckon her back to bed.

And that was not him.

Oh, Carter partook in a lot of morning-after sex, but he viewed
that as necessary...a little like brushing your teeth. You felt better for the rest of the day for having done it.

He wasn't so used to straight-after-sex sex, though...or resisting joining a lover in the shower.

He'd also like to correct her. He was rather certain she could soon be a very noisy lover.

And she was funny—that was new—lying in bed dwelling on another...

He liked her company and that was a whole other type of new.

Climbing out of bed, he picked up a couple of sarongs from his dresser. Covering the evidence of their coupling with the sheet, he left one out for the prior virgin, the other he wrapped around his hips, then walked out through the French doors and onto the balcony.

The sky was still navy, the dawn inching towards breaking. The clouds had drifted away, and the stars were taking their final moments to shine in the moonless sky. The usually muggy air had a morning-fresh tinge.

The recklessness of the night was concerning, but for now, very deliberately, he dwelt on the actual reason he was here.

He had dreaded returning, but it had been made easier by Grace.

This whole situation would be made easier by Grace.

He was certain she needed money for her mother, and he found it endearing that she refused to say.

God knew, he wasn't used to that.

He admired that she had come to his bed with purpose, wanting to lose her virginity. Hell, he completely got that a night that could go nowhere held appeal.

Certainly it had for him, on too many occasions.

And he knew that if there was such a thing here Grace Andrews would already have called for a taxi.

As for pregnancy...?

He closed his eyes. He would not cloud his thoughts with that.

For Carter that was a separate issue entirely.

It wasn't concern about a pregnancy, or a sense of charity, nor guilt that she'd been a virgin that had him considering his options. If he wanted to stop his cousin in his poisonous tracks, then marriage for a year would take care of that.

A year, though?

It had seemed unfathomable—in truth it still did. Yet for the first time he dwelt on that clause he'd so summarily dismissed.

Now it seemed doable.

He'd have to tell Grace why, though—have to share his past when he preferred not to. And he'd have to tell her that this place, even though he'd prefer that it didn't, still mattered to him.

'Hey…'

He turned his head as she came out on the balcony and joined him. Her hair was combed and slicked back.

'Thanks for this,' she said, gesturing to the black sarong he'd left out, then she looked up. 'Wow…' she said, gazing up at the canopy of stars and then staring down to the dark of the thick jungle stretched out in the distance. 'Which way is the resort?' she asked and her eyes followed to where he pointed. 'So, no chance of walking back?'

'None,' Carter agreed. 'Do you want breakfast?' he offered. 'We could take it up here and watch the sunrise. It's pretty incredible.'

He saw her hesitation, knew she really just wanted one night, and it actually strengthened him, made the thoughts in his head take clearer shape. He wanted to be certain before he voiced them.

'Are you going to cook?'

'I don't cook.' He wasn't going to summon breakfast, though. He didn't want anyone else invading, nor his thoughts interrupted. 'But Malay will have it all prepared in the kitchen. We can load up a tray and bring it back.'

'Sounds good.'

They walked through the house she had barely noticed last night, down the curved stairs, and she paused at a photo of a baby smiling.

'Is this your brother?' She looked at the gorgeous almond eyes and spiky hair, the wide smile.

'Why do you think that?' Carter asked.

'Well, he's blond, and far too smiley to be you.'

Carter gave a low laugh. 'You're wrong—that *is* me.'

They wandered down a little further, and they came to an image that had her throat squeezing tight.

His mother was too beautiful for words, with blonde hair and fine features. His father was handsome, but perhaps not as arrogant-looking as Carter. And there he was, smiling again.

Then she looked at the baby Carter held in his arms.

'He's blond too,' Grace said, and then wondered if she should have said *was*.

But all she could see was his soft spiky blond hair and huge eyes. He was such a beautiful baby, and his smile was so infectious that even though she felt her throat grow tighter she found that she was returning it.

Carter could not.

He didn't see the smile. He just stared. Not at his parents, nor at Hugo, but at the silver teething ring his brother held in his hand.

What the hell had Arif been thinking? He should have left it where it belonged.

He walked away, and Grace followed him into the gorgeous kitchen. It was old but very, very beautiful, and as he put some coffee on she took a high stool.

He wondered how to broach things.

How to explain that he was considering asking her to be his temporary wife.

'It looks as if you were a very happy family.' Grace was undoubtedly still thinking of the photos. 'Your parents were clearly in love.'

'It's easy to be happy when you don't have responsibilities,' Carter said dismissively. 'They were happy at the expense of others...' He glanced over. 'I find love to be selfish.'

'Selfish?' Grace checked, and he nodded.

'Extremely. My parents wanted adventure, to travel. To see the Northern Lights, sleep under the stars, trek through the jungle...'

'I think that's lovely.'

'Until it isn't. They had children.'

It had been Carter who had given Hugo his bottle when they'd gone out to gaze at a full moon. Carter who had checked there were enough provisions when they'd set out on yet another adventure.

While waiting for the coffee to brew he loaded a tray with a bowl of fruit and some pastries, and took some jugs from the fridge, scooping out some shaved ice.

'What are you making?'

'ABC,' he told her. *'Air batu campur,'* he explained, adding little balls of pale pink jelly to a bowl. 'Well, the cheat's version. Malay has made it—you just add your own fruit...'

And nuts, Grace thought, then tried to not pull a face when she saw him add to the tray a small dish of creamed corn. 'It looks more like a dessert.'

'Maybe...' In truth, he was unsure whether it was because of his mother's somewhat lackadaisical ways that Malay always served it for breakfast, or simply down to the heat.

There was too much he didn't know, and too many memories. As he walked down the corridor, past the framed photos, he deliberately didn't pause to look at them. He didn't need them, for there were new images dancing before his eyes: a flash of himself feeding Hugo spoonsful of ice-cream.

He was certain now that it was seeing the teething ring that was to blame for this surge in sensation. Arif might just as well have unearthed Carter's deeply buried heart.

There was a deep purple hue to the sky as they set up on the balcony, and he filled two bowls with ice, added the little balls of rosewater jelly and topped them with a red bean ice-cream.

'Choose your fruit...' he said, selecting some berries for himself.

She picked up a dark, heavy fruit, like a cross between a pomegranate and plum, but then, clearly unsure what to do with it, put it back.

Carter hesitated before reaching out for it. 'Give it here...'

She handed him the fruit she'd discarded and he carved it effortlessly, the dark flesh opening to reveal pieces of white swollen bulbs. Carter stared at the lily-white pockets of flesh for a moment. He had always been averse to the delicate sweet scent they delivered—not that he showed it.

'Mangosteen,' he informed her, scooping out the fruit onto her plate, but taking none for himself.

'It's delicious...' she said, popping a bulb in her mouth.

He wrinkled his nose.

'You don't like them?'

'Not particularly.'

He'd lived off them for a week—not plump and ripe, as those ones were, though, but rotten and bitter...

Carter glanced at her, pouring syrup over her breakfast, and knew he had to broach things. But first he watched as Grace took her first tentative taste of the sweet, icy, milky concoction, then went back for a second taste.

She met his eyes and actually blushed.

'What?' he asked.

'It's nothing.'

'Well, you're either having an allergic reaction or...'

'Okay, okay!' She laughed. 'Look, I'd never had sex until last night, but I'm guessing this is the perfect breakfast to have after.'

'I guess I'm about to find out.'

He hadn't really considered it in that way before.

He took a generous taste and nodded. 'Correct,' he said. 'It's definitely a good choice for...'

Then he paused, because if some foods belonged to Borneo, then this breakfast belonged to them, and he would not be partaking with another.

Not that he'd be telling her that.

Instead he moved the conversation to the reason he'd asked her out here—and it was not about sharing a romantic breakfast!

'Those guys staying at the resort—the loud ones... You were right. Their intention is to turn the place into a film set.'

She pulled a resigned face as she put down the jug. 'I thought it was just rumours,' she said. 'Or I hoped it was.'

She looked at him and he could see the disappointment clouding her eyes.

'What sort of work do you do—films or...?'

'I'm an architect.'

'Oh.' She gave a small downturned smile. 'I don't know what to say.' She looked at the lovely old banyan tree. 'Will you keep that?'

'Grace, it's my cousin Benedict who's the one in discussion with them. Arif asked me to come here to try and come up with a plan to stop him.'

'Phew!' She gave him a smile. 'So I don't have to tie myself to the tree to dissuade you?'

'You don't.'

'Is his surname Bennett too?'

Carter nodded.

'Well, his parents didn't put much thought into that.'

He found that he was smiling. 'True…' He even gave a small laugh. 'I've never thought of it before. I tend to use another B-word when referring to him. He's a bastard—always has been. His father was too.'

'Can you say no?'

'Of course,' he nodded. 'And I have repeatedly. It doesn't stop their drones going up, though, or their boats going on the water, or Benedict inviting location scouts to wade through the grounds. They want to make some wildlife adventure show—and that's just for starters. I don't want to spend the next decade in some protracted legal battle.'

'Over the house?'

'It's the land that's the real issue. The division goes right up to the resort. When I first heard, I wasn't that worried. I didn't think they'd get insurance to film here.'

'Oh, people pay a lot for danger these days.'

'It would seem so.'

She smiled then, although not at him, and he turned and saw a tree full of little silverback monkeys.

'They look like Christmas decorations.'

'Greedy ones,' he said, and made a noise to warn off one who was already reaching to jump onto the balcony.

'So,' she said, and he saw her trying to tear her eyes from the pretty babies running along the branches, 'what are you going to do?'

'Something extreme,' Carter admitted.

For Carter, marriage was beyond extreme—and yet somehow, this morning, the impossible felt plausible.

Almost logical.

'My grandfather left the property to us both. I warned him that Benedict was a risk…'

'Yet he went ahead?'

'I guess he considered I was a risk too. He was perhaps worried I'd sell it…turn it into a resort.'

'Would you?'

'No—and I told him that. I said he should set up a trust. The locals know what needs doing. At most I expected to keep an eye from a distance…'

Once again she had him drifting from the point, he thought.

'There was a caveat in his will, though—if I marry here in Borneo, and remain married for a year, then I'll have the opportunity to buy my cousin out.'

'Do you have to live here for a year?'

'No, just marry here.'

'Was your grandfather controlling?'

'No.' He smiled at her odd response. 'He was an old romantic. I told him, clearly, that I would never marry for the sake of this place.'

'Did he put in the same clause for Benedict?'

'God, no. He'd be about to celebrate his one-year anniversary if that were the case.'

For Grace, there was something rather dreamy about sharing a delectably sweet breakfast with Carter and watching the jungle come to life. The birds were singing long before the sun spread its fingers of light. And as the violet sky merged into a vivid magenta laced with rose-gold, she saw that for once it wasn't heavy with rain. Even the few wisps of cloud were already burning off, and the morning was revealing itself to be clear and blue. The chatter from the jungle was loud, and she could almost see the trees stirring, teeming with life.

'Where's the resort from here, again?'

'That way.' He pointed.

'I can't even see the river.'

'You have to be higher up and closer to properly see it, though you can catch a glimpse of it.'

As she looked out there was a loud caw, a flock of birds rising, and then a rare silence fell—one only the jungle could provide.

Grace had noticed it—the sudden hush, as if everything had been placed on mute.

'There's a predator,' Carter said. 'The birds are giving a warning.'

'What sort of predator?

'Take your pick. A leopard, a snake…'

And if he was going to ask her to consider being his wife for a year, then he had to at least attempt to tell her why this inhospitable place mattered…even if he'd rather it did not.

'I was found close to there.'

She glanced up.

'Where you just saw those birds go up.'

'Found?'

'I was missing for a week after my family were killed. It was assumed I'd also died.'

'A *week*?'

Grace stood, the gorgeous breakfast forgotten, and went and gazed out from the balcony to look at the glimpse of river near the resort. He watched as she tried to follow the route they had taken last night, back to here. Then she looked to where he'd been found.

'It's miles from the river.'

'Days,' Carter agreed. 'The locals never gave up, though. They were sure I was out there.'

'How did they know?'

'Tracks…some ground was disturbed. They know every leaf, every bird. My father's body was recovered, and there was evidence that my mother had perished. My brother was strapped to her, so—' He faltered just briefly. 'The official search was called off, but the locals could find no physical evidence that I had been killed.'

He knew his voice was steady, yet he took a breath. The scent of mangosteen was no longer sweet, but pungent, as it had been back then, and he stood up from the table—not just to join her, but to get away from the scent.

'They kept looking. And Bashim, Arif's father, found me.'

They both looked out to where the birds had been startled, and for the first time Carter tried to fathom how an eight-year-old boy had got there.

'Bashim said I was perhaps running to get help, but that makes no sense. I was headed in the wrong direction.' He gave a wry smile. 'It would have been more sensible to wait in the boat, or even head here.'

'I doubt you were feeling very sensible.'

'I blame it on this.' He tapped the scar on his forehead. 'It would seem I fell on a rock. I used my T-shirt to bandage it.'

'Resourceful…' She smiled, but he could see tears glinting in her eyes, and he did not want sympathy, nor to unburden. He simply wanted her to understand the debt he owed to the people here.

'I was very close to death when he found me.'

'How close?'

'Judging from the wounds on my back, they thought I'd been lying there a couple of days…' He'd never told another person that. 'My back was a mess…*kalajengking*—scorpion bites—and fire ants.'

He could see her pallor…he hadn't wanted that.

'It took Bashim a couple of days to get me back to his home. He alerted the authorities and I was transferred to hospital. From the little I remember the best care I had was here. Were it not for Bashim and the people here…'

'You'd have died?'

'Certainly. Sometimes it's good not to be able to remember—'

He halted abruptly, recalling how speaking of his grandfather losing his mind had upset her the night they'd first spoken, and not wanting careless words to hurt her again.

'I apologise,' he said. 'I forgot about your mother.'

'No, no…' She put up her hand. 'They're completely separate things. You can't remember at all?'

He shook his head. 'Little bits… But really, I have no desire to. I thought when my grandfather died that I could move on for good—and then I found out my cousin is intent on destroying the place.'

'You must hate him.'

'No.' Carter shook his head. 'Certainly I don't approve of him, and I really would prefer to have nothing to do with him.'

'I'm sure he doesn't want to completely ruin it.'

Then he heard the doubt enter her voice.

'Does he...?'

'I don't think Benedict gives a damn.'

'Then your grandfather should have made better provisions—I wish to God my mother had. I never know if I'm doing the right thing by her.'

Grace's response surprised Carter. He'd thought she'd get where this was leading by now, but if anything the thought of marrying him to save the place wasn't even on her radar.

'It sounds as if you are,' he said.

'I hope so,' Grace sighed.

She was looking out to the dense jungle and she sounded as lost as he had surely felt back then.

Lost and alone.

Standing next to Grace in the silence of the early morning, for the first time he remembered hauling himself up a tree, searching for the familiar sight of the banyan. Desperate for direction... for some way out...

And he could give her that now.

'Grace?'

She turned at the sound of her name.

'You know I don't do relationships.'

'Carter...' She smiled and it reached her gorgeous green eyes. 'I think we've established that already. Look, I get it.' She gave a low laugh. 'Don't worry. I leave tomorrow...'

'What if I suggested we marry?'

Grace laughed again, only this time she rolled her eyes.

'I'm completely serious,' he insisted.

'I am not getting married to you because of some obscure

clause in your grandfather's will. And if it's last night you're worried about, then don't be. I'm probably not pregnant.'

'That's a completely separate issue,' Carter interrupted. 'What if I offered you two million dollars?'

'Yes, please!' She immediately laughed once more—but then she must have seen his serious expression, because her smile and her laughter faded. 'I didn't mean that.'

'Well, I do. You need to secure your mother's future.'

'I've never once said that.'

'Am I wrong, though?'

Her silence was her answer.

'I need a solution, and fast, and if my guess is correct, you need money.'

Grace swallowed. Only now was it dawning on her that this really was a serious proposal—although not in the least the romantic kind.

'No, absolutely not. Anyway, I'm needed at home.'

'I'm aware. I have an apartment in London, and an office… I tend to spend a lot of time in New York, but in the next few months I'll be in Janana a lot, so we wouldn't be in each other's pockets.'

'That's not a marriage.'

'On paper it would be—at least enough to meet the terms of the will.'

She felt colour suffuse her cheeks at this very cold summing up.

'Grace,' he insisted. 'This is business.'

She frowned, because all the velvet of his words had gone.

He hadn't been confiding in her about his past—he'd been telling her for a reason! Now, when he spoke, he was detached, and although his grey eyes met hers, they looked *at* her rather than beyond. The change was almost indecipherable, but either their gorgeous breakfast had turned into a meeting or, she realised, he'd considered it as such all along.

'I didn't come here to discuss business or money.'

She didn't like this game…whatever he was playing.

Grace was aware she'd already been putting on a bit of a front, shielding her heart from the impact of this stunning man. And now her reckless night, her one-night stand, was offering her more, and it had utterly thrown her.

'Can we please go?' she asked.

'Of course.'

Only they were in Borneo, so it wasn't quite as simple as walking off. The little silverbacks were all waiting to pounce and have a little party with any leftovers, so she gritted her jaw as they both cleared the table away.

'I think you should ask someone a little more…' She didn't know the word she was looking for as they carried the trays down the stairs. 'I am sure there are plenty of women who would be only too happy to take your money.'

'I'm asking *you*, though, Grace.'

'Well, I wish you hadn't.'

Midway down the stairs, she simply halted, glimpsing again the precious sense of freedom she'd found last night, her own reckless abandon, the joy of discovering herself while knowing the jungle would keep her secrets.

'You've spoiled things now.'

'Or…' Carter had stopped behind her on the stairs '… I might just have made things a whole lot better.'

CHAPTER SEVEN

'YOU SEEM OFFENDED by my offer...' Carter commented as they walked across the grounds.

'Of course I am,' Grace stated, even if she did feel like some avatar that kept glitching every time the sum of money on offer popped into her head. 'I was raised to believe marriage meant something...' She paused. 'Till my dad walked out.'

'This *would* mean something,' Carter said. 'Financial security for you, less guilt for me.'

'Guilt?'

'I might not love this place; it doesn't mean I want to turn it into a movie set.' He glanced over. 'This is far less whimsical than marrying for love.'

'You think marrying for love is whimsical?'

'I do. I prefer relationships to be transactional. I don't want the responsibility for another person's safety or happiness, and I certainly don't want another person to feel responsible for mine. I told my grandfather the same. But now here we are...'

He had a point—even if she didn't agree or aspire to his cold, lonely life. She knew that responsibility well...the claw of anxiety when she thought of her mother.

She honestly hated it that she was...just a tiny bit...thinking about the advantages.

He climbed onto the boat and offered his hand. He helped her onboard then, as she took a seat, stored his laptop and the leather cylinder he always carried.

'What is that?' she asked as he carefully tucked it away with more care than his laptop. 'You take it everywhere.'

'Blueprints,' he said. 'Hand-drawn plans. And I am not going to lose them or risk them getting wet... We shan't be long.'

'It's fine. I think I'm already too late for the jungle walk...'

* * *

As he started the boat Carter didn't want to examine the relief he felt. He would never tell another person what to do, yet he'd felt a familiar dread when she'd said she was going into the jungle. The same dread he felt when Arif so casually strolled there, or Jamal said he was in the jungle with their son.

He wanted this solved so he didn't have to think of all that... so he barely had to see this land again.

And he would not lose focus on that.

Grace sat, sulking, as he started up the speedboat. 'I thought you were the one worried about your temporary lovers making demands the morning after.'

She watched his shoulders shrug in a half-laugh.

'True.'

He turned and gave her a smile that would melt the ice from the snow-caps, but she refused to return it.

'It's an offer, Grace, not a demand. You have to have been in the district for seven days before we can put in an application for marriage—that's tomorrow. Twenty-one days after that we could marry and—'

'La, la, la...' She put her fingers in her ears and then removed them. 'I am not discussing this, Carter. What happened to my no-strings one-night stand?'

'He found out she was tough.'

She wasn't, though, Grace thought. At least not when it came to Carter. Right now, her blasé reaction was all bravado.

When she'd realised he wasn't joking, his offer had stunned her. The thought of securing her mother's future had been foremost in her mind for so long, and she'd have been lying to herself to deny she'd glimpsed a solution. More worrying, though, had been a lurch of hope that their time together wasn't quite over.

She'd tried to nullify that thought, of course. To remind herself it was a financial proposal he was putting to her, rather than a romantic one. Yet with her body still tender from their night, and her heart open to a man for the first time, Grace was finding it hard to extract emotion from the business deal on offer.

Sex?

A year…?

Grace stole a look at his broad back as he casually steered, her eyes drifting over the narrow hips and firm buttocks. It was impossible not to wonder if this arrangement included bed.

A year with Carter… As if the years she'd missed out on were all condensed into a delicious one.

As if he could sense her sudden longing he glanced over his shoulder. 'Give it some consideration,' he said, before turning his attention back to the river.

Rather than doing that, she looked at the chipped coral nail varnish on her toenails, wishing she'd thought to bring nail varnish remover.

Oh, and a comb that wasn't falling apart more with each passing day.

It was easier to focus on trivialities than just sit admiring his back, and she was far too distracted by his proposal to notice they were taking a different route from last night.

'Grace?' he said, and she realised the boat had halted.

It was at that very moment she knew Carter Bennett had ruined every future lover for her.

No moment, no matter how perfect, would ever come close to this.

At the call of her name she blinked and looked up, and saw they had come to a halt in a river that seemed to no longer exist. The brown water was spread with dark green leaves and stunning lilac flowers and the sky was the clearest blue she had seen it since her arrival.

It was as if they had landed in the jungle version of Monet's garden.

Better, even, because she wasn't gazing at an image—she was in the midst of it.

It was truly a halcyon moment, the silence broken only by the gentle lap of the water against the boat.

* * *

'Where are we?' she asked him.

'Close to the resort,' he said. 'The tour boats are too big to get down here.' He reached into the water and plucked one of the flowers and handed it to her. 'Water hyacinths.'

'Stunning.'

'They're taking over,' he said.

In truth they were invasive, and clogging the rivers, but he chose not to spoil it for her because, yes, they were indeed beautiful.

Only that wasn't why he had brought her here.

Carter stood up, scanning the trees, then his eyes locked on one close to the riverbank. 'Grace...' he started.

'Please...'

Grace tried to halt him. She couldn't, though, because sitting in a river of lilac flowers, her body tender and her memory fresh from being bedded by him, she was having enough trouble designating this a holiday romance...enough trouble holding on to her heart. So instead, she stared back down to the flower, to the gorgeous petals, their orange tips like peacock feathers.

'I don't want to discuss this any further.'

'Shh...'

'Excuse me?' she checked, affronted at being shushed.

But then she saw that he wasn't looking at her. Instead he was staring out, holding up one hand as Felicity did when she wanted them to be quiet.

'There.' He pointed and she followed the line of his finger. What they'd been discussing faded. 'See the nest?'

She couldn't.

'Come here,' he said quietly, summoning her, his eyes set on the trees as, a little unsteadily, she stood too, and walked over. 'There's movement. Right there.'

Oh! She'd been looking into the distance, but he was pointing to a tree close to the river's edge, and there was a huge nest halfway up.

'See?' he checked, and Grace nodded excitedly as a little head popped up. 'They're waking up.'

The tiny head bobbed down again, but not a moment later two arms stretched up, large hands holding a tiny baby orangutan in the air. She couldn't see the mother, just her arms and hands around her infant, the little baby gazing down. It was such a tranquil moment, a precious moment... A mother raising her infant in the air, playing with her baby as any mother would. Then the baby disappeared from sight, still held in loving arms.

'That was incredible...'

It was a relief for Grace to have a reason to let out a little of the emotion that she'd kept pent up since this morning—to cry a little and wipe the tears with the back of her hands.

'I'd almost given up seeing one in the wild. We've been looking for them all week.'

'They're hard to find—the females make a new nest most nights.'

'What about the males?'

'Oh, they're lazy—more often than not they use the discarded nests.'

Grace gave a soft laugh. 'Typical!'

'Or practical,' Carter countered, and then she felt him looking at her. 'Grace, I may be male, but unlike our primate friends I am *not* lazy. I have built my own nest and feathered it very nicely. I don't mind feathering yours if you'll join me for a year.'

'I think I ought to get back.'

'Are you sure...?'

She was about to nod, but then realised he wasn't suggesting they stay to discuss his proposal, just asking if she wanted to watch the nest for a little longer.

'They'll come down at some point, though it might take a while.'

He was completely content to wait, and she could not understand how he could make such a calculating offer, then moments later stand in silent awe, patiently watching these beautiful creatures.

It was Grace who brought up the topic again. 'I don't see how it could work.' Her cheeks were on fire. She was embarrassed to admit she was thinking about it. 'A fake marriage.'

'It happens all the time.' Carter assured her. 'We'd get an application for marriage here, then fly to Kuala Lumpur... We can meet my lawyer there, work out the details, draw up an NDA and such, then agree on a prenup.'

'In English, please?'

'We try to come to a deal we can both agree on and ensure nobody else finds out.'

He halted as the little head of the baby orangutan peeked out again, as if checking that all was clear.

Gosh, it was so human-looking, so tiny.

'Carter...' she gulped '...what if I *am* pregnant.'

His response was abrupt, even stern. 'This proposal has *nothing* to do with that.'

'But what if I am, though?'

'Shall we cross that bridge if we come to it?'

She looked at the little head, peering from the nest, and knew that no matter what Carter and his lawyer might prefer, she'd already made her decision.

'I *shall* be crossing that bridge, Carter,' she warned him. 'Should the issue arise.'

'Your choice.' He nodded. 'So long as you know we'd still have no future.' His eyes flashed a warning. 'I'll build you a nice bridge, though. Well maintained.'

He took out all the emotion—and, ridiculously, it helped.

She was trying so hard to think of this in practical terms. Using every ounce of logic to stop her heart from dreaming of dangerous scenarios where there was at least some possibility that there was more behind this offer. Some glimmer that this contract marriage held a whisper of hope for them both.

But he'd made it abundantly clear that it didn't.

They waited another ten, maybe fifteen minutes, with the occasional glimpse of hands or a little head, and then there was something she had to ask.

'Would we…?' Her voice was croaky, so she cleared it. 'Does this sham marriage involve us sleeping together?'

It was almost a ridiculous question. Her body was alive to him, she was almost fighting not to move closer to him, and yet it was so vital she asked it. She had collapsed beneath him. One night in his bed had taken her to places she had never known existed.

What would a year together entail?

And what happened when boredom set in and the naïve woman no longer amused him?

Before she even entertained the idea these were details she had to know.

The answers terrified her so.

'Benedict is going to throw everything at me—as I intended with him,' he said. 'So in KL at least we would need to share a suite. It would look odd otherwise.'

'And a bed?'

'Of course—although with that said, sex should never be a chore,' Carter said. 'I certainly don't want duty sex.'

'So you'd go without for a year?' she challenged.

'God, no.' He met her gaze, then. 'If you don't want sex to be a part of our agreement that's fine. I'll agree to be discreet.'

She felt a tremble in her lips and pinched them, reminded herself again that this was a contract…not real.

Then she looked at his strong profile and imagined all that maleness cooped up in a marriage he didn't really want. And she knew that unless she set down some strong rules there was the chance for true heartbreak ahead.

'If you sleep with another woman, then know you'll never again sleep with me.'

'Fine.' He was still staring intently at the nest. 'I'll have Jonathon add that to the contract.'

God, he was brutal. Nothing moved or fazed him.

'Along with my agreement to be discreet.'

He turned his abruptly to her and she saw the male he was, the snap of possession in his eyes, and Grace swore to herself that she would never mistake that look for love.

It gave her the strength to speak on. 'If the relationship falls apart in the bedroom...'

'I've *never* fallen apart in the bedroom.'

'I'm just saying,' Grace retorted calmly, 'that if we go our separate ways, then I too shall be discreet.'

A slight incredulous smile spread over his lips. 'You were a virgin until recently.'

'Thank you for showing me all I was missing out on,' she said, and gave him a tight smile.

She was being brave in words, but she doubted she could ever be so brave in deed. Still, she would not let him see that.

'So we'd have that added to the contract too.'

'Fine.'

'*If* I go ahead.'

They stood quietly. The occasional light motion of the boat meant the tops of their arms brushed every now and again, just a little, and her skin flared at each brief contact, refused to settle.

God, she was really deeply considering it...

'What would I tell Violet?' She could hear herself almost panting, as if on some frantic hunt, stopping breathlessly for clues along the way.

'That we met, fell in love... You can't tell her the truth.'

'I know.' Grace nodded. 'But she knows me. Knows I wouldn't rush into something like this.' She blinked a couple of times. 'I don't think she'd believe me.'

'Then make it so,' Carter said.

She felt his head turn and then his mouth close to her ear.

'Tell her I asked you to marry me in a river of lilac flowers...'

Her breathing was so shallow now she was almost dizzy.

'That we made love in a boat and you said yes...'

She was shaking—perhaps from standing in the morning sun?

Or was it the thought of the two million dollars that would change both her and her mother's life?

Or just lust and desire?

'Does Arif know about the will?' Grace asked. 'Is that why you were arguing?'

'No.' Carter shook his head. 'And we weren't arguing.'

'You looked like thunder when you came out of his office.'

He rolled his eyes. 'If Arif were a woman, we'd have been over years ago. He's that person you can't say no to…or you can't stop worrying about.'

Grace just laughed.

'I think you mean Arif is family.'

'Oh, no. Believe me, I have nothing to do with any of them, aside from legally.'

'I mean family of the heart.' Grace smiled. 'Like Violet is to me…'

She didn't finish, seeing his attention completely on the nest and intently alert.

'She's moving,' Carter said.

And Grace blinked, remembered why they were there, and remembered that this moment—watching a mother orangutan leave her nest—was what she'd been aching for all week.

It still was.

Yet somehow it was made better because she was sharing it with him.

'Where's the baby?' she asked.

'Shh!' he said.

This time Grace didn't take offence.

'It will be with her,' he told her. Then he put an arm around her, pulled her closer as he pointed with his free hand. 'See beneath her arm? Do you want the binoculars?'

'No.'

She really was dreadful with them. But, more, she liked seeing things with her own eyes, and, yes, liked being so close to him, hearing his voice, low and quiet, so as not to carry on the still air.

'I see it.'

Sure enough, she could just make out the infant, clinging on as the mother stretched an impossibly long arm and reached up.

'She's coming this way,' Carter told her, and they both stood in utter silence, watching the mother move from branch to branch with ease, getting closer to the riverbank with each agile swing.

Grace had to press her lips together. It was simply incredible to watch. And there was no need for binoculars, because she came further down, close to the river's edge, till she hung by one hand, no more than a few arms' lengths away from where they stood together in the boat.

'She's watching us,' Carter said.

'I know! I'm trying not to make eye contact,' Grace whispered.

'They don't mind much,' he said. 'They communicate that way.' Then he added, 'And she's not worried by us.'

No, the mother wasn't worried, for she hung there, calmly eating fruit, as the little baby moved onto her chest, boldly peering out at them with huge black eyes, the sun catching on its soft tufts of auburn and gold hair.

'Is it a boy or a girl?' Grace whispered.

'Can't tell,' he said. 'It's very young.'

'How young?'

'A couple of months.'

Then the mother lowered her head, and in the tenderest, simplest gesture she kissed the top of her baby's downy head, then lifted the little one up high on her shoulder, as if she were about to wind her.

And then it was over.

Almost.

The mother calmly dropped down from the tree and walked into the forest, the little baby peering over its mother's shoulder back at them.

'It's so content...' Grace said, stunned at what they'd witnessed.

But then she felt Carter's arm tighten its hold a fraction and she looked up at him, wondering if he was alerting her to something. But, no, it was more as if something had alerted *him*, for even though he stood right beside her, he looked a million miles away.

Carter, in fact, was twenty-seven years in the past, staring at the baby orangutan's huge round eyes that looked back at him just as Hugo's had that last day.

But there was a forgotten moment that had returned...

Hugo holding his fat starfish hand out to him.

Carter had known exactly what his brother's gesture meant.

'Wait!' he'd called, opening his father's ice box, taking the cold silver teething ring and jumping onto the riverbank. *'There you go, Ulat,'* he'd said, handing Hugo his beloved teething ring, gently talking to his little brother as he'd grasped it, ruffling his soft hair, seeing his contented smile...

Then, as if black tar was being thrown over him, the idyllic moment was tainted.

He should have taken Hugo from his mother...carried him back to the boat.

God, this was no memory to stand and savour. Instead he stood there hollowed out with regret.

The only solace he could find as he recalled it was that he'd never know the pain of such loss again.

Ever.

'That was incredible...'

Grace's voice pulled him back to the present and, realising his arm was still around her, Carter removed it, telling himself he'd merely been trying to point out the wildlife.

'I can't believe how close we were.'

'It's very quiet here,' Carter said, and cleared his throat, trying to sound normal while still taken aback by that emergence of the final memory of his mother and brother. 'There's little to disturb them.'

'What will happen if your cousin does get his way?'

'That's my concern. I didn't bring you here to influence your decision.'

Carter would not let emotions override her thinking—they were a currency he did his level best not to deal in.

'Your decision should be based on financial security and providing for your mother. The debt to the people here is my own.'

'Debt?'

'There's a saying here: *Hutang emas boleh dibayar, hutang budi dibawa mati.* One can pay back the loan of gold, but one dies in debt for ever to those who are kind. Unfortunately for me, it's true.'

'I'm sure they don't see it as a debt.'

'Perhaps not a debt, but I do feel obliged.' He saw Grace frown, and then qualified. 'I want to do the right thing, and then finally I can move on.'

'I do too,' Grace admitted, her own words surprising her. 'I don't see it as a debt, though, or even an obligation.'

She wanted to do the best by her mother and she wanted to live her life. This gave her a chance to do both.

'I don't know if can do this, though.'

'That's why there are lawyers...that's why we're not running away to Vegas. If we get the application in then we have three weeks to work things out.'

She nodded.

'Grace, do you love me?'

Her response was immediate. 'Of course not.'

Only Grace recognised her own tone. It was the same one she used when asked if she cared about or missed her father.

She didn't love Carter, of course—she didn't know him—but she stared at the rainforest in the bright morning and knew that she had to stay silent. For she could think of nothing better than knowing this contrary man more.

He clearly hadn't finished checking she could match his cold heart, though. He had another question for her.

'And you understand that I'll never love you?'

How did one even begin to answer that?

'You've made that very clear.'

She took a breath, looked at the beautiful lilacs. There was more tranquillity here than she had ever known, and finally enough peace to think deeply.

Serenity?

Not quite.

But it was enough that she'd found the touchstone of her heart.

'I want real love.' She looked out to the jungle that pulsed with life, to the flowers, to the sky, and she told him the truth. 'I'm so tired of loving people who are incapable of loving me.'

He frowned.

'I'm talking about my father.' She could feel her lips stretch, her chin tremble, but she forced herself to push on. 'My mother.'

'She's unwell.'

'I know—and, believe me, I've had to tell myself that a lot of times over the years.' She took a breath. 'I want someone who can love me fully.'

'It's a no, then?'

'Can I finish?'

She thought of security for her mother and being able to provide the best life she could give her. Of how, if her mother was cared for, she'd get the chance to live her own best life.

Find herself.

Her passions.

She looked over to Carter and, as cold and matter-of-fact his proposal was, it excited her too. Last night she had found all she had missed out on. He'd brought something out in her she hadn't even known existed.

'I shan't be falling in love with a man incapable of loving me back. So, yes.' She nodded. 'I do want to do this.'

'Two million dollars… A wardrobe…'

'I'd need to get to London regularly.'

'Once we're married, I can base myself there.'

It was a minor detail to him, Grace realised. He could uproot to wherever he liked on a whim.

'We'll work out the details of the contract, but…' He seemed to think for a moment, as if pondering what else might be required. 'I think we're both getting a good deal. I like you.' He said it as if it surprised him. 'Although, of course, by the end of the year we'll be desperate to never see each other again.'

Grace hoped so!

She really, really hoped so…

CHAPTER EIGHT

'WHERE WE MET...' Carter said, as they walked through Kuala Lumpur airport and passed the bench where he'd found her sleeping. 'For when you tell Violet.'

'Check,' Grace said, as if she was only now remembering, when that moment was already etched on her heart.

There was a car and driver waiting for them. After a week in the jungle the lights and sights of a busy city late evening were overwhelming. The car was moving at speed through the streets, and there were just so many people.

Carter, clearly delighted to be back in civilisation, had his diary up on a screen and was talking to his assistant, confirming appointments, meetings, flights...

'What ring size are you?' he asked.

'I've no idea. Why?'

He rolled his eyes and got back to his call.

For Grace there was a feeling of excitement that she hadn't expected, and she told him the same as they approached the luxurious hotel. 'I thought I'd feel guilty,' she admitted.

'Why?' Carter frowned.

'It seems wrong. Well, it *seemed* wrong.' She thought back to her abhorrence when he'd first suggested it, yet even before he'd dropped her back at the resort she'd turned things around.

Her last night spent with the group had been incredible.

Arif had been the guide, with Felicity steering the boat, and the pygmy elephants had been at the riverbank as if to wave goodbye...

And then Carter had collected her in the morning.

The story was that she would be working for Carter, collating data for his legal team.

'Thanks for coming on board,' Arif had said as he'd farewelled her. 'I've given some of the data to Carter, but here are my contact details.'

Felicity had even hugged her!

'I'm going to miss the jungle,' she admitted.

'I shan't,' he said, climbing out of the car.

He offered his hand as she went to get out, just as he had on the speedboat, and gave her a begrudging smile.

'Okay, some parts were good.'

Even checking in to such a sumptuous place didn't daunt, when usually it would have, even though for her it was quite an event.

As Carter sat at a desk and spoke with the guest services manager about their upcoming stay Grace sat, sipping pink tea and nibbling gorgeous wafers. And instead of feeling intimidated by the glamorous staff and gorgeous guests, she sat in her black shorts and dusky pink top and called the nursing home.

There was an agency nurse on, whom Grace didn't know, but she told her that her mother was at singing practice.

'Is she settling in?'

'She seems very happy. Maggie's in tomorrow—she'll be able to tell you more.'

'Thanks.'

It was such a relief to know she was okay, and Grace sat back, looking out at the dark city and to the glittering skyline.

'Grace?'

She looked up to find Carter standing there. 'They're still getting the suite ready.'

'Oh.' She'd have expected them to have it ready and waiting for him from the way they were fawning over him. 'No problem.'

'We'll go up to the bar.'

'Carter, no!'

She pointed to her attire, thought of her hair, but he was already walking towards the elevators. Even the doors parted to his instant command, and she stepped into the dimly lit space.

'I'm hardly dressed for a bar.'

'I'm not waiting in Reception.'

'It's dark in here,' she commented, looking around.

'Subtle.' He smiled. 'The corridors are the same—hell when you've had a drink.'

He made the whole thing a little easier, somehow, although as they stepped into a gorgeous dimly lit corridor she tried not to think of Carter and the glamorous beauties who had surely walked this luxurious path with him before.

'Mr Bennett.' He was welcomed with a smile by the greeter. 'Madam.'

They were led outside to some high tables set with pretty lights, where beautiful people were sipping cocktails, enjoying the balmy night. His entrance did not go unnoticed. For the first time in her life Grace felt heads turn as she walked by, and certainly they were for Carter. But then, as they walked to their table, Grace literally stopped.

'Oh, my gosh!'

She'd heard of the Petronas Towers, had seen them in pictures and had been planning to visit them, but standing on the rooftop bar, seeing them close up, as if two giant crystal decanters had been placed in the sky, was simply incredible.

'Like a new moon,' Carter said, standing beside her, his hand around her waist. 'It's better if you don't see it the first time through glass.'

'Is that why you brought me here?'

She couldn't take her eyes off them, yet she had to as they were being led to a private area, a velvet rope being moved aside.

'Thank you,' she said as he gestured for her to take the stool that faced the towers. 'For giving me the best view.'

Carter could have chosen to debate that point.

Her hair was heavy with ringlets, her T-shirt was falling off her shoulder, and her face was glowing. His view was excellent! Her smile and her eyes were bright. He was so used to just a bland re-action when he brought a date here, and yet Grace was enthralled.

Her enthusiasm had him revealing more. 'They were my in-spiration.'

'To be an architect?'

He nodded. 'I used to look out for them when I came home on vacation.'

'To see your grandfather?'

'Of course.'

But as he turned his head to follow her gaze, Carter was starting to recall times long before that.

'My family used to come most summers, but we rarely stopped here. My parents hated the city, but I begged them to take me up. I knew I wanted to design something like that even then.'

'Cognac, sir?'

Carter nodded, and the fact that the waiter knew this nettled Grace a little. As 'madam' was handed a menu, she stared at it, unseeing. There were just too many reminders that, as special as this night might feel, it was commonplace for him.

Carter tried to help with her selection. 'The gin *pahit* is excellent here.'

'Better not.' She glanced at him. 'Mother's ruin and all that. I'm sure I'll be fine, but...' She gave the menu better attention, pleased to see there was something familiar. 'Mangosteen Mocktail, please.'

Grace smiled, only he didn't return it.

God, please don't let me be pregnant, Grace thought.

She rather guessed he was thinking the same thing.

'I am going to Janana soon,' he said.

'Where?'

'The Middle East,' he explained. 'I have a big project there.'

'Oh?'

'Jonathon, my lawyer, is flying in, but before he gets here there'll be time to sort out a few things...'

He paused the conversation as their drinks arrived and the waiter placed a gorgeous pink drink on the table before her.

It was soft, yet fruity, and so icy and delicious. 'It's like peaches.' She pushed the glass towards him, and then frowned, because he seemed about to decline. 'Look, I'm sorry I brought it up.' She was awkward. 'I just don't think I should be drinking.'

'It's fine.'

As if to prove he wasn't annoyed that she might be pregnant he reached for the glass and, almost reluctantly, took a taste.

He screwed up his nose. 'Not for me.'

'I thought you liked mangosteen?'

'No.'

'But we had them…' Her voice trailed off as she remembered he had only peeled one for her, rather than have any himself, and when she'd asked had said he didn't particularly like them.

Carter took a sip of cognac, as if to rinse his mouth,

It was a sickly taste, a familiar taste—only it wasn't this sweet, fruity version he was recalling, but the rotten, decomposing fruit on the jungle floor that had been most of his sustenance for a week.

He took another sip of cognac, looked up at her eyes. He wanted to tell her that memories were starting to come back, his recollections becoming more frequent by the day. Tell her how he'd hoped things would change now they were out of the jungle.

That wasn't part of the deal they'd made, though.

Yet the taste of that damn drink was still on his tongue and churning in his stomach.

As she reached to take the glass he told her what was wrong. 'They were the only food I could find when I was missing.'

She looked at the glass, the condensation trickling down the side, and then up to him. 'You should have said that morning. I wouldn't have asked you to peel one.'

'We were meant to be a one-off then.'

'Yes.'

'And I'd only just remembered then.'

'I'll order something else.'

'No, no,' he said. 'Finish your drink. I just thought it better to say…'

'Before it becomes my nightly treat?'

She made him smile, even with the sickly scent still in the air, and he watched as she called for the waiter and asked him to take the glass away.

'Is everything okay?' the waiter checked.

It was Carter who answered. 'It's fine.' He'd just got a message. 'I believe our suite is ready.'

Their suite was so much more than a suite—it was beyond stunning. They stepped into a candlelit wonder, where the darkened lounge room showed the incredible skyline. But Grace loved it that he'd taken her to the roof to witness the towers first.

'Wow!' she kept saying as she explored the beautiful suite, trying out the low chairs, even dipping her toes in the sunken pool by the floor-to-ceiling windows.

Carter headed to the dressing room just off the master suite.

'Passport,' he called, as he put his own in the safe, checking too that the rings he'd ordered were in there, but without sentiment.

He tried to avoid the churn of feelings as he placed the black pouch in there. Wished to God that the damn teething ring had stayed beneath ground.

'Grace,' he said again. 'Passport.'

'It'll be fine.'

'Said the woman who fell asleep and dropped hers...'

'True.'

He was surprised that after several modes of transport and many hours with her he wasn't aching to be alone, or annoyed by her running commentary as she flitted from room to room, but he caught her tension as she stepped into the candlelit master bedroom.

She gave a nervous laugh. 'We'll spend half the night blowing out all the candles.'

'I don't think you have to worry about that.'

'Here,' Grace said, handing over her passport and then heading back out.

She didn't linger in the bedroom. The vast white bed was daunting. It was so beautifully prepared... There were 'his and her' kimonos draped either side, and just a sensual look to it that made her throat feel tight.

A mocking voice told her that Carter would soon grow tired of his very inexperienced lover, especially in surroundings as sophisticated as this.

It was all so subtly sexy and dark. Like Carter, she thought as she went behind a glass wall and saw more candles placed around a deep stone bath already filled with soapy water.

'Look,' she said as Carter wandered through, and dipped her hand in. 'It's hot!' she exclaimed. 'How?'

'They would have prepared it while we were at the bar,' Carter said, breaking the romantic mood and flicking the lights on.

'I wish you hadn't done that,' Grace muttered, seeing not just her tatty toiletry bag on the gleaming marble, but her tatty reflection in the equally gleaming mirror. And, yes, she looked as if she'd been dragged through the jungle backwards. 'My hair!' she groaned, for it seemed to move as one. 'Are the mirrors in Sabah kinder?'

Carter found the mirrors kinder here.

The world was in neat order—unlike in the jungle.

He liked Grace brightly lit, so he could see the dusting of freckles on her nose, and how her T-shirt gaped as she leant forward and moaned about her eyebrows. He liked her bare feet on the marble floors...

'I'm going shopping tomorrow,' she told him, taking tweezers from her toiletry bag.

'I'll leave a credit card for you. Or charge it...'

'I didn't mean that.' She stopped plucking her eyebrows and caught his eye in the mirror. 'I was always going to get rid of these clothes and buy some new things.'

'I don't think the high street is going to cut it.'

Her eyes narrowed. 'Are you saying I'm to be more "Carter Bennett's fiancée" suitable?'

'I'm saying exactly that.' He nodded. 'Tomorrow night I have to meet with a senior financier.'

'Am I to make small talk with his wife?'

'No, I shall be doing most of the talking. Simi's the one who I need to sweet talk—you get the husband.' He watched her get back to her eyebrows and could not resist adding, 'They're in the top one hundred of the most successful, beautiful people.'

'Shut up!' She smiled. 'Are you serious?'

'Very.' he nodded.

'If you're already so rich, why do you need to impress a financier?'

'Because I intend to stay rich,' he retorted. 'Get some nice clothes, and whatever else you need...'

She might have been wholly offended, but staring at her woolly hair and dusty clothes she felt a shiver of excitement. It felt as if she'd spent for ever dressed in yoga pants, with her hair in a ponytail, having dinner in front of the television. Rarely going out, let alone dating.

This wasn't dating, though, Grace reminded herself.

Carter began to strip his top off—as uninhibited as that—and she wondered if she was about to be summoned to the bath...

Could you use condoms in water?

She had no clue. So for something to do she opened up all the freebies and brushed her teeth with a very nice brush, selected all the lovely shampoos. She was delaying, nervous...

'Grace...'

He turned her around. He was naked from the hips up, and he wiped a little toothpaste from her lip.

And she thought he must seriously hate mangosteen, because his gaze had changed, and it would seem her mouth was kissable now.

This wasn't love, she thought as their mouths met, but nor was it shame. It was finding out how good a kiss could be, discovering her body, feeling wanted and sexy when she'd wondered if that side of her even existed.

His tongue tasted of cognac, and when it mingled with hers she tasted mint. And her hands were on his chest, feeling the dark hair, the flat nipples. And she didn't want this kiss to end. But he was more measured than she...pulling that sexy mouth back from her own.

'Why don't we lose the jungle?' Carter suggested, pulling at the hem of her dusky and also rather dusty pink top.

The tops of her thighs ached and her breasts felt tight with anticipation as he lifted her arms and removed her top, tossing it towards a basket. She watched her very tatty bra fly that way too, and then he left it for Grace to take care of the rest. Possibly because he needed to be naked as much as she.

Although not for the reasons she'd first thought.

'Enjoy,' he said, taking her hand and helping her into the bath.

She watched a little bemused as he headed to the shower, and perhaps he saw her blink of surprise.

'Did I tell you I'm not romantic?'

'Many times.'

'That means I don't do candlelit baths. I'm going in here.'

'Bastard!' She laughed and lay back, still semi turned on, but finally relaxed, letting the fragrant water wrap around her body. Sometimes her eyes would open and drift to look at his magnificent physique, his lean legs, the indentations at the side of his taut buttocks. And it was intimate to watch him from a distance, to see the thick length that had been inside her and to feel her throat go tight. He turned and she saw the scars on his back... She closed her eyes on the vision of scorpions and fire ants, knowing he'd hate the tears that had suddenly filled her eyes.

He turned off the water, came out and wrapped a towel around his hips, and flicked through all the toiletries. He started to lather up several days' worth of growth on his chin, not even bothering to look at her when she asked, 'Is there any more conditioner? My hair's all knotted.'

'Book a hairdresser tomorrow.'

'Please!' Grace mumbled, lying back in the bath and letting the water wash over her, knowing he couldn't possibly understand how awful it was going to be to face a hairdresser somewhere as gorgeous as here. She usually trimmed her own hair, and the humid air really had wreaked havoc with it, as well as the near toothless comb.

* * *

Carter was now watching Grace.

The efficient extractor fans meant he didn't even need to wipe the mirror to shave. Still, rather than his own reflection there was a far more appealing sight in the mirror, as Grace lay back in the bath and floated. Her hair fanned out, her eyes closed, and he saw her usually pale skin was pink from the warm water. The dispersing bubbles revealed her soft breasts and his eyes moved to the dark triangle of hair.

He thought of their one night...the heat they had made.

He understood a little of what Grace meant when she'd said she kept expecting shame to kick in... In Carter's case, though, he was waiting for regret to arrive.

Waiting to rue the offer he'd made.

Even as they shared the bathroom he kept waiting to feel as if she was invading his space, and yet it was Carter who wanted to invade hers... To climb into the bath and feel that slippery body... to be with her again. *Now!*

'What about this?' he asked and she glanced over. 'It says "Hair Masque".'

She sat up and held out an impatient hand, but just as she grabbed it he pulled it away. 'Please...' he reminded her.

'Please,' she said, and with slippery hands tried to open it.

She soon gave in and now it was she who held it out, for him to open.

'Please!' she repeated, and then she caught his eye and they both smiled.

This was the smile she gave only now and then, and he found himself giving back a new smile.

Then the smiles faded, but their eyes remained locked.

The water was still, as was Grace, and there was no fan powerful enough to erase the unseen mist of desire descending.

As he handed Grace the opened hair masque he saw that her flush was darker and that the nipples that had been flat were now puckering and pointing as if the steaming water was cold.

'Do you need help?' he offered.

Carter loved the way her neck corded in tension as she nodded.

He didn't do this, Carter reminded himself as he collected a comb from the selection on offer. Usually women arrived dressed and scented…or he woke to the spritzed version.

'Move.'

He gestured and she scooted forward, and as he climbed into the bath behind her there was just a little slosh as his six-foot-three frame lowered. She leant over to survey the spillage, her skin gleaming, wet, and he reached for her waist, pulled her between his legs.

No, he had never done this, Carter thought, massaging the thick cream through her hair, then slowly combing it through.

'My comb broke,' Grace explained, feeling a little embarrassed, but far less so than she would have been under the critical eye of a hairdresser tomorrow. 'Well, it kept snapping,' she told him. 'I'm nervous about tomorrow,' she admitted, somehow finding it easier to talk as he combed her hair, to admit her thoughts. 'Not just about the hairdresser.'

'Why?'

'I don't know anything about make-up, clothes…not lately anyway. I feel like there's a big gap in my knowledge—a six-year yoga-pants-and-baggy-T-shirt-shaped gap.'

'Let the stylists here help?' he suggested.

She nodded, but the gentle mood changed when he must have hit a rather difficult knot. 'Ow!'

'Sorry…'

He paused long enough to kiss her shoulder and the last traces of awkwardness and embarrassment simply faded away. Even if he thrilled her, there was something incredibly relaxing about Carter—a quiet knowledge that he wouldn't be doing this unless he chose to. He wouldn't be combing her hair and holding her between his thighs for any reason other than that he wanted to.

And she wanted him there too.

'I'm not used to long hair,' he explained as he resumed.

* * *

And perhaps it relaxed him, too, because he seemed to be dwelling on that thought.

He'd only ever combed his own hair.

Certainly he wasn't used to combing long, thick, curly hair until it hung heavy, smooth and glossy down her back.

'There,' he said.

But as she went to turn around, he pulled her to lie back against him. Lifted her hair so it lay over his shoulder rather than in the water.

'The packet says fifteen minutes.'

And he used every one.

Several of them spent with large slippery hands sliding over her breasts, toying with the peaks.

Grace lay there, feeling him so turned on behind her. She ached to turn around, to touch him, too, and yet it was bliss to just lie there.

To feel one hand slide down and part her legs a little, to rest her thighs against his and for his fingers to explore her.

She turned her head and he kissed her mouth. 'I want...' She was tense with the need to turn, but too laden with pleasure to move.

She felt guilty, because the focus was so much on her own pleasure, was unable to accept that the pleasure was also his.

'God, you fight,' Carter said, and he gripped her thighs closed with his, and then there were no more kisses, just moans as she leant her head forward and beneath the water gave in to the pleasure that rippled through her.

His thighs parted and she folded, clutching her knees, sated.

As he climbed out, he offered his hand. 'Give me a moment...' Her legs were shaky, but Carter wasn't waiting.

'Come on,' he instructed. 'We need to rinse your hair.'

She would have gone to his bed with the masque still in, every thought except for him seemed to have floated out of her head.

He took the gold shower attachment from the bath and she

knelt on the towel he had dropped to the floor a little later than the fifteen minutes stated on the pack.

No regret as to her decision to come here.

Still no shame.

None.

'We could go back in the shower,' Grace suggested as she leant over the bath.

'We could,' he said, his voice with a thick edge, 'but then you'd have to move and I don't want you to.'

She felt his finger run down the length of her spine, opened her eyes to her hair dripping into the bath, to the feeling of his deft fingers in her scalp, then the tug as he squeezed the water out.

'Do you want to go to bed?' he offered. 'Or…?'

'Here,' she said, her voice a bit of a squeak. She was just not wanting to lose the exquisite feel of his hands low on her back, sliding to her hips and moving her just a fraction. 'Just here,' she affirmed.

'Good,' he said.

She rested her head on her forearm, almost shaking with trepidation as he leant over her body and turned off the water. The feel of him aroused and erect matched her own swollen pleasure. She could feel his hand moving down, closing around himself, and she felt a desperate, delicious impatience flood her veins.

'Hold on,' he said.

And that desperate, delicious feeling flicked into frustration as he remembered to keep both of them safe this time. He stretched to the counter behind them, his other hand on her stomach, and there should have been relief that he'd remembered protection, or a little quip about the thoughtful placement of condoms, but the only thing she could think of was the gap placed between their bodies, the air that did not belong there.

Then he was back, his knees between her calves, his hands on her breasts. 'Look,' he said, and she lifted her head. But he corrected her. 'To the side.'

She could see them in the mirror.

Grace barely recognised herself. Her skin was pink, her eyes dark and wide as they watched his hands on her breasts as they move to her waist.

'Oh…' She was shivering—a little from the cool air on her wet skin and a lot from the sight of Carter kneeling up, holding himself, rolling a condom on.

She raised herself higher, her bottom pressing backwards.

'Are you still sore?'

'No,' she said, as he slid in his fingers.

She had been prepared to perfection, and his deft check was soon completed, fingers replaced. She felt the nudge of him.

'Maybe a bit,' she gasped, realising she was still a little raw from their first time. But the return to bliss was swift. 'Don't stop!'

'Shh,' he said, as if he were concentrating, and then she realised the effort he was taking to enter her slowly, felt the tension in his body and heard it in his breathing as he eased in.

Certainly it hurt less than the first time, and it allowed her to fully feel the stretch. And then he repeated the thrust, and repeated it, until it was she who moved her hips back a little, wanting more, ever more. Because he'd moved deeper, and she felt him nudge at her cervix, and she groaned at the decadent places he took her, slowly and very deliberately,

Each thrust had her closing her eyes tighter, and then he took her hips and moved her, and Grace found that she was back to looking in the mirror.

'You like watching?'

She nodded, as he confirmed another thing she hadn't known about herself, and then he pulled out, enough to move them so that she was kneeling facing the mirrored wall, with him behind her. He entered her again, and there was nothing to lean on, but he guided her arms behind her, so they were locked under his, and she watched as his hands explored her body, both saw and felt the pleasure he gave. And then his cheek came to hers, and he watched them for a moment, his hand in her most intimate place.

'My knees hurt,' she told him, because there was pleasure in every other pore.

And he laughed. And, carefully holding the sheath, removed himself again, spinning her to face him.

'I'm going on the pill,' she blurted out in her frustration.

How she wanted his skin…even the tiniest of barriers felt too much.

For Carter, her words took him back to the feel of her naked and tight around him, to the one time he'd been careless, and he adored how his inexperienced lover already craved that again.

He had never, ever wanted this closeness, this much of another person—not just the press of her naked on his chest, her hands on his shoulders, but on his back, where the scars were no longer a novelty, or something to avoid, just a part of him.

He kissed her hard, relieved that she did not know that he did not always kiss as passionately as this, that she was unaware that the feel of her wet hair on his face and sex on the bathroom floor, as inconvenient and hard as the marble felt, was a new discovery for him too.

He was a controlled lover, although he was losing control now—but then she could not know how rare this was, because she was falling apart too.

Her arms were locked around his neck, and she could feel his hot breath. His movements were urgent and intense, and then there was an incredible sense of being still. She was trying not to tremble, she felt the energy that was coming, and yet her body was already alight.

Grace gasped and screwed her eyes closed as he held her steady, moaned as her orgasm met his. He shuddered in a breathless shout and then moved her slowly, tender and aching, the length of him.

She could hear their breathing, her own heart and possibly even his. It was the most incredible, selfish feeling. Such a rich, giddy pleasure, and yet it felt like a shared one.

'You're cold…' he observed, and it took a moment for Grace to acknowledge that she was.

For the first time since she'd landed in Malaysia her skin was cool, and with her hair still drenched she really was shivering.

'Finally!'

Her legs were almost numb as she stood, and he took her hand and led her through the stunning rooms.

The bed was already turned back and it was such a relief to sink into it.

'What are you doing?' she asked as he went to the dressing room.

'I meant to...'

He came out with a box—a flat black velvet and rather large box—and sat on the bed and unclipped it.

There were so many things about Grace that surprised him, thought Carter, and her reaction to the black velvet tray did too. For even though there were diamonds, sapphires, emeralds and rubies, and even though most of the women he'd dated would have squealed, she just stared.

She was like no one he'd met.

And the clinical proposal was a little nicer than he'd intended, what with the candles putting themselves to bed around them, fizzing out one by one, and her chest still flushed from orgasm and her soft, naked breasts a diversion for him as she stared at the selection.

'Choose one.'

'We haven't even spoken to the lawyer.'

'The marriage application is in; you need a ring.'

It wasn't just that. The meeting with the lawyer could very well end them, Carter knew.

Grace was proud, and he wanted her to have something. Something she could sell. And this was the best he could come up with.

He flicked on the lights, hoping that would help. But now he could see the pucker of her areolae, so he moved his gaze up and saw that plump mouth.

'What one would you choose?' She met his eyes then. 'After all, I'll be returning it to you in twelve months.'

'You get to keep it.'

'Why?'

'Gifts,' he said. 'Jonathon will explain."

He watched her fingers hover over the diamonds, the rubies, as the lights caught the precious gems and they sparkled beguilingly. And then he watched her pause over a magnificent teardrop emerald. It was beautiful, yes—stunningly so. But if she was thinking of her future...

'The diamond next to it is exceptional.' He pointed to it, several carats worth, and the one she was supposed to select. The one every other bride marrying for money would swoop on like a magpie.

'It's too big,' Grace said, then frowned, because of course the emerald was even bigger, yet just so gorgeous. 'Anyway, we're not for ever,' she said.

And, selection made, she took out the emerald ring, looking at the beautiful stone set in white gold, and felt as if she'd been struck in the throat.

She had never thought that selecting a ring for a fake engagement would cause her heart to implode—that she might have to keep her head down so he wouldn't see the tears that filled her eyes as she examined it.

'It's beautiful.'

Her voice was a tremble as she looked at the stone, at the flashes of yellow and green, like tiny fireflies, and for a second, she was transported back to a time when all she had wanted was one night. Deep in the jungle she'd felt on the edge of for ever, utterly alone with him and without agenda.

'I love it.' She told him the truth. 'I'll want to keep it for ever.'

'Don't get romantic,' he told her.

'No, but I'm allowed to adore it.'

'Grace, you're going to sell it. For now, though, if it's too big it can be resized,' he said, taking her hand.

He looked at the gorgeous ring, slipping a little on her slender finger, and he felt something deep inside. What he felt, he didn't quite know—but it was unwelcome.

Was it the painful thaw of black ice cracking?

It wasn't desire, yet it was laced with it…

He did not want to care.

Not too much.

He snapped the box closed. 'If you change your mind, they're not going back till tomorrow.'

'I shan't change my mind.'

Grace wouldn't. She was under the covers with one hand out, admiring her ring, when he came back from the safe. But when he climbed into bed she turned and faced him, ran a newly bejewelled hand along his smooth jaw. It was almost the same Carter she'd met that first day.

'I forgot how good-looking you are,' she said, and her honesty surprised her—it was as if she'd forgotten how to be shy.

'You prefer me shaved?'

'No,' she admitted. 'I just…forget sometimes.'

She examined his features and they were as gorgeous as they had been that very first day, and yet then it would have been rude to fully stare, or to reach out and touch.

'The first time I saw you…' she smiled a slow, satisfied smile '… I thought I was dreaming.'

'Really?'

She nodded. 'I mean it. I thought you were part of my dream. I had no idea where I was. Bear in my mind I couldn't hear a thing. I thought it was a very nice, almost inappropriate dream.'

He smiled. 'The first time I saw you I thought of Sleeping Beauty.'

'Liar.'

'No.' He pushed her damp hair from her face. 'Well, actually I thought, when I saw your passport on the floor, that you were not my problem.'

'I'm *not* your problem,' Grace said.

Possibly, she pondered, that was the beauty of them. They

weren't each other's problem—instead they were each other's solution.

Maybe that was why it felt so right.

It was a nice thought to fall asleep on.

Grace woke up alone.

Well, she heard the door close and realised there were to be no morning kisses goodbye or...

Staring at her ring, she told herself she was being ridiculous, and rang for tea and pancakes. And then, as she always did, she took a breath before checking her messages.

None from the care home.

Phew.

And just as she was about to call Carter, ask what the plans were for tonight, her phone rang and it was the Ms Hill she'd heard mentioned several times.

'The stylist is booked for midday, but I've left hair and make-up till five, given you're meeting Carter at seven.'

She gave Grace the location.

'He's not coming back here?'

'No...' She seemed to be checking. 'Seven p.m. reception. The car will be booked for six-forty-five.'

'Thanks so much,' Grace said. 'Do you know...?' She stopped. 'Actually, I'll call him myself.'

'Excuse me?'

'I'll call Carter.'

'If you need Mr Bennett for any reason, then you can contact me.'

'I meant for a personal reason.'

'You can contact me any time.'

Grace felt her lips stretch into an incredulous smile. 'What about in an emergency?'

'If I deem it an emergency, I'll be certain to pass it on.'

Oh, my gosh!

Grace wanted to be Ms Hill, she truly did—even if she was cross.

So cross that the moment the call ended she called Carter directly—just because she could.

Or, she thought she could—'How can I help you, Grace?' Ms Hill answered.

Grace gritted her teeth. 'Is it very formal tonight?'

'I've given Mr Bennett's schedule to the stylist. She'll be able to direct you.'

'Thank you.'

It was unexpected, and it jolted. She'd thought she had his number, had slept with him last night, and now she had to go through his PA in England to find out what to wear for dinner...

Her perfect dream makeover day was—oddly—not quite so.

'Wow!' Grace said, because her hair had been straightened and looked like silk.

Then she was shown it from the back, and if she hadn't known, then she'd never have guessed it was her own reflection.

She glanced at her toenails which were no longer painted a faded coral—in fact they were back to their natural colour, only buffed and polished, as were her fingernails.

It really was like a theatrical production, with a break for light snacks before wardrobe was called.

Grace felt an odd pang of disappointment at the underwear selection. It was gorgeous, she was told. Sheer and so barely there...

She felt barely there.

She felt as if she'd been dipped in ink stain remover as she tried on endless clothes.

There were pale dresses, cool linen suits and beautiful shoes. But for someone who had lived the last two years in yoga pants or cargo pants, it was a little less thrilling than she'd imagined.

'Beige?' She flicked through the dresses. 'Grey?'

They were 'wheaten' and 'pewter', apparently, but there was just no colour anywhere, save for a very pale blue trouser suit—so pale it was almost off the spectrum.

'We're just building a basic wardrobe,' the stylist informed her. 'You can then add your own signature.'

So she chose suitable outfits for day—cool linen trousers and light jackets—and then her hand hovered over an oatmeal linen smock with spaghetti straps that would be gorgeous to throw on after the pool.

'That's stunning,' the assistant said, but then Grace looked at the layering, the beauty of the garment and the designer tag, and hastily put it back. No, that was *not* a dress to throw on when she was damp from the pool. Instead she turned her attention to the evening wear.

Ms Hill had indeed given the stylist Carter's schedule—business dinners, performing arts, restaurants… She even had to choose outfits to wear should she have to join him in the Middle East…

And as she tried on clothes she felt as if she were dressing for a man she didn't know—certainly not a man who didn't seem bothered by shorts and tatty tops or bright red sarongs…a man who stood so quiet and still watching the dawn break…nor one who handed her a lilac flower.

Finally, it was time for make-up.

Or rather for her foundation to be matched and lessons on application to be had.

She rather failed with eyeliner and looked at the gorgeous eyes of the beautician, wanting them!

'How do I do wings?'

'You don't,' she was sharply told. 'If you want a smoky-eyed look then it is better to call us.'

The car was there, as arranged, and it took her to another very nice hotel. She sat in Reception, nervous and unsure, leaping on her phone with relief when it rang with a video call.

'Violet!' Grace quickly changed hands so that she held the phone with her left one, so as to hide the enormous ring.

'Oh, my God!' Violet said, when she saw her. 'Grace, you look….'

'I just got my hair done.'

'You've had *everything* done! Where are you?'

'Waiting in Reception at some fancy hotel,' Grace admitted, but then played it down. 'I'm just going for drinks…'

'With…?' Violet asked eagerly. 'Come on, Grace.'

'Some guy I met on the tour.'

'You look incredible!'

Violet was excited, and Grace wished it were a little more infectious.

'Different,' Violet said, cocking her blonde head to the side. 'But amazing. I hardly recognise you.'

Neither did Carter for a moment.

Her curls were gone, swept in a slick chignon, and he'd never noticed Grace's excellent posture before.

Correction. He'd examined her spine in detail, but he wasn't thinking about that now. Just her legs, long and slim in heels, nicely toned calves…

The dress was…well, a dress. But to his surprise he missed the curls.

And further to his surprise was the fact he'd noticed.

'Grace.'

She looked over, and as always her smile was more than her mouth. She smiled with her body, stepped towards him and raised an arm—a whole welcome with a smile.

'They're already here,' he told her.

He handed his laptop and the precious blueprints that barely left his side over to the concierge, and asked him to lock them away.

Grace was waiting for him to comment—on her make-up, her hair, anything—but he didn't.

'Simi and Tengku,' he told her as they walked through.

'I tried to call you…'

'Ms Hill said.'

She stopped—just stopped walking. And that was another thing Grace did—another damn thing he'd noticed.

'If you ever do that on the underground in London you'll cause a pile-up.'

He saw her angry face beneath the perfect make-up and found he missed her freckles too.

'Grace, I don't take personal calls at work.'

'Ever?'

'Never.' There was no one important enough—he very deliberately kept it that way. 'Now, are we going to do this?'

'Yes.'

Grace nodded, wondering how to 'do this'—how to sleep with someone at night who was completely unavailable by day.

A man who didn't even notice the effort you'd made.

Even if he'd paid for it.

A man who, without effort, always made her smile.

'Simi, Tengku—this is Grace.'

'It's lovely to meet you.'

They were surely *not* in the top one hundred most beautiful people—they were portly and happy and normal… Well, apart from their surroundings and their wealth.

And as she took a seat, and Tengku tucked a napkin under his ribs, she caught Carter's eyes.

Got you! said his smile.

He very possibly had.

CHAPTER NINE

'*CARTER, LOOK!*'

It was his father calling to him again, and he turned, saw Hugo looking back at him. Only it was Grace carrying him into the jungle rather than his mother.

And it couldn't be his father calling out, Carter realised, because his father lay face-down in the water with his arms spread out.

Or was that Grace floating?

His eyes snapped open. He was unsure for a moment if he'd shouted out, but presumably not, given that Grace lay wrapped around him like bindweed.

He'd have to remind her again that he liked space in bed.

Especially if they were going to be doing this for a year!

Carter gulped in air, went to move her so he could sit on the edge of the bed, catch his breath and drink water. But his heart was slowing down, and her skin was warm and alive.

'Carter…?'

She lifted her head from his chest, and it was like the first time they'd met. For her eyes were open, yet she was more asleep than awake. 'What time…?'

'Early,' he said. 'Go back to sleep.'

He felt the weight of her head as it sank back down on his chest, and the tickle of her hair on his chin didn't even irritate him.

He'd thought the nightmares had returned because he'd been in Borneo, yet he'd been back in KL for more than a week.

It was the teething ring unsettling him, he was certain, even in the dressing room and behind the solid walls of the hotel safe, it was pulsing like a radioactive alarm.

It was the anniversary of his family's deaths coming up, and he was seriously considering once more asking Arif to return it to the jungle.

He'd been too sideswiped at the time to think straight, and had let him load it onto the boat.

No, he would not be asking.

He would be telling.

In fact, he might call Arif and ask to meet him. Give it back to him and tell him to damn well return it to where it belonged.

Arif's father might have saved his life, but he was surely no longer beholden? He'd taken that week off work to look into things, and now—not that Arif knew it—he was possibly going to marry a woman when he didn't want...

Except he did want.

Constantly.

Usually, sex was a like a prescription for him.

To be taken as required.

Necessary, pleasurable, it relieved an ache, took care of a basic need.

Now he was seeking her needs, turned on by her climaxing, feeling her at times holding back...

Her thigh was over his now, her hand low on the side of his stomach, and he was hardening as if he were reaching for her, almost willing her hand to slip further down. Wanting her to react to his desire as his more vigilant lovers would have...

And yet he liked the chase, the flirtation, and so he lay there, feeling her even breathing, her inhalations so deep she was on the edge of a gentle snore. The horror of the nightmare had faded, it was nice to simply lie there and hold her...

'Carter?'

He frowned at Grace's groggy voice.

'We've overslept.'

'No.'

He turned to the clock. He never overslept. And neither did he fall back to sleep after a nightmare.

It was a bit of a rush.

Grace forgot to wear a shower cap and, no matter how brilliant the hairdresser, there wasn't a product invented that could tame her curls. To see the lawyer, she settled for the very pale powder blue trouser suit, and pulled on the awful underwear—a little bandeau bra thing that she had to put on over her head, and knickers that were sheer enough not to be noticed whatever she wore. The unfortunate pay-off being they came up close to her belly button.

God, she'd have preferred red velvet and suspenders, she thought, or at least she'd thought Carter would have preferred that.

She added a little cami, and then the suit, and slipped on some heels.

'We need to get a move on, Grace,' Carter warned.

'Then lucky for you I'm ready.'

'Back to curls?'

He looked at them, all pinned up, and was about to say he preferred them—though that wasn't his place. Nor was it for him to say that he missed her red sarong, and the dusky pink top, the coral on her nails.

Grace had said she was sorting out her clothes and her hair herself, and who was he to debate her choices? Even so, he did comment on her tension.

'Are you okay?' he checked. 'You look nervous.'

'Well, it's not every day you sign a contract for two million dollars.'

'It's just the NDA today.' He waved away her concerns. 'Then he'll walk us through the prenup. He might get a bit personal, but it's necessary.'

'Why?'

'Because...' he tried to keep his voice patient '...we are going to be marrying, and divorcing, and presumably sleeping together.' He was not going to startle her before they even got out of the stalls. 'Let's get some breakfast.'

They headed up to the restaurant, and as they were led to their table Grace looked at all the busyness and inhaled the scents. He seemed so at ease here.

'I don't know where to start...' she admitted, eyeing the gorgeous buffet.

As it turned out, his schedule was too tight for a buffet, and she was back to looking at menus again.

'I just want toast,' she said.

'No coffee?' He frowned.

'Tea,' Grace said. She was a bundle of nerves as it was.

She ordered exactly that when the waiter came.

Carter, though, appeared starving—from all the sex they *hadn't* had this morning? He ordered *nasi lemak*, and she wondered how he had the stomach for such a spicy dish so early, and how he had not even a hint of the nerves she was feeling...

'We're having dinner with them after,' he told her.

'Who?'

'Jonathon and Ruth—my lawyer and his wife.'

She shook her head as if to clear it. 'Seriously?'

Carter saw her shaking hand as she attempted to add marmalade to her toast, and knew he needed this to work.

'He might ask about your father,' he warned her.

'He can ask,' Grace said. 'I have no idea where he is.'

'You know once this hits the news there's a chance he'll get in touch?'

'I don't care.' She shrugged. 'Honestly, I have nothing to say to him.' She poured some tea. 'I last saw him in the interval of a pantomime. He popped out to get a drink.'

Carter waited. 'And...?' he prompted.

'That was it.' She added sugar to her tea. 'I must be boring company, because I haven't seen him since. I don't care if he gets in touch, or pleads for money, or tells whatever lie he comes up with...'

'So, I don't have to ask his permission?'

'No!' she replied hotly, and then looked up as if she'd realised it was she who had missed a small joke.

This time she didn't smile back.

'Excuse me for a moment,' Carter said.

He didn't explain where he was going and neither did she ask. There were several meeting rooms off the corridor just down from the restaurant—places to withdraw for private discussions or to toast success…

Jonathon was already there, of course.

A gleaming desk was all set up—there was a delicate floral arrangement as well as a jug of iced tea and pretty glasses, water and notepads. But for all the luxury and creature comforts he knew that to Grace this would appear as clinical as a hospital… Or rather that the topics about to be discussed would not be softened by the surroundings.

'Ready when you are,' Jonathan informed him.

Despite his somewhat genial appearance, Carter knew that Jonathon's mood could and often did quickly change. He had been on his side since he'd come out of the jungle, an orphaned eight-year-old with a fortune ripe to be misused by others.

'We can expect some pushback from Benedict, but—'

Carter cut in. 'I want you to listen to Grace.'

'Of course,' Jonathon said. 'But we shan't budge—'

'No.' Carter interrupted again. 'She has no one representing her.'

'Excellent.'

'There's a small possibility she's pregnant—'

Now Jonathon stopped leafing through the preliminary draft. Perhaps he saw Carter's grim expression, because it was Jonathon who interrupted now. 'Should the situation arise, it will be dealt with.'

'Go easy,' Carter warned.

'I don't play softball.'

'Just…' Carter made a gesture with his hand. 'I want the marriage to go ahead. There's a lot at stake.'

'Oh, I'm well aware,' Jonathon warned—and Carter knew he wasn't referring to the land, more his client's vast fortune. 'You need this to be watertight.'

'And I'm telling you to tread gently.'

Those were his instructions.

It was for the sake of his grandfather's legacy that he was reining Jonathon in, Carter told himself as he walked back to where Grace sat.

'Ready?'

She nodded and stood, and he watched as she blew out a breath.

Perhaps, he considered as they walked towards the meeting room, Grace was right. He should have chosen someone more suited to a world of convenient marriages.

They took their seats across from Jonathon and, as always, Carter started to leaf through the documents at his place. Grace sat ramrod-straight.

'It's fairly straightforward…' Jonathon kicked things off. 'Anything you don't understand, feel free to interject. First things first, though: we can't proceed without an NDA.' He glanced to Carter. 'Has this already been raised?'

'It has.'

For something 'straightforward', Grace soon found out the devastating price she would pay if she broke her silence. And after reading through the first of the contracts she broke her silence now.

'All proceeds? A percentage of my future earnings? You know I'm struggling…' She shook her head and stared aghast at Carter. 'I've already told you I don't want anyone to know.'

Carter stared ahead. He knew he was an utter bastard in negotiations but he was trying to hold back, so he left Jonathon to do the talking.

'If you don't divulge, then there's no issue.'

On and on Jonathon went, explaining that things could go no further until the document was signed. That it was to protect them both. That Carter's previous partner had taken out a two-page spread in a magazine…

'So?' Grace asked. 'I'm not carrying the can for something one of his many exes might have done.'

Carter glanced at Jonathon, who'd clearly expected the NDA to be a trifling matter. In truth, so too had Carter—he'd thought this was the easy part!

'Indefinitely?' she checked, the reality of that single word dawning. 'I can *never* tell anyone?'

'It's quite standard,' Jonathon said.

Not to Grace.

Oh, it wasn't the wedding, nor even the year they would spend together.

It was after.

Grace caught a tiny glimpse of the future then—a life after Carter, all her problems seemingly solved. But he'd be gone.

She pushed the chair back and stood. 'I'd like to take a break, please.'

She felt a little giddy, and the dim lights of the corridor did nothing to soothe her—they annoyed her, in fact.

She took the elevator down, and even if Kuala Lumpur wasn't the best place for cool air, it was so vibrant, so alive, it was still a relief to be out of the formal surroundings, to watch the busy city, the people, the cars, the noise...

'Grace.' Carter had come out. 'What the hell? If you're going to storm out over every clause this is going to be a very long day.'

Her response was silence.

'There has to be something in writing to ensure this remains between us, but I'm hardly really going to go after your wages.'

'Violet's been there for me every step of the way—and, believe me, given how I doubted her, it has nothing to do with *obligation*,' she sneered. 'That ran out a long time ago... It's about friendship...love.'

She looked at Carter then, a man who actively turned his back on the things she treasured the most.

'You couldn't begin to understand,' she said.

For someone who tried to be kind, she was possibly being mean now—but, hell, this morning had made her so.

'I know you lost your family, and I can't ever fathom how dreadful it was to lose them all in an instant.'

She stared at his granite features, saw now why he preferred the cold world of business, the towers, the noise.

'But I lose my mother a little bit more each day, and my friend is there for me. A year or so from now you'll be gone...' Grace said.

Her voice trailed off as she glimpsed the devastation she might feel and, frantically not wanting him to see, she reminded herself that emotions—at least deep ones—were not, nor ever could be allowed.

'What do I tell her?

'Just say that we didn't work out.'

'Please...' She gave a mirthless laugh. 'That's not going to work with Violet...'

'Then it's up to you to make it work,' he warned. 'This isn't a game, or about placating friends.'

Grace swallowed as she suddenly got a front seat row to his ruthless edge as he very succinctly reminded her that this was a business arrangement, not a cosy deal.

She thought of her mother, reminded herself that was the real reason she was even sitting down to sign a contract. And yet there was a lump building in her throat.

Pulling herself away from the wall, Grace simply refused to let him see how deeply this was affecting her. 'Oh, well...' she shrugged '...at least I'll be rich.'

'And Grace...?' He called her back, waited till she'd turned around. 'If we do somehow manage to get past the NDA without you melting down, then we move on to the marriage contract. That won't be getting signed today...'

'What does that mean?'

'It means there's no need to argue every point or storm out.' His eyes never left her face, and his voice was curt. 'Some personal details will be raised—don't get all offended, just make a note on the paper provided and we can discuss it between ourselves later.'

'Fine.'

'Grace, I told you right from the start you couldn't tell Violet.'

'I thought that meant while we were married.' She looked at him. 'I don't even know if I'll ever want tell her, but maybe in time...'

* * *

Carter arched his neck when she'd gone.

He loved the sounds of a city—any city. Usually they drowned out the thoughts in his head. But now all he could see was the sight of her strained features. And, no matter how self-sufficient *he* chose to be, he knew that Grace was close to her friend and that they relied on each other. He wasn't used to that. Not just for himself...all the women he generally dated would know the score.

This was a business decision.

He thought of Arif, impatient at eight, wanting to know what had happened to his friend.

Of Bashim telling him to give it time.

And, no, he'd never been ready to talk to his friend...

Yet here he was, taking that right away from Grace.

Damn.

He took the elevator up, walked back into the meeting room where she sat, taking a long drink of water. And the ridiculous thing was that he missed her small smile when he entered. The tiny moments of eye contact they had started to share. The feeling they were both in this together.

It would seem that he had the business meeting he wanted.

'Are we ready to resume?' Jonathon checked.

'Sure,' Grace responded.

'It's a standard agreement,' Jonathon started. 'And not just for your own protection. If the press or Benedict attempt to approach your family or friends, this ensures they don't know anything.'

'I understand,' Grace responded, her voice almost a monotone, but she frowned when Carter spoke.

'Add an exclusion...' He turned to Grace, and knew he didn't even need to ask if she trusted her friend—she'd already told him her life's regret was a brief moment in time when she'd doubted her, simply to save herself from the reality of facing her mother's diagnosis. 'What's Violet's surname?'

'Lewis.'

Jonathon was less than willing, pointing out that Violet would need to agree to sign her own NDA, that there was no guarantee otherwise.

'Violet Lews is to be excluded at Grace's discretion.'

'The consequences remain,' Jonathon warned.

She must really trust her friend, Carter thought as finally, one hour and forty-seven minutes after the meeting had commenced, Grace picked up her pen.

Now came the hard part.

He glanced up as Jonathon took his jacket off.

It would be some considerable time till they were alone…

If Grace lasted that long!

CHAPTER TEN

'WELL DONE,' CARTER SAID, steering Grace, who was almost fizzing with silent anger, to the elevator.

It was close to midnight as they left the restaurant, having had a long dinner with Jonathon and his wife.

Somehow she had held her temper and made notes throughout the long meeting. Somehow she had not stood up and walked out as extremely intimate details had been discussed. Then, the audacity of having to sit through dinner!

No room full of candles was going to fix this, she thought, as they stepped into the suite.

'DNA!' She was as close to slapping another person as she had ever come as—now they were in private—she raised the points that had hurt the most. 'I thought the NDA was bad enough, but…' She looked at him in abject fury. 'You laughed when he said you'd insist on a DNA test and I had to just sit there.'

'I did not laugh,' Carter corrected. 'I smothered a smile.' He took her by the arms. 'Grace, he was just saying that if you are already pregnant…'

She finished for him. 'You'd demand a DNA test.'

'Did you want me to tell Jonathon that you were a virgin? That we both got carried away? Because I could have—and do you know what? He would have still insisted the DNA clause remained.'

'In case I spend the next few weeks frantically trying to get pregnant so I can blame it on you because you're such a big shot?'

'Something like that,' he said.

He moved away and punched out two headache tablets, adding another and swallowing them down with a drink that she was sure wasn't the one recommended on the packet.

'Then we had to sit through dinner afterwards…as if I hadn't just been insulted.'

'He's just doing his job.'

She kicked off her shoes. 'I am *so* not suited for this.'

Then she took off the horrible pale jacket, and the trousers, too, and decided she wasn't suited to suits either.

'I agree,' Carter nodded, tearing off his tie as if it were choking him, and his jacket and shoes too, and then his socks. He lay back on the bed. 'Believe it or not, it's your unsuitability for this that makes marriage doable for me.'

'I don't get it.'

'Grace, I take my dates to the theatre, so I don't have to talk to them. I can't imagine getting past time in the jungle with any of them, let alone them agreeing to a wedding there, without exclusive photos and a freaking string quartet and white chairs with bows, a few celebrity guests...' He covered his eyes with the back of his arm and groaned. 'At least you just want money and a peaceful life.'

Grace was almost terribly pleased he was deep in migraine land, so that he could not see her awkward swallow.

Even as she denied it, even as she ignored it and told all the thoughts to go away, as she sat on the bed and looked over to where he lay she knew the reason for the sudden clarity that had struck her when she'd agreed to this madness. How the impossible decision had been made so easily...

She was more than a bit crazy about him.

Fascinated by him, really.

Trust her to go and fall for the one man who actually *was* an island...well, at least most of the time. Because now he pulled down his forearm and gave her a half-grimace and a half-smile that almost felt like an apology.

'Seriously, I know it was hell in there.'

'I hated it,' she admitted, still appalled at all that had been discussed, right down to those awful 'discreet affair' clauses. 'All of it.'

There were so many things that had upset her today, Grace thought as she headed into the bathroom. Finally alone, she took the clips from her hair and then washed the make-up off her face.

She was too weary to take off her cami, let alone her colour-less underwear, and she just stared in the mirror and didn't know who she was any more.

By night she felt safe in the decision she was making. Making love with Carter, she felt giddy with desire, safe to take risks, to watch in the mirror as he took her as if seeing herself come to life.

Right now, she didn't even know if she liked him.

But that question faded when she saw him dozing on the bed. He was why she was here—not that she was going to admit that. And she really was the luckiest—not for ever, of course, but for now. She felt lucky to be able to climb up onto the bed, to take a little of his *don't give a damn* attitude and curl into him.

'What are you doing?' he asked, pulling away from her touch as she laid her head on his chest.

'Checking there's actually a heart in there.' She felt his half-laugh. 'I don't like Jonathon. I don't get why we had to sit down to dinner and make small talk with him and his wife…'

'Because…' he said. But, as was so often the case with Carter, he didn't elaborate. He tried to peel her off him. 'Get undressed and get some sleep.'

'I don't want to.' She was too tired even to move, but after a day of having details discussed such as their having no love, no involvement afterwards, no expectations, she could not turn her mind off. 'He seems *very* familiar with your private life.'

'Of course he is. About ten years ago there was a lawsuit about twins. I think the woman was just hoping I'd pay up, but Jonathon shot that down very quickly. Look it up.'

'I already have.'

'Then you'll know about the guy I supposedly dated?'

'Yes.'

'An attempt to bribe me. Look, Jonathon knows I don't want a relationship, he knows that I'm straight, and that my family are useless. I don't have to repeatedly tell him that I never want kids, and he knows without asking that I don't have unprotected sex. So, yes, it's probably a surprise to him that I'm suddenly engaged and forgot to be cautious.' He gave her shoulder a squeeze. 'Don't take it all so personally.'

'Oh, it feels personal. But why did we have dinner with them?'

'Aren't you supposed to be calling the care home? Wasn't that meeting today? It's almost four in London.'

'You're like one of those time zone walls at the stock exchange…' Grace grumbled, half relieved he'd reminded her, but also certain he was trying to avoid the discussion. Still, if she wanted to catch the manager before she went home then now was the time to call.

Peeling herself from the reprieve of his arms, she sat up on the edge of the bed.

His arm had gone back across his head, and she was certain he was dozing—anyway, she doubted her mother's care plan meeting was high on his list of priorities.

'Maggie!' She was relieved to reach the manager, especially when she heard it was all good news. 'They're reducing her medication?' Grace blinked, thrilled to hear that her sedation was being cut back.

And not only that…

'That's so sweet of her,' she said, when she heard that Violet had been bringing in a chocolate éclair each Sunday, just dropping it off at Reception so as not to upset her mother.

Oh, and she needed new lenses for her glasses… Grace chose not to ask about her hearing tests—not just yet. Anyway, there was something more that had been worrying her.

'Is she still asking for me all the time?'

The response was one she hadn't expected, and she wished— oh, how she wished—she'd taken the call in the lounge, or some other area of the opulent suite.

It was ridiculous to get good news and want to cry.

Carter knew damn well he'd changed the subject rather than answer her question, but behind his forearm he frowned at Grace's long silence in response to whatever the answer to her last question had been.

'Oh,' she finally said. 'That's good… I guess.'

'Everything okay?' he checked when she'd ended the call.

'Yes,' she said, just a little too brightly.

Carter removed his arm and looked to where she sat, her back to him.

'Are you sure?' Carter checked.

'Just leave it.'

'Grace?'

'She's stopped asking for me. Apparently, she refers to me being at school, but…' She swallowed. 'It's good news, I guess.' Then her voice changed from falsely upbeat to hollow. 'I didn't expect it.'

For a moment the false wall she'd put up had nothing to support it, and he reached out, completely on instinct, to put a hand on her shoulder. But she brushed it off.

'I don't want to talk about it.'

'You can.'

'I don't want to.'

'Come here,' he said again, and pulled her, tense and yet yielding, back into his arms. Only it wasn't the same relaxed space as before. 'She probably—'

'Carter,' she interrupted. 'It hurts to talk about it.'

'I know.'

'So can we change the subject? Like you did when I asked why we had to have dinner with your lawyer?'

She lay there.

'If I get my own, will you sit through a chummy dinner with them?'

'No.' He gave a soft laugh, realising now how odd it must have seemed. 'Jonathon does a lot for me.'

'You pay him to.'

'Not just that.'

He loathed sharing anything personal, but he'd just asked for the same from her. More, he'd asked her to sit through dinner with two people who were not only clearly on his side, but actively suspicious of her.

'I don't expect you to get it, but they have both looked out for me. A lot.'

'How?'

He swallowed before he told her something very few knew— and it had nothing to with the fact she'd signed the NDA.

That wasn't even a thought in his head.

More, it felt right to reveal it.

'I lived with them for a couple of months while it was decided where I'd end up. Jonathon wanted to be sure I had a say—well, of sorts. I wasn't talking then.'

'At all?'

'Not much. I could hear, though.' He gave her shoulder a squeeze, making another little joke, even if the topic wasn't funny. But it seemed they had this new language they shared, because she looked up briefly and smiled.

'What did you hear?' Grace asked.

Her head went back to his chest, her eyes open as she listened. Usually she'd close her eyes to picture things. Only now she needed every detail—how one hand held her arm, and the other found her fingers and toyed with her ring as he spoke.

'My uncle was prepared to have me,' he said.

'Benedict's father?'

'Yep,' he said. 'Well, he wanted to get his hands on my parents' money. We'd be lying in a cheap motel now if he'd got his hands on it.'

Grace found that she was smiling, wishing she was in a motel with him for gorgeous, uncomplicated sex. Pull-up-the-car-and-get-a-room sex. And she found that she blinked in shock at her own thoughts, especially when they were discussing something so serious.

'What's funny?' he asked, and it dawned on her that he, too, was aware of even her tiniest movement.

'Us in a motel.'

'What about it?'

'You were talking about your uncle…' She nudged him, knowing he would happily stay off track and wanting to know more.

'Jonathon threatened my uncle with an exposé, so he soon pulled out. Really, you can see where Benedict gets it from. Then there was my grandfather… He was eccentric, at best, and grieving.'

He fell silent for a moment, and she watched his finger hover over the stone of her ring.

'As well as that, I didn't want to go back to Borneo—it was a couple of years before I did. And it was Jonathon and his wife who stepped up.'

'So they took you in?'

'They did. And I think I could have stayed for longer. But then my aunt in New York decided she needed to be seen doing her part.'

He told her about his mother's sister, and how she really wasn't 'mommy material'.

'That lasted a couple of years before she shipped me off, back to boarding school in England. Jonathon's always looked out for me and, as expensive as he is, he has never once taken advantage…'

'Do I have to like them now?'

'No, just understand where they're coming from.' He played with the edge of her cami. 'Get undressed?' he suggested.

'I honestly can't be bothered.' She liked being sad in his arms.

'Nor can I,' he admitted. 'I'm sorry you're upset about your mum.'

'Thank you.'

She knew he'd possibly shared with an agenda, but it was a nice agenda—to give a bit of himself, to know her some more.

'I've been worried the whole time I've been away that she'll think I've forgotten her. I never gave much thought to her forgetting me.' She took a breath, but it shuddered. It was five staccato gasps just to get one breath in, and it was the closest to crying she'd come. 'I don't want to be forgotten…'

'I know.'

There was something else that had upset her during the discussions today. 'Why are you having a vasectomy?' she asked.

'I've been meaning to.' She watched as his hand moved to his crotch, as if to protect it, but then moved away. 'Though it didn't seem urgent until the other night.'

She lay there, trying to tell herself it was ridiculous to be upset about something so sensible—something he clearly wanted. Or rather to think about babies he didn't want, and certainly not with her.

He picked up her hand and looked at her ring and she knew he was about to change the subject again—but at least she understood why. It was too painful for him to recall.

'Why the hell did you choose this one?'

'Fireflies.' Grace smiled and let him talk about nothing rather than desperate hurt. 'When we were just a one-night stand...'

'Seriously?'

'Mmm...' she said. 'Then you had to go and propose, and bring in lawyers and stylists.'

'I thought you wanted stylists?'

'Not any more,' Grace admitted. 'I miss us.'

'Do you?'

He looked down at her pale leg, lying over his. 'I miss your coral toenails,' he told her.

'So do I.' She liked the *thud-thud* of his heart and how neither of them moved. 'I love coral... I love colour.'

Carter frowned, unsure how to respond. If he *should* respond!

'So why all the...?'

'They suggested I start with a neutral palette and then add my own signature.'

'You already have your own signature.'

'I don't think so?'

'Oh, you do,' he assured her. 'Well, you did.'

'What is it?'

'Sunset colours. Sunrise, maybe. I don't know... But it's not neutral…' He actually gritted his jaw. 'You're more vibrant…a bit…'

Careful Carter, he thought.

'Dishevelled…'

'I was dishevelled when we met because I'd been travelling and was asleep. Then the jungle…'

'I like your curls,' he said. 'And how your top falls off your shoulder. Always…' he stuck with his chosen word '…dishevelled.'

'Slatternly, as my mother would say.'

He liked her soft laugh.

'Though not any more. Even my underwear is sensible.'

He frowned, pulling at her cami, stretching his hand around her back.

'It's a bandeau,' she said. 'No hooks.'

He pulled her up onto his stomach, took off her cami and looked at the little strip of material, and her dark nipples all squashed by the fabric.

'Like a bank robber,' he said, and they laughed. 'I like these,' he said of the glossy knickers. He could see the darkness of her triangle of hair and tried to unfocus his eyes. 'You look naked.'

'I thought you'd be more into velvet and lace.'

'You so have the wrong impression of me,' he said. 'I am not really bothered by underwear…' He was almost too tired to speak now, so his words were sort of a drawl. 'More what's under the underwear.' Then he pushed her breasts together and changed his mind. 'You have the best breasts…'

He moved down to her invisible knickers and dusted her thighs with his hands. And then he pulled her head down.

He had never expected a kiss like this when they'd walked through the door. Certainly, he had not expected for all the tension that had built through the day to be erased by deep and real conversation. Nor, as he'd led her angrily from the restaurant, had he envisaged this slow intimate kiss. Their mouths were too tired to talk, their bodies almost too tired to move, but somehow he was in deep discovery, because his hands were peeling down the knickers she loathed.

'I hate them too,' he said, for they refused to tear.

There was something so inherently pleasurable watching her sensual nature emerge. 'I was worried they'd get rid of this,' he told her as he stroked her triangle of hair through the flimsy fabric.

'They suggested it…' She blushed so deeply the colour speckled her neck. 'I refused.'

'Good.'

'Get what *you* want, Grace…'

'I want this.'

Perhaps he heard the urgent note, because Carter tried again to tear at the fabric, but they were better designed than that, and Grace didn't want to get off his sexy hot body.

He lifted her bottom, brought her towards him and raised his head, and she held the bedhead as he tore the fabric with his teeth.

It was the sexiest thing she'd ever felt…his head on her stomach, his hand on her bottom and the tearing of her knickers.

'There,' he said.

It was a very slow start, because he'd managed only to rip the fabric to the edge of her thigh, then it was back up again for another nibble from his teeth.

He slid them down one thigh and didn't go back down. He slipped a little lower and tasted her. It was something she had never thought she could enjoy. In truth, as she closed her eyes, she was too tense to know if she actually did.

'Grace…' He probed and he licked and he relished, and she felt herself pressing down a little for more of the bliss. 'Give me a little climax…'

'I can't—'

Famous last words, because he pulled her down onto him till she was gripping the bedhead and fighting not to cry out, such bliss he delivered with his mouth.

'That's it…' he said, stroking her bottom with his hand as he stroked her with his tongue. She gave him a little, a flicker of orgasm, but he knew as she lifted from him, that she held back a lot.

He sat her down on his thighs, felt her hand close around him, and not shyly, just so blissfully.

They were both panting, both turning the other on, but with more than just touch—they were crossing into each other's thoughts. 'Why did you smile when I said motel?' he asked and her flushed face darkened, yet she stroked him still.

'The thought of...' she shook her head.

'Go on?' he invited, deeply curious to hear more.

'The thought of wanting another so much that you simply have to stop the car...' she gave a half nervous laugh. 'Or meet in your lunch break...'

Carter had never wanted anyone in that way.

Yet he wanted her in that way now.

He reached for a condom and saw her eyes briefly close in frustration as he tore the wrapper.

If she had been anyone else it would have alerted him. He'd just been lectured by his lawyer, after all, to be very careful in the coming weeks. Instead it made him reckless. Their wants matched...this desire could not be contained.

'In a moment,' he said, and she nodded in weak relief.

And then it was Grace who knelt up and held his thick, unsheathed base, and together they watched her lower herself down onto him.

'God...' she moaned. Because he made her crave.

And she looked at him, half dressed, resting up on his forearms, as fascinated as she, she rested her hands on his chest and moved.

It was a dangerous, dangerous game and they both knew it, but they were in this together, this *folie à deux*, this shared madness, and she felt for the first time in her life completely free.

And also looked after, because he nodded and said, 'I won't come,'

He gave her his word, and with it she had permission to move again.

He stroked her breasts, pinched them, and he stroked her stomach, then round to her bottom. He didn't guide her, just inflamed her. He stroked her thighs and then, when she bit her lip, he thrust up into her, and she could not believe his control. How he could lie there and thrust and observe.

'Carter...'

She was holding the bedhead and moaning loudly, and then he started to pull her down hard, again and again, and Grace could hear herself shout. She was suddenly frantic, deeply orgasming and trying to lift off of him, yet he held her firm. Pulsing and making sounds she never had before. Then, when he could hold back no more, he took her by the hips and lifted her, and she watched him spill onto her. Breathless, she watched as his palm cupped her where she ached with the void he'd left.

He pulled her head down and they kissed as if it were their first time...wet, deep kisses. And in between he told her off...warned her not to play that game again...

'I won't.'

She could barely breathe. Her sex felt heavy and her stomach was still tight, as if unfulfilled. Yet she had never been more satisfied.

Carter wasn't faring so well. He rarely made mistakes, and certainly not the same one twice. Okay, he hadn't come inside her, but he was taking risks he never had before.

He wanted Grace more than he'd thought he was capable of.

But she deserved someone who could love her—completely.

He knew he was incapable of that.

Knew he had to pull back.

CHAPTER ELEVEN

IT WAS THE scent rather than the sound of Carter coming out of the shower that awoke Grace.

She knew his scents now.

He worked hard for his millions—or billions—and at the end of his working day there was just the last trace of bergamot on his jaw, and the masculine scent of Carter as he peeled off his shirt.

Possibly that was the one she loved the most.

Even so, the heady mixture of clean male, deodorant, and his sexy cologne was such a potent hit to the olfactory system that Grace was smiling even as she opened her eyes.

She thought of their lovemaking last night and lay watching as he pulled on his shirt and suit. He was clearly trying not to wake her, because he sat on a bedroom chair to put on his shoes, but then he must have seen her watching him.

'You're awake,' he said.

'It's early.' She frowned, peering at the time.

'I've got a flight at six.'

'You never said.'

'Didn't I?' He paused, then slipped on his second shoe. 'I thought I told you I had to go to Janana?'

He wasn't used to giving times and dates to anyone other than Ms Hill, who then did her usual magic with his schedule, but even so he was certain he'd mentioned it.

'The council's meeting. We have to make some last-minute changes to the plans.'

'For the palace?'

'That's right.'

It blew her mind that he was working on the restorations for some ancient palace while she was filling her days with designers and having her hair straightened, her nails or make-up done.

'When will you be back?' she asked.

'Depends.'

Carter moved his luggage out of the bedroom suite.

Seeing Grace stretch was like watching a flower open, or seeing how the giant ferns at the river edge unfurled.

But he didn't like the way his mind kept drifting to the river, and he kept waiting for boredom to kick in, for her to annoy him.

For her to stop creeping into his heart.

'You look tired,' she commented.

'No,' he disagreed, even though he knew he looked like hell. 'You've got Ms Hill's details. Any problems that Guest Services can't handle just call her.'

'Why can't I just call you? What if I—?'

'Grace.' He halted her right then and there. 'I've told you I don't take unscheduled calls during working hours. If there're any issues while I'm away then call Ms Hill, because you won't be able to get hold of me.'

She was tempted to ask, *Am I to tell Ms Hill if I get my period?* But she just lay back on the pillow, telling herself she wasn't even late yet.

He snapped on his heavy watch and frowned when he saw the time. 'There won't be any internet,' he told her. 'At least not if we go into the desert.'

'I thought it was just the palace?'

'There are some desert abodes he wants me to look at.' He shook his head. 'They look pre-biblical.'

'Seriously?'

'Apparently so. Sahir thinks they'll work better than a tent for his retreats.' He went to the safe to collect his passport. 'I'm going to—' He halted, suddenly feeling the silk of the pouch, then just grabbed his passport and turned around. 'It depends how quickly the council decide. I'd better go.'

'Sure.'

He picked up the plans and she pursed her lips as the man who had made such thorough love to her last night went to walk out through the door.

And then she reminded herself of his warning that they would never be close. She lay back on the pillow, feeling the tension in her own lips, holding back from telling him that she expected...

What *did* she expect? Grace chided herself.

Better than this!

And Grace was suddenly angry. She wasn't asking for love, or affection, just for him not to leave her feeling discarded.

Grace pulled on her robe and ventured out of the bedroom, saw the breakfast waiting for her. Bypassing it, she wrenched open the door.

'Carter...'

He was standing at the elevator when she walked down to him in her robe, still tying it.

'What?'

'You forgot something?'

He frowned. Had the audacity to check the inside pocket of his jacket.

'Back in the suite,' Grace said, her voice shaking with anger.

Because if he thought they could make love all night and then he did not even have to tell her his return date on the way out, then he could forget it.

'I get that it's a sham,' Grace told him, before the elevator doors closed, 'but if you don't want things to fall apart in the bedroom very quickly, then you'd better damn well learn how to say good-bye properly.'

'Poor Grace...' He had the audacity to smile. 'You want a kiss?'

'Not especially.' She stared at him. 'But I do expect basic manners.'

He made two kissing noises. 'See you soon, my darling...' he mocked, turning to go.

But possibly he then saw her furious eyes, because he bent his head and kissed her hard, forcing her lips apart, pulling her in.

'Better?'

'Screw you.'

'No,' he said. 'Neither of us are getting screwed, Grace. I have a long flight, and an important series of meetings. I haven't got the head space to play happy families in the morning, and don't expect me to come back bearing flowers.' He held up his hands in exasperation. 'What do you want? For me to pretend?'

'No.'

'To lie?'

'That's the last thing I want. I never want you to lie.'

She felt stupid. For pulling on the robe and running after him. And for not understanding that the intimacy they'd shared at night could be gone by morning. How, like a conjurer, he could whip away the cloth and leave everything standing.

Only the cloth was her heart, and she was starting to realise that she didn't know how to give it one moment and claim it back the next. Make love with him at night and be roommates by day.

'Grace...'

'It's fine. Go.'

Of course he did just that, and she stood there, tears filling her eyes.

She was scared that she was falling in love with a man incapable of love.

And worried too. Because while she wasn't technically late, her breasts hurt like hell. Or could that just be from sex?

She would go for a swim, Grace decided, slipping off her ring and looking at the pretty glinting lights. She'd go for a swim and then head to the Batu Caves. She would not spend the day dwelling on him...

That was all she was thinking as she went to pop her ring in the safe. Her hand brushed against something cool and, widening the door, she felt her mind leap at the brief distraction of a black silk pouch. She frowned as she lifted it, saw the fabric opening, and a glint of metal.

A silver bangle was her first thought as she slipped it out and weighed it in her hand. Only it was far too chunky and there was no hinge, no give in the gap that would allow it to slip on her wrist. It was heavy, too, and quite, quite beautiful.

So lost in the mystery of it, so relieved by the temporary re-prieve of thoughts of Carter was she, that she didn't hear the door.

'What the hell do you think you're doing?'

She jumped at the whip of his voice and swung around. 'I just…'

She swallowed, unsure what to say. After all, she'd been caught snooping and it just wasn't like her.

'I don't know,' she admitted, trying to cram it back into the pouch. But she was all fingers and thumbs and so she just held the bangle out to him. 'I'm sorry.'

'Just put it back.'

It was as if he didn't even want to touch it.

'Christ, is there no privacy?' he demanded. 'I would *never* go through your things.'

'I wasn't…' Only that wasn't strictly true, and Grace knew it…

Seeing him so angry, so defensive, she guessed the bangle was meant for someone else.

'I hope she likes it…' She tossed him the damn thing but he made no attempt to catch it, just stood there as it fell to the floor.

As Grace headed to the bathroom, Carter stood, eyes closed.

He held the cold metal again for the first time since he'd handed it to his brother, fighting not to look down, to trace the scratches, doing all he could not to recall Hugo's trusting smile as he'd reached out to take it.

He'd let him down so badly…

Replacing it in the pouch, he returned it to the safe and then closed the door, breathing out as the lock bolted closed.

He was bizarrely conflicted. Because if it had been anyone else going through his property, touching something so private, he'd have had Security throw them out by now.

But he knew it had been a mistake, or just…

Some hotels were great for romance and sex but simply dread-ful to have a row in, he thought. Because he could see her out-line through the glass dividing door, see her back was turned. He knocked on the glass and she didn't need to turn. He could see her strained face in the huge mirrors.

'Grace...'

'I wasn't snooping...' Her voice was shaky. 'Well, clearly I was. But I didn't intend to. I just...' Her green eyes were anguished. 'I was putting my ring away and I saw the bangle...' She stopped. 'I saw the pouch.'

He smiled at her honest correction. 'I get it.' He nodded 'I overreacted.'

He could apologise for that and leave it there, but he knew more was required.

'It's not a bangle. It's a teething ring,' he told her. 'It was my brother's. It's been in the family for years. Polished up for each baby.'

'I'm so sorry.' Her eyes filled up and she looked at him, "It's lovely that you keep something of his..."

'No, Grace,' he corrected with a slight smile, 'I don't drag it around the world with me.' His smile paled. 'Ulat had it with him when he died.'

'Ulat?'

'Hugo. Ulat is what the locals call their babies for the first few months. He was just starting to be known as both. Arif goes back to the site each anniversary. It turned up last year and he gave it to me that night at the resort.'

That night.

'Was that why you were arguing?'

'In part.' He nodded. 'I told him he should have left it where it was.'

'You don't want it?'

'No.' He shook his head. 'I don't.'

He'd been in turmoil since it had been handed to him—the nightmares, the feeling of dread...

For years he'd settled for being numb—outwardly successful, inwardly dead.

Now he was thawing, and the agony it exposed was spreading beyond him.

Everything had changed since this teething ring had been in his possession, and he wanted it back where it belonged.

'Arif thinks I should take it back myself.'

'Go into the jungle?'

'He's offered to take me.'

'Maybe it would help?'

'How? I watched my family disappear before my eyes. Believe me when I say I don't want to relive it.'

It was the first time he'd really spoken about it, and she felt her heart squeeze. 'You saw it?'

'I don't know,' he admitted. 'I guess I must have. I should have stopped it.'

'What were you supposed to do?' she asked. 'What could a child do?'

'Kept him in the boat with me.'

'Hugo?'

'Believe me when I say that I was the adult in that family.'

He was still furious with them; she could feel it.

'I was taken out of school—not just to travel but to take care of him. And I didn't.'

'You can't let guilt stop you living your life.'

'I don't let guilt stop me,' Carter said. 'I've built the life that I want.'

She nodded, but she felt it wasn't enough, that something should be said. But she knew Carter would not have that conversation.

'Anyway,' he said, 'it's a double apology. The reason I came back to the room was to say you were right.' He looked at her. 'I am not used to sharing my day with any other—calling, saying goodbye.'

'I know.'

'I'm new to this, too, Grace.'

She nodded.

'I'll try and call, and I should be back by Sunday.'

'Thank you.'

'Very well, I hope to see you on Sunday.' He looked right into her eyes. 'Preferably with no knickers on...but I'm guessing I'm not allowed to say that.'

He made her laugh even as she pushed him away, even as he blew her a kiss at the door.

'Oh, God,' she said, when he had safely gone.

Grace knew she was in trouble.

Big trouble.

Because she didn't want Carter to lie and pretend that he loved her.

The more time she spent with him, the more she wanted it to be for real.

She couldn't be falling in love with him.

That wasn't the plan...

CHAPTER TWELVE

CARTER'S CONTRITION DIDN'T LAST.

He really was the worst fiancé, even allowing for the fact their engagement was fake.

Not a single call or text.

Even if he was in the desert, there were a couple of airports in between, and when she looked up Sahir and the opulent palace... Oh, she was rather certain there would be the odd occasion when he could call.

But nothing.

So, she'd shopped, as any good Carter Bennett fiancée would.

And Kuala Lumpur was incredible. The shops were airy and beautiful, and the cakes.... Oh, her mother would have loved them. Every afternoon Grace carefully selected a treat and brought one back with her. And she visited the Batu Caves and climbed the coloured stairs, stood at the top and looked out onto the glorious view.

But there was only so much shopping and sightseeing she could do.

And she hated lying to Violet, so their conversations were a little short.

'What's happening with you and that guy?' she'd asked.

'I like him,' Grace said. 'A lot.'

'And?' Violet prompted. 'Does he have a name?'

'Violet...'

'God, you're mean.' She laughed. 'I'll wait for all the gossip when you're home. I popped in to find out how your mum is getting on today.'

'Thanks for that.'

'They're thrilled with her,' Violet said. 'Please don't worry. I peeked in and saw her line dancing...'

Grace laughed. 'I know. I'm trying to buy her a Stetson...'

Grace was still smiling as she took out the folder Arif had given her and read detailed notes about the gradual rise in the number of orangutans on Carter's land, the rare birds they were encouraging, the decline in saltwater crocodiles...

Felicity's work was fascinating—tracking endangered birds, some exclusive to the area—and Grace found herself all too often straying from her task.

Instead of inputting data, she was looking things up. And rather too often she found herself looking up Carter.

It was unsettling to see evidence of his decadent past, and a lot of it seemed rather recent. And it served her right for peeking, because she found out that Sahir was a playboy, and he and Carter had been hitting the social pages since their university days.

She tried not to feel a little tense that he was in the company of the playboy prince now...

It took a lot of scrolling to get further back into his past and when she did, she thought her heart would break.

A miracle. That was what they'd called Carter.

There were pictures of a helicopter, and him being stretchered out.

And Grace, who really didn't cry, wept right there in the hotel's business centre when she saw his scarred face and dark eyes.

Then, in an article a couple of years later, Carter had been photographed standing in a short coat beside a Christmas tree with his glamorous aunt.

She scrolled on, but it didn't help matters. Because there was an image of Carter coming out of a theatre, rumoured to be engaged, and he was with the most beautiful woman Grace had ever seen...

She peered at the date.

Last month!

At that moment, as if he knew she was snooping again, her phone rang and she saw that finally it was him.

'Hey...' She attempted to sound normal. 'How's it going?'

'Stalemate,' Carter said, and let out a breath. 'It's the most beautiful building I've ever worked on, but one wing of the palace was destroyed by an earthquake more than a century ago. We've been going off old plans and drawings, but a lot of the design is based on astronomy—a first for me.' He sounded incredibly tired. 'Most of the council don't even want it done.'

Carter had reverted to his usual tactics and withdrawn—but, given the serious nature of the project, and given that Sahir was a friend, he hadn't simply walked out. Instead he was cooling his heels, sitting in the opulent royal lounge at a private members' club.

'What are you up to now?' Grace asked.

'Watching a sandstorm.'

'Sounds spectacular.'

'From behind glass, it is. Sahir wants to head out...'

He paused, not really wanting to discuss Sahir's methods for solving an issue.

For so long he'd wondered why Sahir would disappear into the desert for days or weeks on end. Yet a part of Carter understood the search for answers.

Those damned dreams now featured Grace, disappearing on a plane, or sinking beneath the water. It was now always Grace rather than his mother holding Hugo, who was gnawing on that teething ring as they walked into the dense forest...

'Head out?' Grace asked, but he didn't elaborate, and she felt an odd sinking feeling.

They hadn't parted on a row, they'd spoken afterwards and he'd been kind, but she had doubts leaping in her chest like salmon...

'So, what are *you* doing?' he asked.

'I'm trying to find a Stetson for my mother?'

'Excuse me?'

'She's taken up line dancing, apparently...' Grace gave a small laugh. 'I need to find a sparkly shirt and a hat for her. Oh, and I'm working on that data Arif gave me.'

'You don't have to do any of that.'

'I like doing it,' Grace admitted. 'There are reams of information about the conservation work being undertaken. I don't see that Benedict stands a chance if it's taken to court.'

'Careful,' he warned, 'you might put yourself out of a job. I need a wife so I can inherit the property.'

But then his voice changed and he was serious.

'Look, I agree. If it goes to court, we'll eventually win— "eventually" being the operative word. However, there is damage being done now.'

'I know.'

She went quiet, aching to admit just how very nice it was to hear from him. And to tell him that from her digging around in his past she knew the anniversary of his family's deaths was fast approaching. She wondered if it was on his mind. It had to be, she decided, even while knowing the phone wasn't the place to bring up something so deeply personal.

Still, she took a breath. 'It will be nice to go back there.'

'If the talks with Jonathon go well, and the contracts get signed, we soon shall be.'

'For how long?'

'Just for the wedding—one night.'

'We could stay for a bit longer…'

'The point of this marriage is to end my obligations, so I can spend as little time there as possible.'

'I know.' Grace sighed. 'But that doesn't mean I can't go by myself.'

'Excuse me?'

'You've said yourself you'll be away nearly all the time, and I'm enjoying collating the data. I don't mind going.'

'It's data entry,' he snapped. 'You can do that remotely.'

'I like it there, though.' She looked at the meticulous notes spread before her. 'I wouldn't mind getting more involved.'

'You're supposed to be acting as my wife for a year,' he said, pulling rank. 'If I'd wanted Jane Goodall I'd have asked her to marry me. Or Felicity…'

The sound of Grace's laughter down the line actually brought a reluctant smile to his lips.

'I'm not suggesting throwing darts at wildlife and tagging them,' she said.

'Good.'

But despite his smile, he could hear her interest ramping up. A couple of weeks away from the jungle and already she was longing to return. It was all too familiar. His grandfather had never left, and his parents had been drawn back over and over again…

Carter got it.

For all it had taken from him, the place, and the people, the jungle still held a certain allure.

And now Grace was becoming ensnared…

'That type of work is best left to the experts—that's what I'm trying to secure.'

'And my job is to be Carter Bennett's adoring wife?'

'Correct.'

'Carter, about the wedding…'

'What about it?'

'If you want to go out with Arif and take Hugo's teething ring back, I get it…'

'Grace,' he snapped. 'I'm at work.'

Damn. There was a reason he didn't make personal calls. But once he'd rung off he sat staring at the sandstorm, and there was a part of him that wanted to call her back, admit that he was thinking of going…

Hearing Grace talk about Hugo, he'd felt everything coming back to him. That time standing in the boat, watching the mother and baby orangutans disappear, the mangosteens… And he didn't know if it was the teething ring or Grace that was unlocking him.

Or both.

And he didn't know what he was going to find out. Certainly he didn't want witnesses when he faced whatever demons lay waiting there.

But only a local or a fool went into the jungle alone.

Carter was neither.

So that meant things needed to be taken care of.

Places and people too…

He pulled up a name on his phone and called his assistant. 'Tell Jonathon I need him in KL. I want the wedding contract signed and my estate sorted…'

Damn. For someone determined not to care, there was an awful lot to sort out.

He just wanted the teething ring buried…to make his peace with the land, or whatever.

And he knew he had to deal with things the only way he knew how—alone.

And neither Arif nor Grace could know.

CHAPTER THIRTEEN

'HI, HONEY, I'M HOME…'

Grace thought she was hallucinating when Carter appeared three days earlier than her vague expectations—completely unannounced, ever gorgeous in a suit, and wearing a Stetson.

'What on earth…?' She blinked, not just at his unexpected arrival, more at the fact that Carter didn't do 'cheery'. 'I thought you weren't back till Sunday?'

'I got fed up, sitting around waiting. They can call me when they've finished debating. You have no idea how hard this hat was to find in the Middle East. Actually, Ms Hill had it sent to me.' He took it off and placed it on her head. 'For your mother. Though it suits you…'

'Thanks,' Grace said. 'I think.'

He wasn't looking at her, Grace noticed. He was talking, but not actually looking her way, and she had an awful sinking feeling.

He'd been out with Sahir.

And that wasn't just her insecurity talking.

He didn't love her.

He'd told her.

'Also,' he said as he threw off his jacket, 'Jonathon's coming in.'

'When?'

'He should be here soon.'

'Now?' she asked. She was pleased to see Carter, but unsettled by the surprise and the sudden changes. 'I thought that wasn't until Monday?'

'That was the plan, but I might be called back to Janana at any time. It's like waiting for the smoke at the Vatican. We'll just get this marriage contract done…'

'Why?'

'Why not?' He shrugged. 'You have your questions ready?'

'Yes.'

'Then why wait?' he asked, tossing his passport into the safe. 'I want this sorted.'

'But why the sudden rush?' she asked. 'We can't get married for another week, so it's not as if we have a wedding date.' And perhaps she'd been peeking into his scandalous life too much, because she couldn't help but ask, 'Is some scandal about to hit?'

'What are you talking about?'

'I don't know...'

Something had changed, but Grace didn't quite know what. And when he stripped off to shower she found herself looking at his back, his chest, telling herself she was being paranoid.

'It's to your advantage,' he said as he dropped his trousers. 'You get a quarter of a million on signing.'

'I'll remember that,' she said, and smiled, though it faded as he headed off to the shower.

She felt ridiculous for being suspicious, and a bit teary too, and she couldn't work out why. Oh, other than the fact that she was crazy about a playboy who was only marrying her to release some assets.

And today her period was due.

She pulled on her new knickers and bra, floral and lacy this time, and of her own selection. Then she put on a new dress—a gorgeous russet linen that was cinched in at the waist.

'New stylist?' he asked as he came into the bedroom.

'Yes,' Grace said as she glazed her lips orange. 'Me.'

For the first time it was as if he'd actually noticed what she wore, and he ran his fingers through her curls as they were about to head out.

'You look incredible.'

He looked at her, right into her eyes, held her cinched waist and looked at her glossy lips. 'Slatternly...'

'Thanks.' She smiled. 'I think...'

'Come on, then,' Carter said, and they walked together but apart to the elevator.

* * *

It was a different room from the one they'd sat in before, and displayed were different flowers—a huge vase of pink orchids was the centrepiece this time.

'It's a late start,' Jonathon said, all polite smiles.

Carter watched as Grace took out her notepad, and he saw about twenty yellow tabs sticking out...

Of course Grace would be taking this seriously.

So too was he.

But he wanted her signature tonight. He wanted this document signed. He wanted them to exist on paper before he went into the jungle.

And if she was pregnant he'd be taking care of that too.

As well as his grandfather's property and land.

Jonathon would be earning his keep tonight.

They went through the financial figures, and all were as arranged before.

'Agreed,' Carter said.

'Grace?' Jonathon checked.

'Agreed.'

'The wedding will take place in Sabah?'

'Agreed,' Carter said.

'Agreed.' Grace nodded. 'However...'

Carter watched as she took a breath, looked at the notes she'd written.

'If this is to appear real, then I'd like to have a small reception. At least let my mother see me.'

'A reception in London?' Jonathon glanced at his main client, who nodded. 'It might help our case with Benedict.'

'Agreed.'

Jonathon went through everything, point by endless point. Grace would receive a quarter of a million on signing the contract, a further sum after the solemnisation of their marriage, followed by serval payments through the year.

The words blurred on the page as Grace was taken through them, her heart pummelled and torn by seeing something that should be beautiful reduced to clauses and subclauses, but she gave nothing away.

Did that make her just as calculated and hard-hearted as Carter? She hoped so.

She actually hoped that for the next year she would be able to place her emotions in deep freeze, tell herself she was agreeing to this only for the sake of her mum.

But she could think of no other man with whom she could even contemplate doing this.

She fiddled with the ring, just a little loose on her finger, as more intimate details were relayed.

'Agreed,' Carter said, accepting his responsibility for contraception.

'Agreed,' she repeated, and it felt as if they were ticking boxes, racing to get this over and done with.

'Jewellery and gifts…' Jonathon intoned, instructing her to turn the page.

On and on…

There was an offer to break for afternoon tea, and Grace was about to nod when Carter cut in.

'I'd rather push on.'

She felt rushed, and she didn't know why. She felt as if the man who had turned her world upside down a few weeks ago had walked in this morning and upended it all over again…

And then they were done, and a new contract would be drafted.

Only as much as she wanted things wrapped up, Grace wasn't done. 'I do have another question.'

'Of course.'

'What happens if I am pregnant?'

'Have you had a positive test?' Jonathon asked.

'No.'

'Well, let's not deal in hypotheticals.'

'Let's,' Grace said.

Carter closed his eyes. Because while he could sort out the financials, where the rest was concerned he had no answers.

He knew he had to sort out his head.

'Excuse me.'

He stood and let his lawyer deal with that question—exactly the way he would have done three weeks ago, before everything had changed.

They were in there for a full forty minutes, and he saw her pale face when she came out.

'Grace…'

She brushed past him. 'I'm going to have tea up in the suite.'

She could barely look at him.

But it was nothing she didn't already know.

Carter didn't want a baby.

All decisions on a pregnancy would be hers. She'd be provided for financially. If she continued with the pregnancy the baby's way in life would be paved with gold.

Everything he'd told her from the start.

Except she knew him now, and had thought he was better than that.

She couldn't keep it in, turning back on her new heels at the last moment.

'At least my father made *some* attempt.'

She took a breath, trying to get her head around Jonathon's breakdown of the figures around Carter's complete abdication of responsibility.

'Not you, though. Not one piece of that black heart…' She shook her head, her temper rising, and hit her fist into her palm. 'Hit and run.'

'Grace…'

He knew she was hurting, but he didn't want to offer any solution, or tell her he was heading into the jungle and hoping to fix that black heart.

He honestly didn't think there were any answers there, but he would try. He'd bury the teething ring, wish his family peace, or whatever, but he just didn't see that going back to hell would work…

How many times and how many ways had he said it over the decades and years?

He. Did. Not. Want. Love.

Now it was staring him angrily in the face, and he was just a bit angry too.

'Don't compare me to your father, because I shall take care of my child, and you. But not—'

'I get it.' She put her hands up. 'I don't think I can do this…'

'Your period is not even late.' Carter would not let her end things here. 'And we're going for dinner,' he told her.

'With your lawyer and his wife?'

He didn't correct her—didn't tell her that it would only be Jonathon. He just nodded when she gave a bitter smile.

'I might give it a miss, thanks.'

CHAPTER FOURTEEN

In NO MOOD for candles, Grace flicked on the *Do Not Disturb* light and took off her clothes and curled up in bed.

It was pouring again, the rainwater cascading off the towers and sliding down the glass windows. It looked cold and wintry outside, though she knew it was hot.

The reverse of Carter.

Sitting in that room with Jonathon had hurt, but she'd already pretty much known Carter's take on fatherhood.

And she didn't know if she was angry because he didn't want a baby that might not even exist, or hurting because he could not, would not, did not love her.

It felt back to front to be considering saying no to marriage because she loved the groom—far too much!

Carter didn't exactly rush dinner, and the towers were in darkness by the time he came back to their bedroom.

He saw Grace close her eyes as he undressed.

'I know you're awake,' Carter said.

She didn't answer.

He climbed into bed and lay there for ages.

'Definitely awake…' he said into the dark silence.

He was going back into the jungle to find hope for them, but he might be losing her in the process. Only he didn't know how to reach out. How to explain that he didn't know what he'd find there—or, worse, would come back the same? Closed off and cold. Great for sex and money, just not for the love she silently demanded.

She finally fell asleep. Carter knew because she rolled into him. And he lay there trying to work out the route he'd be taking in the jungle.

Every time he closed his eyes he felt as if he was perched up high, flying over Kuala Lumpur, or high in the jungle, looking for the banyan tree, or some familiar sign…

He snapped his eyes open, felt the relief of her limbs around his and her head on his chest, and he didn't even attempt to lever her off.…

Damn you, Arif.

If the windows here opened he'd take that damn silver teething ring and toss it out now…

He closed his eyes, only he saw his brother again, peering over his mother's shoulder. Hugo's fat hand reaching out. And there was a scream building, his body paralysed as his heart beat a tattoo in his chest, and he shot awake, felt the icy drench of sweat as he gulped in air.

Grace could feel his hand on her arm, and she felt as if her body was a cheat—because it disobeyed her strict orders to turn away, or return to its corner and come out fresh for the next round. She didn't want this fight, if that was what they were having.

'You're lying to me,' Grace said into the dark. 'I don't know about what, I just know that you are.'

'Grace…'

He didn't deny it, instead he silenced he questions the best way he knew how.

For the first time she felt guilty at the pleasure of his kiss—as if her hurt should somehow erase her want.

But not guilty enough to stop.

It was a temporary solution, but she would take the relief, and she sank into him and kissed him back as if they were lovers who'd been parted for a decade. Or strangers who'd met in the dark and would be gone by light.

When he rolled her onto her back she was possibly forgiving them *both* their careless mistake that first night, because she was panting as he sheathed himself, holding the sheet rather than grabbing at him as he rolled it on, and she moaned in relief when he slipped in.

It was eyes closed and private, neither wanting to look at the other as they pushed hurt aside and caved in to desire, and in that Grace knew they were agreed.

She had never thought she could want and feel wanted, could trust another person the way she trusted him when she was in his arms, could feel—for now, at least—together with him in a place they could meet and agree.

'Grace...'

He was not holding back, and he pushed her to new limits. And he made her a noisy lover.

The only thing she held back were the words from her heart. Because she would never, ever say it—never admit it, even as he came deep inside her, even as her body arched and orgasmed at his bidding.

She would deny to his face, if she had to, that this was love.

CHAPTER FIFTEEN

GRACE WOKE TO the sound of Carter dressing, and the snap of the catch on his watch told her he was almost out through the door.

She rolled over in bed and watched as he pulled on his tie. He barely glanced over as he spoke.

'The council in Janana has called us in.'

'When will you be back?'

'I'm not sure.'

'I wish we hadn't had sex last night,' she told him.

'Really?'

'No…' Grace admitted. 'But I don't think I want this marriage. I don't think I can fake it for a year.'

'Fake what?' he asked, with all the confidence of someone who knew she wasn't lying when she was in bed with him.

Then, to her quiet surprise, he came and sat on the bed, took her hand and looked at the ring.

'Listen to me. On your phone you should have the new contract.' He picked it up and handed it to her. 'Check.'

She squinted. 'Yes.'

'Sign it,' he said. 'We'll work out dates as soon as I'm back.'

'I don't know…'

'Stay till I get back?' He gave her thigh a squeeze through the sheet. 'We could have a very nice year.'

He kissed her on the cheek, and then he looked right into her eyes. And she knew that fifty years from now, if she met that gaze, he would melt her again.

He kissed her both deeply and nicely, and she breathed him in as he held her. 'If I do leave, I'm stealing your cologne.'

'I've got to go.'

'I hope the council approves.'

He smiled, and then he was gone, and she realised she could lie in bed for an eternity and still be no closer to working him out.

She should get up and shower and then go to a pharmacy...buy a pregnancy test and find out once and for all.

Unless it was too soon.

Or there was nothing to find out.

Grace bought her first pregnancy test kit and then came back to the hotel, but she had to wait for room service to finish before she dared used it.

She came out of the bathroom and willed herself to wait the requisite minutes.

Of course she paced.

And then she glanced at the open-plan shelving near the entrance.

Carter had forgotten his plans.

She took her phone out to text him, wondering if he'd boarded yet, or was about to dash back through the door, or send some-one more likely.

But then she stood stock-still.

He surely wouldn't forget the blueprints.

Even on the boat, deep in kisses, he'd made sure to drag them to and from the house. Even the first time they'd met he'd been holding them.

She called him and got sent straight to Ms Hill. 'I'd like to speak with Carter.'

'Mr Bennett's unavailable. I can pass on a message.'

'He's left his blueprints.'

'I'll let him know.'

She sounded utterly unperturbed, and as Grace took a breath it dawned on her that possibly he hadn't forgotten his plans...

For someone who'd been caught red-handed before, Grace didn't hesitate to punch the numbers into the safe.

Yes, his passport was gone. But what made her swallow was the fact that the black pouch was missing too.

Her heart was fluttering in her throat, panic building, and she wasn't quite sure why. It was just that it was the anniversary in two days, and she knew he wanted that teething ring back where he thought it belonged.

Carter had been lying to her.

He wasn't heading to Janana. He was going into the jungle...

Her hands were shaking as she went through the folder, took out the card and called Arif. But his number kept ringing out.

In the end she called Felicity.

'Arif's at a conference,' she said, all efficient and cheery. 'He should be back at the weekend.'

'You're sure he's at a conference?'

'He's the guest speaker.' Felicity gave a jolly laugh. 'So I really hope so.'

Grace shook her head. 'I thought Carter was meeting with him?'

'Not that I've heard.'

He was going alone.

Grace sat on the bed. Her head was all jumbled, and yet she was utterly certain that Carter was returning the teething ring.

Alone.

He would never go with Arif—she could see that now.

Nor would he go with her.

There were some pains so private you dealt with them alone.

She thought about how she'd shut Violet out rather than tell her what was going on at home. How there were some things you didn't want others to see. And yet they wanted to be there...

She looked at her ring and was taken back to the fireflies and that wonderful night...and the tension in Carter, the flashlight skimming the water.

And, no, she couldn't go with him—he wouldn't want her to, that much was clear.

But she could be there waiting for him.

The biggest problem she'd thought she had had been relegated, but it was remembered now and, feeling oddly calm, she walked back into the gorgeous bathroom.

Yes, she was going to be a mum.

Only Carter didn't want to be a dad.

But she'd tell him anyway.

To his face.

She'd never once regretted telling her mother she loved her.

It was time to tell Carter the same.

Even if he didn't want her.

They deserved a proper goodbye.

CHAPTER SIXTEEN

CARTER COULD HAVE approached from the river, sat in the safety of the boat and tossed the teething ring in, but he'd never been going to do that.

And so he'd taken the long way, setting off at dawn and approaching the river from his grandfather's property, retracing the steps he had taken with Arif as a child.

Although the incident had taken place further up river from where they'd used to turn around and head home.

A lot further.

Hot, humid, dense...

He hated the place, and every step was taking him closer to a place he didn't feel he needed to be.

He reached the spot where Bashim had found him, but he knew that only from what he'd been told. There was nothing he could remember here.

Or maybe a little...

Hot...thirsty...his head throbbing...

He walked further in and he could hear the chirps and sounds of the jungle. Looking up, he knew he'd climbed a tree, his limbs aching, pulling his puny body up. Searching for the banyan tree... knowing he was lost.

He also saw the spot where he'd fallen.

He recalled the taste of blood, and remembered he'd known he had to stem it...

Some were his own memories, some were Bashir's tales, but nothing helped.

Yet as he got closer his pace picked up.

He was following the line of the river, but well back from the mangroves.

And he'd been right, Carter decided, when he saw the silvery striped mangroves. Even if he'd done his best to avoid this spot, he knew it exactly. Yet there were no answers to be had here.

This place that had tormented him for a lifetime was not the stuff of nightmares.

Birds flashed like red jewels, and where the dense canopy of trees thinned there were glimpses of cloudy blue skies.

As Carter drank the last of the water he'd brought, he decided it had been a mistake to come.

Hunger gnawed. He picked up a mangosteen and stared at it, then tossed it away, deciding he would never be that hungry again.

Yet he bent to retrieve it, and as he held the rough waxy orb the desperation he'd felt as a child was revived…the fatigue and hunger as he'd bashed it on a stone, the purple wax seeping in, the usually sweet white parcels stained and rotten, bitter on his tongue.

Yet he'd eaten them.

No wonder he couldn't stand them now.

He took one and peeled it open, saw the pretty white parcels like the ones he'd opened for Grace that beautiful morning. He thought of that cocktail, and how she'd simply put it down when he told her.

She'd brushed her teeth before she'd kissed him—and that memory felt like her smile.

He tasted the fruit and it was sweet…like peaches.

He tossed it away.

The heat and the low-hanging branches made it a fight at times to move even a few steps further. His shirt was torn, a heavy branch swung back, and he felt the tear of the flesh on his cheek. He reached for his water bottle, but of course it was long empty, and he knew he was on his own with the elements. But still he was not concerned. This had been his and Arif's playground. The boys had often gone further than his grandfather would have permitted, and it had been a regular outing throughout the summer, with overnight treks a frequent adventure. Even a couple of nights at times.

They'd always stopped here, though.

Arif would put out his arm and halt them, telling Carter they should go no further.

'But the river is just through there…' Carter would protest, for it was just a couple of miles ahead, and he'd known someone there might give them a ride back, or take them to their home for a meal.

But Arif had always pointed to the still, shallow stretch of water, sometimes high from recent rain. 'Mortal danger.'

Even at eight years old, Carter had known what that meant.

'Idiot!' he muttered, his lip curling on the word.

For how the hell had his father thought it safe to bring his family here? To watch as his wife carried his infant into infested waters?

He came to the edge of the mangroves, their silver branches like bony arms stretching skywards, beyond the river. They looked eerie, yet beautiful in the pale moonlight, and he scanned the water for the glint of eyes or any movement. But it was peaceful. And there was a rope over the river that hadn't been there when he was a child, put there for the orangutans.

It had been dusk when his mother had said she wanted to take the perfect photo—to capture the setting sun and the little king-fisher perched over the water.

'Sophie!'

He could hear his father warning her to stay back, telling her that the water in the mangroves was deep from a week of tor-rential rain.

It was comparatively dry now, but he looked at the water and knew the dangers that lurked beneath. He stood there numb, re-fusing to feel, but it was as if he was witnessing again the stealth of the beast approaching.

He'd attempted to shout—'No!' But the sound of the word hadn't carried, and his mother had suddenly plunged lower in the water, as if she'd stepped off a ledge.

He felt again his relief when she'd seemed to right herself, ris-ing up in the water again.

Then he'd heard one desperate shout from his father, seen the whipping water his father had rushed towards.

And now, as he had all those years ago, Carter stood horror-struck and silent, watching, waiting for his father to sort this out, to save his mother, for she and Hugo to emerge.

Apart from that single shout from his father there had been no screams, no noise, when surely there should have been?

The thrashing, beating water had gone still.

Carter had gone in.

He felt again that blind panic. Holding his breath...searching the water...shouting to his father who lay face-down, urging him to help find Hugo...

'Papa!' He'd urged him to wake up. 'Hugo... Ulat...'

His hand had closed on something, and he'd frantically pulled—but it had just been roots and leaves, and he'd screamed to his father again. 'Find him!'

Even then there had been the first stirrings of anger at his father, who lay motionless and incapable of helping find his son. Anger at his impetuous mother, who had stepped out of the boat without thought or care for the precious infant in her arms.

At some level he'd known his mother was dead, but he'd told himself the baby would have slipped out of the sling, that Ulat would rise, smiling like he did when they played in the pool. Surely? After all, there was no blood in the water...no sign that anything had occurred.

Then he'd looked to his father, still face-down, his arms spread, and it had been then that Carter had realised he stood in infested water.

His own sense of survival, the lessons from long days spent in the jungle with Arif, had kicked in.

Mortal danger.

He'd waded out, still searching the water with his hands, scanning the muddy edges for Hugo, calling out to him, unable to fathom that he was gone.

All of them were gone.

Gone.

He'd never cried, or screamed, and he didn't now. He just sat there feeling again the winter, and the emptiness, the finality. And that was the part of the nightmare he never wanted to get to.

No, he hadn't run for help. He'd wandered, dazed, knowing they were gone for ever.

And he'd loved them—his floaty mother, his hapless father, their passion and their slight craziness...

He thought of his father, his brief eye-roll before he'd called out to stop his wife. But it would have been like trying to halt the wind. Her passion, her longing for adventure, had been impossible to contain.

Carter's anger was misdirected. It wasn't at his family, nor even the animals who had simply been being true to their nature.

It was at himself.

He hadn't stopped them, hadn't called out, and he'd failed to protect his baby brother. Little Hugo, who had brought so much delight into the world, who in the chaos of a somewhat nomadic existence had, for Carter, been like a little beacon. Hugo's routine had been a welcome dose of normality in a disorderly existence.

His heart thumped in his chest. And now there was nothing to show for his existence.

One thing.

Carter pulled the silver teething ring from his pocket and opened the pouch. His intention was to somehow return Hugo's beloved teething ring, his comfort, to him. He saw the little teeth marks...and now he ran a finger over them and cried the tears he never had before.

It was the teething ring that had caused this. This place had been calling to him the night he'd been with Grace...

And now Carter knew why he was here.

Love had returned to his life even when he'd tried to deny it had ever existed.

A bird landed on a branch—a blaze of colour in the silver and grey—and, yes, all these years on he knew it was the kingfisher his mother had hoped to capture in her photo.

He looked down at the silver teething ring, at the scratched surface, and thought of Hugo's bright smile, how trusting he'd been...

His milky breath and gurgles of laughter.

His contented smile.

Contentment…

He thought of Grace…how she was terrified of being forgotten by those she loved.

'You'll never be forgotten, Hugo,' he said aloud.

He wouldn't let a single memory fade for as long as his life allowed.

He could almost hear his brother's bright smiling laughter and, pocketing the treasure, he knew now where he was headed…where he'd been trying to get all those years ago.

He had been going home.

CHAPTER SEVENTEEN

'*SELAMAT.*'

Arif offered peace as he greeted him, just on the edge of dawn.

'*Selamat,*' Carter said. 'I thought you were away…?'

'I heard you were back…'

And, like a friend, he'd dropped everything the moment he'd found out.

It had taken Carter a full twenty-four hours to get back, and he'd eaten more of that damn fruit—but thankfully not rotten this time. Or was it that the world was a bit sweeter this day?

'You need to bathe,' Arif said. 'Eat…'

'Sleep?'

'Soon.'

And as Carter ate a light meal he was grateful that he did not ask how it had been.

Only as Malay cleared his plate did Arif tell him he was in trouble. 'You left the plans behind.'

He frowned.

'Your blueprints. Grace was calling everyone…'

He would have to come up with a suitable lie, Carter decided. Or simply tell her the truth about where he'd been.

'She's asleep,' Arif told him.

'Who?'

'Grace,' Arif said, and told him his brother had picked her up last night.

'She's here?'

'Pacing all day.' Arif smiled. 'I told her to get some rest, that you might not be back till tomorrow. You made good time.'

'You mean she's here now?'

'In your residence.'

Carter wasn't sure if he was sleepwalking, or if he was having some delusion and would wake with a fever, but this was not like the last time. He felt invigorated, rather than collapsed. Curious, rather than frantic, as he walked through his part of the property.

Climbing the stairs, he found he wasn't avoiding the pictures now. He could see his parents smiling, and Hugo too.

Then he pushed open his bedroom door and indeed Grace was there, lying on her back, wearing a muslin nightdress, the fan blowing.

He could not quite believe she had followed him here.

That she was waiting at his home.

And then he could—because he knew she loved him or he'd never have come here.

She was still wearing the ring.

'Grace…' He sat on the bed, and this time when he reached for her slender shoulder he did not pull his hand back. 'Grace!'

Her eyes shot open, and so did her mouth, but she said nothing, just wrapped herself around him, coiled around him, more sweet pea than bindweed.

'I thought you were dead…'

'You were having a very good sleep,' he teased, holding her and breathing her in. 'Perhaps you fell unconscious with panic?'

'Stop!' She pulled back. 'You lied…'

'I did—but I had to.'

'No.'

She wanted to tell him it didn't work like that—except he'd climbed into bed and, given it was *his* bed, she couldn't really refuse him entry.

'I'd have come with you.'

He shook his head, tried to explain, but Grace had been waiting a long time to say what she'd come here to say.

'I know you don't want anyone, but…'

She'd thought he had died every moment since she'd seen the plans he had left behind, and her biggest regret was the one thing she hadn't told him.

'I love you. I'm sorry, and I know you don't want to hear it…' She put her hands up when it looked as if Carter might say something. 'But let me speak. I want you to know that. And I want to say a proper goodbye.'

'Why would you come all this way to say goodbye?'

'Because goodbyes are important.'

'I know,' he told her. 'But this was never about goodbye, Grace.'

Carter lay down and the bed was like a pillow, and then she was running her fingers over his eyes, and his scratches, and he was aware of just her fresh air scent.

'I hated the thought of you here,' he told her. 'I didn't want you on a jungle walk… I didn't want you coming back…'

'Don't be—'

'I mean it. I hated the thought of you here… I had to go into the jungle to find out that I don't hate the land, and I don't blame my parents. I thought I did, and I even hated myself. But I didn't know what I feared till now.'

She looked at him.

'It was losing another person I love to this place.'

'You love me?'

'From the moment we met.'

'No, from the night we came here.'

She kissed his dry mouth and then she got up, and he lay still as she put orange gloss on his parched lips.

He shook his head. 'The moment we met,' he confirmed. 'I felt obliged to go over to you…obliged to pick up your passport—the same way I feel obliged to this place. I think it's a little like love.'

'No…'

'Sometimes it seems that way,' he insisted.

And she breathed, and he nodded, because there were obligations, and some were hard to keep, but when you loved someone you stepped up.

'I couldn't tell them apart,' Carter admitted. 'Obligations and love. I didn't want to tell them apart. But I know for certain this is love.'

Grace rested her head on his chest. He loved her—she knew that from his kiss, from the way he held her for a full moment, just breathing together.

But then another wave of panic at what might have been hit.

'You could have died.' She said it again. 'Even Arif was worried.'

'Grace, I've been dead for almost thirty years. I haven't felt a damn thing since I watched them all disappear.'

Now he felt everything. This sensory overload, this pain, the fear, the warmth of her smile…

His kiss was rough and yet tender. He felt the scratch of his unshaven jaw, his swollen lips, and then the balm of her tongue.

'Grace, I had to get my head straight.'

He lifted her hand and looked at the ring, then at the woman who had chosen the cheapest ring in the box.

'Fireflies over diamonds?'

'Every time.'

'Marry me?' he asked. 'Not because of this place, and not to take care of your mother.'

He saw her close her eyes.

'I shall take care of your mother whatever your answer. I shall fight Benedict through the courts. I am asking you to marry me because I love you, and because I believe you love me.'

'Would that change if I told you I was pregnant?'

'Not one single bit,' he said. 'And as for all I said before, I regret every word. *Are* you pregnant?'

Grace nodded, scared not of his reaction but because it was all so new.

All of it. Being in love, being loved, being pregnant…

'It's too soon,' she said.

'Would it help if I told you I am brilliant with babies?'

She looked at him.

'I got up to Hugo all the time. We would laugh and sing…'

He reached over and handed her the silver teething ring.

'I adored him…he was the light of this place. And now we're going to have our own Ulat.'

She smiled and examined the teething ring. 'What about its teeth?'

He laughed—he'd clearly worried about the same.

'How soon can we marry?' Grace asked.

'I'm not sure of the rules in London.' He smiled. 'I'll ask my PA.'

'I meant how soon can we get married *here*?'

He frowned, clearly unsure what day it was.

'Twenty-one days after the application.'

'That's today.' She looked at him. 'We can marry today...'

EPILOGUE

It was to be the tiniest wedding, with a small celebration to follow when they returned to London.

At least, that was what Grace assumed.

The hotel staff, when they'd packed for her, had included the strappy oatmeal linen dress, and it was gorgeous to slip on,

Her hand was shaking as she tried to tie her hair, but Malay came in and helped her twist it and pin in a water hyacinth.

'Everything is ready.' Malay smiled at her. 'How romantic to get married at sunset…'

'I shan't be long.'

She picked up her phone. Gosh, this was going to be a surprise.

'Violet!'

'Grace, you look—' Violet stopped. 'Oh, my God, I don't even know his name. Grace, you cannot get married. Honestly. Whatever—'

'Violet…' Grace gave her dear friend a smile. 'I love you, and we're going to have a proper reception in a few weeks.'

'Grace…' Violet gave in then. 'I'll be here for you.'

'I know.' Grace smiled. 'And I love you for it.'

She took the stairs and saw Jamal, dressed in pale shimmering pink. She handed her some flowers.

'Don't be nervous,' she said.

'I'm not,' Grace said, but then her hand went to her chest. 'Perhaps a little…'

Or was it just excitement? They walked towards the ancient ballroom, but as she stepped in she saw, instead of Carter, the French doors wide open.

'Your groom is waiting for you outside…'

She stepped out and gasped. The pool was lit, and the pathway too, all the trees dotted with lights, and she walked with Jamal through the beautiful grounds to an ancient banyan tree where Carter stood waiting.

And he was so loved… For it wasn't such a small wedding after all—there were many of the local people, dressed exquisitely, playing soft music, as she walked to be by his side.

'How did you do that?' Carter asked, and kissed her. 'Do you travel with a wedding dress?'

He made her laugh, and they kissed again before they were man and wife.

'You look perfect,' he told her.

And for someone who had spent three decades numb, Carter could never have envisaged being surrounded by so much love.

He knew there was no one else he could have shared this with.

The gorgeous tree, the scents and the moonlit sky, and the sounds of the jungle settling for the night. The caws of birds, the chatter of monkeys, and then a certain quiet, as if thousands of eyes were watching them.

The celebrant welcomed everyone in both English and the local dialect, and Carter translated when needed.

And then he took a breath.

'Bashim, Arif's father, is going to speak…' Carter told her, and watched as Arif helped his father to the front.

The man who had searched for a missing boy and carried him home.

Carter's voice was husky as he translated. 'He says that no one is ever lost here…that souls remain…' He squeezed her hands and she squeezed it back. *'Gotong royong,'* Carter said. 'It means life is lighter if we share the burden together.'

And now it was Carter who wanted to speak.

'Grace…' He thought for a moment. 'This morning, when I saw the sunrise, I knew I wanted to spend the rest of my life with you… To come back home and find you waiting here for me was the greatest gift of my life. I shall never stop loving you.'

She believed it,

'Carter…'

She looked up at the man who had claimed her heart the day he had woken her to hand back her passport.

'I have loved you from the moment I laid eyes on you…'

She would never forget opening her eyes to this man, and knowing, somehow, that he was the one for her.

'You have my love.'

For ever…

That was how long true love lasted.

* * * * *

Were you swept off your feet by Bride Under Contract? *Then you'll love these other passion-fueled stories by Carol Marinelli!*

The Greek's Cinderella Deal
Forbidden to the Powerful Greek
The Sicilian's Defiant Maid
Innocent Until His Forbidden Touch
Virgin's Stolen Nights with the Boss

Available now!

FORBIDDEN ROYAL VOWS

CAITLIN CREWS

MILLS & BOON

This one is for Nicole, who was halfway through
Carliz's book when she said she couldn't wait to read
Mila's… The one it hadn't occurred to me
I should write until then!

CHAPTER ONE

QUEEN EMILIA OF LAS SOSEGADAS was perfect.

She made sure of it.

Las Sosegadas was a tiny country between France and Spain, all mountains and sparkling alpine lakes. Her family had ruled it for centuries, mostly in peace. And her people were consistently at the top of all the polls that measured the happiest citizens in the European Union.

And unlike some other kingdoms, support of *her* monarchy was always robust.

Because, she knew, she was perfect.

Perfection wasn't simply her job. It was her calling. Her duty.

She spent hours every day discussing exactly how the Queen could appear to her best advantage in all things, not because she had an ego, because she didn't. What she had was a crown and what she owed her subjects was to keep it untarnished.

In private, she could be a person. Even a woman.

In private, she still thought of herself as Mila, the nickname only her sister still called her. Even her mother called her *Your Majesty* now, likely to remind herself as much as anyone else that it was her daughter on the throne now instead of her late husband.

There were a lot of things Mila liked about being *just Mila*, but that was always a temporary state, mostly when she was asleep.

The moment she left her rooms and let anyone lay eyes on her, she was the paragon of a modern queen she always was. In public, Mila was only and ever *the Queen*.

She had promised herself to her country and that was that.

A life of service suited her perfectly, she always said, and she meant it.

Tonight her service to her country had involved the sort of dress fitting that had taken most of the afternoon. It was always necessary to make sure that she looked the part, of course. She had an entire wardrobe team dedicated to the task and they were good at what they did.

What Mila had to do in turn was always and ever appear *relatable*. But not *too* relatable. Subjects wanted to love their Queen, but they certainly didn't want to know her *too* well. A simple flip through the headlines of any European kingdom on any given day told her as much.

Mila had to strike a balance between seeming *almost* approachable while never actually letting anyone near enough to get any fingerprints on the symbol she'd become in her short reign.

Figurative fingerprints, that was. Or the Royal Guards would get involved.

Tonight's event was a banquet to honor service to the crown, an annual gala that also raised money for various charities. It was the usual collection of aristocrats, Mila saw at a glance as she arrived, her foot hitting the exact stone that she had promised it would hit at the exact time it had been announced she would.

Because it was always important to be a *dependable* icon, no matter what else she was.

Sometimes Mila thought it was all she was.

If so, she thought now, *there are far worse things I could be.*

And she did not list off what those things were, as she sometimes did. She already knew that did not lead to perfection. It went the other way, rather precipitously.

She swept through her usual protocols for these things. The selected greetings after her entrance. The few, carefully chosen comments to make it clear that she knew the people she was speaking to. Even a smile now and again.

Mila had always been good at these things. She'd always known how to make these little connections, over so quickly, feel bigger than the sum of their parts. Because she had not been thrown into the royal life in a turbulent fashion. She'd had the gift and curse of knowing that her father was not only going to have to die *someday* for her to succeed him, but that the doctors had given him a date by which they expected that to occur.

There were very few good things about that, but one of them—maybe the only one—was that he had taken the time to prepare her appropriately for what was to come. And not in the abstract, as she'd been taught as a child.

She had no regrets, she told herself.

What was there to regret? She was the Queen.

"You are looking splendid, Your Majesty," said her mother from her side as they left the receiving line and processed through the party, headed for the Queen's usual spot on a dais up near the throne. Mila inclined her head, lest anyone think she was engaging in something as base as small talk or gossip while the trumpets were playing.

Was it ostentatious to have balls take place in front of the throne of the kingdom? Certainly. On the other hand, she had been told many times that most people appreciated the touch of glamour.

Besides, it was expected.

No point going all the way to a palace and not experiencing anything palatial, now, is there? her sister, Carliz, would have said if she was there.

Mila let her lips curve with great serenity as she passed the line of bowing subjects. But inside, she felt that surprising pang again.

She didn't know why it had not occurred to her that she would miss her sister.

When Carliz had gone off to university, the first one in the family to leave the kingdom to do so, she had been younger and consumed with learning her duties as Crown Princess. It wasn't that she hadn't missed her then, because she had.

But it was different this time.

She had gotten used to having Carliz here, was the thing. She had gotten used to her sister slipping into her room at night, when Her Majesty was left at the door and Mila could simply be Mila again. They had spent most of a summer that way and Mila had gotten used to it. She had come to rely on it, even. That was all.

It wasn't that she would change a thing. She was too happy for Carliz, who had gone from being one of the world's greatest sparkling It girls to about the happiest wife and mother Mila had ever seen.

But she could be happy for Carliz and sad for herself, it turned out.

I contain multitudes, she thought as she moved, practicing the dignified inclination of her head which she could often use in place of actual speech, or even a smile.

This was one of the great many ways she got people to forget how very young she was.

Only twenty-seven, though that was rarely mentioned in the way it had been at first, when her father had died and the whole of Europe had acted as if they didn't know what an *heir apparent* was.

Now when they said *"only twenty-seven"* it was in tones of awe, as if no one could quite credit that she was still something less than the formidable dowager of indeterminate years she would be one day. The one she had gotten so good at pretending she already was.

If everything went according to plan, she would simply grow grayer but otherwise remain exactly the same.

The Queen, nothing more and nothing less.

As ageless as the currency she graced.

Her mother was murmuring to her as they walked, the usual comments about this noblewoman's dress or that aristocrat's wandering eye, because nobody minded if the Queen Mother offered commentary. And the dancing had begun, so there was no shortage of things to look at.

"And, of course, we are treated to the next regrettable stop along Lady Paula's road to ruin," her mother was tutting at her side. "I often look at her and think, there but for the grace of God above did your poor sister go."

Mila was entirely too well-trained to react broadly enough that anyone could see it. All she did was slide a look her mother's way. Nothing more. She did not even have to raise an eyebrow.

Still, the Queen Mother blew out a breath, aware that she had stumbled into one of the places she should know better than to go.

As Mila had made her feelings on this clear. As the Queen.

"My sister," Mila said softly, smiling magnificently at a set of honorees as she passed them, dipped down low into their curtseys, "would never dream of embarrassing me. And she never did. Lady Paula, who I think you know I quite like, has a different goal entirely in mind."

She did not go so far as to say, *I support her.*

But she was defending her, so that should have been obvious.

"You may judge me if you like," her mother replied in that particularly aggrieved tone she was so good at pulling out at moments like this, as if Mila had thrown her in the dungeons. If the palace had actually *had* dungeons, which it did not, she might have considered it—for the express purpose of watching expression on her mother's face. But that was childish. And the Queen could never be childish. Even when she'd been a child, it had been discouraged. "But I cannot for the life of me understand what it is Lady Paula is so upset about. Many women of her station are called upon to make life choices that honor their family legacy, not their own wild impulses."

It was well known that Lady Paula's father wished to marry her off to a man of his choosing. Lady Paula had made certain that no one in the whole of the kingdom could think for one moment that this was something she approved. Or would ever approve. She had gone to great lengths to make sure that her disapproval was recorded in the starkest possible terms in every tabloid that could be found.

With as many inappropriate men she could find, to her father's fury.

"Maybe it's time that we allowed women of whatever station to choose their own destinies," Mila said.

Reasonably enough, to her mind.

The look her mother shot her was sharp. Too sharp for a public setting, Mila would have thought. "I hope you do not intend to follow Lady Paula's example. Your Majesty."

That was a shot and they both knew it.

Mila smiled as they came to a stop before the throne, because it was considered gaudy and inappropriate for her to guffaw. Or so she had been told, never having given in to the urge in public before.

"I know my duty, Mother," she said softly. "I daresay I know it better than most."

"Of course you do, my dear," her mother replied, though they both knew that if it were up to her, the Queen Mother would be planning the sovereign's wedding here and now.

And when she turned away to talk brightly to the people who came up on the other side, as if she hadn't been squabbling with the Queen herself, Mila took a moment to gaze out at the whirling mass of dancers before her, looking for that telltale flash that was always Lady Paula's orange-red hair.

When they'd been girls, Paula had won her friendship

forever by wrinkling up her nose and laughing too loudly at a party where they were all attempting to out-ladylike each other, and then announcing quite boldly that as her hair was already problematic, she saw no particular reason not to make sure her behavior matched it.

Mila heard Paula's laugh before she saw her. She was already smiling as she realized her friend had drawn near the way she usually did, moving along the sides of the ball that was in full swing across the floor of the great room. She turned her head, expecting to see what she normally did when Paula attended one of these parties.

Her friend always dressed *almost* inappropriately, but not quite, because it drove her staid and quiet family mad. And she took pride in always presenting herself in the company of some or other wildly inappropriate date, and then presenting said date to her friend—the Queen.

Usually Mila made it worse, according to her mother, by indulging Paula in this. Meaning she only smiled at her friend's behavior when, as queen, she could also have indicated her displeasure.

That would not have stopped Paula, but it would have meant she had one less friend, and Mila had never seen the point.

She had so few as it was.

"Don't start," she warned her mother beneath her breath as Paula drew close.

Her mother sniffed in reply.

But then the crowd parted way and the man Paula was leading toward the throne stepped into full view.

And Mila froze.

She wondered for a moment if she'd simply died where she stood—or possibly it was only that she wished she had.

Because tonight it wasn't just any old inappropriate man on Paula's arm. This or that baronet from some country Mila hardly knew.

Tonight, it was the most inappropriate man Mila had ever met.

And he was looking right at her.

With that trademark near-smirk in the corner of his appallingly sensual mouth.

Because he was the only person in the entire world who knew the truth that Mila preferred to believe only she knew. That Queen Emilia of Las Sosegadas was not the least bit perfect.

He was, in fact, the only one who knew that she was capable of an epic, life-altering, unforgivable error of judgment.

Not just *capable* of it.

He was one of the last great European playboys in the old style, a recent article in a non-tabloid magazine had claimed quite seriously. And had backed it up.

He was famous for his long string of astonishingly beautiful, powerful, and famous lovers, his mesmerizing charm that Hollywood actors tried and failed to replicate onscreen, his deeply mutable moral code that some found charming, and the great fortunes he'd inherited from all branches of his enormously complicated family tree.

A tree, the article had claimed, that has its roots in every grand old family in Europe.

Worse than all that, he was impossibly, disastrously attractive.

A description of him would involve dark hair, dark eyes, and those cheekbones, but it would fail entirely to capture the way he moved through a room like the world was nothing but a crock of creamery butter waiting for the edge of his knife.

And she knew that he always, always, had that knife.

He was always perfectly dressed for every occasion, yet managed to provoke all the same. It was that swagger. It was that hint of a smirk. It was that lazy wit in his gaze, and his inability to show even the faintest bit of humility to stations higher than his own.

It was the fact that he could be so incisive. That he was so intelligent when there should have been nothing but air and smugness between his temples.

It was the formidable way he could gaze at a person and make them forget who they were without even seeming to try—

Mila had to remind herself to maintain her composure. She had to *order herself* not to lose her cool, right here in the middle of a gala.

Something she had not had to do since she was a child of eight who had accidentally indulged in too much sugar one Christmas.

But he was a whole lot worse than too many sweets at a holiday party.

He was a *catastrophe*.

He was Caius Candriano.

Mila's one and only mistake.

And he was also, though no one knew this but the two of them nor ever would as long as she drew breath, still— legally—her husband.

CHAPTER TWO

CAIUS CANDRIANO HAD waited for this day for a long, long time.

Five years, to be exact.

Five whole years, and there was some part of him that expected to find her…different, perhaps. Changed entirely by what she'd gone through and who she'd become these last few years—perhaps because that, at least, would be some kind of explanation.

However little he wished to accept that explanation, at least it would exist.

After all, she was a queen now. *The Queen.* Not merely the Princess he had met with the whole of her weighty future yet before her. Not that young woman with too much maturity and luminous eyes, and a deathly ill father who had ordered her to in that sense that she was only marking time before her whole world changed.

But Mila looked entirely unchanged.

Maybe that was not entirely true, he thought as he swept a gaze over the whole of her magnificence, when the woman he'd known had been dressed as casually as he had been on that long-ago climb up a remote stretch of California coast where there had been no one at all but the two of them. Though the drama of the gown she wore would have been epic even if he wasn't comparing her to his memories.

Caius should not have been surprised. He was fully aware that designers from all over the fashionable world clamored for the opportunity to dress the young, beloved Queen of Las Sosegadas.

It was his own curse that he knew too well that, left to her own devices, she preferred simpler, less theatrical fare.

Not that anyone could have guessed that by looking at her.

She *gleamed* with her own consequence. The palace arranged around her, complete with the throne placed *just so* behind her, only made her glory more apparent. He might miss the days he'd known her out of time and place, but there was no denying that gown suited *this* version of Mila. Her team had clearly chosen it to make her seem to glow as if by virtue of her own sovereign power.

The Queen had been the only thing anyone had looked at when she appeared. The Queen had been gazed at in varying degrees of awe and adoration from all corners as she'd made her way across the floor of the long ballroom, the traditional signal that the festivities were to begin.

The gown helped, though Caius found himself simmering with what he decided could only be the same old pent-up *fury* that really, she could have sloped across the ballroom floor in jeans and trainers and had much the same effect.

He focused on the gown, because that was smarter than looking straight at her when he could not be entirely sure that he had his face in proper order. When he had been born the chameleon he was today, a necessity in his family, chock full of narcissists and pathological liars—and that was just the people he was related to that he liked.

Caius took in the sophistication and elegance of the damned dress. He focused on the full skirt and fitted bodice that should have made the dress too undignified for a queen, but was saved by its deep, dark shade of purple. It suited her. Something about the conversation between the dress's serious color and merrier shape made Mila's regrettably perfect beauty all the brighter.

He wished it did not still light him up from within, damn her.

Though that was not the point of this.

This, he reminded himself, was about *a reckoning*, nothing more.

Because Queen Emilia was suitably untouchable and all the more breathtaking for it. But Mila was the kind of woman a man looked at once and found himself intoxicated evermore. She was like a flickering flame. Once a man singed himself on the edge of that fire, he could never come back.

He had never come back. And she had never looked back.

So Caius had come to her little palace in the mountains instead.

She wore a tiara tonight, in case the throne behind her did not give away her status. The bejeweled concoction sat on her smooth, glossy dark hair that looked like ink tamed into a sophisticated twist and dared any man brave enough to reach out and try to touch her.

Though he did not. And not because he was lacking in bravery. On the contrary, he had only recently taken a step back from his more high-octane activities, all of them death-defying, and only because he had done them all.

Even adrenaline got boring if you had too much of it.

But he had chosen this battle specifically, and there was no point getting ahead of himself now when he'd gone to all the trouble to ingratiate himself with half the aristocracy in this tiny country. Something that had involved him deigning to notice them, since he was, being himself, far more famous and sought after than a host of interchangeable blue bloods.

That was not arrogance on his part. It was a simple truth.

He had often been called the most beloved guest in modern Europe. That was partly because he was a great delight, if he said so himself. But it was also because his attendance at any given party made it *the* party.

That, too, was simply a fact.

Really, the monarchy of Las Sosegadas should *thank him* for deigning to attend at all.

Caius lifted his gaze to hers at last, taking no small amount of pleasure in how stunned Mila looked. There was no trace of anything he would call *thankful* on that gaze of hers, a perfect oval saved from any insipid sameness by that strong, Roman nose that made her something else than simply *pretty*. That and her mouth, a wide, sensual feast that she mostly kept pressed into a dutiful line.

Though not now, he was pleased to see.

And there was something in the gray depths of her gaze, rimmed in a darker steel, that he recognized. It shot through him like more of that inescapable flame, though he doubted she would appreciate it if he reminded her where and when he'd seen a look like that before.

That made him want to tell her even more.

Because none of this was about what she appreciated.

If she had wanted him to consider such things, she would have handled the past five years much, much differently.

On the other hand, he did have a plan. Such as it was.

So he only held her gaze, which was not exactly good etiquette. Not so directly. Not for so long. But more tellingly, she continued to stare back.

And Caius had watched enough videos of Queen Emilia's much-swooned-over perfect manners to know that this was unusual.

As it damn well should be, he thought then.

Next to the Queen, her mother, once Queen Alondra and now the Queen Mother, clearly noted that something was amiss. She drew herself up with a sideways glance at her daughter for only the briefest, nearly imperceptible instant before stepping forward and claiming Lady Paula's attention.

"I trust your parents are well?" the older woman asked, with a bite behind her words that even he could hear. Clearly Paula could as well, because she let out that high-spirited laugh of hers again, infectious enough to make Caius almost wish that he had it in him to move on.

But he could not seem to break his stare. He could not look away from Mila.

And as he watched, he saw the Mila he had known five years ago first bloom in her expression, then disappear again.

Until *the Queen* took her place.

She made the transition very clear and unmistakable. It was something about her posture. Something about the tilt of her head, or perhaps the elongation of her neck. One perfect dark brow rose, just slightly.

Yet still elegantly.

"I forget myself, Your Majesty," Caius said, and he could see that his voice affected her. He saw the faint hint of color on her cheeks. That glimmer in her gray gaze.

He still got to her. That was good.

Caius had not exactly planned what he might do if she looked at him as if he was a stranger. He had not allowed it as a possibility.

Instead of interrogating himself on that topic he executed a bow so deep and so perfect that it bordered on parody. That was the point. She had once accused him of using his grasp of excruciatingly proper and gloriously correct manners as a weapon. So efficiently and so ruthlessly that he was already bludgeoning the haughty and the arrogant before they even realized there was a weapon in the room.

Guilty as charged, he had said.

And it felt like a bit of poetic justice that he was now using those weapons on her.

He could see that she remembered that same conversation when he rose and met her gaze again. He could see the knowledge there, the memory. He could almost smell the sea air and feel the crackle of the fire they'd built, the flame a wild heat against his face.

He was not the only one recalling what had come after.

"Your Majesty," said Alondra from the side, warningly, though Caius did not bother to look away from Mila, "Lady Paula has kindly come to present the Honorable Caius Candriano, late of Italy."

Caius looked at the Queen Mother then, and bowed again more shallowly. "I am afraid I have not been to Italy in some while, ma'am. Nor can I claim to be anything like honorable."

He lifted his head and grinned at Mila's poor mother, who was very clearly both unamused by him...and yet amused despite herself.

That was the Caius effect.

"Your mother does not approve of me," Paula was saying to Mila with more of that laughter, because she was a free-spirited thing and had no qualms about showing it, a rarity in these circles. She looked back at the Queen Mother. "You may wish to remove yourself from this conversation. I do not censor myself in front of my queen."

"Or anywhere else," said the acerbic older woman, but she did move away at that—with shoulders set to angles of pure umbrage.

Paula gave the impression of moving in close to the Queen, though she did not actually scale the dais or step up, or even encroach particularly on Mila as she stood there in all her state. Close enough to the great throne that not sitting on it seemed like more of a power move than sprawling there might have.

He had no doubt at all that it was deliberate, and more, that it was her doing.

"You've heard of Caius, of course," Paula was saying happily, and did not seem to see the nearly pained look on Mila's face. "My grandmother had a *conniption fit* when I announced that I would be attending with him. A proper fit of the vapors. Though I maintain that if she knows of his exploits, that must mean that she has the very lowbrow taste she *claims* to abhor."

Mila made a low sort of noise that Caius supposed could be taken for assent. Paula leaned a bit closer and continued chattering on about her own reputation, and making shocking asides about Caius's—shocking, that was, only because he had been *much worse* in the time period she was referencing, and had worked hard at being that notorious.

It was only when Mila still kept standing there in the same way, looking dumbstruck at Caius—though he supposed it was possible no one else understood that he was the cause of it—that Paula subsided.

"You seem a bit out of it tonight," she said in a different tone. One that indicated, immediately, that the woman who had been nothing but laughter and fun thus far was, truly, the friend to Mila it was rumored she was. "Are you all right? Is it Carliz?"

Mila looked away from him at last, and he hated that.

But then she smiled, and the smile made him forget where he was. "Carliz is fine. More than fine. Carliz is *great*."

Caius remembered himself, despite that unexpected shine and the way it was as if all the light in the room had clung to her like that. He did not shake it off, not physically, but he stood there, calculating. Taking stock of the fact that Mila clearly favored Paula, as some had said and others had debated. She *liked* Paula.

And he wasn't sure he liked the part of him that was

glad of that. He remembered too well the confessions she'd made to him on that long trek they'd taken together. How little she could trust that anyone truly liked *her.* That the specter of the queen she would become was always there between them.

"She seems deliriously happy," Paula was saying. "Truly happy, not simply a bit of Carliz sparkle."

The two of them spoke for a few moments longer, and he watched her eyes light up the way they always had at the mention of her sister.

But then it was time for the best part of this entire scene he had gone to such trouble to engineer.

No one got to stand and talk to a queen for long. There were always interfering ministers about. There were always haughty people who thought it was their *right* to demand a moment with her. There were long lines of those who only wished to curtsey before her and see if they could get a small smile, a kind word. Like she was an art installation.

It was not a surprise when Alondra reappeared, tugging on her left earlobe in what seemed like a casual gesture. But Caius knew it was a sign to her daughter that it was time to move on.

"We must catch up properly," Mila said. "Have you seen all of Carliz's baby pictures?"

Paula sighed. "She keeps promising to send them."

"Something will have to be done." But as Mila said that, she straightened, and Caius watched with interest as she became *the Queen* once again. Not chilly, but remote.

Paula understood at once. She reached for Caius's arm and stepped back, then curtsied yet again. Beside her,

Caius bowed, a gesture replete with all the mockery he could manage.

And then he had the very great pleasure of walking away from Her Majesty, Queen Emilia of Las Sosegadas, and not looking back.

He didn't have to look back.

Caius could feel her eyes on him no matter where he went in the ballroom. When he danced with Paula, or the much older ladies who he always liked to favor with his attention because they saw right through him and basked in him anyway. Even when he loitered about near the bar, making pointless conversation with interchangeable nobles.

He made certain to spend the night paying her not the slightest iota of attention.

But just as he, and everyone else, knew exactly where Queen Emilia was at all times, he knew full well that she was returning the favor where he was concerned.

Caius could feel it like her hands on him.

When the banquet was over and all the speeches had been made, and more dancing had taken place until well past midnight, he offered his date his arm as they walked out of the palace with the rest of the guests.

And he felt pure triumph kick in him when an aide stepped smartly to Paula's side. "Lady Paula, if you'd be so kind, the staff have assembled a selection of Princess Carliz's private photos for your perusal at the behest of the Queen. If you have a moment."

"For Carliz, I have all the moments," Paula proclaimed grandly. She was slightly tipsy and even more boisterous than before, and she waved Caius off as she followed the aide away. "Don't get yourself in any trouble," she called back over her shoulder.

Then laughed as she disappeared out of sight.

But even if Caius had been intending to get himself into trouble, he could not. Because another aide appeared at his side, then. This aide only bowed and indicated that Caius should follow him. Then, wordlessly, led him away.

It did not occur to Caius to resist.

He thrust his hands into his pockets, and sloped along after his guide. And he was not the least bit surprised to find himself taken away from the public areas of the palace and into a quieter, lusher wing.

The aide led him down the long, intricately decorated hall and stopped abruptly at a particular door. He knocked three times, then waited for a signal only he seemed to hear.

But hear it he did, for he clicked his heels, bowed his head, and pulled open the door to let Caius inside.

He found himself in a small salon that did not look as if it saw great deal of traffic. And Caius could admit that he was surprised to find himself alone—

But no. Not quite.

Across the room, there were doors that led outside. He went over, looked out, and there she was.

She was standing out on a balcony, her back to him and her gaze focused on her kingdom's capital, arranged neatly below the palace and marching in tidy lines around the first of the many alpine lakes that were considered the beating heart of this country.

Or so he had read.

Extensively.

He stayed where he was, on his side of the glass, because everything in him was a drumbeat now. Blood too hot in his veins. Pulse pounding like he'd jumped from a plane. She was leaning forward, her elbows propped on the stone railing, and if he was a painter his hands would have itched to capture this moment. The Queen in a moment of reflection. The Queen's quiet contemplation of the weight of her crown.

Though he knew what she was actually considering just now was the weight of him.

His body hard over hers. His mouth to hers. His—

Caius made himself pause. He made himself *breathe*.

And then he stepped out onto the balcony himself. And thrust his untrustworthy hands in his pockets as he moved to stand beside her.

She did not look at him. He did not look at her.

But for a long moment, there was only this. The two of them, breathing in the same air after so long.

"I can only assume that this is some kind of a threat, Caius," she said, eventually. Softly, even.

She was still looking away from him. When he glanced at her, he could see the line of her face, the nose that defined her face and made her so stunning, the shape of her lips. But he could not read the expression in her gaze, or even if there was one.

"I'm not a man who needs to issue threats, *Your Majesty*." He even laughed a little. "I would have thought that you would know this already."

"It's been five years. I assumed that you'd slithered off, never to be seen again. To be clear, I hoped you had."

She turned then, straightening from the rail and folding her arms over her chest, which he understood in an instant was as close as he would get to an outward expression of her emotional state. *The Queen*, obviously, did not cross her arms.

Yet he had known her as a woman first. He could see the things she hid. The sheen in her gaze that spoke of her feelings. The barest, faintest hint of a tremble in her lush lower lip.

This was likely to be all the temper she was willing to show him.

He'd take it. Because he could see the truth of it.

"Careful," he murmured. "That is no way to speak to your husband."

"What is it you want?" And her voice was so cool. Her gaze was frosted over. But he was close enough, outside on this clear fall night with the canopy of stars above, to see the pulse in her throat that gave her away even further.

"What is it you think I want?"

They stared at each other, and it was as if the earth and the sky switched places. As if he was standing half in each, not sure if there was solid ground above his head or stars at his feet.

"As you might imagine, the pressure to marry is intense," she told him in that grave, measured manner that he had studied, these last few years. He'd seen it in so many news programs. In every clip of her speaking that he could locate online. "At a certain point, my protestations that I wish to stand on my own two feet will have to give way to the best interests of the kingdom. Those being, of course, that I will be required to produce my own heir."

"Mila," he murmured, and it was possible he moved a bit closer, too, "that sounds a great deal like your problem, not mine."

Her gaze was dark and gray. "I understand that vows mean nothing to you. But I'm afraid I take mine rather seriously."

"Nothing has changed since the last time we had this delightful chat," he said in the same quiet way that tore at him, so he suspected it shredded her, too. "I invite you to divorce me, as I have done from the start."

"You know that I can't."

"Then I can only repeat what I told you five years ago. If you do not wish to divorce—"

"Of course I want to divorce." And whatever it was that flashed in her gaze, that slap of emotion, he could feel it in him, too. Low. Deep. Much too dangerous, the way it always had been between them. "But you refuse to sign the documents that I would need for that to happen."

"I've already kept our marriage confidential," he said with a shrug that, very likely, did not match the edge in his voice. "I do not see why you cannot simply trust me to keep our divorce equally private."

"I have never understood why you insist on playing these power games." But there was no heat behind the words. If anything, she sounded weary, and that felt like a weapon of her own, sunk deep. "What do you hope to gain? At the end of the day I will always be, until the day of my death, the Queen of the Sosegadas. And you—"

"Yes, me," he said when she paused. "There's nothing about me that is not indiscreet, is that not so?" He made himself a portrait of sheer indolence, standing there so languidly, and perhaps it was for the sky above. Perhaps it was for her. Perhaps it was entirely self-referential—or perhaps it was that or put his hands on her the way he deeply, darkly wanted to. "My own parents appear to be engaged in a competition to see who can collect the most spouses in one lifetime. Mine is less a family tree, and more…a collection of misbegotten sticks that someone gripped in a careless hand, then threw up into the sky, not caring at all where they might land. This must be so distressing for you."

"Again." And this time, her voice was resignation and steel at once. "What is it you *want*?"

"Perhaps I think it is time you finally recognize me," he said. And then he tilted his chin down so he could look at her and not the stars. So he could bask a little in that look of sheer horror on her face. "Oh, dear. Does that not fit into your plans? What *would* the good people of your kingdom think if they knew you had married so disastrously? If they had any idea you were swept away like a foolish girl, enslaved entirely by your body's demands? What will they think of their spotless queen then?"

"They would assume what I have assumed ever since," she said in that same calm voice, but he could see her eyes. He could see the way they'd gone a little hectic. "You are a master seducer, as you have proven repeatedly. I succumbed, as many do regularly, according to your rather overactive tabloid profile. Life is filled with regrets. The end."

"I can see that you put thought into that one," Caius said, sounding almost congratulatory. "No doubt you practiced it in the royal mirror. But the tragedy remains the same, does it not, my queen? In order to brand me a base seducer, you must cast yourself as the seduced. And who will consider you an icon above all others then? You will be but one more pathetic creature, ensnared like so many women are by men so unsavory that any association with them leaves a mark."

Mila only raised a cool brow. "How lovely that at least one person on this planet appreciates my dilemma."

He laughed at that, a low sound that the stars stole away. But he saw the color rise in her face, and then everything was fire.

"Poor little Majesty," he murmured. "It appears that you remain hoist securely on your own petard."

Her cheeks were aflame but her voice was still cool. "We will have to find a solution, Caius. You must know that."

"I require no solutions. I am perfectly content."

"Then why are you here?"

Caius laughed again. "When have I ever given you the impression that I'm the sort of person who would not enjoy a moment like this?" Her face looked hotter, and he could feel his own temperature rising. He told himself it was temper. Well-deserved temper. "You can't control this, Mila. You can't control me."

"I have no wish to control you. The world is yours, Caius. Go be as uncontrolled as you like, with my blessing. Only let me end this marriage first."

But he was on a roll. And he didn't believe in her blessings anyway. "This palace is yours. All of these people, yours. Yet you and I know that where it matters, Mila, you have been and always will be mine."

Again, he saw the way her gaze flared with temper, though there was otherwise little sign of it on her face. Maybe her jaw was more firm, but that was all. "This isn't a game, Caius."

"But to me, everything is." He leaned in then, so close but he did not reach for her. And the sharp pleasure of denying himself almost gave way to the bright flame of indulgence. *Almost.* "Have you forgotten when you said that to me? Because I have not, Mila. I have not forgotten one word."

"I was not trying to insult you. I was trying to explain."

And years had passed. He believed her. She had, truly, simply been explaining her position to him, but in a way, that made it all the more insulting. Had she been *trying* to insult him, he would have been able to dismiss the things she'd said. Standing there so earnestly before him after the time they'd shared.

But she had been trying to be kind. He remembered that part too well. That had made it worse.

That had made it unforgivable.

"You have had the opportunity to change," she said now, and there was a different sort of tension in the way she held herself, then. "It is impossible to avoid your exploits, and believe me, I have tried. So instead, I watched them. I watched you. I waited to see if even the slightest, faintest hint that anything I'd said to you had landed. If you'd thought for even one moment about my position, or what I need—"

"There was a time when I thought of nothing else." And it was not perhaps the greatest strategy to say something like that so boldly, with so little finesse.

Then again, maybe it was the best strategy, because he heard her breath hitch. He watched, transfixed, as she lifted one hand and held it to her neck as if attempting to conceal the way her pulse pounded.

But he could see the way her fingers shook.

It should have made him feel small, the way that echoed in him like a new heat. Like a blessing all its own.

Luckily Caius was not that kind of man.

There was nothing small about him.

"You can't want money," she said after a moment, insulting him anew. "Can you?"

"Perhaps you have forgotten that I have too many fortunes to name," he said, and this time, he forgot to keep the danger from his voice. Because she was even more maddening up close than she had been from afar all these years. He had not expected that. "Perhaps you have forgotten everything."

"I have forgotten nothing," she shot back.

"All the same," he said, turning toward her at last and feeling that same electricity flood him the way it had since the moment they'd clapped eyes on each other, all those years ago and now again, too, "I think a small reminder is in order. To remind us who we are, *Your Majesty.*"

And he did not wait for her raised brow, her queenly armor.

He did not wait for her response at all.

Caius simply hooked a palm around the nape of her neck, aware that she still fit him perfectly.

Then he pulled her to him and kissed her the way he'd wanted to for years.

CHAPTER THREE

MILA TASTED HIM again and died.

Or maybe it was that she came back to life.

It was that intense, that glorious, the way it always had been. The way she had known it would be from the start. The way he had showed her it could be between them.

And tonight his kiss sent her spiraling back through time.

Straight back into all the things she'd forgotten—or tried her very best to forget, with failures she only admitted to in the very dark of night. Then tried to deny come morning.

He took her mouth the way he always had, as if he knew her body and its needs better than she ever could. It was deep, familiar shock of pure desire, as expansive and overwhelming as all of that California sunshine mixed in with days of intense fog that they'd once walked through together.

It was everything she missed and pretended she didn't. Because she couldn't.

And it was also a deep and enduring grief, washing over her, through her, making the intensity of the kiss seem to roll through her so hard and wild she was surprised, on some level, that it didn't knock her off the balcony.

Mila forgot all these years of duty, just the way she had before. She forgot the promises she'd made, the vows she had spoken with such deep solemnity in front of the country and the world.

She forgot everything but the magic of his mouth on hers, the way their lips fused together and their tongues danced, as if their bodies had not forgotten a thing.

As if all this time she had simply chained this dragon deep inside of her, but now she'd roused it all over again, fire and fury.

And she could see the edge of that cliff that she'd leaped off once before. She could see how easy it would be to simply throw herself over the edge, allowing this impossible kiss to sweep her away. It would take nothing at all on her part to simply surrender to the storm, to the bright, gleaming dragon that was this passion she'd so deliberately pretended she'd never known—while all the time it had been coiled up inside of her.

But she wasn't the girl she'd been five years ago.

Mila no longer had the luxury to forget who she was.

That had been true five years ago, too. Eventually. It was even more true now. She couldn't block out the simple, undeniable facts that governed her entire existence. She was a queen now, not a princess whose father had given her leave to go out there and find the taste of something normal before it was her turn to take the throne.

She was *the Queen* and this was her palace, and sooner or later, someone would see them here if they hadn't already. And even though she knew that her staff supported her, and some even adored her, there was always the chance that someone would think a hefty tabloid payment was well worth a simple phone call and the queen's lost trust.

Mila put her hands on his chest, though that was its own mistake. Caius was already too beautiful, too impossibly gorgeous to bear, and that was simply *looking* at him. Touching him was a tragedy and once again, that grief slammed through her.

Because once, long ago and so far away now it seemed like a dream, she had imagined that things could be different.

Once, she had dared let herself *hope*—

But reality had come for her with a vengeance.

She remembered that, too. It was impossible to remember any part of what happened with Caius without remembering how it had ended.

Mila could picture it all too clearly. She had been standing in a hotel room in a haunted city high in the redwoods, staring in complete incomprehension as the guard she had come to view as more of a friend did not smile back at her. The way Noemí always had done before, every time she officially entered Mila's presence on this adventure of theirs, where no one could suspect who Mila was.

Noemí had taken to smiling in place of any curtseys or bows.

That day, her bodyguard had instead dropped into a deep curtsy that had seemed alarmingly out of place in this faraway place that had nothing to do with monarchies or palaces. And seemed absurd given that Noemí had been wearing hiking clothes, adding a kind of madness to the traditional curtsy that had only etched a kind of grotesque hyperreality to the scene.

The King is dead, Noemí had said, her voice gravelly and not like her at all. *Long live the Queen.*

And one of the secrets that Mila held deep in the darkest part of her heart was that for a long, disorienting moment, she had forgotten that *the Queen* was…her.

That the day she'd been preparing for the whole of her life and yet had never wanted to arrive, had come at last.

All this while Caius took a long, hot shower, unaware that everything had changed. That Mila's much-loved father was dead, that she had not had the chance to say goodbye, and that she would now have to mourn him under the searing and inescapable lens of the public.

Many of whom would be looking to their new queen to lead them through.

Their new queen who had done exactly what her father had told her he trusted her *not* to do—and shamed the entire family with an impetuous marriage.

She remembered staring back at Noemí in a silence that seemed to drag on for whole lifetimes, thinking, *What have I done?*

There was all of that pounding through her now, as if it was new, and then there was the reality of Caius. Caius himself, in the flesh. Not the memory of him that had taunted her and tangled itself around her on too many nights she refused to think about come morning.

Caius, who looked down at her when she finally managed to pull away, that mouth of his already moving into its mocking twist, and all that bright, hot fire in his eyes.

Eyes that were a dark, impossible amber ringed in black.

Like he was made of magic.

She had always thought he was.

Not helpful or productive, she scolded herself. "Things are very different than they were back then," Mila managed to say after a moment, grabbing at the remnants of her dignity as best she could.

Instead of letting herself get carried away by his *magic*.

Not that it seemed to affect Caius at all. He reached over and brushed the back of his knuckles over her cheek, as if it was his dearest wish to light her on fire. Then he carefully tucked a piece of hair that should not have fallen from her elaborate updo behind her ear.

"I would not say that *everything* is different," he said, his voice little more than a low rumble.

And to her astonishment and great despair, Mila wanted to cry.

She could feel it rush through her, then rebound as if it meant to drown her where she stood, and for a moment she really did wonder if her knees might buckle.

Because there it was again. The faintest shadow of that sliver of hope she should have known better than to hold on to, all these years later.

The sliver of hope she would have sworn she'd long since extinguished.

She tamped it down, ruthlessly. The way she had learned how to do long ago, because it was that or perish beneath the weight not of her crown, but the piles upon piles of expectations heaped on top of it.

"It is not a simple problem to solve," she told him,

when she could be sure she sounded calm. Even. "And I know you disagree. But it has never been simple, no matter how many arguments you mount."

His wizard's gaze gleamed in the dark. "I have made it simple, Mila. You may thank me later. After all, the damage is done. There is only the announcing it."

She'd forgotten too many things, that was the trouble, like how much she wanted to simply *melt* into this man. And she blamed herself for that, too, because ignorance was never something that a queen could allow herself to wallow in, but she'd chosen it in this case. It seemed like valor, all those years ago.

Because she had been reeling from the loss of her father and the loss of this bright magic she'd found with Caius that had seemed as if it might kill her, too.

When she should have known that sooner or later, he would come back. Because people always came back to collect on promises.

Promises she should never have made in the first place.

Mila made herself take one step back, then another, and it felt as excruciatingly painful now as it had that last day. More, maybe, because she'd tried very hard since that day to tell herself that she'd made all of that up. Or, more charitably, that she had been stunned by her father's death and sideswept by all the ramifications of it—all of which had felt very different now that it was more than a theoretical protocol to be discussed while her father was still safely alive.

But no. It just hurt. Everything about Caius was the same agony, no matter how she looked at it.

The difference, she told herself sternly, *is that now you do not have the luxury of showing anyone your feelings,* especially *him.*

Mila pulled herself back into character, though these days she thought it was less a character and more simply who she was. The Queen. Always *the Queen.* She folded her hands in front of her in as regal a manner as possible. She arranged her face into polite impassivity. She managed to look down her nose at him though he still towered over her, and she was not a short woman.

And she pretended that she could not hear that low, mocking sort of laugh of his.

"What announcement do you think we should make?" she inquired with deadly calm and the faintest hint of something almost like interest. Almost, but not quite. "That the man recently seen as the paramour of an old childhood friend is in fact having secret assignations with the Queen? The people will be delighted, I am sure."

"I know this is a long shot," he drawled, in that way he had, with that particular accent of his that was all accents and no accent. And somehow entirely him. "But we could always try the truth."

She shouldn't have mentioned Paula, because now all she could think about was her friend. Her poor friend, who she had betrayed. There was no other way to look at it. Paula could have had absolutely no idea that Caius was secretly married, much less married to her friend and queen. But Mila knew full well whose arm Caius had arrived on this night.

"The truth is impossible." She almost allowed herself to frown at him. "And now you have made me not only betray myself and my country, but my friend. I think that's a hat trick."

"And to think," Caius replied as if this was all terribly amusing to him, "I'm only getting started."

And that terrible desire, that impossible dragon, was still coiling around inside of her, lighting her up in ways she'd forgotten was possible for her to shine. Just as she'd forgotten what it was like to have someone *touch her* the way he did.

So casually, as if she was a person. As if she was like everyone else, and could be jostled casually, touched carelessly, brushed up against by mistake.

These were things that did not happen to the Queen of Las Sosegadas. These were things that were not allowed to happen. Ever.

These were more things to grieve when she was alone.

"If you'll excuse me," she said, very sternly so that perhaps she would listen to herself, "your date is waiting for me. And likely for you."

"If that's how you want to play it, My Sweet Majesty."

The way he'd used to call her *Princess*. The way he'd whispered *my princess* while he was deep inside her, filling her so completely she could not imagine how they had ever parted.

Somehow the *My Sweet Majesty* was even…worse.

"I know that you think—" she began, in the sort of placating tone she often used on fractious ministers and unduly contentious politicians.

"I'd be careful with that," he interrupted her, and that, too, was a revelation and a memory all at once. No one else dared speak when she did. No one had in five years, not even her mother. "You don't know what I think. I believe you never did. I would try not to make a fool of myself by pretending otherwise, if I were you."

Mila opted not to inform him that it was impossible for the Queen of Las Sosegadas to be a fool. By definition, tradition, and the odd royal decree.

"An interesting tack you're taking, Caius," she said instead, not letting herself fold. Not even *considering* something like folding, come to that, because it had been a long time since she had ever been required to entertain surrender as a possibility. "I watched a program on this. It's what men these days do, is it not? Perhaps men have always done it. They fear that no woman would ever want them, usually because they are substandard and unworthy. But instead of working to better themselves, they prefer instead to insult women so that they will feel grateful for lowering their standards to men so far beneath them that it's almost amusing that they even try."

And for a moment, then, she simply smiled at him. Not quite sanctimoniously.

"The first thing you should always remember about me," he replied, with that quirk in the corner of his mouth and his eyes entirely too bright, "is that I do not suffer from low self-esteem, a lack of self-confidence, or any of the maladies the men you're talking about do. I am not short, nor am I dull. I am well aware of the way I look and how avidly my company is desired wherever I go. I do not need to play games to get women. I need only exist."

"I see your arrogance has only grown."

"Is it arrogance or simple truth?" He shrugged. "What you need to ask yourself is if you're prepared to deal with the version of me that is no longer interested in keeping your secrets."

She held his gaze as if that little speech did not terrify her, and she did not cower. She did not even blink. After a moment, she inclined her head the faintest bit. "I appreciate you laying out this mission of yours in such stark and unmistakable terms. I will take this opportunity to remind you that I'm not a lost princess on a lost coast any longer. I also know exactly who I am, and I think you'll find that the girl you knew was never anything more than a daydream in the first place."

Mila did not say, *And now I am the Queen, who you would do well to treat more like a potential nightmare.*

She felt it was implied.

"A daydream who had the misfortune to sign legal documents, that is," Caius countered. In that mild way of his that was at complete odds with that blazing fire in his eyes. "Lest you forget."

"Barring that," she said cheerfully, "there are always the dungeons."

And staying here any longer, interacting with him like this, was beginning to feel like an indulgence, so she turned and marched away. She did not wait to see what he would do, because she was the Queen, damn it.

What mattered was what *she* did.

Accordingly, Mila swept off, back into this remote and little-used room. She strode past the guard—sadly not Noemí, who had been rewarded for her extraordinary service and friendship by being made a Baroness of the Realm as one of Mila's first duties, and was now the Minister of Security.

Once she cleared the guard, she raced down the hallway—or her version of racing, since it was undignified to break out into a run. And she checked the clocks standing here and there in all their state as she went. It could not have been more than a handful of minutes that they been together. Ten on the outset. They could not possibly have engaged in anything *too* scandalous in so short a time, and she was in no way disheveled—apart from that one rogue tendril of hair.

Not that she expected that particular guard to betray her, but that was the thing. Anyone could and it wasn't even personal. Because Mila wasn't a *person* to them.

She hurried along to a salon off a different hall, where Paula was waiting. She was seated on a couch, surrounded by all the pictures of Carliz and her growing family that the palace had been able to find, both in Mila's personal collection and from all the press sources.

"I'm so sorry to keep you waiting," she said as she hurried into the room, waving off the aides that waited unobtrusively, because someone was almost always watching in the palace. "I could lie and tell you that I was swept up in matters of state, but the truth is, I was vetting that date of yours."

Paula laughed. Mila hated herself.

She hadn't even planned that lie. It had simply slipped out. Because she'd had just enough time on her dash over here to think about the fact that Caius could very easily tell his own tales, and start with Paula when he did.

This was who she was now. It was second nature to play elaborate games of chess, whether or not anyone else was playing.

"He is my escort tonight," Paula told her, waving a languid hand. "But he is not a *date*. Can you imagine? Who could possibly take the likes of *Caius Candriano* seriously?"

"I rather thought the point of him was to take him as extremely unseriously as possible," Mila heard herself say. Because, apparently, she couldn't stop.

"It's not that I *wouldn't*," Paula said with another laugh. "If it were the right bad decision I wouldn't hesitate. But I'd sooner jump into bed with a comet than Caius Candriano. I think he would burn a mere mortal to a crisp without even trying."

Mila had never heard a better description of Caius. It was his reputation, certainly—but she rather thought it was simply a primal truth any woman who ventured near him understood at once. In their bones.

And she could feel that comet inside her, burning her alive, even now.

Had she only been pretending, all these years, that she had somehow escaped that fire?

But there was no time to wonder these things. Not now. She turned to the pictures before them, some on the tablet the staff had brought and some printed out. And for another half hour or so, they talked about when they were younger. When they'd stood on opposite sides of ballrooms, Mila exuding duty from every pore while Paula and Carliz had gotten themselves into different sorts of trouble. Paula had always been more about giving her father white hairs and near heart attacks. Carliz had always promised not to embarrass her sister, so she was simply…irrepressible.

Some years Mila had been jealous that they were allowed to behave as they liked, even within the strictures of their class and its expectations. Other years she had felt quite serene in her choices, and her future.

And now here she was, living out that future, only her past—the one she thought she'd hidden away, far from view, where no one could ever find it—had reared its ugly head.

Well, drawled a little voice inside, as if he was still part of her, *not* ugly. *I think you know better than that.*

By the time Paula took her leave, Mila was almost tempted to pretend that she couldn't remember that part of the evening. She said goodbye to her friend and did not accompany her out into the public part of the palace, where she knew Caius would be waiting.

She told herself that discretion was the better part of valor. That she had nothing at all to fear. That she was not, for that matter, the least bit afraid.

But it was also true that she walked a bit faster to get back to her rooms.

Because once she said good-night to her staff, once she closed her door, she could be *Mila* again until morning.

Just a person. Just herself.

And tonight she had her own mission.

Mila smiled and thanked her staff as they withdrew. She closed the door behind them to her private rooms and stood there a moment, her heart telling truths she didn't want to listen to as it beat much too hard in her chest.

She forced herself to go into the dressing room and take her usual meticulous care of herself, the way she did every night. She had needed help out of the dress, but the rest she could do on her own, and so she did. She changed into what her sister had once called *princess pajamas.* It was a lounging set of the finest, softest cashmere that floated like a whisper over her skin.

And did not in any way remind her of the way Caius had once skimmed his fingers down the length of her—

"Stop it," she chastised herself.

She sat in front of a mirror and took down her hair, brushing it the way she did each night. Her mother had always told her that it was not only her crowning beauty, but would be looked at more than most women's, by virtue of the actual crowns she would be called upon to wear.

Like every other part of the vision that is the Queen, *your hair must gleam with health and vitality*, Alondra had declared. Repeatedly, throughout her girlhood.

Health and vitality, Carliz would whisper, twisting her own hair in a knot on the back of her head some years and acting as if she'd never seen a brush.

Mila took off her makeup, cleansed and moisturized her face. And only then, only when she had attended to the physical body of the reigning queen as was her sacred and sovereign duty, did she surrender to that wild and consistent beating thing behind her ribs.

Only then did she dart back into her bedroom, go over to the desk that stood in one far corner, and dig into the back of one of the drawers. She wedged her hand inside, reaching with her fingers until she could push just the right spot.

The drawer pulled out then. And she could pull off the envelope that she had taped there years back. She held the envelope in her hands as if, were she not careful, it might bite her.

Mila took it over to the bed, climbing up into the center of the mattress on this bed that the staff was forever trying to make more ornate and she was always asking them to make simpler. It had four posters, it didn't need a canopy. It had enough pillows, it didn't need a thousand more throw pillows to adorn it. It was already fitted with a soft mattress set to her precise specifications, about which she was quizzed with regularity, lest she spend even one night in discomfort.

And yet she wasn't sure that she'd ever sleep again.

Mila turned the envelope over. Once. Again.

She blew out a breath and then she opened it up, shaking out the content onto the coverlet before her.

Then there was nothing to do but stare down at the delicate gold chain that held only the simple gold ring that she had worn on her finger only once.

Only briefly.

She had thought she might wear it on the chain instead, but had known even before the plane had landed back in Las Sosegadas that she couldn't risk it. It would invite comments at the very least. It would demand speculation.

Mila had hidden it away. And she had not allowed herself to look at it since.

Now, once again, she felt all the same things that had charged around inside of her earlier. That wildfire passion. That intense, impossible connection.

The coiled, golden dragon of the way she longed for him and all the grief and hope and loss that went with it.

There were other things that she could do to handle

this situation. She knew that. There was a team in the palace whose job it was to anticipate bad press, or any kind of scandal, and get out ahead of it. She should have been on the phone to them right now.

But Mila didn't pick up her extension.

She stayed where she was, sitting cross-legged on her bed.

She thought of that kiss, that glorious kiss she should not have allowed, and eventually she picked up the gold chain and let the ring dance there on the end of it in the soft light of her bedroom.

Here, only here, where no one would see her and no one would know, she slipped that ring on her finger the way she had years ago.

And for the first time in a long, long while, let the memories wash over as they would, until her mouth tasted of salt and there were no tears left to cry for the man she couldn't have.

The man she shouldn't want.

The man she would have to make herself forget all over again, come morning.

CHAPTER FOUR

A FEW WEEKS later Caius helped himself to a drink at the latest party he had been invited to personally and not as an escort to someone else, looked around yet another crowded ballroom, and congratulated himself on a campaign waged well.

He had single-handedly made Las Sosegadas a premier destination for the very rich and very, *very* bored set, who were always listlessly trailing from yacht to beach, complaining that the dog days of August were tedious in the extreme.

Now they were all cavorting about this pretty little jewel of a mountain kingdom instead, swanning up and down the boulevards and talking in their disaffected drawls as if they'd spent their whole lives holidaying in the kingdom.

"Why broil on the beach when we can be in the mountains instead?" brayed one pouting, supposedly fashionable heiress with a breathlessness she considered her trademark. She waved her cocktail in a manner designed to draw the eyes of her rivals and friends, clustered near the looming pillar. It drew Caius's gaze too, though not for the same reasons. "Besides, I prefer my skin to look like porcelain, not leather."

Hotels were suddenly overbooked all over the kingdom. Housing prices skyrocketed as the sorts of people who liked a fashionable *pied-à-terre* wherever they might find themselves found their way here.

And all Caius had to do was the same thing he always did: wander about these same parties with a smirk on his face. Very much as if he knew something everyone else didn't, the better to drive them all mad.

Because without exception, they all threw themselves into a frenetic competition to pretend they knew exactly what it was that Caius Candriano knew. Whatever it happened to be.

It worked like a charm every time.

That was the power of the mask he'd learned to wear.

It had taken very little time to ingratiate himself with the grand hostesses of the realm, who, naturally, quickly found him indispensable. Was it even a party, they queried each other both in public and private, if Caius was not in attendance?

But he was always in attendance. And he had merited his own invitation shortly after that first party at the palace, followed by every invitation. To everything. It was child's play to make certain that he turned up wherever the Queen was expected.

Sometimes he even got to talk to her, though he made no effort to do so.

Because he knew she expected him to do just that. To *push*. To *encroach*. And the more she expected him to do it, the less he tried.

The glorious result of that was that every night he went out to an event where the Queen was expected, he could feel her temper rise as if she was holding the flame of it to his own skin.

A flame that grew higher and higher each evening he wandered through rooms she was in, pretending he was unaware of her presence. Or better yet, uninterested.

Tonight it was nearing inferno levels, that temper of hers he could feel from clear across the ballroom.

It was possible that he enjoyed it a little too much. Particularly because he knew that he was the only one who could see it. To everyone else, she might as well have been a portrait of herself, stood in her usual place so they could gaze at her from afar.

There was something about that notion that got under his skin, worrying its way deep.

"You should make me your one-man tourism board," he told her later that night when they ended up seated next to each other at the long, sumptuous banquet table.

Not because he had asked for such a manipulation, because he hadn't. He wouldn't. But because the hostess thought she was doing Her Majesty the great favor of bestowing Caius's much-sought-after company upon her. He was the *prize* at these gatherings.

Accordingly, he beamed at Mila and smiled lazily as she committed acts of restrained violence against each and every course that was brought before her.

"We already have a tourism board." She stabbed a succulent shrimp with the tines of her fork. Hard. "And I was unaware that you had ever worked for a living. Or at all."

"You can be sure, Your Majesty, that I'm very good at…" He waited for her gaze to find his, clearly against her will. He let his smile get even lazier and tinged with wickedness. *"Working."*

He should not have taken so much pleasure in making

her react. But he did. There was something about watching the hint of color bloom in her cheeks. About tracking the precise tautness of her lips. Because Caius liked that he could see beneath her mask when no one else seemed aware it was there.

Having seen beneath it, how could he keep himself from trying to pry it off?

Or pretending he might pry it off, anyway. Out here in public, where anyone can see—something he was certain she sat up nights worrying about.

Just so long as you think of me, he'd said when she'd said something like that, though in a way that suggested her worry was cool and rational. Not hot and bothered and *yearning* at four a.m., the way he often was.

"How curious," she said now, in that cool, repressive tone that he could feel directly in his sex. It made him grin. "I was under the impression that you were nothing but a dilettante. Flitting about Europe like an intoxicated butterfly."

"I have also spent rather a lot of time on the West Coast of America," he said, grinning wider at that faint narrowing of her gaze that was as loud as shout to him. "It's the most interesting place. A very rugged sort of beauty. Not nearly as manicured as the Continent can be." He let his smile go guileless. "Have you been? On a state visit, perhaps?"

She did not dignify that with either a glare or a reply. She turned to the person on her other side instead, engaging the older woman in what sounded like a very dull discussion of economic programs that had failed to achieve their stated goals.

When the next course came, she returned her attention to Caius with a baleful sort of glare. Because, he knew, she would have continued to ignore him all night but that would elicit as much comment—maybe more. She was expected to divide the favor of her notice equally and Mila was scrupulous when it came to managing the expectations put upon her.

He would have made a terrible queen, he had often thought.

"How long do you intend to grace the kingdom with your presence?" she asked.

"I had originally thought to stay only a day or so." He leaned back in his chair so he could *lounge* at her, boneless and unfazed by her regal consequence, which was not strictly polite. But then again, he was already the darling of society here, and everywhere. He was allowed leeway and what was the point of such allowances if he couldn't take advantage of it. "I am looking into buying some property here."

"Whatever for?"

"Surely your kingdom's charms advertise themselves, Your Majesty."

"I have always found the charms of the kingdom profound. It is the kind of place that becomes a part of a person's soul." That smile of hers flashed then, and he saw how easily she could make it a weapon. She aimed it straight at him. Then held it to his throat. "Are you in possession of one of those?"

Caius should not have found himself disarmed. So easily.

But he was.

Later, maybe, he would piece together what happened just then. That flash of the girl he remembered there in that gleaming gaze of hers, for only him to see. And the joy of it, that unexpected attack.

She'd enjoyed it, and so he had, too.

"I doubt I have ever known the touch of a soul," he answered honestly. And quite without meaning to. "Yet somehow I muddle along."

"Pretending, is that it?" Mila was no longer stabbing at her food. And though he knew better than to indulge this in public, he could feel the current between them then, blocking out everything else. When that was nothing but dangerous. "Just preening in the dead center of whatever stage you can find? Playing whatever role will get you whatever it is you want in that moment?"

He forgot himself entirely. "I thought that was your role. Your entire objective is to disappear until you become your own statue, is it not?"

And they were both lucky, he thought, that the hostess chose that precise moment to surge to her feet and start making proclamations in the form of a deferential speech, so that no one heard him.

But Mila did.

There were cheers all around, applause and toasts, but their gazes seemed tangled together with too many ghosts in between.

Until she tore her gaze away and cooled back into her preferred state of flesh become stone, the perfect queen.

The next morning, he woke before dawn, as was his custom. Though he went to great lengths not to let that sort of thing get out. It would ruin his reputation as a debauched hedonist entirely.

Caius slipped out of his hotel before the sun's rays fully penetrated the grand valley. He went on a long, hard run, out there beside the sparkling alpine water of the Royal Lake.

But no matter how many kilometers he ran, or how fast he ran them, he couldn't outrun Mila.

And it was only when he was out there with his legs pumping, his heart pounding, and his breath coming hard and fast to remind him that he was alive, that he accepted the fact that seeing her like this—all the time, but never close enough to touch, not really—was perhaps backfiring.

Because the truth was that he'd expected that he would have one or two interactions with her and no longer find it necessary to even play these games. Or he had hoped. He had assumed that the girl he had known was the part she'd played, and that there would be no trace of her in the dauntingly serene *Queen Emilia.*

Instead, he could see the girl he'd known peering out of the Queen's eyes sometimes. Every time her cheeks flushed, but only slightly. Every time there was that snap of temper in her gaze that no one else seemed to notice.

He could see her there, peering out. Reminding him that he hadn't made her up. That she had existed all this time. She was *just there*, just out of reach.

With only the small matter of a throne and a crown between them.

He ran for hours and when he made it back to his hotel, he wasn't surprised to find all kinds of messages on his mobile. He ignored them. And when the phone rang as he stood there, gulping down water and staring out the window at the palace that rose on the hill, he almost ignored it.

But that would only make call *more*.

"Caius," said his sister when he answered, "what in the world are you doing? Since when do you hunker down in one place like this? I've never known you to turn your back on your vagabond ways. It's chilling."

"Good morning, Lavinia," Caius replied mildly. "That's a bit dramatic, don't you think? It's been a few weeks. Not years."

"You once told me that anything more than a long weekend in a place was dangerous. Roots might spring up when you least expected it and hold you there forever."

"That sounds like teenage poetry and I, happily, never wrote such trash."

Though he had almost certainly said exactly that when he was an adolescent. It sounded like him.

Lavinia laughed at that, because the two of them were the only members of their sprawling, complicated, maddening family who had always gotten on. Probably because they had endured such a nomadic existence when they were young, forever being dragged from one hotel to the next, in service to their mother's bottomless need for attention.

In those days, the Countess—as his mother preferred to be known, though her pretensions to the title were questionable at best—had in fact been homeless. But that was not a word anyone used when the person in question was of a certain social strata.

Or when she was a particular strain of attractiveness. The right width. The right way of dressing. The right friends, the right parties, the right way of manipulating events until she got what she wanted.

Another word for his mother was *grifter*, but it was so impolite to say such things out loud.

Along with other words like *narcissist. Alcoholic.*

Countess was easier.

"I know why you're calling me," Caius said. "I would have thought my not answering was its own clear message."

Lavinia laughed again. "The Countess is becoming alarmingly tedious about this. She refuses to ask you herself, but she will be absolutely devastated if you don't come to this wedding of hers."

"I was at her last five weddings. Speaking of tedium."

"She claims this one is different."

"She always does," he reminded his sister. "And why are *you* accepting her calls? Last I heard, you vowed not to be a party to this nonsense any longer."

"Someone has to answer her calls," his sister said, with the sort of defeated sigh he recognized only too well. Having made that sound himself more than he cared to recall.

He could hear some city or other in the background of wherever she was. Honking horns, spirited snatches of conversation. Whole lives that were conducted without the slightest interest in what one deranged woman they happened to be related to was or wasn't doing.

"That is false," he told his sister. "Someone always *does* answer her calls, but that doesn't mean you need to be that person, Lavi." He pronounced it *Lovey*, as he had since they were small. An unfair weapon then and now. "Besides, she has other children."

"None of them would dare call you," Lavinia said with a cackle. "They are far too protective of their own skins. I find it absolutely hilarious that the papers are filled with all the stories of *'Caius Candriano, the most beloved and delightful guest at every society event,'* but anyone who knows you knows the truth. You're a holy terror."

"There is absolutely no difference in my behavior anywhere I go," Caius told her with great dignity. He took another swig of his water, still glaring out at that palace. "I can't help it if our family doesn't like the way I tell a truth."

"Tell yourself whatever you need to," Lavinia said with an audible eye roll. "The Countess is getting married again, whether we like it or not. I don't even know what number it is, because I have chosen not to process the final tally. As it so often changes."

"I cannot for the life of me understand why you're engaging with this, Lavi."

But she continued as if he hadn't spoken. "It would be one thing if you were simply unreachable, forever here, forever there. But it seems as if you've settled in this place. You're in the papers every day. How would it look if you couldn't come to your own mother's wedding?"

"One can only hope it will be seen as a complete lack of interest in a very boring subject, as we all know there will be another wedding to attend." Caius rubbed his hand over his face but the palace was still there, looming, when he opened his eyes again. Mila might as well have been on the other side of the glass, staring him down with that look of hers, unknowable and imperious at once.

"Have you met him?" Lavinia asked.

"I don't need to meet him."

"Anyway, Caius," she said in the resigned tone of one who is forced to soldier on despite unforeseen and obnoxious resistance, "it will hurt her feelings if you don't make an appearance."

"You and I both know that the Countess does not have any feelings."

"Forgive me." This time the sigh was aggrieved and aimed directly at him. "What I meant to say is that you are by far her most famous offspring. She will be humiliated and outraged if you don't turn up the way she wants. You know how she gets when that happens."

"Goodbye Lavinia," Caius said in the same mild voice he'd been using all along, because he knew it would annoy her. "Stop doing her dirty work."

And he could hear his laughing as he rang off.

He stayed where he was for a moment, frowning down at his mobile and wondering if he should add insult to injury and give his father a call. Just to see how badly the old man was messing up his life these days, what with his addictions to fast cars, too much gambling, and making a mockery of his family's once good name.

It was enough to give a man a complex, if Caius was the kind of man who allowed himself such things. But that was another thing that had never been allowed when he was a child. Only his mother was permitted feelings.

And hers were operatic.

He and Lavinia were the oldest of his mother's five children. Each of them was the product of a different father and all of those fathers also had other children elsewhere. This had led to what Caius liked to call the dark comedy of family events, not that anything was ever very funny. But because the Countess had kept Caius and Lavinia with her for the longest period of time—there being at least ten years between Caius and the next in line, which had led to all kinds of bonding between him and his older sister—the two of them had always considered themselves their own family.

As for the rest, he sometimes had to do a bit of research on his Wikipedia page to figure out all the ins and outs of who he was related to.

If asked in public, he liked to make a joke of it. There were all kinds of unflattering terms to describe a woman like his mother, who was forever jumping from one man to the next and having babies many of them as possible, so that they were forced to feel responsible for her forever. There were many ways to describe the kind of woman who made her living that way, but because the Countess came with a pedigree and had a claim to exiled royalty of one form or another, no one ever used those terms. No one would dare.

The fact that she was a cruel, vain, vicious woman seemed to trouble absolutely no one at all. She wandered from man to man, dragging her kids along as props and abandoning them to hotel staff when she bored of them, or might be asked to *parent* in some way. She threw them into schools then yanked them out again, without caring at all how they might feel about it—and woe betide anyone if they complained or so much as drew her attention when she was not in the mood to remember their existence.

She had left Caius on his own in a hotel room in Berlin once for *bothering* her. She'd sent for him ten days later, and had punished him for the inconvenience. He had been eight.

Caius had hated every moment of his childhood.

But he had made that same kind of lifestyle his entire personality as he grew older. He was a man who followed his limbs whoever they took him. He had not allowed himself to stop and attempt to fix his childhood, because if he did, that might indicate that it needed that fixing in the first place. That *he* did.

And he had decided at some point in his adolescence that he was perfect as he was.

There was absolutely no need to change a thing.

One significant benefit of growing up the way he had was that he could charm anyone. He'd had to do it more times than he could recall—at his mother's command or to get out of a tricky situation—and now he chose to use that skill all the time. He could charm anyone. He could fit in anywhere. He could be anything to anyone, and he had taken pride in that.

Until Mila.

And that was the part he couldn't forgive, not even after all this time. She had looked at him as if she could see who he *really* was. Not the person he pretended to be. Not the role he'd been playing all his life.

She had spent only those few months with him and she had been a revelation.

And all of it was a lie.

Maybe, he thought as he looked out the window at her palace, he shouldn't blame her for that. Maybe it was his fault for imagining that what had happened between them could be real once they let the world back in. Because he really should have known better. He had always prided himself on being a realist.

And then one look at her and it was as if he'd never learned a thing.

Maybe he needed to accept that even though he'd vowed that he would never marry—so he could never divorce, much less as many times as his parents had—he had gone ahead and done it anyway.

And maybe he really should go to his mother's latest wedding, where he would learn her husband's name just in time for them to separate, because it might teach him a valuable lesson that he'd never wanted to learn.

He was exactly the same as everyone else in his tangled and embarrassing family tree. He was certainly no better than the rest of them.

It had been madness to think so.

Caius stared out at the palace where Mila was, there and yet gone the way he should have known she always was and ever would be, and let out a kind of groan that seemed to come from deep in his bones.

He would give her that divorce. He should have done it long ago.

Then he would leave this pretty kingdom of hers and he would never come back. He would never stay put anywhere, ever again, because that was what he knew. That was who he was.

Slow down and your devils can find you, his mother had liked to say when she was drunk. *You'll meet yours soon enough, my boy. You* are *one.*

And he thought that really, he should never have imagined that he could be a different kind of man than the one the Countess had raised.

Just a pretty face, a charming smile, and the good sense to never overstay his welcome.

That night, he dressed exquisitely. Everywhere he went in the ballroom *du jour* women watched him, laying down palm fronds with their covetous gazes.

Caius knew he was resplendent. Just as he knew Mila would be able to see him even if he wasn't, the moment she entered the gala.

He would simply have to take comfort in the fact that she would read about him in the tabloids forever. And that he would do the same.

It was more than some people had, but at least he could make sure she would never forget him.

"Have you heard?" one of his companions asked him. When he only looked at her and shook his head, she clapped her hands together. "The Queen is looking for a husband at last. *Everyone* is talking about it."

"Is she indeed."

And the woman beside him saw only his charm. His smile. Not the chasm that had opened wide beneath him and was filled with sharp teeth that were now sinking into him, deep.

"Maybe you should apply for the position," the woman said, laughing shrilly. She even put her hand on his arm, as if they were friends. As if he was alive. "Wouldn't that be a laugh? Can you imagine *King Caius*?"

But that was going to be a problem, he thought, his gaze on Her Majesty as she entered the room in a sweep of deep lavender and gray serenity.

Because it turned out, he could imagine *King Caius*. Vividly.

CHAPTER FIVE

"COULD YOU PLEASE tell me why it is," Mila said in an undertone to her mother, her perfect smile never wavering, "that every man on the palace grounds who does not work here appears to be looking at me?"

"You are the Queen of Las Sosegadas. Pray, where else should they look?"

"They are looking at me less like I am their beloved sovereign and more as if I am a piece of meat hanging in a marketplace," Mila replied, bestowing her smile upon a group of women, who did not make her want to check to see if she'd accidentally walked out of her dress before exiting the palace. "And what is more, I believe you know it."

Beside her, Alondra was gazing serenely about, with an air of satisfaction that boded ill. "Your Majesty, forgive me, but I am unaware of any time you have spent in any marketplaces. Particularly marketplaces that have raw meat hanging on display."

Mila was far too well trained to give her mother the look that comment deserved. "If I'm not mistaken, old Lord Stefano, who I believed entirely too withered and ancient for such sport, licked his lips in my direction."

Alondra sniffed, gazing censoriously in Lord Stefano's general direction. "How terribly uncouth."

They continued walking at the usual sedate pace that Mila had been told her entire life was the appropriate speed at which a queen should cover ground. Sometimes, like today, every muscle inside her body fairly *hummed* with the need to do something...explosive.

That didn't mean blowing up her life, the way she would have done if she'd returned home from the far reaches of America to announce to all and sundry at her father's funeral that she had taken the notably unsuitable Caius Candriano as her husband. Not just as her husband, but as the future king.

That was not the sort of explosiveness she meant. She had no intention of stumbling over that sort of landmine. She wasn't sure she knew how she'd done it in the first place.

What she thought sometimes was that it might be quite pleasant indeed to take up an actual sport of some kind. She had always been discouraged from such pursuits because, her mother had told her icily years ago, no one wished to see the future Queen heaving about on a court in a red-faced sweat.

An image so horrifying that Mila wasn't sure she'd allowed herself to perspire for years afterward.

On days like today, however, she rather thought that whacking something with a racket sounded like nothing short of a delight. Especially when she thought about Caius—something she forbade herself and yet she found herself doing it anyway—who had taken up...lurking.

If anyone that dramatically beautiful and attention-getting could be said to lurk, that was.

Today was an annual late-summer event in the kingdom. The Royal Gardens were opened to the public once in spring, once at the end of summer, and once not long before Christmas when the gardens were done over into a veritable pageant of a Christmas card. Mila was currently doing her usual August promenade from the sweeping steps of the palace down the long, paved walk that cut through the heart of the gardens and allowed for press pictures, meet-and-greets, and the like.

But unlike all the balls she threw and attended throughout the season, this was the sort of event that was open to the entire kingdom. Not simply the aristocracy and the usual touring heirs to this and scions of that, where a certain level of snobbish hierarchy was expected.

These were the three events a year where, once her initial promenade was finished, she could simply…wander as she liked. She could talk to her subjects more freely when she encountered them. She did not have to work as hard on seeming approachable and relatable because, for once, she did not have to exude them through a smile. She could simply *be* those things one-on-one.

Normally she loved everything about the Garden Galas. But today she could not say that she liked the way a great number of the particularly high in the instep were looking at her. Something that did not go away as they walked.

"This is not the first time I've noticed this, Mother," Mila said from beneath another smile. "It's been going on for at least a week. What have you done?"

"I have done nothing at all, Your Majesty, except what I have always done. Which is to adhere, as ever, to your every stated wish."

Mila nearly forgot herself and laughed. "That has a rather ominous ring."

A sideways glance from the Queen Mother indicated that it was finally occurring to her that Mila was losing her patience. She cleared her throat, something she managed to make sound delicate. "It was at one of our private dinners the other week. You were brooding down at your game hen and said that you were thinking of marrying."

Mila actually did laugh at that, and had to cover it by pretending that she was *that* engaged in the antics of a set of squealing children who stood along the path. But as soon as they walked past she actually turned her whole head and pinned her mother with a glare, and she wasn't even certain she managed to keep a smile on her face while she did it.

"I am absolutely certain I said no such thing."

Her mother looked startled. But the Queen Dowager Alondra was made of nothing soft, inside or out. She lifted her chin and barreled forth the way she always did. "You may not have used those words, I grant you. We were talking of your sister. And how impossible it seemed that Carliz would ever settle down. How can you not recall this?"

"I said that life is endlessly surprising." Mila's voice was quiet, but she knew her mother did not mistake the hint of steel in it. "That it was impossible to say what the next turn of the season might bring. We were speaking of *Carliz*, Mother."

"And then Your Majesty said, and I quote, *'The mistake we make is believing anything can be set in stone.'*"

Alondra looked at her in triumph.

Mila gazed back. "I am waiting in breathless anticipation to see how you interpreted that to mean that I would like to walk about my kingdom being slobbered over by every man who dares look at me. Truly. I cannot wait."

"There has only ever been one thing you have declared set in stone," her mother said primly. "I merely whispered in a few ears that perhaps, after all this time, the stone has begun to shift."

Mila fumed for the rest of what was normally her happy promenade.

When it was finished, she took the requisite photos with the gardening team, shook the hands of expected dignitaries, met the people who had been selected to receive her special notice this day, and then lost no time setting off for her wander when it was all done.

But she didn't follow her normal route. Usually she made her way through the summer flowers, happening into conversations as she found them, with whoever she discovered along the way. It was one of her favorite things to do.

Today, however, she headed for the maze.

Unlike some garden mazes that were built as follies and design elements and would not have confused a toddler, the palace maze here had been the brainchild of one of the kingdom's darker figures. Prince Clemente had poured his animosity for his long-lived and famously unpleasant father into this particular creation on the palace grounds, where it was said he preferred to tarry so as to avoid the intrigue of the royal court as much as possible.

Much of the maze was made of tall evergreens that did not fade away with the seasons at this elevation, but continued to stand tall and impenetrable all winter. Its narrow little passages twisted this way and that as it rambled about in its dizzying manner. It was impossible to see into it from above, and entirely too easy to get lost in it on the ground. Some even claimed it was haunted, and the routes to the center some believed did not exist changed at the whim of the maze itself.

But for Mila, the maze had always been a place of refuge.

Because of its reputation, most people avoided it, so filled was it with superstition and all the whispered stories of dark things that might have happened within it.

What that meant, she knew from experience, was that very few people braved the narrow, thorny, gnarled little pathways. Most people never made it to the center. But she knew where it was—she could get there blindfolded—and she headed there now.

And the farther she moved away from the sound of all of those voices—all of that polite laughter, the buzz of gossip, speculation, and apparently, now, talk of marriage—she felt more and more like *herself.*

Like the Mila she got to be when she closed the door to her bedroom each night.

The Mila she was when Caius looked at her and the world fell away.

The farther she went, the better it felt, so she actually let herself move faster, then faster still, until she was running flat out.

Until she was breaking a damned sweat.

As if she was just a woman. Just a human being, hurtling unseen and yet protected by these hedges. Just out here running on a pretty summer day because it felt good to run. Using her body because it was hers. Because she wasn't simply a figure stamped on the side of a coin. She breathed. She bled.

Every once in a while, she even wept.

And for a few months, long ago, she had let herself feel every single thing a human could. Every beautifully mortal sensation, on every centimeter of her body, and she hadn't cared what she looked like while it was happening. She had spared not one thought for the sounds she made or the position of her lips on her face.

She had been *alive* in a way she hadn't been before or since.

Mila ran faster and faster, filled with a kind of mad, desperate exultation.

She burst into the center of the maze at last, skidding to a stop in the sweet-scented grove and blowing out a long breath that seemed to take from every part of her. As if it was scooping out everything inside of her, all those old ghosts and long-held fears and regrets, and releasing them all into the sacred geometry of this hidden place.

Here in the center, the grim hedges gave way to flowering trees. They cast shade, dancing over the sparkling pool that gleamed there in the sunshine. As if that long-ago crown prince, despite his dark feelings for everything within the palace, had been unable to prevent himself from showing his soft center to the very few people who ever made it here.

Mila was panting a bit as she walked to the edge of the pool. She gazed down at it, looking less for her reflection and more for the sense that she could, if she wished, be the woman she had only ever been in a real sense for a scant few months on the other side of the world.

I want to feel as if I chose *not to be her*, she thought fiercely.

Then she said it out loud. "I chose to come home. I chose to be Queen. I *chose* this."

Her dress felt heavy all around her after running as she had in it, but she didn't mind. Because for once, for a moment, she felt light. Airy.

And the same old dark thoughts pressed in, but she ignored them. Here, now, she shoved them aside.

Because she did not need to spend more time litigating her own behavior. Or her choices. That was in a past she could not change.

She had *chosen* to marry Caius long ago in a civil ceremony on a beach during a golden sunset, presided over by stranger who had never heard of either one of them.

And she had kissed Caius here in her own palace, though she certainly knew better. She could pretend that he had *stolen* that kiss, as if she had been a piece of candy in a store somewhere that someone could palm on their way out the door. Instead of what she actually had been, a grown woman, a literal queen, who had known exactly what he intended to do and had let him do it.

If she was honest, she had wanted him to do it.

Mila could lecture herself about what she owed her country and do a few more rounds about what her duty was and what she owed her family and her people and the very ground she stood upon, but not today.

Not here, where no one could see her.

Because this was the only place on the palace grounds

where she ever felt like that anonymous girl she'd been for only those very few months of her life.

That was the gift her father given her before his death. That was the magic he had bestowed upon her.

It is too dangerous, she had said at once when he'd called her into the bedchamber where he'd spent his last days. She had sat on the edge of the bed as indicated when he'd inclined his head toward the mattress and had frowned at him. All the while ignoring that fluttering, leaping thing inside her at the very idea. *What if I were to be kidnapped? What if I were to get myself into trouble? It would reflect badly on you and the whole kingdom.*

You will not travel with an entourage, he had said quietly. *Only one guard who has been training for the position. She will be tasked to look and act the part of a friend. The two of you will fly commercial. You will drive a rental car, eat in regular restaurants, sleep in unsecured hotels, and at no point will you do a single thing that would make anyone imagine you are in fact the Crown Princess of a royal house.*

That fluttering thing was threatening to take her over, but she had learned her lessons well. But…

The King had reached over and rested his hand on her leg. *My father sent me off to do the same thing when I was about your age. It was his belief that no one can fully commit themselves to this life without experiencing a different one, however briefly.*

But the risk… She'd tried again.

I trust you, Mila, he had said simply. *I trust you to take care of my kingdom when I am gone, you know this. But I trust you to take care of yourself, as well. I'm certain you possess discernment enough to track your own course and the wisdom to do so in a way that shames neither you, this family, nor the crown.*

He had paused as if he'd expected her to mount another argument, but she couldn't.

This is the greatest gift I could give you, he'd said then. *A small window of anonymity before you become, as you inevitably will, public property in almost every way.*

She had wanted to cry, though she hadn't.

And then she had gone and planned not simply a trip, the way many did for gap years and the like. Mila had planned a mission. She had reveled in the challenge. She'd had Noemí collect the items they would need from shops where normal people went. Things the Crown Princess of Las Sosegadas would never possess.

When it was time, they had snuck out of the palace under cover of night, and Mila had laughed as they'd crossed the border. That had the last time someone had recognized the name on her passport. After that, even if there was a second look, she was instantly dismissed.

Because it beggared belief that a woman with the name Emilia Christiana de Las Sosegadas could possibly have anything to do with a princess or a crown far off in the mountains between Spain and France.

They had spent two months wandering where they liked, through cities Mila had never had the opportunity to explore on her own, before they decided to take that particular guided hike through a dangerous stretch of the Pacific Crest Trail.

Nothing but nature for weeks, Noemí had said. *Hard to be more anonymous than that.*

That was where Mila had finally met Caius, who she had certainly heard of before. And had possibly even seen at some or other event, though they had never interacted.

Someone had likely seen to it that they never crossed paths.

She could admit that she hadn't known whether to be thrilled or disappointed that he hadn't seemed to recognize her at all.

It was only later, when they had been telling each other truths at last, that he'd admitted that he'd known who she was at once. That he had hoped that if he didn't indicate that he knew who she was, she wouldn't say anything either, and none of the others in their group would be any the wiser. None would know that they were in the presence of two extremely famous people in a place no one would think to look for them.

They had spent the last few months of her six-month adventure completely inseparable. To the point where Noemí had allowed them time to themselves, and Mila had not thought twice about taking it.

It was something she had never had before. Something it had not occurred to her to treasure—though she knew, even then, that she would miss it. For days on end she got to feel what it was like to have no eyes on her at all save those she loved, from morning until night.

It was like a prayer she hadn't known she needed answered.

And it was only here in this quiet, secluded place where no one knew she liked to come to see her real face in a pool no one else could critique, and breathe her own breaths with any expression on her face she liked, that she could let herself remember those months.

Really, truly remember them.

And that person she'd been then, when she'd been as close to free as she'd ever come.

It wasn't the freedom she missed, Mila knew. It was the way she'd felt in her own skin. Invincible. Entirely herself.

Not subject to any whim but her own.

Her fist clenched involuntarily, as if she was still holding the ring he'd given her. As if she hadn't carefully tucked it away again, back behind the desk drawer, vowing not to give in to the urge to take it out again.

Vowing she would leave it there for future generations to wonder over when they found it, a mystery forever unsolved.

She stayed there until her breathing slowed. She smoothed down her dress and composed her features. Only then was she ready to be *the Queen* again. Only then did she turn, shoulders straightened, to head back out and face the music.

"The music is your life," she said under her breath. "You love your life."

But before she could launch into a series of fierce affirmations to remind herself of why that was true, she stopped.

Because he was there.

He was *right there* and there was no telling how long he'd been there.

Caius stood in the opening to the hidden central grove, seeming to gleam like sunshine though he stood in the shade. He was dressed like the perfect male fantasy of a garden party. All creams and whites, yet slightly rumpled, as if he was far too uncontained, too languidly danger-ous, to suit such elegance.

He didn't say a word.

She didn't ask him how he had managed to follow her through the maze or if he'd simply found his own way. He was capable of either, she knew.

"I suspect you heard that I'm looking for a husband," she said, because he would have to have heard. And there was that certain glinting thing in his gaze that made ev-erything in her...*tremble.* "Never fear. I'm not planning to set off on a bigamist excursion. That is the precise op-posite of anything I would ever be tempted to do."

Caius still did not say anything.

And Mila had spent more time that she would like to admit thinking about this man in the years since those months together. Every time she'd seen his picture in a tabloid, with the inevitably stunning women falling all over him in front of a cameras, she'd imagined what it would be like for the two of them. Against her will, she'd let the images of him and all of them into her head.

Because she knew. All of that fire. All of that lazy intent.

Mila knew what he could do. And how he did it.

He drifted farther into the small grove, seeming to both take it all in and yet never shift his gaze from her at the same time. He kept his hands thrust deep in his pockets, which made him look slouchy and disreputable, and seemed nothing more than an extension of that little curve that was always in the corner of his mouth.

"So this is where you come," he said in that low voice of his that seemed to hum inside her on a frequency all its own. "Where you can simply be Mila."

He might as well have taken out a stun gun and fired it at her. It seemed to hit her with the force of that kind of weapon, dialed up to the highest possible voltage. She hissed in a shocked breath.

"There is no *Mila* to be, simply or otherwise," she told him, though it felt like a sacrilege, here beside the pool. For now she could see not her reflection, but theirs. Together, like a memory.

Like a warning, she tried to tell herself.

"No?" he asked, but indulgently. As if he knew better. "Not anywhere?"

"There is less and less Mila every day," she told him quietly. "That's a good thing. There is no room for anything else but the Queen. Anything that is not the Queen is a distraction."

"You get to be human, you know." And he did not sound indulgent then. It was much more intense than that. Or maybe it was the way he looked at her with that wizard's gaze. "Because you are actually human, Mila. All the palaces and crowns and fancy dresses in the world can't change that."

It was so close to her usual line of thought when she was here she wanted to cry. And that made her want to throw something at him, because queens did not cry. Not in the light of day. Not where anyone could witness that sort of breakdown.

She felt her fists clench again and had to stop herself from looking down at her left hand to see if that circle of gold was there. She knew it wasn't. She *knew* it wasn't, and yet still, she glanced.

The worst part was that he did, too.

"What do you *want*, Caius?" she asked. *Again.* "If it is something I can give you, I will. But I can't allow this to keep happening. I can't allow myself to be fractured like this. It serves no one. Like it or not, being *the Queen* is my role on this earth, no matter how human I am. I'm here to serve the people of his kingdom, irrespective of any wants or needs or dreams. Much less any ill-advised adventures I might have had in a different lifetime."

"It was this lifetime, Mila." His voice was gravel then. His eyes were fire. "I was there."

She shook her head. "Neither one of us was really there. It was a dream. A beautiful dream, but we should have let it stay just that. A *dream*."

She thought he would argue. Instead, he bent down and found a pebble, then tossed it across the smooth surface of the water with an easy flick of his wrist. Together they counted the skips.

The pebble bounced five times, then sank.

He swallowed, then spoke without looking at her. As if the ripples on the pool were too fascinating to turn away from. "I heard that after this flower show—"

"It is the August Garden Gala," she interjected coolly. "A great favorite of the people."

Caius acknowledged that with the faintest crook of one brow. "After this, I am told you retreat for the month of September."

"I do indeed." Mila looked back over her shoulder to where the palace rose in the distance. It seemed so far away, here by the pool. "It's a place called, creatively enough, the September House. And it is not exactly the stately affair some might imagine. It is quite wild. And very remote. The sovereign generally spends some time there at least once a season." She tried to aim her usual public smile at him, but it felt strange on her mouth. Stiff and unwieldy. "A time for reflection, some say. My father liked to hunt. His father was a keen cross-country skier."

"What do you do?"

She found herself turning to face him. And it was different here, where there was no one watching. When it wasn't the middle of the night and she was still reeling from the shock of seeing him at all.

When Mila looked up at him, she knew better than to allow herself to yearn for things she couldn't have. She found herself wishing against wish that she could be someone else.

Only for a moment. Another stolen span of time.

"I do very little," she told him, hoping her wishes did not show on her face. "There's a daily call with certain ministers, of course, and a government to run. Other than that, I am left to my own devices."

When Caius only gazed back at her as if he truly wanted to know, as if he was still the man she had considered her only truly safe space on earth, if only briefly, she sighed a little. "At first I took my mother and my sister with me when I went. But I stopped that after the first time. I didn't want to be anything while I was there. Not a queen. Not a daughter. Not even a sister, which I would say is the easiest role of the three." She lifted a shoulder and let it drop. "I just wander about as if I'm anyone. As if I'm no one. I cook my own meals. I clean up after myself. Doesn't that sound silly, that a grown woman could find these things transcendent? Transformative?"

"Not at all," he said, and there was too much memory in his voice then. Too much of the Caius she'd loved so recklessly, so heedlessly, so fast. "I was there the first time you let yourself be anyone and no one. I'm glad to know you still do it."

In the distance, she heard a swell of laughter on the breeze. It was the waning days of August now. And the summer was always stuffed full of events, so that she usually couldn't wait to set off to the September House.

But she knew that this year would be different. Because she knew no matter when she went, she would take this aching thing inside of her along with her.

"I did hear that you planned to start looking for a husband," he confessed, maybe to that ache. Maybe to the memories they shared. "I was incensed."

"Let me guess. You assumed I was throwing down the gauntlet. Directly at you."

"Something like that." It was the way he looked at her, the way no one else ever did or ever would. As if he saw the things she worked so diligently to hide. It was the way he saw *Mila* first, always, and had to look for *the Queen*, when for everyone else she knew—including herself—it was the opposite. It was the way he seemed to have no notion of the reverence he was meant to show in her presence. All the deference he was meant to display. Not Caius. He only reached out and brushed something from her cheek as if she could just...*be touched* like that. Then his mouth curved, likely because he could feel the same heat that she did. "I set about plotting how best to disrupt this process immediately."

She laughed, despite herself. And the glory was, she didn't have to try to hide it. "How marvelous. I can't decide if I think you would go for a big, splashy sort of disruption, for maximum scandal and rippling aftereffects. Or if you were looking for something more stealthy, for more of a seismic, earthquake effect."

There was a flash of his teeth and that smile of his he used far more rarely than people thought. They always remembered him smiling, laughing, but in reality, it was usually that smirk. He was witty, not funny. There was a difference.

And when it came to Caius, all of it was sharpened to a point and wielded with precision.

"I haven't decided yet," he told her, still smiling. "It was all going to depend on what lies you told me."

"And now?" Her hands ached with the effort of keeping them to herself. "Have you decided my fate?"

"Before I heard about your dating plans, I had intended to divorce you." But he was still standing so close to her. He found a tendril of her hair and was wrapping it, ever so slowly, around and around one finger. "I was going to tell you that I would sign whatever papers you needed signed, so that we could dissolve the legalities as if they had never occurred in the first place."

"I think," she whispered, "that you don't actually know what you want, Caius."

He tugged the bit of hair he had wrapped around his finger and they both made the faintest noise, as if they were singing in a kind of harmony.

Mila knew that harmony. It was that ache inside of her. It was that grief.

But it was less and less like grief the longer they gazed at each other like this. It shifted. It became that long, lingering, golden heat.

She recognized it. The way it wound around and around inside of her. The way it lit her on fire and the flames seemed to reach every part of her, only to settle between her legs. The way it made her soft and needy in an instant.

Oh, yes. She remembered the song too well.

"I have always known exactly what I want, Mila," Caius told her.

"You only want me because you know that you can never truly have me," she replied, and she hardly knew where those words were coming from. But they felt true as she said them. And she wasn't hurling them out. She wasn't even upset. If anything, it was another part of that same golden heat. The part of her that grieved for having to give him up. Again. And always. No matter what she wanted. "It's much easier to blame it all on me, isn't it? Then we don't have to ask ourselves what you might have done to change the landscape." He stared back at her, something like affront in his gaze, or perhaps all that magic was laced with a kind of acknowledgment she doubted either one of them wished to face, or speak out loud. "You could have made yourself into a paragon, Caius. A saint among men."

"What would be the point?" he returned, and he didn't sound intense or furious, either. "Each and every strand of my bloodline is shiny in its way, but altogether? It's a whole lot of mud. And we know you can't have that."

"Just remember that you get to make choices. I am bound to fulfill my duty. No one ever said it would be *pleasant*, I assure you."

He let out a breath, or maybe it was a curse too soft to hear. "What's the point of having all this power, Mila, if you only wield it to make yourself miserable?"

"What are my options?" She leaned in close, because that felt like power. Then she reached up so she could set a palm on each side of his jaw, holding that beautiful face fast between them. And that felt even better, even if it hurt. "This was always better as a dream, Caius. The more we do this, the more we tarnish it. Is that really what you want?"

She felt his hands cover hers, but all she could *see* was the way he looked at her. The way he had always looked at her.

As if their hearts beat in the same rhythm, even now.

"So which is it?" she asked him, keeping her gaze trained on his. "Will you expose me to all of my people, making them all question my judgment forever? Will you attempt to seduce me so you can cause a new scandal in real time? Or will you simply say goodbye, and let us both remember what this was fondly?"

Mila didn't know how she managed to say that so calmly, when inside, she felt ravaged. She felt torn into ragged little pieces, but that didn't matter. That had never mattered. She could rip her heart out of her chest and hurl it out of the highest window in the palace, and it still wouldn't matter. She would still be *the Queen*. She would still have the same duties, the same responsibilities, the same expectations.

And the anguish she saw on his face didn't make it any better.

"I don't like any of those options," he said, as if the words cost him. As if this all hurt him as much as it hurt her, and the funny thing was, she believed it did. Not that it changed anything. Not that anything could. But her foolish heart jolted all the same when he smiled again, just for her. "What if I had a better idea?"

CHAPTER SIX

MILA WASN'T SURE that it was a better idea at all.

In fact, she thought a few days later as she quit the palace for the September House, she was fairly certain that she had taken leave of her senses completely. And this time she did not have the excuse that she was off on a journey to experience a different sort of life, as prescribed by her own father.

This time she did not have any excuse at all.

Her mother fussed at her about everything and nothing, the way Alondra always did when one of her flock was leaving her—something Mila had to chant to herself to keep her smile welded to her face and the spirit of empathy in her heart.

"The kingdom has soldiered on through this very same crisis a number of times a year since antiquity," she reminded the Queen Mother.

Also my *mother*, she reminded herself, *who calls me only my title so she won't slip up and call me an endearment in front of government officials.*

"And we no longer have to send messengers by horse and cart. You can call me. If you must."

Alondra did not miss her daughter's faint emphasis on the word *must*.

By the time Mila sank into the back of the armored SUV that had been prepared for her, she was only too happy to sit back, close her eyes, and start counting the minutes of the drive that would take her to a month of something far closer to freedom than usual. That was as normal as her retreat itself. It wasn't that Mila didn't enjoy her life and her role. She did. But she also liked this tradition—the only version of a holiday a queen could have.

She was driven out of the city before the car started making its way around the lakes. One after the next. The car wove a path from lakeshore to rolling field to lake yet again, giving Mila a tour of the country itself.

It looked like a painting. It always had.

She supposed it was down to her to make certain it always would.

The car began to climb once more on the far side of the great valley. They took the steep switch-backed roads until the air grew colder and she could see that snow had already fallen on the highest peaks. Only then did they turn in through a set of unmarked but sturdy gates, then take a slightly less steep zigzag of a drive until they reached the house itself.

It had been built to be a kind of mirror of the palace that stood all the way down on the other end of the valley. It was too far to see with the naked eye, though she'd seen artists' renderings of the two buildings and the valley many times, as it was considered an iconic representation of Las Sosegadas. But the two royal dwellings couldn't have been more different.

Where the palace was a collection of spires and turrets, rising high above the kingdom's capital city like a beacon of prosperity and peace, the September House was more of a brooding affair. It had been built as a hunting cottage, but the word *cottage* didn't really apply. It had been expanded over the centuries so that now it was a cluster of different buildings that shouldn't have gone together at all.

Yet they always seemed to do so beautifully, to her eye.

Mila could feel the tension in her shoulders melt away as they pulled up and stopped before the stairs that led up to the heavy wooden doors.

The house was ready for her. All the lights were blazing against the bite of the cold this high up. She knew that the kitchen would be stocked full and that the staff who lived on the grounds would give her the space she liked. There would be deliveries of perishables twice a week and otherwise, unless she called them in, she would be left to her own devices.

Mila felt the lick of a familiar flame, deep within.

She let the driver carry her bags inside, because he would have been offended if she did not. And then she stood in the warm, welcoming hall that smelled the way it always did—of a hint of cinnamon and something citrusy—and waited until the car disappeared back down the long drive.

The flame within her danced higher.

The house had been built as a place to relax on a grand scale. The library flowed into an atrium, then flowed out onto the terraces that were lovely in warmer weather, then seemed to roll off into the woods. She walked that way, but instead of heading outside she took the turn that would lead her into the rambling kitchen. Then to the old door that led down into the cellars.

The cellars housed some of the kingdom's finest wines, and many gifted bottles from abroad, but she walked past them. She kept on going down a long, cold corridor carved into the mountain, then down another flight of stairs that a scant few people even knew was there.

It had been hidden, deliberately. It was far off in the back and looked as if it should be little more than a closet. Mila pulled the keys from the pocket of her long skirt that she'd brought with her from the palace—another item she hid away in her private effects. She opened the door that looked like a forgotten closet and switched on the lone light that did little to beat back the shadows gathering there on the spiral stone stair. It looked and felt medieval, and her father had told her—when he'd told her about this family secret in the first place—that there were some arguments to be made that it might, in fact, date from that period.

But it had been put to great use in the last century's great wars.

Mila followed the cold stair down and around until she got to the heavy iron door at the bottom. She fit a second key into the lock there, and threw the dead bolt. Then she pushed back the other bolts with her hands, and slowly, carefully, opened the heavy door.

And then smiled.

Because he was there, right where she'd told him to be.

Better yet, he was lounging against the wall of the tunnel that wound down for a mile or two and came out in an abandoned tomb in the nearby village. And even here, in the faint light from that single far-off bulb, Caius looked...

Perfect, Mila thought.

Rakish and beautiful and his gaze met hers, bright and hot, and warmed through with that particular spell work that was only his.

That same gleaming dragon deep within her stirred, and its tail seemed to snake through her, sending sensation spinning into every last cell.

"I feel like a spy," he told her, with that grin that suggested he quite liked that idea.

"You are now in possession of state secrets," she told him. "Use your power wisely."

"I think you know I always do."

And they were both smiling too much, Mila thought. She actually felt *giddy* and that could only be dangerous, because she couldn't pretend it was something to do with the pent-up air down here.

It was *her*. It was *him*.

It was the fact that he had suggested he join her here and she had immediately figured out how he could.

And here he was.

Giddy barely covered it.

Mila tried to cover up her reaction by motioning for him to come in. He did, with his usual nonchalance and nothing but a bag slung over one shoulder. She started fussing around with the bolts and the locks again, before she realized that all she'd done was leave them both crowded on top of each other.

At the bottom of a spiral stone stair.

With only the faintest little bit of light.

She cleared her throat. "The tunnels were built a very long time ago," she told him as if this was a tour of the September House that he had signed up for, the way tourists could do at the palace. "They have been used in any number of wars and minor skirmishes, as you can imagine. It is never a bad idea be difficult to find when people are calling for your head, or for a revolution, or are looking for simple and effective way to occupy a country."

"I always thought of the kingdom as somehow above the whims of war or invading armies," Caius said.

"We would like to be," she replied. "The tunnels help. So do the mountains."

And she was afraid, suddenly, that he would be able to hear her heart pounding in her chest if she stayed still any longer. Mila turned abruptly, as if she had never had a lesson in comportment in her life, headed back up the stairs. *Sprinted* back the stairs, more like.

She cautioned herself to slow down, but she felt as if she was some kind of mythological creature, granted a wish. All she had to do was lead Caius up from the underworld.

Mila wanted to glance back, but she didn't dare. Everyone knew what happened if she did.

Back in the main part of the house, she found herself buffeted by the strangest feelings. And it took her some while to realize that she felt...out of place. As if she didn't quite know what to do with herself.

The moment she identified that sensation, she very nearly laughed. Because she couldn't recall feeling like that in a long, long time.

And the last time she had, she had been setting out on the adventure that would lead her to him.

"Well," she said, all formal and stiff after she'd led him on a small sort of tour. And felt as if her skin was seven sizes too small on her body while *he* seemed only to become more boneless with every step. "I don't know what your intention was when you suggested this—"

"Yes, you did," Caius replied.

They had made it to the low-slung, relaxed living area, all soft, aged leather and a fireplace stocked with wood, ready to light.

He tossed his bag on one of the sofas, and then turned toward her with a look of intent.

And everything in her flashed into a white-hot coil of need. Desire.

That dragon testing its gleam, stretching out inside her.

"We can't possibly just *leap*—" she began, almost desperately, though she didn't step away. She didn't move a single inch.

"We can." He stopped before her, his bright eyes alight. "Take the leap, Mila. Let's see if we can find our wings again."

Then Caius simply pulled her into his arms, lifting her high above him so he could slide her back down the length of his body.

Mila's mind went blank with delight, though it seemed as if her mouth still wanted to form words. As if there was an argument waiting, there on her tongue.

But her body knew exactly what to do.

She wrapped herself around him as he slid her down the length of his torso. And so by the time he settled her, his hands gripping her bottom and her legs around his hips, she could no longer tell who was kissing who.

It felt too good. It was a *catastrophe*.

A cataclysmic eruption of everything she had put on hold, everything she had tried to forget, everything that had always been there, waiting.

And this was no kiss stolen on the balcony where anyone might happen along.

Mila knew that both of them were fully aware that no one was going to interrupt them here.

That for the first time since she'd looked up and seen that he'd walked back into her life with that same smile on his face, they were well and truly on their own.

And this was what that meant. What that had always meant.

That blazing fire. The dragon's mighty roar.

And the sheer, impossible joy of it.

She dug her hands into his hair and found herself rocking against him, to make it better. To make it worse.

And also because she couldn't stop.

He didn't wait another moment. Caius toppled them both down onto the nearest couch, and then everything seemed to implode even more.

One implosion after the next, as if they might die like this, wrapped up in each other—and Mila wasn't sure she'd mind.

He pressed her down into the embrace of the sofa, and she *bloomed* beneath him. Had she worn this particular airy skirt in the hopes that it would go this way? Had she known that it would be like this—that his hands would be on her thighs, smoothing their way up to the V where her thighs met, so he could stroke his way into her soft-ness while his tongue did the same dance with hers?

Maybe she'd only dreamed it, for years, but now it was real.

Neither one of them spoke. Because this was the same wildfire that had always consumed them, only this time, it was…*more.*

More intense. More demanding.

More dangerous, Mila managed to think, but that didn't stop her.

Her hands were beneath his shirt, finding their way to those muscles of his. She was alternately clinging onto him or digging into him, depending on what he was doing with first one long finger, then two.

And the thing about Caius is that he knew exactly what he was doing.

He threw her over the cliff too easily and she found her wings there, laughing as she shook and shattered.

That he moved over her, reaching down between them to free himself, before thrusting his way home.

For a moment, then, there was only *this.*

The sheer, impossible glory of it.

He filled her completely. It had been so long.

They were locked together, their gazes, their bodies. It was as if there was no telling where one of them ended and the other began.

She clenched around him, unable to stop herself, and felt him as he shivered in response.

And then that shiver seemed to roll through her, so that suddenly she was shattering apart all over again, but he stayed where he was, hot and hard and still so deep inside of her.

She slid her hands around the front of his chest, still tucked there under his shirt, and for a long, long while, there was only shaking apart. Shaking back to life.

Shaking and shaking and shaking.

When she opened her eyes again his magical gaze, like nothing short of spell work, was all she could see.

"I want to see you." She swallowed, hard. "I'm still protected. But I want to *see* you, Caius."

She had never been more grateful that she had taken her sister's advice and gone on birth control when they were still teenagers.

I don't... Mila had blushed. *I mean, I haven't...*

It isn't about what you're doing or not doing, Carliz had said. *It's about setting a precedent so that no one but you ever knows if you need it or not.*

Mila made a mental note to send her sister a gift.

Caius blew out a breath. He rested his forehead against hers, holding himself there for one breath. Another.

Then he withdrew, and that felt like grief all over again. It rolled through her too much like a sob.

But he was only shrugging out of his shirt. He wore some kind of chain around his neck but he pulled that off too, crossing over to his bag and tossing it all there, followed by the rest of his clothes. Mila followed suit, and he crossed back to her he made a very low, very male sound of appreciation that she was naked, too.

Then he rolled her with him as he lay back down, so that she ended up between the back of the sofa and the glorious wall of his body.

She thought he would say something then. But there was no curve in the corner of his mouth. His eyes were like magic, and they were all she could see, still.

And suddenly everything felt sacred.

Caius smoothed a hand over her face, this thumb moving over her lips. Then he pulled her over the length of his body as he turned on his back, settling her astride him.

And then, with his hands at her hips to encourage her, to command her, they both seemed to hold their breath at the same time she braced herself against his torso and angled her body to take the full, thick length of him deep inside her once again.

"*My* Majesty," he growled.

Then Mila tipped back her head, arched her back, and lost herself in the rhythm he had taught her five years ago.

It was the same dance, but it felt like new.

They were the same people, but five years' difference had changed everything. And nothing. And somewhere in the tension between those two things, there was *this*.

The way she rocked against him, half blind with need and pleasure and spinning out on the sheer beauty of the heat they made together. On her softness and his hardness. On all the ways they fit so well, so perfectly.

Just like five years ago, he met her as she moved, until the dragon was in flight and everything was fire.

"You had better hurry, my queen," he told her as the fires built. "You're running out of time."

Mila laughed at that, throwing back the hair he'd taken down with his greedy hands. She moved faster, wilder. And then, finding his gaze and holding it, she reached down between them and found the center of her own need.

And she hurtled herself toward that edge.

But he was there with her as she leaped—

And then it was nothing but a soaring, sweet flight with fireworks all around, comets and shooting stars.

Until she floated back down to earth and caught herself right where she wanted to be, with her face tucked into the crook of his neck.

Just like coming home, she thought.

Or maybe she said it out loud, because there was an echoing rumble in his chest.

But there was no point worrying about that now.

She drifted off to sleep, in a way she knew she hadn't done since Noemí had walked into that room in California and curtseyed to the new queen. She slept the way a monarch never could, because she knew that with his arms around her, he would protect her from whatever came. That she could trust him to take care of her.

And as she drifted there, half awake and half asleep, she knew too well how dangerous it was to think these things. How they had led her to marry him in the first place, which was the cause of all this trouble.

But it didn't feel like trouble today.

It felt like lifetimes later when she stirred and found that he had disentangled them, but still lay there with her, his gaze on the ceiling. She took stock, finding tiny little remnants of sensation like undercurrents, running beneath her skin. There was the endless list of things she ought to have been worried about—but this was the September House. Unless and until there was a pressing matter of state to deal with, she did not have to worry about anything.

That was the whole point.

So she propped up her chin on her hands and looked at him, at those impossibly artistic lines of his beautiful face.

"So," she said.

She could feel laughter move in him though the only sign of it on his face was the shift in his gaze, that dark amber lightning. "So," he agreed.

There were too many things she wanted to ask him. But all of them were huge. Weighty and impossible when she had the feeling that this thing between them, just now, was like spun glass. It would be easy enough to hurl it to the floor and watch it shatter into shards too small to ever put back together. Too easy.

Alternatively, she could go the other way and blow the glass into shapes and colors, just to see. Just to make something different.

Or possibly because you can't face the truth, a voice inside her scolded.

But she accepted that.

"Where did you go?" Mila asked instead. "After California?"

It was a risky proposition. She knew that before he slid a gaze her way, one brow lifted. As if to ask, *Do you really dare?*

But she gazed right back at him, steadily.

And he could have been the one to take that little bit of glass and throw it against the wall, but he didn't. "I needed a project," he said. "Something to lose myself in."

She did him the courtesy of not asking what he meant. Because looking back, she supposed that that's what she'd had, too. The project of becoming *the Queen*. Of morning her father. Of planning her coronation. Of turning herself into the sovereign.

There had been no time to think about what might have been.

Or perhaps it was more accurate to say that every time she had thought about it, she had chastised herself for losing focus.

And despite all of those other things to focus on, it had still been so hard she was sometimes surprised she'd survived it. Though she didn't like to think about that.

"I started a production company," he said, with a self-deprecating sort of laugh. She remembered him sitting in the firelight on that long hike, talking about his childhood and how his parents had never been there for him, but that there had always been the cinema. There had always been movies to watch and characters to depend on instead. "Such companies are thick on the ground in Hollywood and most of them fail. Usually because of the enormous ego of the person whose vanity is funding the project in the first place. I could easily have taken that route, with my rather robust ego. But I chose instead to have an ego about the projects, not me."

"That is the only way," Mila agreed. "Vanity is a mirror. True confidence is a path forward."

"Indeed." She had forgotten the way he liked to run his fingers through her hair, letting the silken strands dance over his palm. "The company still exists. We are small, but so far, have a not-unimpressive track record." Another self-deprecating sound. "It is something to do."

It would have been easy to laugh at that, and the way he said it encouraged that, clearly.

But Mila didn't. She studied him instead. "You're proud of what you've done. You should be. It's not a small thing when you make a dream come true, Caius."

His expression was wry. "It is not a big thing either, not when one is encumbered with a portfolio like mine."

"Don't worry," she said, smiling at him. "I won't tell anyone that secretly, deep down, the famously jaded Caius Candriano cares deeply about the things he makes."

And she was surprised, then, when he shifted, moving to sit up. And she had a moment of something like dizziness that they were sitting there, disheveled and undressed, and she didn't have to worry about how it would look should someone stumble in.

About what she would do or how she would explain this away.

Something seemed to clutch at her, but she didn't know what it was. She pushed it aside, because Caius had his elbows on his knees and was shoving his hair back from his brow with both hands.

"This is the part I try to forget," he said in a low voice. "I don't want you to understand me, Mila. Not when that understanding doesn't go anywhere. Not when it's like throwing stones at the moon."

She sighed, and that clutching thing inside her intensified. "Do we have to do this now?"

But he didn't answer her. He raked a hand through his hair instead, and the laugh he let out twisted in her, too sharp. Too hard.

"I made the films for you." When she didn't respond

to that, or not with words, anyway, he turned so he could look at her. "You must know that, surely. I made them all for you. Love stories, writ large. Like love letters I did not dare send to your palace."

He gazed at her. And she shook her head, slowly.

Then again. "I didn't know," she told him. When he looked incredulous, she lifted her hands. "I do not watch as many television shows or films as other people do. I hate to stumble over some or other representation of myself, or royalty in general. I prefer books."

And for a moment, she thought he might explode. She'd seen his temper before—always a bright flare followed by instant regret. As if he bubbled over sometimes, could not contain it, and then wished that he had.

But then, she thought the next moment, that was a different version of him.

This version looked at her with a sad curve of that sensual mouth of his and a kind of bleakness in his gaze. "That sounds about right. I am nothing if not predictable. Forever tilting at windmills when you have no use for wind, or mills, or down-market knights of any kind."

She moved closer to him so she could take his face in her hands. She pressed her lips to that space between his brows. To one eyelid, then the next. She pressed kisses everywhere her lips could touch, from temple to chin to that corner of his mouth where that mocking little curve lived. She kissed him over and over, until she felt the tension in his big, rangy body ease.

And when she pulled back, there was something sweet there between them. Something new.

"What I can give you," she told him quietly, solemnly, "is September. Will you take it?"

And she knew he would. They were twined together again, tangled up tight. She knew he wasn't going to storm back out of those tunnels. Not today.

Because they were nothing if not trapped here together.

Maybe she wanted him to admit to it.

"I will take it," he said, as if they were making vows again. "But Mila, I warn you, that will not be the only thing I take."

And she chose, then, to misunderstand him. She made her smile go sultry. And then she licked at his mouth, kissing him deep.

Chasing that dragon once again.

"Challenge accepted," she whispered, and then she wrapped herself around him once more, and set them both into flight.

CHAPTER SEVEN

SEPTEMBER WAS LIKE a dream—the kind of dream that Caius had woken up from, wild with desire, unsettled, and without her, more times than he could count over these past five years.

This high in the mountains, autumn was already making its appearance. The mornings were cold, though they warmed into achingly blue days and crisp nights that came earlier all the time. The trees were turning bright, bold colors, as if gripping on tight to the long summer days already past. Caius could relate.

It was a dream, these September days, but Caius could not fool himself the way he had once before. Because this time, he knew how this dream was going to end. There was no point in imagining otherwise, the way he had once before.

What he couldn't understand was how, knowing what was to come, he still couldn't bring himself to change a thing.

"I thought you were going to enact some kind of dastardly revenge plan," Mila said one evening as they moved around the kitchen together. They had taken to playing music as they assembled their meals, the kitchen brightly lit against the dark that waited there outside the windows, music dancing in the air like some kind of spell to keep the world away.

The kind of spell Caius had wished he'd known as a child, forever languishing in hotel rooms and dreaming of exactly this kind of life. Of becoming the kind of person who was capable of this kind of life. This ease and sweetness instead of his mother's chaotic rages. This pervasive wave of something he thought might be happiness, instead of the battle to assess his mother's condition in any moment and figure out how to pretend to be whatever version of her son she might have decided he was that hour.

It was easy, here, to pretend they were other people. People who did not play vicious games with one another and call it *family*. People who did not fight nasty little wars for supremacy, imagining that somehow they might escape the Countess's notice—that too-sharp focus that always boded ill.

Here in the September House, they did none of those things.

Here they were different people entirely. People who prepared food because it was good and put out table settings because they were pretty, and then enjoyed each other's company when they sat down. People who talked of the weather, not because they had nothing else to say, but because even the most innocuous conversations were layered and textured with all the ways they took each other apart and put each other back together when they were naked.

As if it was all the same thing, in one form or another.

Mila did not cook in the classic sense. But she was a deft hand at putting together ingredients that were pre-prepared for her. He discovered that she was a big fan of a hearty soup or a stew, accompanied by freshly baked bread with a liberal application of butter. That she would eat it night and day, if possible.

Caius contributed his own skills, which were not inconsiderable—because he had developed a deep loathing of delivered food when he was young, so had taught himself to cook—to add a bit of variety to the menu.

And this was how they sank in deep to this long September dream of the kind of domestic bliss neither one of them was likely to have, and certainly not with each other. They prepared all their meals together and ate them slowly while having wide-ranging conversations on every topic under the sun. They fought, not always amicably, over the books they'd both read. They avoided the news and laughed at each other's stories. They took long walks around the property, taking in the mountain air. They even did a bit of hiking the way they had all those years ago.

And they feasted on each other, at every opportunity, as if they could never get enough.

Because, he supposed, they both knew the inevitable end was coming. They both knew there was no future. Caius had to make sure that every moment of this month was memorable enough to last them both a lifetime.

He took that calling very, very seriously.

And so they indulged themselves in every scrap of sensuality they could find. The stately old hunting lodge offered an endless array of places to explore. From the hot springs that some enterprising member of the royal family had erected an entire bathhouse around in centuries past to a wide selection of beds and showers, including his favorite of those—the outdoor shower that let the stars shine in.

Yet she wanted to know if, through all of this, this banquet of the senses in all its forms, he was plotting revenge.

"You really do have a dim view of me, don't you," he said.

She was stirring the night's big meal, a crock of lamb stew that filled the kitchen with its rich scent. She turned, looking around at him in surprise, the steam from the simmering pot making her cheeks red.

And Mila was always beautiful. There was no denying that. Queen Mila was a study in contemporary elegance. Every outfit he'd seen her photographed in reached new heights of sophistication, as if she challenged herself daily to redefine chic for the modern world.

But her ability to casually, offhandedly achieve the same result without a cadre of attendants amazed him daily. She was a wonder. Today she was wearing her hair in two braids, each one wound into its own bun on the back of her head. He had watched her fix them that way herself. She was still wearing the sleek leggings she'd worn out on their walk, with colorful knit socks pulled halfway up her shins. And an oversized sweater in a fine, lush wool that managed to make all of that look not like a lumberjack or even all that casual, but like royalty.

He acknowledged the possibility that this was just... her.

"A dim view of you?" she repeated. She shook her head as if he wasn't making sense. "I...don't?"

"You do." Caius had been slicing one of the fresh baguettes that turned up at the kitchen door like clockwork and needed only to be baked through. He set the knife down, then propped himself up on his hands against the great butcher block on the island in the center of the sprawling kitchen. "You do, Mila. That's not an indictment. I've spent my entire life making certain that I'm underestimated at every turn. I can't get angry when my efforts are successful, can I?"

She studied him with those solemn, clever gray eyes. "Yet you seem angry."

"What I am," he said, and it was a challenge to keep his voice calm when he knew it should not have been, "is viewing everything that happened between us with new eyes."

They had danced around this topic since he'd gotten here, after trekking miles through underground, clearly little-used tunnels, hoping that she hadn't sent him off to march his way into the dungeons she'd mentioned. But this was different. She didn't cross her arms. She didn't straighten her shoulders and tip her head in that regal way of hers—to let him know *the Queen* was in the room.

She only waited, studying him, as if she didn't know what he was going to say.

It was strange how cheering that notion was.

But he didn't speak. And the silence stretched out between them. Eventually, she swallowed. "Are you going to say something?"

"There is nothing to say." He shrugged. "I have said it."

"How ominous," Mila murmured.

Caius pushed back from the butcher block and returned his attention to the bread. "My mother is getting married."

He sensed Mila's confusion at that change of subject but when he glanced at her, she had already turned back to the stew bubbling on the range, stirring it again. "I don't know whether to offer you congratulations or condolences."

"She wants me to attend, of course. My sister—"

"Lavinia," Mila said, warmly enough that it made something in him squeeze tight.

He nodded. "She keeps calling to tell me how important it is to the Countess that I be there. How devastated she will be if I don't turn up."

"Will you go?"

Caius set the knife down on the cutting board. "It's not that my mother wants my emotional support or has tender feelings about gathering the family together. That's not her style. I'm not entirely certain she's capable of tender feelings. She wants my presence to raise her profile. She wants to make sure that the paparazzi, who must be as tired of tracking her marital status as anyone else, will be there to cover it. Because nothing makes my mother feel alive like seeing herself in newspapers."

"I thought that's what you liked." Mila glanced back over her shoulder at him, and there was nothing accusing in her expression. If anything, she looked...concerned. For him. He didn't like how that sat heavy on him, then pressed down hard. "You used to talk extensively about what it was like to be seen as a kind of conduit for people." She put the big wooden spoon to the side of the pot, and then drifted over from the range so that she faced him directly across the center island. "To be perfectly honest, I think I drew on that quite a bit in my first days as queen.

You once told me that the most important skill you'd ever mastered was being the kind of mirror that anyone who looked into believed was bespoke." She shrugged, giving him a small smile. "See? I've never forgotten it."

He was stunned by that. If she had picked up that pot simmering away behind her and whacked him with it, he could not have been more stunned—but there was an urgency in him, now. There was something winding its way through him, past the heaviness of her concern for him and the conclusive proof she'd just given him now, that she had not forgotten him. That she had held on to things he'd told her.

That it had mattered, those stolen weeks in California too long ago now to bear.

There were a great many reasons to keep his counsel in this moment, Caius knew, but he didn't. He couldn't.

"I have never been more surprised in my life," he said quietly, "then when I learned that what I considered my superpower—the ability to read any room I went into— was a product of being raised by the kind of terrible people who would, years later, hound the child they'd neglected for clout." But he didn't want to talk about his mother. He was studying Mila's face. "I've never asked you how hard it was. It must have been nothing short of terrible for you, to have no time to prepare."

He remembered that day in the sort of detail he would have thought usually reserved for, say, terrible accidents. He'd walked into the shower a married man, not unaware of the challenges ahead of them due to their different stations, but secure in what they were to and for each other.

He'd walked out to meet the Queen.

"You prepare for the ceremony," she told him in a hushed voice. "For the steps that you'll take and the way that you'll present yourself. You don't do it alone. My father planned it with me. His team and mine talked all the time about the plans. Always the plans. Always making it sound like a great festival of some kind." She gave him a wry little smile, then, that broke his heart. "But you never talk about how much it hurts."

One of her hands drifted to her chest, directly over her heart, in a gesture that he knew, somehow, was unconscious. It made his own heart ache even more.

"It would be unseemly to talk about how it feels. And so you rely on all of that planning, and all of the pomp and circumstance. You're busy thinking about how it looks, and what message you're sending, and how the people are perceiving you… And it turns out that it's a crutch." Mila looked almost lost, for a moment, but then her gray gaze found his again. So at least he could be lost with her. "It's much easier to think about how to become a queen than it is to mourn the death of your father. To be honest with you, I'm not sure I ever have."

"And one day, if you do your duty, your child will have to do the same thing."

He realized after he said it how she could take that. How she might see it as a jab, but she didn't. If anything, her smile grew deeper.

More wry, if that was possible. "I don't think that's the privilege of royalty. I am fairly sure that's just life. We will all of us mourn our parents, if we are lucky."

"You consider that lucky?"

"The alternative is that they would have to mourn us," she said quietly.

"Mila." He said her name so urgently. There could be no mistaking that. He saw the way her eyes widened. But then again, if he wasn't mistaken, she was holding her breath. "Mila, why did you leave me?"

"You know the answer to that. We are discussing the answer to that right now."

"That's not what I mean. You know it's not."

He thought she would default to an instant denial, but she didn't. Instead, she looked away for a moment, out toward the windows, where the night was already dark and seemed to press against the glass. She looked…softer than usual.

Caius realized that it was surprising to think of her as fragile. He never had. She was so good at exuding all that regal energy. She was so good at making it seem as if she was far too iconic to be human at all.

He was going to have to think about the fact he'd let himself believe that, when he knew better.

"Putting aside all the many heart attacks the palace would have over your presence in the tabloids," Mila began.

"Because the tabloids are bastions of truth, of course. Everyone knows that."

He couldn't seem to help himself.

Mila only held his gaze. "Whether the stories are true or not isn't the issue. The issue is the regularity of your appearances and the kinds of places and people you have frequented over the years." Her eyes were so gray. So grave. "This isn't a lecture. It's an explanation. But that's an excuse, I think."

"You think."

"It's *this*," she said, and waved a hand back and forth between them.

He thought of the way that same hand had wrapped around the hardest part of him earlier in the shower, las she'd looked up at him so boldly while taking him into her mouth.

"This…intensity. How does that fit into my life? Or your life, for that matter?"

She could hardly *think* around the man. Much less *rule* in the way that was required of her. Or she couldn't imagine how she might go about it, anyway. It felt impossible.

"Do you know what I often wonder?" But she didn't wait for him to answer that. "If I hadn't left you, you almost certainly would have left me. If I had to guess, I would say that you would have found a way to manufacture some scandal or another so that I would have no choice but to leave."

"Again." His voice was a mere scratch. "It really is a dim view, isn't it?"

He could see she didn't like that by the way her chin inched up. "It's who you are. It's who *I* am. Those things can't mesh."

"You mean your pedigreed status and the fact I am a mongrel, I suppose."

"I mean that you like to immerse yourself in intensity. You like projects with a beginning and an end, and when it's done, you move on. And I…" She sighed, and shook her head a little as if the sigh was a cold wind and now she could not shake the chill. "Everything I do must be sealed in eternity. I must be a walking, talking study in permanence. How could it ever work?"

"It does work, Mila. Behold, it's working right now."

"We are magic," she agreed, though her voice was rougher than he'd heard it in years. Since she had looked at him with the same gray eyes but a stranger's face and had said, *There has been some news. My father, the King, is dead.* Here, now, she leaned a little bit closer over that island between them. "But it can only be a temporary magic, Caius. Like before. I thought you understood."

But she laughed—looking startled—when he came around the island, swept her into his arms, and then demonstrated how powerful his *temporary magic* was, right there on the old wood table.

More than once, for good measure.

Still, Caius found he continued to brood over that a day or two later.

She'd had to take an extra call that day, in the alcove off the main living room that she'd told him at least five of her predecessors had sat in to do the work of the kingdom. He stayed nearer the fire, but he could hear the cool, collected way she spoke to her ministers. Not the words themselves, but her cadence. Her tone.

It didn't matter what she was saying. It was all regal.

Every single thing that made Mila who she was, he understood, was another nail in the coffin that was the two of them. And this month that was winnowing its way out.

He pulled out his mobile and didn't bother scrolling through his messages. He knew what he would see—that his voicemail was full and there were so many texts that he might as well toss the bloody thing off the side of the mountain, then start over.

The way he did several times a year, usually without explanation. Everyone he wanted to talk to always found him again.

But he didn't get rid of his mobile just yet, though the mountainside beckoned. Instead, he looked up a number he rarely called, then pressed the call button before he could think better of it.

Well. Not *before* he thought better. Just before *think better of it* could stop him.

It rang and rang. And when it was finally answered, it was in a great flurry that shouted *drama is occurring and you might be the cause* and he could feel himself tensing already. Before she even said a word.

Though it was always the same word. Lavinia and he had long ago decided that she could not recall their names. Not in a pinch.

"*Darling.* I was beginning to think the worst."

"Hello, Countess," Caius drawled. Because his mother did not take kindly to the term *mother.* Or any other version of that word. Or anything that suggested an age differential of any kind.

The last time he'd tried he had been six. He had gone racing into her room, called her Mama, and had gotten slapped soundly across the face.

After all, she'd been entertaining. It had been his fault.

She had made certain he knew that he'd done it to himself.

Now, his mother was prattling on, the way she did. It was always so tempting to think of her as insubstantial when she wittered on about dresses and wherever she was living now and the cost of something after which he hadn't inquired.

But Caius knew that she was a shark and this was how she circled, looking for blood.

"I will come to your wedding," he said abruptly, cutting her off. "But only on the condition that nobody knows I'm there."

His mother laughed in obvious incomprehension, and there was nothing about that sound that anyone would describe as *insubstantial*. "I have no earthly idea what that means."

"It's very simple." He sat back in the old, soft leather couch and stared up at the art on the wall before him, a finely rendered landscape painting. Likely of a view from this house. "I will attend to support you, as your son. But I don't want the papers to catch wind of it."

"Darling, the papers don't *catch wind* of anything." Now she sounded like the shark she was, teeth and all. "They follow you around. Surely you know this."

"Sometimes they follow me around, and sometimes people call them to let them know where I'll be," Caius countered. "I'm going to need you to promise me that won't happen this time."

"Caius." When it mattered, apparently, his mother did actually know his name. "This is all very childish. You are a public figure, like it or not. And there's a certain expectation when it comes to our family. The people have come to require certain things of us. It's the least we can do to give them that."

But he was sitting in the September House, in the company of a queen. An actual queen who lived her life for her people. Who had walked away from him for them. Who would do it again.

A woman who did these things for duty, not fame.

"You have my permission, indeed, my encouragement, to seek out that attention all on your own," he told his mother. "With my compliments."

"Don't you dare do this," his mother seethed at him, and he thought, *There she is.* It was that instant flip from one face to another that he remembered so well, and he could hear it in her voice. He didn't have to have eyes on her because he knew exactly what it looked like. One moment, his beautiful mother, all that was lovely and graceful. The next, the monster who wore that shining vision as a costume and was never too far from the surface. "After all I've done for you."

"And what was that again?" Caius asked, making sure he sounded bored.

He wasn't. Because he supposed there was still that little six-year-old inside him somewhere, wishing he'd had that *mama* he'd gone looking for. But if the Countess ever got wind of the possibility he might have actual feelings, she would hunt him down and try to eat him alive. That was her favorite pastime.

Caius knew her well enough to know that for a certainty.

But maybe, as he sat in this royal hunting lodge as the Queen's guilty secret, he was starting to wonder who *he* was.

"I was in labor for seventy-two thankless hours," his mother railed at him. He thought she was slipping, or confusing him with his half siblings. Usually she said ninety hours, for the drama. "And raising you was no walk in the park, Caius. Your father was a horrid monster. You can't imagine the things I suffered!"

"Surely if that's true, you would have seen it before the wedding and shouldn't have married him," Caius drawled, because he had not let her wind him up in a long, long time.

Maybe his father was a monster, too. He had always seemed deeply sad and ineffective to Caius, but then, people were different with their intimate partners. But there was nothing he could do about a marriage she'd left when Caius was small. None of the things she claimed she'd suffered excused her.

And he couldn't help but notice that she only used her excuses to land what she hoped were mortal blows.

"And this is what I get," the Countess snarled, switching tacks yet again. "As if it is such a hardship to do the only thing you've ever been any good at. Simply show up. Smile. Practice that empty charm of yours that you throw around like confetti." And she laughed as if she could see him. As if he'd let his guard fall when he knew he hadn't. She was good at that, too. "That's all you've ever had to do, Caius. No one *wants* anything from you. No one *expects* anything from you. You drift through your life as meaningless as the day you were born. All that's needed from you—ever—is that you stand still long enough for the right pictures to be taken. How can that possibly be a trial? Even for you?"

He didn't mean to hang up on her. Or he didn't think he did.

But he found himself staring at the mobile in his hand, the call ended, and a selection of some very unflattering thoughts taking space in his brain.

She'd like that, he knew. She'd like to think she'd gotten to him.

If I could slap you again, she'd said at one of her weddings, *I would do it harder, so it taught you something.*

In case he'd been tempted to believe that she might harbor regrets. Or have amnesia about her own behavior.

In case he took his sister's position and tried thinking of her as a flawed human who had used what few, poor tools she had—instead of the shark she had always been and always would be.

Caius could still hear *the Queen* from the other room. Cool. Commanding. When this was the same woman who had sobbed in his arms only an hour ago, digging her fingernails into his back and leaving her trademark trail of half-moon crescents down the length of his spine.

One of these times, she had said later, sprawled out beside him and panting wildly, *you will break me down into too many pieces. They'll never put me back together again.*

But then, at the appointed time, she had risen from the bed without question or any excuses. She had pulled herself together in a flash, requiring no one's help to put her own pieces back, right where they belonged.

Something deep inside of him seemed to tremble at that, as if the ground beneath his feet was giving way.

He punched the button again to ring his sister.

"She's already on the other line," Lavinia said crossly, in lieu of any greeting. "What did you expect would happen, having a go at her like that? I'm not sure I'll ever talk her down."

"Then don't," Caius replied shortly.

His sister was quiet. He heard her mutter something, as if excusing herself, and then the sounds around her changed. He heard a door shut and imagined her walking from one room to the next, leaving whatever social situation she was in. Taking his call the way he would if taking her call in similar situations. A roll of the eye. A few choice words, mouthed to her friends.

All of these performances.

"I have a novel idea," he said into her ear. "What if you don't try to talk her down? What if we ignore her?"

"I didn't realize that was an option available to us," Lavinia said dryly. "Ignoring her and hoping she'd go away never bore any fruit that I can recall."

"All I did was tell her that I didn't want my picture in the paper if I went to her wedding," Caius said.

His sister sighed. "Why on earth would you tell her that?"

"Because I don't want my picture used as currency to buy things I don't value," he bit out, and there was a different sort of silence then.

And he knew why. He hadn't laughed. He hadn't sounded lazy, or amused, or deeply jaded.

If anything, he had sounded stern and *that* was something he never did. Not with Lavinia. Not with anyone, really. Not even with himself, if he could avoid it.

"Are you…?" He heard Lavinia blow out a breath. "Are you all right, Caius?"

"I would like to see what my life looks like if it is not a

performance," Caius told her, the words welling up from within as if he had prepared them. Or as if they had been trying to come out for a long, long time. "If I am not the poster boy for the bad behavior of every single person I am related to, through no fault of my own. It occurred to me to wonder what it must be like not to have pictures of myself staring back at me from every newsstand, no matter where I go."

"You've done this before. The last time, you wandered off into the wilderness, as I recall. Did you learn something then? Because my memory is that you wandered back out of the mountains and became a tabloid darling all over again, overnight."

His sister sounded exasperated, but Caius looked up. Maybe he'd sensed something. Maybe she'd made a faint noise.

But either way, Mila was there. She was standing in the doorway, watching him.

And her face was caught somewhere between the Mila he had been with all these weeks and the Queen. He wanted to ask her which one was real, but she wasn't like him. She hadn't created her role in response to a mother like the Countess. She had been born to be the Queen.

She was both Mila *and* the Queen.

He'd gotten that wrong, last time.

Because last time he'd been so sure that he knew himself that well, too. He'd been wrong about a lot of things.

"I will tell you what I learned," he said into his mobile, his eyes on Mila. "Wandering around this planet with only my own two feet to guide me from one place to another made it clear that I have more to offer than a photo op. The Countess is under the impression that all I have to bring to the table is a smile. In which case, I suggest she find a cardboard cutout of me. She can use that at her wedding, with my compliments. Because what I learned all of those years ago, hiking around in places where nobody recognized me at all, was that anonymity is a gift."

"Oh, Caius," Lavinia said, laughing now. "You only think that because it was a choice. You've never seen a stage you didn't climb up on, then position yourself dead center. Why pretend otherwise?"

"Lavinia," he said, almost gently. "I'm not going to her wedding. Or any future weddings. Ever."

Then he hung up on her, too.

"That seemed intense," Mila said after a moment, when all they did was look at each other across the expanse of the long room. "Families always are, I know."

He wanted to tell her all the things that were swirling around inside of him, all of the odd thoughts and new understandings that he wasn't sure he really wanted. He wanted to tell her that he wasn't temporary, that he didn't *want* to be temporary.

That just because he was good at center stage didn't mean he liked it.

"Do you know why I like producing?" he asked instead. And he must have looked as rough as he felt, because all she did was shake her head, *no*.

And the tiniest little frown appeared between her eyes.

"I like fitting the pieces together," he said, and he knew he was losing it because he sounded so vehement about it. Not the faintest hint of an incoming joke or any small drop of self-deprecation. But he couldn't seem to stop.

"I like putting the right people into the correct rooms. Making sure the trains run on time. That everyone is paid. That everything works the way it's meant to work. When most people see a beautiful sports car, they *ooh* and *ahh* over the shape of it. The form. How it looks when it drives. But what fascinates me is what's under the hood. That's what I like."

He stopped himself from saying, *That's who I am.*

For a moment, they held each other's gaze.

But then, Mila laughed.

And he didn't know how to tell her that the sound splashed over him like acid. "You have always been a great many things, Caius. But I would never consider you a *mechanic*."

He should have told her then. He could have. He could have dug down into that trembling place inside, where everything was unsteady and new, glaring and terrible. He could have torn herself open, and *showed* her who he was.

That it was no laughing matter—

But his mother's voice was in his head, snide and harsh, telling him exactly what he was good at.

So all he did was smile when she came closer, and laugh along with her, careful to make sure he was charming. So goddamned charming, because that was the only thing anyone ever saw when they looked at him.

Even Mila, apparently. After everything.

CHAPTER EIGHT

MILA KNEW THAT something had changed after that day she'd heard him on a call she wasn't sure he'd meant her to witness. Something was different, though she couldn't put her finger on it.

She wasn't sure she liked that *yearning* thing inside her that wanted to know him inside and out in ways she certainly didn't want to be known herself. She wasn't sure she liked any of the messy, impossible things she felt these days, come to that.

Then again, September was waning all around them no matter how they filled their stolen days. It felt to her as if both she and Caius were on edge.

It was there in the way they devoured each other, but talked less. Everything was heat and flame, until she began to wonder if they would both burn to a crisp up here on her month away. The kingdom would look up and see nothing but a bright and burning torch where the September House had been.

Some part of her, she was unnerved to discover, actually craved that. As if self-immolation was that perfect solution she still hadn't been able to find. Instead of a daydream of pure, outrageous selfishness. Not to mention anathema to everything she'd always believed she was.

But that was the trouble with spending time with Caius. She began to imagine that almost anything was possible.

When she knew better.

No matter how she agonized, no matter all the what-ifs that sometimes kept her awake at night wrapped up in his arms—thinking through one implausible scenario after the next—she knew better.

Her life had been planned from the start. It had never been her own, no matter those stolen weeks with him. It wasn't hers to give away to her *feelings*—something she'd seemed to understand more fully the last time.

Yet the more torn-up she felt that their end was nearing, the more ravenous he became.

And though she prided herself on never shying away from a difficult conversation, that, too, was different when it was Caius. She tried to tell herself that was only because they had both known, this time, that there would be nothing else.

Maybe this was simply how it would be between them this time, in lieu of any unpleasant scenes.

She told herself she ought to be happy with that. But what she felt, instead, was that she'd miscalculated. There would be no grand ceremonies to throw herself into on the other side of him this time. She had nowhere to ascend now that she was already Queen. She did not have to race home to the palace to comfort her sister, who had never enjoyed as peaceful a relationship with their father as she had. Or to perform her duties seamlessly and beautifully for her mother, who would not speak of her grief, only the future that Mila needed to embody to make it all right that her husband, the King, was gone.

It was beginning to seem clear that she might find this parting more difficult to bear than the last, and with less distraction. Fewer great griefs.

There would be no state funerals or coronations to concern herself with once September ended. There would only be whatever was left of her heart in his wake.

"Where will you go next?" she asked him on one of their last nights in the house, though neither one of them had mentioned *next*.

Until now, she supposed. Obliquely.

They'd thrown together one of their typical dinners tonight and she was trying her best not to let herself get too emotional—something she had never had to worry too much about and was now going to have to learn how to tuck away again, out of sight, if perhaps not as out of mind as she might wish—over the *ease* of it. Of simply being in the same rooms Caius inhabited.

After all these weeks they could predict each other's movements, in the kitchen as well as in bed. And there was something poignant and marvelous about the dance of that kind of intimacy. They hadn't experienced that before. There had been too much camping, too much hiking, so that everything was always new. Including them.

Mila had not expected the romance of familiarity. Handing him the utensil he needed before he asked for it. The way he moved around her, with the brush of his hand against her hip to let her know where he was, or the touch of his arm to hers because they were close.

The truth she did not know how to process was that she didn't know how she was going to do without this.

This forbidden intimacy she hadn't known she hungered for so deeply.

And this time she couldn't tell herself that the memories she had of him were overblown, that he was just a madness induced by those months of living a life she could never have.

Now he gazed at her as they sat before the fire. They had eaten, speaking in their new, slightly *careful* manner about things like history, change, and the march of progress, even in monarchies like hers. When she had suggested something sweet to finish off the meal, they had decided the best dessert around was each other.

He had risen, eventually, to bring the wine over and now they were sprawled out on the plush, cozy rug that was tossed out before the fire. She rather felt that they were in some kind of a cave tonight. As if they could as easily be ancient people doing ancient things, with only the light of the fire as witness.

More lives she could only daydream about, she knew.

"Are you throwing me out already?" he asked, mildly enough, but she didn't much like that, either. It was the way he sounded now, no longer all that marvelously textured gold. There was something like flint in it.

His wizard's eyes still gleamed, he was *right here*, but she couldn't reach him.

Mila hated it.

And she was making herself sick with all her *decorum*. With how much it cost to maintain her composure when they talked, if not when he was inside her.

It made her *ache*.

But, "I'm not throwing you out at all," she told him, and took more pride than necessary in how calm she sounded despite that ache, that sickness. How serene, with a glass of courage in her hand. "Yet in two days' time, like it or not, I will have to return to the palace. In all of my state. There will be no nudity near the fireplace, because what if the servants saw me? There will certainly be no *unmarried cavorting* of any kind." *Ever again*, she thought, and she meant to laugh. But the sound that came out didn't quite qualify as laughter, and that ache in her hardened into something far more precarious. "It doesn't seem like there's a whole lot to recommend it, if I'm honest."

"But you must do your duty."

Mila didn't much care for the way he said that, with that unmistakable edge to it.

Or maybe she didn't like it because it was true. "I must," she agreed.

And when he reached over and tugged her close, so she could sprawl across his body and he could set his mouth at her collarbone, she was grateful.

Because this fire, she understood.

Maybe it was better to stop talking altogether. That the way they devoured each other, rested as briefly as possible, and then went back for more was the only conversation that was necessary.

The next day they stayed too long in bed together in the morning. He rolled her beneath him, stretched out over her, and broke her into very small, very jagged pieces by taking it slow.

So slow there was nothing to do but *stay there*. In that gaze of his, all that lost magic she couldn't bear to lose again. In his arms, where she fit so beautifully. In the sheer, glowing wonder of this thing she couldn't have.

Caius set a pace that made her want to cry, it was so devastating. It was so shattering, so demanding, so intensely *revealing*.

He wrung every bit of emotion from her, brought her close to relief and then kept going, and Mila thought it was possible she would never recover.

That she would never feel clothed again, having let him strip her so naked.

She couldn't tell if she wanted to rejoice in that, or collapse somewhere and sob.

In the shower, before he joined her, she could pretend it wasn't tears on her face. She could prop herself against the wall and ask herself if it was possible for her to die from all this vulnerability.

Or if its curse was she would only feel as if she might.

As if she had.

She was the one who suggested a long walk to get the blood pumping more productively.

"You and I have very different definitions of the word *productive*," Caius told her darkly as they set out.

But she let the mountain do the talking for her. They hiked up one of the trails that led straight away from the back of the house, winding in and out of the woods and then out at last to what Mila believed was the most beautiful view of the kingdom in existence.

It never failed to soothe her. Even now, she could feel it sink into her, the sight of the lakes far below. The green hills. The villages dotted in the far reaches of the valley and then, far off where she couldn't quite see it, the palace she knew waited on the other side.

"It looks so beautiful from up here." They stopped at the bench one of her ancestors had installed a long time ago, because she wasn't the only one who loved this view. "It's beautiful down there, too, but from up here it's like a sparkling little jewel of a country, isn't it?"

Beside her, Caius said nothing.

And she was…less soothed. A bit raw, in fact.

That vulnerability did not seem to be going away.

Instead, it seemed to wind its way deeper and deeper inside of her, like a grief all its own. It made her wish that she was someone else. Anyone else.

It made her wonder, for the first time in all her life, why she was so certain she couldn't be—

But it was nearly October. This high up they were well into the fall already, and gearing up for the long winter ahead. There was a hard, crunchy frost on the ground, and it had already snowed while they'd been here. This high up, the air was bright and crisp, no matter how cold. The mountains ringing the valley were capped and white and more than ready for the colder weather that wasn't hiding its approach any longer.

Yet all she could think about was the man beside her, whose eyes glowed with more and more secrets by the day.

While she felt splayed wide open.

And it was something much deeper than an *ache*.

She thought back to that first night in the house. When she had let him in through the tunnels and he taken her right there on that couch. How when he'd stood up to get rid of his clothes he'd tugged something over his neck, then tucked it away before she could see what it was.

That was what she'd told herself anyway. That she hadn't seen it.

And she couldn't tell, out here in this confronting cold, if it was true that she hadn't laid eyes on it at all and had merely filled in the blanks in her own imagination, or if she really had glimpsed it.

She wasn't sure which one should worry her more, since both seemed tender. Both hurt her, if in different ways.

"You normally wear a chain around your neck, don't you?" she asked.

He let out a sound then. Too low, too ripe with the very shadows she was pretending she didn't see. "Be careful where you tread, Mila. You might find something you can't ignore. And then what will you do?"

She could already feel the different parts of herself fighting for supremacy inside her. It was easy to be *the Queen* in the palace. Just as it was easy to be *just Mila* here. But this close to leaving the September House, both of them were inside her, pushing and pulling.

It was the Queen who sat straighter, lifting her chin. But it was the Mila who had been here this whole month who gazed at him, sure that all that vulnerability was splashed across her face.

"If it was a chain," she said quietly, so very quietly she almost wondered if the wind might steal her words away, "I think I know what normally hangs on it."

He stood up then, thrusting his hands deep into the

pockets of the coat he wore. Like everything else that was his, it had been made by the finest craftsman and tailored to make him look even more effortlessly heroic than he normally did. Maybe it was simply that he stood at the edge of a cliff, his eyes out on the beautiful valley so far below while the cold wind moved through his hair. Maybe it was the distance she could see in his gaze, even though she didn't feel that distance between them, not entirely. Not when her body was still warm from his.

Not yet, something in her warned. *But you will.*

"How do you think I should answer that, Mila?" he asked in a growl, when the misery inside of her seemed to be at a boiling point. "Should I wrap it up into some kind of charming anecdote that we could tell at a boring dinner party? Is that really how you think this should go?"

She felt a kind of panic, then. It was the only way she could describe the sensation that washed over her. It was the only explanation for the way she opened her mouth to speak, but then couldn't find the words.

As if her own hand was clenched tight on her own throat.

He turned back to her then and his eyes were glittering, as bright as the jewel of her country behind him. Brighter, somehow. Because her kingdom was something Mila gazed upon. But Caius's eyes tore into her.

Because he was the only person alive who saw every part of her. Who knew every bit of her.

And she was going to have to give him up.

Again.

"It's my wedding ring," he said in that uncompromising way of his, so at odds with the Caius he showed everyone else in public. But she had no doubt that this was the real him. She knew this version of him. This was the Caius she knew in bed. "But I suspect you know that. I wear it next to my heart. Isn't that a laugh? While I have seen no evidence to suggest that you possess a heart, I still think it might matter if I keep the ring you gave me warm with mine."

She was surprised she didn't topple over, that blow hit her so hard. "That isn't fair."

"I didn't realize that fairness was a part of this." He shook his head. "I rather thought this was an extended torture session. I will admit that I had aspirations for more in the beginning, but that will never happen, will it? You decided who we were to each other long ago. And heaven forfend the great Queen of Las Sosegadas change her mind once it's been made up."

Mila found herself on her feet, her whole body shaking as if she'd just run up the side of the high peak that towered above them. "That is quite a characterization. Insulting, but I assume that's the point. We've had this whole month, Caius. That's something I never thought would be possible. Why can't we take it for what it was?"

"I study the laws of your kingdom," he told her, that glittering thing still in his gaze. It made her shake even more. "It's become something of an obsession of mine. Did you know that the legal spouse of the heir apparent ascends right along with the crown prince or princess on the very day of ascension? A coronation is just icing on the cake."

When she only stared back at him wordlessly, the corner of his mouth twisted into that famous smirk of his. She hadn't seen it in weeks. She hadn't missed it.

"All this time I have already been your king," he said, and his voice was mocking now, with that bright fire in his gaze. Once again, she almost wished he would simply let her burn. "Some countries demote a man when he's married to the sovereign. But not here. This country has always understood who is in charge, as do I." He even sketched a sardonic bow. "Your Majesty."

Not *My Majesty*, she noted. As she was meant to.

And they both knew it was a demotion.

Her throat hurt as if someone really had choked her, but she made herself speak. "So we will end as we began, then? With more threats?"

"I don't want to threaten you," he threw back at her. "But I don't know what to do with the fact that I've been walking around with a wedding ring all these years. I don't know where to put that, Mila. At least before I came here I could pretend to myself that it mattered. That those months mattered, even if nothing came of them. That maybe you were out here living on that memory the same as I was, but you weren't. You won't."

He walked toward her then and for an exhilarating, much-too-telling moment, she thought he would sweep her up into his arms—

But he didn't.

Caius passed her instead and started for the trail back down to the house.

"I never forgot you," Mila said then, foolishly. Recklessly. And when she turned around, she could see that he'd gone still. He'd stopped right there where the trees were about to swallow him whole, though he didn't turn back. "And I still have the ring. I could never throw it away. I keep it on a chain myself and hide it away in a safe space, but I always know where it is." She wanted to stop there, but there was something inside of her that couldn't. That wouldn't. Maybe that was why she felt as if she was choking—maybe it was happening from the inside out. "I always know where you are, Caius."

She saw something go through him, like another gust of wind, though the branches of the trees around him did not move at all. And he looked back over his shoulder, his eyes brilliant there against the backdrop of evergreens.

"I would like to tell you that I would find it an insult if you thought you could call me up once a year to play house with you, *Your Majesty*." And her title was even sharper and more damaging this time. "But I think we both know that's not true. All you need to do is call and I'll come running. Like the little lapdog I suppose I've been to you all along."

He stared at her for another long moment, then he turned and disappeared down the trail. And Mila wanted to run after him, but her knees stopped working. They gave out completely.

She sank down heavily on that bench again, looking out at the kingdom. It was beautiful. Truly it was, but how had she never noticed how *distant* the kingdom seemed from here?

Because that was the point of all of this, she understood as she sat there, feeling far worse than simply *vulnerable* now. Thrones and crowns, rituals and schedules. The demands of aristocracy. The expectations of royalty.

All of it was to create that distance. And to keep that distance, day after day, year after year.

And this time when she cried, her tears turned her cheeks ice cold.

Her body followed, as if he'd never warmed her at all.

She couldn't stand it, so Mila got up and headed down that path herself, but she should have known before she got there that it was too late.

Because Caius was gone.

He'd taken her keys and left them in the door to the tunnels. She stood down there in the dim light, using the thick walls to prop herself up, for a long, long time.

It seemed to take a lifetime to climb back up that spiral stair. To wind around and around without him. To make her way through the cellars and back up into the kitchen that seemed to echo all around her without him.

Everything was too big, too empty. Nothing fit.

Mila decided that she couldn't face staying here for the last little bit of time she had left without him. The remaining time stretched out before her like a prison sentence. What would she do? Just float like a ghost through this house, missing him with every step?

The very idea felt like torture.

So instead, she called for her car and headed back to the palace early.

That meant she had extra time to turn herself back into *the Queen*.

She had to ride down from the September House and put her mask back on. Her armor. She had to root out every soft place, inside and out, and wall it up. She had to wrestle her body back under control, because the way she wanted him was *physical*, and still forbidden.

With every kilometer, she forced herself to remember who she was.

The closer they got to the palace, the more she reminded herself of what her life was, would be, and always had been. Who it was promised to. And what her duty required of her.

Mila is dead once more, she told herself as the car pulled in through the palace gates, and they shut tight behind her. *Long live the Queen.*

She woke up the next morning and surrendered herself to the team of aides who tended to her wardrobe, her skin care, her hair, and everything else concerning her appearance. She let them sigh and cluck over her as they repaired the damage of her month away, muttering over her cuticles and giving her hair what they called *a little gloss.*

Mila presented herself at a private dinner with her mother. Then she sat there while Alondra, seeming not to notice her daughter's mood, launched into her usual recitation of gossip, innuendo, and scathing commentary on everyone and everything Mila had just spent a month forgetting.

Back in her rooms, she could feel that ring in the back of its secret drawer, seeming to pulse like it had its own heart. Like it was beating to its own rhythm. Like it was shooting out light and heat, daring her to keep ignoring it.

But she did.

She got up and went out to her little viewing room instead. She wrapped herself in quilts. She got into her personal supply of wine, and she watched Caius's films.

In chronological order.

They were love stories.

But they were not happy. They were textured and complicated. They were tragic and they were beautiful, and she could see him and her stamped deep into all of them.

And so there, on her favorite couch, alone at last, she cried.

That terrible ache. That impossible grief.

Oh, how she cried.

The next day, she was absurdly grateful to throw herself into her usual roster of meetings and appearances, and only slightly puffy and hungover after her aides were done with her. That night, she went to a dinner where she sat between two equally tedious self-styled *titans of industry*, where all she was required to do was nod sagely and make the odd opaque remark.

And it was fine, she told herself back in her rooms again that night. Once again refusing the siren call of her ring. The ring that *he* wore around his neck. Right there, next to his heart—

But it did her own heart no good to think of it.

It did her no good to think of him at all.

All thinking about him did was keep her up at night, watching the films he'd helped make. The films he'd tinkered with, like a mechanic after all, to create art while all *she* could do was sob.

And then suffer through her aides clucking all around her as they tried to repair the dark circles beneath her eyes the next day.

It did her no good to dream about him, either, because her body refused to understand that he no longer slept there next to her, that long, rangy body of his sprawled out beside hers, with a muscled arm tethering her in place.

A dream just like that woke her on her third night back in the palace.

He wasn't there, she knew that, but it took a while before she could do more than stare at her ceiling. Before the tears stopped sliding down her cheeks to make her ears wet.

And she couldn't fall back asleep.

But it was productive, Mila told herself, because she used the time to plan. Who she would call in her legal office to come talk to her about what had happened long ago in America. Who she would trust with that information, and who she thought would give her the best advice in return. Who, then, she could trust to hunt Caius down and handle him appropriately. So that, whatever else happened, they could legally be separated. As quietly and under the radar as possible.

Something she should have done five years ago.

Mila told herself that the emptiness she felt, that stunning desolation, was nothing more than a quiet certainty that she was on the right path at last.

And that was why she was particularly unprepared for the morning papers.

They were delivered without comment with the breakfast that she always took in her private sitting room. It took her a few more moments than usual to stop staring pointlessly out the window and to unfold the paper on top.

It took longer to stare at that picture on the front page.

Without a shred of comprehension.

Because she recognized the people in that image, but she couldn't let herself understand what she was seeing.

She was slow to put that puzzle together. Possibly because her brain rejected the possibility that she could be looking at such a thing at all.

It was a picture from the Garden Gala. She recognized the hedge towering there in the background. She stared at that hedge for a long while.

A very long while.

But she was quite certain that the only thing anyone else saw were the two people in the center of the photograph. Mila and Caius, doing absolutely nothing untoward.

That was what was almost funny about it. Of all the pictures that could have been taken, this was the most innocent.

They were simply walking side by side, coming out of the maze together.

But it was the *way* they were looking at each other.

She could see that immediately.

It was the way *she* was looking at *him*.

Mila had a look on her face that made three things abundantly clear:

One, that Queen Emilia of Las Sosegadas was a woman, made of flesh and blood and *desire*, not simply a monarch.

Two, that there was something unquestionably electric and charged and even *carnal* between her and Caius. The fact that the evidence was simply *right there* in the way they gazed at each other, even though they were fully clothed, somehow made it all the more blazingly obvious.

And three, the thing she'd been dreading since California had finally happened. The proverbial had hit the fan, with a vengeance.

She had finally caused the scandal she had vowed to her father she wouldn't. She had finally become the very thing she had worked so hard to avoid. She had betrayed herself in every way and worse, she had betrayed everyone else, too.

And now they would all know it.

While Mila knew that it was only the tip of the iceberg.

Caius Candriano, her one and only mistake, was going to take her down after all.

CHAPTER NINE

CAIUS FIRST HEARD the news that he was having a scandalous affair with his wife, a shock to all and sundry as neither all nor sundry had the slightest idea that Mila was his wife, at an arthouse film festival in Manhattan.

He had been working overtime. Not to promote the film he'd worked on that was being shown at the festival, because he felt the film spoke for itself. What needed his fierce concentration and total commitment was returning to his expected form.

Because Caius had never felt less charming or personable in his entire life.

One of his business partners had even commented on it the night before, looking at him askance as they'd circulated a private party in Gramercy Tavern, filled with all manner of gleaming, glittering people who were not Mila.

What happened to you? he had asked.

Nothing ever happens to me, Caius had replied, aware that his smirk was a tad more cutting than necessary for the sort of party that was all about creating connections and behaving like instant intimates, the better to extend their spheres of influence. *Ask anyone.*

In that case, let me talk to people tonight, his partner had said. *Why don't you just let them look at you. They like that.*

He couldn't even work himself into a temper about a comment like that. He'd brought it upon himself. He had lived down to the version of him that people wanted to see for so long that it was now all they saw.

And Caius knew perfectly well that the longer he inhabited that character, the harder it would become to tell the difference between the character and the man he really was, deep inside. He would forget it was possible. He would erase himself, one laconic bit of wit at a time, and this time, he wanted that.

The quicker he could disappear into everyone's favorite guest—the kind who never stayed too long in any one place, could be depended upon to provide the entertainment wherever he went, and never demanded anything of anyone—the better. He had let one person see that there was more to him and it didn't matter. She didn't care—

But he tried to stop himself when he thought things like that. There was no need to be unfair to Mila. Caius knew full well that she cared. The fact that she'd recognized the ring he wore around his neck and still had her ring too ate at him, with sharp little teeth and the occasional claw...but it hadn't mattered.

She could care about him enough to spend a month with him the way she had and it still didn't matter.

He needed to stop letting it matter, too.

He would. He was sure of it.

Any day now.

Caius had been prepared for the flashbulbs when he stepped out of the theater tonight. He was an old hand at paparazzi scrums and usually engaged them in conversation, got them all laughing, and generally did not behave the way some famous people did, as if this necessary evil that kept them a household name was a personal attack upon them.

As an old hand at fending off personal attacks, Caius knew the difference.

It was his habit to laugh off or ignore the suggestive things that paparazzi yelled at him, looking for that reaction shot. Sometimes he planted new stories while refuting the old, simply to entertain himself—because there was only one woman alive, as far as he knew, who did not want her name linked to his.

Tonight, that was the name they were yelling.

He shouldn't have stopped, but he couldn't credit what he was hearing. It took him a few moments of looking around to see if there was another Mila about to accept that this was really happening.

But how?

No one had seen him go in or out of those tunnels. He'd been scrupulously and excessively careful. *He* was not going to be the cause of any of her problems, whether he agreed that they were problems or not.

He did have some pride.

But only where she was concerned.

"How long have you been sleeping with the Queen?" screamed one fool who clearly did not value his life and would never know how close he came to a swift end, there on a street in New York City.

But Caius knew better than to react the way everything in him demanded he react. With prejudice. Because he could not protect Mila without making this worse, whatever this was.

So he laughed, the way he always did. He smirked and posed for pictures with actors and directors and the people like him, who usually preferred to stay behind the scenes but could always smile for a camera.

Still, they kept at him with *The Queen, Queen Emilia, weren't you there all* summer and the like.

"Come on, Caius," a paparazzo he'd known for years complained as his car pulled up. "You need to tell us what's up between you and your queen."

"I would describe every woman I've ever laid eyes on as a queen," he replied smoothly, and with a grin. "You'll have to be more specific."

And he kept that grin on his face as the car pulled away, out of the pack of them, pounding on windows and shouting his name. He kept it there until it was clear that there were no paparazzi on motorcycles following them, as sometimes happened.

Then, when he was certain no one was looking at him, he let his face...do what it liked. Whatever it liked. He didn't even look at his reflection in the window to see what that was. Instead, there in the safety of his car on the way to a private airfield outside New York City, he pulled out his mobile and stared at it in frustration.

Because the sad truth was that he couldn't do the thing that every cell and atom in his body wanted him to do. Reality reasserted itself like a slap upside the head.

He could not simply *call* Mila.

There was no reaching the Queen of Las Sosegadas on a whim—that was why he'd gone to all of that trouble to find his way into her palace by other means.

The mobile phone she'd used in America had long

since been disconnected and redistributed. He had checked. Years ago.

Though he checked again now, just to be sure, and hung up when he got the voicemail of a surly-sounding American man with an accent he couldn't quite place.

He had always known that he could reach her in person if he needed to. That was the story that he'd told himself for years, and he'd proven it in August. He could do it again now. It was easy enough to direct his plane to fly him back to Las Sosegadas. This time, he wouldn't need any kind of intermediary to bring him along. He was well enough known there now that he was certain he could show up, like an honored guest, with or without an invitation.

But what he couldn't do was call Mila himself and ask her if she was okay.

He knew she wasn't. There was no way they were coming after him and not her. She had to think her world was crumbling, and here he was, incapable of doing a single, solitary thing to help.

It was hard not to think that his mother had been right about him all along.

And that maybe he should have listened.

That wasn't even a round of self-pity. The person he was sorry for in this was Mila. He should have known that going anywhere near her would taint her with the same slime that he only got away with because he'd always acted as if he was in on the joke. The joke being him.

Now she had to pay for that joke, and he couldn't so much as text her that he was sorry for it.

The grief of that sat heavy on him for the rest of the drive, and it only got heavier. Once his plane was in the air, headed for his meetings in Hollywood instead of a tiny kingdom across the Atlantic where he was quite certain Mila did not wish to see him, he opened up his laptop and started looking for the story. Whatever it was.

It didn't take long to find.

There was one tabloid article after the next, videos from every outfit he'd ever heard of, and a great many he hadn't. Not to mention the user-generated content, which was far more scathing.

All of them using that single photograph to springboard into speculation.

He could remember walking out of the maze with her, but he'd been so certain they were discreet. It was something like an out-of-body experience to look at photographic evidence of the last five years of his life when for so long, the truth about the two of them had been something he'd thought only he even remembered. It was locked away, down deep, and had remained there until the summer. And even then, he hadn't really imagined that they would ever stand in the light. Not where anyone could see them.

But here was a picture that told every truth he never had.

Here it was, displayed in color for everyone to see.

He had to sit with that for some time. Because for all his brave words to Mila in the September House and up on that trail with the view of that valley she would always love best, the truth was that he'd never believed that she would ever truly acknowledge him. He had never believed that anyone would ever know that they had this kind of connection.

And it was hard to reconcile how resigned he'd become to that with...*this*.

He felt inside out.

With a sense of impending doom, he switched on his mobile.

A queen, Caius? came a message from his sister, almost at once. I should have known there was a reason you were suddenly so interested in that random kingdom.

Thank you, Lavinia, he messaged back. Your support at this time will not be forgotten.

It makes no sense unless there are ulterior motives, she wrote. But I know you always have more than enough of those!

Then she added a spate of emojis that he supposed were meant to indicate that this was a lighthearted response from her.

And this was his sister. The only member of his family he actually liked.

Caius sat back in his seat, staring out at the patchwork quilt of the American continent far below, wondering why his chest felt tight, his heart was pounding, and sitting still felt more and more oppressive by the moment.

Then he made it worse. He started looking at the comments.

And by the time his plane landed in California, he had saturated himself with more dire opinions about himself than anyone should. Or could, really, without going a bit mad.

He had meetings to attend, but when he got into his

car, he didn't drive toward the studios. He drove for the ocean instead, feeling that same tightness in his chest. That same driving need to *do something.*

When he got to the water, he turned right on the Pacific Coast Highway and headed north.

Except he didn't stop in Malibu, where he lived when he was in town. He kept right on going.

It was like something was chasing him, but he was pretty sure that the biggest threat to him was sitting right here in the car, inhabiting his body.

Everyone thought so.

Literally everyone. His so-called defenders, if such they could be called, thought he was attractive. That was it.

He had read hundreds upon hundreds of comments about himself and Mila on too many sites to count, and had not encountered anything he could construe as positive, save that.

Caius had expected to be called names. He could even have guessed the names, without having to look. He'd made those kinds of names the basis of this character he'd been playing all this time.

Given that the Countess had often called him a great many of these names herself, they didn't really have the power to bother him anymore. He had cultivated his own image, after all. He wanted people to think of him as entirely insubstantial, so they could never be disappointed by him. And would never expect anything of him, either.

He was, as one scathing commenter had put it, *A man whore of epic proportions whose only talent seems to be*

showing up next to cameras where other, more talented
people happen to be standing.

That was all fair enough. But the more he read about
people's disappointment in Mila for lowering herself to
the likes of him, the less *fair enough* it felt.

Because it wasn't simply that they didn't like him looking at everyone's favorite queen. And they really, really
didn't.

It was more than that. Her proximity to him in one
photo made her a disappointment. It made the entire
world question who Mila really was.

Caius could not think of a greater torture, and there
was nothing he could *do* about it. There was nothing he
could do at all.

The last time he had felt this powerless, he had been
a child in his mother's neglectful care. He had vowed
he would never let this happen again, and now it was
not only happening in real time—it was happening to
Mila, too.

His phone kept ringing and ringing, but he didn't answer. When he drove through Santa Barbara, he chucked
it in a bin and bought himself a fresh new phone that no
one could reach.

And then he drove. Low and fast, in a sleek little sports
car that made him even more of the flaming cliché that
he was. An embarrassment of such epic proportions that
a single photograph of him with an otherwise beloved
queen meant that there were calls for her to abdicate, so
thoroughly had she stained the crown.

It wasn't his history splashed all over the papers that

bothered him. He knew how much of it was made-up. It was the one they'd created for her.

As if he was so infectious—*A virulent strain of cringe*, one young girl said in a widely circulated video—that it was obvious she had to be some kind of liar and deceiver to have concealed this kind of thing.

He called only his assistant, to update her on his new mobile number and the fact he was not available, at all, to anyone.

Though he knew that if Mila really wanted to reach him, she could.

But she didn't.

Mile after mile, she didn't.

And that was why, in a tiny little town up north, he bought the supplies he needed, stashed his flashy car, and hiked his way back to the Pacific Coast Trail.

Because everything in him rejected the character he was reading about in the papers, because he knew that wasn't him.

But all he could think was that this was how Mila saw him.

This was the reason she'd walked away from him five years ago—and even now, after their month together, assumed without any question whatsoever that the only logical thing to do was separate again.

It hadn't even been a discussion.

And now he knew why.

He should have expected it.

The truth was that Caius had already been tired of the games he played. Reading about them was even worse.

Cataloging the entire series of a lifetime of misdeeds made him feel sick.

It didn't even matter that more than half of the suppositions about him weren't true.

This was who people thought he was. Like his mother, they might have valued him for his proximity to fame, but they didn't value *him*.

He had turned into the Countess, he realized now. Entirely without meaning to, he had become a parody of himself. Just as she was.

And he knew that if he said this to Lavinia, she would encourage him to go talk to their mother because she still believed that there was some sort of conversation they could have that would fix their childhood. Caius knew better. He knew who his mother was. And better yet, he knew that the Countess would never see what she'd done to them. She would never admit that she had been in the wrong.

As far as he knew, she never had.

And showing her that they cared would be a weakness she would try to exploit.

There was no point talking to his father, either, because while the man might eke out an apology, all he really cared about were his highs. Caius had never been sure if his father remembered that he existed between visits.

All he was, to anyone and everyone, was that character he played.

Smirky, salacious, dismissible.

DISGUSTING! more than one commenter had typed. In all caps.

With every step, he thought about the fact that this

was who Mila believed he was. This was the man she thought she'd married.

This grasping, empty, cardboard cutout of a creature, dead behind the eyes and good for absolutely nothing but the clout the entirety of the internet was certain he had not earned.

Hell, he agreed.

But for a short while, he had been a man that he was proud of. In a lifetime of make-believe, playing characters to manipulate people and situations to survive or to shine, there had been one stretch of time when he had only been himself.

That was what he hadn't forgiven her for leaving.

Their marriage was a symbol of that. The ring hanging there around his neck, still and always, reminded him with every step. It wasn't just that she had promised to love him forever. It was that when she had made that promise, she'd meant *him*.

The real him.

Those months had been extraordinary. No one had known who Caius was, and therefore, he'd had no influence whatsoever. There'd been no performance to put on. They had all simply…walked. And hiked. Camped and slept, then hiked on some more.

He and Mila had gotten to know each other as *people*.

Nothing more, nothing less. They had never spoken about their lives off the trail, not for a long while. Not until they'd left their guided hike and gone off on their own.

Caius had liked that version of himself.

Mila had fallen in love with him.

And this last month in her September House had been a reintroduction to that man. It had been a sharp reminder of why he'd long ago decided he hated what he'd become—the reason he'd gone on that long hike in the first place.

He hadn't wanted to return to that in the five years since, but he couldn't put the fact he had on Mila. That was what he'd done to survive the loss of her. He'd gone out and frolicked in that spotlight, acting like it had never happened and he was incapable of caring either way if it had, and this was what he'd won.

He'd made himself what he hated.

He'd become exactly what his mother said he was.

So Caius took himself back to the woods. Step by step, he walked away from the spotlight and the speculation and that goddamned smirk, and he vowed that he would walk until he found himself again.

Until he became that man that he admired once again.

That man that Mila had loved before she'd become *the Queen*. The man he knew she didn't believe he was now.

But he was. He wanted to be, for her, but mostly so he could find a way not to loathe the very sight of himself.

He vowed that he would walk until he found that man again, no matter how long it took.

And when he did, he would go back to Las Sosegadas and he would figure out how he could save the love of his life.

From himself.

For good.

CHAPTER TEN

THE PALACE WENT into crisis mode and stayed there. Teams of outward-facing staff huddled in the corridors, whispering to each other about *the situation*. The crisis management battalion took over all palace communications. There was a sudden influx of very serious people having very intense meetings, throwing around buzzwords and PR phrases.

Mila sailed about pretending she didn't notice. Or perhaps that it was all *beneath* her notice, which was not quite the same thing.

But when Carliz arrived, a few days after that picture hit the papers when it was clear that the scandal was not going away on its own, she was grateful.

More than grateful, even though her sister had left her baby, not quite a year old, at home.

"We don't get to see him enough," Mila chided her as she greeted her with a hug.

"This visit is not about him," Carliz replied in a fierce whisper, hugging her back.

Hard.

"How can you travel without your child?" Alondra asked that first night as they gathered for a private family dinner. "I know I never did. Not when you were both so small."

"You and Father did a round of extended state visits all over Europe the year I was born," Mila said mildly. "And again when Carliz was eighteen months." She smiled when her mother glared at her. "I've had to study the history of state visits, of course. What worked, what didn't, goals versus outcomes, the usual."

Carliz, on the other hand, smiled in that way she had that was precisely calculated to drive the Queen Mother mad. She had cultivated that smile, Mila knew. She had spent years working on it.

She had once told Mila, *If you can't be the heir, be annoying instead.*

"It is actually not necessary to live forever tethered to a child," she told Alondra languidly now. Deliberately giving the impression that she let her infant fend for himself on his Mediterranean island home when Mila knew she did no such thing. "As you apparently decided yourself in your day, Mother. I always knew we were secretly alike."

Alondra did not care for that comparison, as the way she gripped her utensils made clear. "I suppose that husband of yours can afford a fleet of excellent nannies," she murmured, quite as if her two daughters had not spent large swathes of their young lives in the care of staff.

"We do have some help," Carliz agreed. Serenely. "Though Valentino prefers to care for Centuri himself, whenever possible."

The Queen Mother blinked. "How singular that he is willing to babysit."

"He is not singular, he is a parent," Carliz replied, and

she no longer sounded languid. Though she was still *sparkling* at her mother. "A *parent* cannot *babysit* their own child. By definition."

"You will argue about anything, Carliz," Alondra said, as if this conversation had already exhausted her. "My goodness."

"If you're asking if the man I married, the love of my life, is a good father? Yes, he is. And lo, just as he is perfectly capable of making empires out of all he surveys, he can also take care of *our baby*. Sometimes he does so when I am right there."

Alondra did not respond to that. Mila glanced at her sister. "I'm not sure she can take that on board."

"I'm sure you're both very droll," their mother replied. "I am certain there must be *someone* who would find your humor entertaining."

That person, she made clear with her tone, was not Alondra. She started talking of incidental things, deftly leading them all away from powder keg topics like anything involving Carliz's husband and Mila's *scandalous photo*.

So mostly she discussed the plans for the holiday decorations in the palace.

Later that night, when Carliz slipped into her bedchamber the way she had that summer she'd lived here—and every single night when they'd been girls—Mila felt herself relax for the first time since she'd walked down that trail behind the September House and found Caius gone.

Just…gone.

The crisis team had suggested he'd planted that photo, but she'd shut them down.

I am more likely to have planted that photo than Caius Candriano could ever be, she had said dismissively. *For one thing, he does not* plant *photos. He doesn't have to.*

But she had almost wished she could believe that he had. It would have felt like a message. It would have felt like *something.*

"So," Carliz said breezily, taking her place on the chaise. "It sounds like we have some catching up to do, no?"

Mila blew out a breath, and decided, what the hell, she wasn't going to brush out her hair. *Such a rebel*, she told herself sardonically. What she did instead was crawl into her pajamas and then curl up on the chaise with her sister.

Wine in hand.

She'd poured a glass for herself, and handed a glass to Carliz, who made an exaggerated face of shock.

"I see it's serious," she murmured.

Mila smiled. She took a gulp. And then she opened up her mouth and told the truth about her life.

She spared no detail. How magical it had felt to escape the palace all those years ago, and how she delighted in the so many ordinary things that her position had always kept her from experiencing. Being jostled on a street. Being spoken to sharply by a stranger. Being made to wait in a queue with everyone else.

Carliz was shaking her head. "I would not have thought that you would get off on people being rude to you, Mila."

"It wasn't the rudeness that was delightful." Mila shook her head ruefully. "I was being treated the same way as everyone else. Not like a precious heirloom that has to be carefully transported from place to place as if a loud noise might tarnish me forever. I liked it. It was novel and exciting."

"I personally prefer an upgrade," her sister drawled. "But to each her own."

Mila held her wine in her hands, frowned at it, and kept going. She told Carliz about her decision to do that long hike. The lure of going out into the woods and up into the mountains, away from everything that she was and would become. She told Carliz how hard it had been at first and how she'd second-guessed her choice—but hadn't wanted to prove that she deserved the cotton wool treatment by changing her mind. How she had made herself keep going, and had kept her complaints to herself, until the day she'd found she'd hit her stride.

"I didn't know that was an actual thing," her sister said.

Mila nodded. "From horse racing, apparently."

"Well," Carliz said over her wineglass, her eyes sparkling, "you have always been quite the thoroughbred, haven't you?"

And then, because it was time, Mila told her what it had been like to meet Caius for the first time. How it had happened like the weather. One moment she had been contemplating her brand-new hiking boots and questioning her skills and desire to do this thing and the next he'd been there, drowning out the universe.

He had been like a shooting star. She had been dazzled.

And they hadn't exchanged a word for days.

"You must have known who he was," Carliz said, her eyes wide. "Everyone knows who he is."

"Of course I knew who he was. I only pretend to live under a rock."

Her sister laughed at that and waved her hand at the palace all around them. "At least it's a pretty rock. Let's brush past how you never told me any of this, shall we? Tell me everything."

And Mila felt guilty about the fact she'd hoarded all of this to herself, so she spared no detail. How they had gotten to know each other in a way that she knew she would never get to know someone else. Because the situation could never be repeated. She would never have that kind of time or space or anonymity. She would never be on her own again, not like that.

Back then she hadn't even been the Queen.

"He knows you in a way that no one else can," her sister said, with a certain wise look that told Mila things she wouldn't ask about her sister's marriage. "That's magic."

"There was something about being so far away from everything," Mila agreed. "I'm not sure that it could be replicated. Even if I wasn't who I am. Because he's who he is, too. And there was such an intensity to it—as if that kind of anonymity was sacred. Maybe it was simply that both of us were there for the same reasons. To be outside our skins. To find out who we were when no one knew who we were supposed to be."

Maybe her eyes got the slightest bit misty as she said that, too.

Carliz pressed her shoulder to Mila's. It felt like solidarity.

"You must hate me for not telling you," Mila said in a rush.

"Mila." Carliz shook her head with a certain gleam in her gaze. She reached past Mila and refilled her wineglass, then topped up Mila's, too. "Remember all those tabloid stories about Valentino and me?" When Mila only nodded, remembering that she'd thought back then that her sister would be the only not-quite-scandal of her reign, Carliz shrugged. "I planted them."

Mila gaped at her. But queens did not *gape*, so she snapped her mouth shut. "What? What do you mean?"

"It wasn't true," Carliz said. "We didn't have a relationship. We didn't *continue* our affair the night that he was supposed to marry, we started it that night. He would have ended that, too, but I got pregnant. That's the dirty truth. Do you hate me for not telling you?"

"As your sister, yes," Mila said, her head spinning, and not entirely from the wine. "As your queen? I'm delighted you didn't let me know that any of that was happening. My God."

"That's what happens when you fall in love," Carliz said in the same soft tone. "All of the noise, all of the trouble, it all disappears. And all that matters is the bright light that shines between you two."

"I did more than find it," Mila told her then, though her throat constricted as she spoke, so used was she to keeping this secret. "I married it."

And it took some while after that to settle back down. Because first there was the squealing. And enough shrieking that she had to assure the guards that all was well.

But Mila couldn't really blame her sister for this reaction.

It was actually…comforting. Validating, somehow. Because it meant that it was the big deal—the *huge deal*—that she had always thought it was.

She couldn't beat herself up for hiding this if her sister, who was usually impossible to rile up like this, was having this kind of reaction. Imagine what her mother would have done five years ago?

"I'm sorry." Carliz wiped at her eyes, still shaking her head. "You were far more composed when I told you my tiny little secret. But I can't believe you managed to hide something like this not just from me, but from the whole world. *For years.*"

"I kept thinking it would come out. I kept thinking that I would wake up one day to find that he'd told the entire planet." She blew out a breath. "But he never did."

They both sat with that for a while.

"What are you going to do?" Carliz asked. "I know you were leaning in the direction of being the apparently not at all virgin queen for the rest of your life, but sooner or later...?"

She didn't have to finish that thought. They both knew what family they were in, and what each of their responsibilities were.

"There is no question about what I will have to do." Mila couldn't look at her sister anymore. She stared at the wineglass instead. Ferociously. "I must do my best to provide the kingdom with an heir. And, really, I was always meant to find the perfect king while I was at it. They have a list of the attributes this paragon should possess. He should be quiet and self-effacing. He should be weighted down by his own pedigree, someone who fades into the shadows while standing in plain sight, so as never to detract from my sovereign magnificence, blah blah blah."

Carliz reached over and hooked her hand over Mila's

wrist. She squeezed until Mila found her gaze. It was too bright. Searing. "What's the point of being *the Queen* if it means a life of lonely misery? Isn't that just a nun? That's not your job description, Mila."

"Maybe," Mila agreed, astounded both that her voice was noticeably rough and that she did not feel compelled to hide it. "But what can I do?"

Carliz laughed at that. "Have you confused yourself for someone else?" When Mila only looked at her without comprehension, she sighed. "What if you just said, *Guess what? I love him. And I'm the Queen, so I'll love who I want*. What could they do?"

And it was easy, in a happy red wine flush and the joy of her sister's presence, to tell herself that was a good idea. That not only was it a good idea, but that it would be easy. A wave of the nearest scepter. A royal inclination of her queenly head.

But when she woke up in the morning her queenly head ached, her royal heart was sore, and she had to sit in on another endless meeting about *approaches* to the scandal. She had to nod sagely at the discussions of crisis management, sinking relatability scores, and *messaging*.

None of this was new. Only the intensity of these discussions were different.

And maybe she had changed—or it was the hangover that lingered at her temples—but it sat heavily on her that what they were talking about was her *life*. This roomful of people, mostly men in dark suits, was carrying on a rather heated *debate* about how she should proceed to live out what no one directly called her ruined life. Though it was heavily implied that it would all be picking up pieces and hoping for divine intervention from here.

All it took was one photograph that was in no way salacious to overshadow her otherwise entirely spotless reign, and the exemplary life of excellent behavior that had preceded it.

What she needed to do, she thought when the interminable meeting was over, was not listen to these crisis counselors. They were worried about a photograph and internet chatter. They didn't even know the real crisis, which was that she had given her heart away five years ago. Then frozen herself solid when her father died.

Only Caius had come back, and nothing in her was frozen any longer, and she was finding it hard to remember why she had decided that the only way she could exist was to disappear into her role. Become a statue of *the Queen*, like the one that would no doubt stand somewhere in this palace one day, instead of a person.

She knew she needed to find that statue again, no matter what she could remember. It was past time to pull herself together. Get her armor back in place. Figure out how to wear *the Queen* like a mask again, but this time, never take it off again.

But first she enjoyed every moment of her sister's company. They saw old friends, like Paula. They spent as much time as they could alone together. Carliz had her speak to Valentino on the video calls she made and took to check in with him and the baby, so that at the end of the week or so she stayed, Mila felt as if she knew her brother-in-law in a way she would not have otherwise.

Better still, she had a sense of her sister's relationship

with her husband, which, after all the studied formality in their family, felt like fresh air.

And on the last night of Carliz's visit, they once again indulged in a private family dinner. Because tradition always won out, no matter how many times the three of them had proved that sharing meals was a fraught exercise.

"I hope," Carliz said over the fish course, with a sparkle in her gaze that told Mila she was about to cause trouble, "that if we can agree on nothing else, we can agree on this. At least everyone can understand why even a saint like Mila would trade in her reputation for the likes of Caius Candriano. It doesn't need an explanation. Pictures of him exist."

"Carliz." Alondra looked appalled. *"Really."*

Mila tried to look stern and queenly, but heard herself laughing instead. That did not make her mother any happier.

"The pair of you go too far." She pushed back from the table. "This can only embarrass the crown, no matter what the man looks like. *I* was never taken in. And I'm surprised that you, Mila, would allow yourself to stray so far from the path your father laid out for you."

"So you can call her Mila after all," Carliz murmured, eyeing Alondra. "But never affectionately. Only to chastise her. No wonder she had to keep a secret or two."

Mila should have stepped in then. She should have ended this with one of her usual serene asides that were actually commands…but she didn't.

"You don't understand, Carliz," their mother replied icily. "Thrones and crowns and the family legacy do not concern you. You've made that clear enough."

"By not marrying some terrible, boring man the palace selected for me?" Carliz laughed. "Guilty as charged."

Mila realized too late that this was a wound that needed cauterizing. "Mother, please sit down. It's Carliz's last night."

But there was no stopping her mother tonight. "You promised your father that you would never embarrass him, and what do you think this is? How do you think he would react to your involvement in such a tawdry scandal?"

"Returning to reality, it could be significantly more tawdry," Carliz pointed out. "All they were doing was looking at each other. Everything else is base speculation."

"If he was any kind of man, he would have immediately countered the situation. Instead, what is that clip that keeps running again and again?" The Queen Mother made an aggrieved noise. "Speaking of all his bedmates and calling them queens. It's disrespectful. It's beneath your station, Mila. I thought you understood that."

Mila stared down at her plate, biting her tongue. Something she was not sure she had ever literally done before, and it hurt. Maybe that was good. She was tired of her heart hurting, so might as well spread the wealth.

Carliz did not hold back, however. She fixed their mother with a direct, unflinching gaze. "Which sovereign's station are we concerned about here? Mila's? Or Father's? Because they're not the same person."

"Your father would never cause a scandal," Alondra belted out. "I can tell you that."

"I can't take this seriously." Mila didn't know she meant to speak.

Or maybe she did. Maybe something else inside of her was taking control at last. It wasn't that mask. It wasn't *the Queen*. But that was the trouble with all of this, wasn't it?

She was tired of *the Queen*.

She liked the woman she was when she was alone with Caius. She always had. She hadn't thought that she could ever access that woman again—but it had been easy. All had taken was the way he looked at her.

All it had taken was seeing herself in his eyes.

Maybe she was having trouble remembering why it was she couldn't have that all the time. Why it was the end of the world to even want it.

She realized that her sister and her mother were gazing at her, waiting for her to explain herself.

That meant she had to try. She sighed. "I question why this is the greatest scandal of all time. It seems a bit unfair, if I'm honest. I have been a literal paragon of virtue my whole life. There are very few members of royal families who can say the same. And there's nothing untoward about that photo. We could have been discussing the weather."

"It's because you're such a paragon," Carliz said quietly. "People are so desperate for you to have a secret, dissipated life—one that makes them feel better about not living up to your standard of untouchable virtue—that they've created one out of a single photograph."

"People are horrified at what it means," Alondra argued. "That a woman whose passion has always been her duty to have her head turned by such a…wastrel of a man." She made a face as if she was disgusted at the very thought. Or as if it was Caius himself who revolted her, and something in Mila…chilled straight down to the bone. "It's beyond comprehension."

"You can comment on my behavior, Mother," Mila said quietly. And very, very coldly. "But I am not interested in your opinions on his."

"Hear, hear," Carliz muttered.

But Alondra waved a hand at her. "And now this. You are the Queen of Las Sosegadas, Mila. It is a little bit late to start acting out one of your sister's teen rebellions."

Carliz made a sound at that. But Mila found herself looking at her mother in a way she normally reserved for uppity ministers.

"Excuse me?" she asked, very quietly.

The Queen straight through.

But her mother's face was flushed with emotion. "I don't understand how you could let him do this to you," she cried. And when Mila started to speak, she didn't stop, which, from Alondra, was akin to flipping over the table. "Duty is everything. Duty is all that matters or ever will. It is the *only* thing you will be remembered for. Because we, your family members, will pass on and no one will know who you were behind closed doors. They will speculate. They will imagine as they please. But all they will *truly* know is whether or not their Queen did her duty. Duty is all that's left."

As she stood there, her face crumpled, just slightly. Just enough. But she caught herself before she could dissolve entirely.

Then, as her daughters watched, she pulled herself together in a manner Mila knew all too well. Because she did it herself. That deep breath. The straightening of the shoulders. And then, at the end, the determined rise of her chin.

"Love dies," her mother told her, in that rain-soaked voice she would never acknowledge. She had never cried in public. Mila and Carliz had assumed she'd cried in her bedchamber, but they had never seen it. If she asked about it now, Mila knew Alondra would say that was the tribute she was paying the late king. "All that remains is your legacy, and that only comes from your dedication to your duty."

Mila felt winded. She and her mother stared at each other across the table, and Alondra's chest might have been heaving as if she'd just run uphill, but her gaze was clear.

"And that is why, my favorite queen, only sister, and very best friend on this earth," Carliz said quietly, from where she was still lounging in her chair, "you must love while you can. As hard as you can. For as long as you can."

She shook her head when Alondra started to speak, and harder when Mila opened her mouth to do the same. "Yes, even you. Especially you."

Carliz looked at her mother, then at her sister, with compassion and something else in her gaze. Something like pity, Mila thought, though that stung more than she wanted to admit.

But then, Carliz was the only member of the family who had picked her own path. She had gone to university outside the kingdom, the first in the line to ever do such a thing. She had not toed the family line, married a palace-vetted candidate, and quietly produced children to bulk out the blood claim to the throne. She had declined the offer to take royal engagements, because she wanted the chance at a different life.

And Mila couldn't help noticing that she was the happiest person in this room.

Possibly in the whole of the palace.

"You have to make the duty worth doing by living a life worth claiming," Carliz told them both, with a kind of wisdom in her voice that made everything inside of Mila seem to ache. In rejection, she tried to tell herself. But she thought it was likely recognition. Her sister seemed to pin her with that gaze of hers. "Or what is the point of living at all?"

CHAPTER ELEVEN

CAIUS WALKED OFF the trail some two weeks later.

It turned out that he wasn't quite the callow younger man he'd been the first time, unable to imagine a life or a world that wasn't the same endless merry-go-round of notoriety and exposure. He hadn't needed months to come to his senses.

"Besides," he muttered to himself as he took the last long walk back into the nearest town. "The company this time was severely lacking."

With a couple of phone calls, he arranged everything he'd decided he needed, out there where his clarity had descended when he was finally alone in the wilderness. No comments section. No paparazzi. No one clamoring for his money or his notice or what he could do to *raise their profile.*

He could breathe again, and getting that back made it clear he'd lost it sometime over the past five years.

Maybe the moment Mila had walked away from him.

But out on the trail with only the sky and the earth, the weather and his heartbeat, he could think through the implications of everything. Every single thing that had happened to the pair of them since they'd met. He could see it all clearly. He could cut through not only the excuses he'd made to himself, but his own deeply ingrained, knee-jerk reaction to be only what was expected when people looked at him and nothing more.

How, the stars above had seemed to say, *can you ask for a change you are not willing to give?*

He had turned that over and over inside of him.

One day it had rained. On and on, relentlessly, and yet he hadn't quit. He hadn't even considered it. Caius had marched grimly on, determined to keep going until he found what he was looking for. That unidentifiable thing inside him that would indicate it was time to leave the wilderness and face the world.

Why, the mountains had seemed to whisper, *can you commit yourself so wholeheartedly to a* hike *no matter the adversity you face, when you accepted the end of your marriage without so much as a whimper?*

Caius had walked until he'd found the answers.

He'd walked into that last town, met his assistant, and drove the rest of the way to that same hotel that he and Mila had stayed in so long ago. Once there, he cleaned himself up. He restored himself to form, though part of him would miss the ease of the wilderness. The beard that grew without his notice.

The lack of any reflective surfaces.

He thought a lot about that, too.

And he decided that he could not let himself go so long again. That the moment he suspected the real him was retreating from his own gaze in the mirror, that was his call to take himself off until he found himself again. Until he remembered that he wasn't who they said he was. That was a role he played, and anytime he liked, he could step off that stage.

He'd had ample time to think through all those parts of his childhood that had led directly to where he was now. Caius knew full well each and every incident that had created the empty vessel he'd made himself into.

And he'd worked so hard on the particular quality of that emptiness, was the thing. He'd learned how to bend any room to his will from a master. His mother was a pro at it—it was only those who knew her who truly saw her for what she was. But her charm, used only on strangers, was a useful tool. It had helped him immensely in his business dealings, which was likely one of the reasons all the rest of his half siblings were in awe of him. Because they relied on his mother's fickle regard to fund their lives.

It had been good to walk until he remembered that he'd chosen the tools that he would take from her. That he had vowed when he was sixteen that he would never rely on her for anything material again. And he hadn't.

Caius had developed his pretty-as-a-picture, delightful, and profoundly empty persona instead.

He had used it well.

And now it was time to see if he could fashion a different role altogether.

Because he didn't need to return to this hotel room to remember all the things that Mila had said to him here on that last day. In their last hour. How she had laid out the gulf between them calmly, quietly, and had explained that the palace would never stand for it.

I am so young, she had said, though she had not seemed the least bit young then. Her gaze had been old and wise and sad. *They will question my judgment, and once they start down that road, there's little hope of coming back. I owe my father's legacy more than that.*

We all owe our parents' legacies something, he had thrown back at her, reeling from the shock of what was happening. The impossibility that he had found her, the own person in the whole world who looked at him and saw all him. And the agony that he could not keep her. *Most of us discuss these issues in therapy, Mila.*

Her face had changed then. It had grown sadder. Kinder.

Everything is a game to you, she had said, and it had devastated him. *That is what you know of the world, and you play these games well. But what I do can never be seen as a game, because that would make me nothing but a toy. And should that happen, how can I rule?*

Nothing that has happened between us is a game, he had gritted out.

But she had only gazed back at him in that same earnest, sorrowful way. *Caius. I am a pr—* Her voice had caught then, but she'd gone on anyway, with a certain resoluteness that he had thought might kill him. *I am a queen. It's time we stopped playing games of hide-and-seek, don't you think?*

"I do think," he said now, to the bathroom mirror.

He had not thought so then. There had been a part of him that insisted, always, that he had dispensed entirely with games and that she had treated him cruelly.

Now, all he could think of was the fact she had waited for him to come out of the shower when she could easily have left without a word. She could have had one of her staff deliver the news. She had not had to stand there and talk it through, no matter how upset they both got.

He couldn't understand how he'd been too busy thinking of his own bruised heart, because she was walking away from him. When her father had just died. And she was going home not just to bury a man she'd loved and admired, but to take his place.

"You," he told his reflection, "did not deserve her kindness."

In fact, he had not forgiven her for it. Until now.

When he had set himself to rights, he crashed out on the hotel room bed, thinking that he would get a good night's sleep in an actual bed. Tomorrow was soon enough to set his various plans in motion. Tomorrow was the earliest he would even consider dipping a toe back into the life he'd walked away from again.

Another thing that sat heavy on him was how easy it was to do that. To simply walk away. This was the second time he'd done it so completely, but then, he'd been doing it all his life. Whenever something got too bothersome or too intense, the Countess had moved them on. He'd adopted the same habits, though he'd told himself it'd been for different reasons.

He couldn't settle. He was easily bored. He was always looking for the next great thing, and that meant a lot of moving...

At a certain point, a man had to face himself. He had to stop running away and decide, at last, who he was going to be. The geographic cure was a lie.

He clicked on the television, flipping absently through the channels, though it was almost offensive to try to focus on flashing lights and gaudy colors after the serene stillness of the outdoors.

Though when he saw her face, on the screen and not only in his head, he stopped.

And then sat up, because it turned out that Queen Emilia had decided to make a speech.

He had plugged in his long-dead mobile when he'd entered the room, and he switched it on as the news desk of the channel he'd landed on talked about the possible reasons for the Queen to speak.

He found an avalanche of messages forwarded on by his assistant, but none from her.

Still, something in him felt called to attention as the screen changed.

And she was there.

Right there.

"It is not the habit of this palace to comment on the scandals of the day," Mila said in her calm, serene way, looking directly into the camera. She was sitting quite smartly in a chair in what was clearly the palace, that made her look as if she was seated on a throne without actually reverting to the Las Sosegadan throne itself. The light that fell upon her was splendid, but then again, so was she. Her dark hair gleamed, pulled back into an intricately braided bun at the nape of her neck. She was dressed, as ever, to perfection. He wondered if he was the only man alive who could see the passion that glittered in her gray gaze. He wondered if she knew that he could still see *her*. "But I find that I cannot remain quiet."

Halfway across the planet, Caius sat up straighter.

"I have been made aware of the photograph that so many have taken such liberties in dissecting," said *the Queen*, with more than a hint of frost to her tone. "I quite understand that there's an extreme level of interest in me and great speculation about my life, and I accept that. My personal wishes must always be held up against the best interests of the kingdom, and I can only hope that these things align. And that I always act with the country foremost in my thoughts."

She did not seem to move, but her gray eyes cooled considerably. "What I cannot countenance is the savaging of a man who did nothing to deserve these attacks but walk beside me at a garden party."

Everything in Caius went still. As quiet as if he was standing at the top of a mountain, with nothing but a sea of forever stretching out on all sides.

"This is a man who graces the covers of magazines with regularity, because he is a household name, almost entirely because of the genetic gifts that make him so pleasant to look upon. He can also boast a direct, hereditary link to almost every noble house in Europe," Mila was saying. "He is a favorite of style-setters and old guard watchdogs alike, because he is not merely pedigreed, he is kind. He is amusing, but never at the expense of others. By any standard, he would be a perfectly appropriate escort for any woman, including a queen. Indeed, the only reason he is held to be a disgrace, as I read to my surprise this morning, is because of the speculation in the gutter press about how he spends his personal time."

Caius felt almost…outside his own body. As if he was looking down from far, far away. As if perhaps he had actually died, hearing these words he had not understood until now that he had waited his whole life to hear.

The woman he loved, defending him. And not simply

defending him, but painting a picture of him so that all the world would see him that way.

The way she did.

He found himself gripping his chest at that. *The way she did.* The way she must, or she would not have said those things.

To the world.

Mila did not seem to move, and yet the way she looked at the camera changed. It was as if she was demanding that anyone watching look within themselves and ask, *Is this fair? Is this right?*

And she wasn't finished. "I ask you, who are we as people if we believe every rumor we hear, hold it as fact, and judge each other harshly because of it? I am not certain who among us could stand tall in the face of such an onslaught. I am appalled that anyone should have to. I am deeply saddened that his association with me has apparently opened the floodgates to this sort of shocking behavior on such a widespread scale." She paused for a moment, then leaned slightly closer to the camera. "I have read a great many vile things about both him and myself in these past weeks. For myself, I understand. I am a Queen. I am public property. But a man who smiles at me in a photograph is not."

She did not *say* anything like *You should all be ashamed of yourselves.*

But Caius was sure everyone heard it.

"Furthermore," she said, all stone and ice, "the world will know when and if the day comes that the Queen of Las Sosegadas requests romantic advice from the tabloids. Until then, I will walk in gardens as I please, with whom I please, and will expect my subjects to understand that I, too, have a life to lead. I hope to live it in a manner that will make them proud. But I cannot—I will not—live it to anyone's standards but my own."

For a long time after Mila's face disappeared, Caius couldn't move. He wasn't sure he breathed.

It was entirely possible, in fact, that he was really, truly having a cardiac event.

Or several.

When he ascertained that he was still alive, somehow, he swiped up his phone once more so he could watch that statement over again.

To make certain that he was not hallucinating. That Mila had said what he thought she had.

That she had defended him to her kingdom. To the world.

She had not spoken to him at all since he'd left the September House. She had not had her people chase him down to see if he had somehow released that photo, as he'd thought she would.

There had been no contact between them.

And that meant that Mila didn't know that he'd gone off into the wilderness, or come back a changed man.

"She doesn't know," he said out loud, in the quiet of his room.

She didn't know, and yet she had sat there and told the whole world not only that she would do what she pleased with him, but that he was an excellent choice. That he was a good man. That he was a worthy escort of an honest-to-God *queen*.

Caius felt as if something walloped him, hard.

As if he was a different man all over again because it walloped him so completely. He was surprised he wasn't tossed backward out of the room, across this haunted city, and into the Pacific Ocean.

When he stood at last—when he was *able* to stand—he felt drunk. And wild with it.

This time when he picked up his phone, he barked out more orders. Then he had to check the mirror more than once to see if he was in a proper state before he left the room.

Because he was fairly sure he was somehow wearing that statement on his face.

Caius wasn't sure he thought clearly again until he was in his plane, winging his way toward a tiny little jewel of a country tucked away in the mountains of Europe, and the only woman in his life who had ever defended him.

Not even his sister had done that. Not when her own neck was on the line.

In his family, it was always every man for himself.

The plane landed while it was still dark. Caius had slept very little, preferring to rewatch that video of Mila again and again. This time, he didn't read reactions or comments—because he didn't care.

He cared about what she had said. He kept rewinding, looking for more nuance. Basking in her voice. Wishing that he could have reached through the screen to curve his hand over the elegant line of her neck. To feel the strength in her even as she spoke so softly, yet so resolutely.

Once in Las Sosegadas, he headed directly for the palace, prepared to charm his way in. One way or another.

Or cause a scene.

He wasn't picky.

Caius presented himself at the gates, expecting to be turned away. He was already formulating plans for that—

But it was unnecessary.

They made him wait, but after a while he was let in and ushered through the battlements, until he found himself in the palace's architectural wonder of the forecourt.

Where the woman waiting there, arms crossed, smiled when she saw him.

It took him only a moment.

"Noemí," he said, with genuine pleasure. "It's been a long time."

"Too long," the woman agreed. She still held herself like the guard she'd been pretending not to be when he'd known her. He'd instantly assessed her as someone with martial arts training and perhaps a military background, which was why he'd taken a closer look at Mila. And realized he knew exactly who *she* was.

Then hadn't looked away again.

"I never had a chance to thank you," he said now. "Those were magical days."

"They were," the other woman agreed. "And between you and me, I think we could all do with a little more magic, don't you think?"

Caius found himself grinning ear to ear. "I do," he said. "I really do."

Noemí grinned back, then nodded toward the path that wound around the palace and into the gardens.

"Her Majesty is enjoying an early-morning walk in her maze," she said. "I believe you know the way."

Caius started to walk, but something occurred to him.

He stopped, looking back over his shoulder. "There were no paparazzi here at the Garden Gala. There were only official photographers." The older woman only gazed back at him. "And you are the Minister of Security, are you not?"

"I am."

"I would have thought that you would know of a photograph like that. That you would have seen to it that it did not slip out into the wrong hands."

Noemí smiled. She seemed to take her time with it. "Sometimes," she said after a moment, "magic needs a little help."

With every step he took, Caius couldn't help but feel the portent of it all. Back in the maze but this time, he knew where he was going. Back at the palace but this time, he wasn't pretending to himself that he was here for any reason at all save this one.

It was time to do what was right in the soul he'd always claimed he didn't have, and maybe he hadn't until five years ago. Nor since, as he was fairly certain he'd handed it over into her keeping.

But the good news about that was that he knew exactly where it was.

The maze was a blur of high, imposing hedges and his own impatience. Until, unerringly, he stepped out into the grove at the center the way he had once before.

Though it was changed now.

Summer had turned to fall. The flowering trees were bare. The pool looked cold and uninviting.

But Mila sat there anyway, as the first rays of the dawning sun peeked over the mountains and then tumbled down into the valley, lighting up the maze.

And bathing her in all of that shine.

"You defended me," Caius said.

He watched her go stiff. Then she whirled around and her jaw dropped open. Her gray eyes went wide.

"You're here," she whispered. "You're really here."

"How could I be anywhere else?" he asked. He searched her face, looking for clues. Answers. His own heart. "Why did you defend me, Mila? I thought I was your dirty secret."

And to his surprise, she turned all the way around, and then came to her feet. Or maybe he met her there in the middle. He would never know. It was all a brand-new sunrise and her gaze, wide and gray and fixed to his as if she was drowning and he was safety.

Caius had never managed to be safe for anyone, including himself. But for her, he would do it. He would figure it out.

"I hate myself for making you feel that way," she was saying, and there were no echoes of *the Queen* that he'd watched so many times on his race across the world. This was Mila. This was his Mila. "I hate that I wasn't strong enough to admit what you were to me years ago. I hate that it took all of this, all of this separation and all of these games I was so sure I wasn't playing, to understand what I needed, without question, a long time ago."

They drew closer together, in this secret place that felt like freedom to him. Because it was the first place he'd understood he hadn't lost her. That even if he had, he could find her again.

It was the first place he'd *hoped*.

"There has never been anyone for you but me," Mila

told him. She blew out a breath. "And I don't care how many times you might have sampled those other queens you mentioned, because—"

"I'm a married man," he said, cutting her off. He caught her gaze and held it, because this was what mattered. This was a truth that had nothing to do with masks or charm or any of the smoke and mirrors he knew how to use so well. "I have never broken our vows. There were times I wished I could. But I couldn't. I didn't."

"Caius…"

And the way she said his name was like a song.

Something shifted inside him, then. All those blows he'd taken since that photo was published. All the things that had become so clear to him out there on the trail.

There had only been one path in his life and it had always led here, to her.

"I'm happy enough to be your secret," he told her now. "I don't need you to claim me in front of the world. That you would think to defend my honor is a gift too sweet to bear."

"But bear it you must," she replied. "For it is a gift freely given. And I do not think it is the last of the gifts I will give you."

"I understand who you are," he told her, holding her gaze, because these were vows far more important than the ones they'd made five years ago on a beach. These were the ones that counted, because he understood the two of them better now. "I always did. Of course you had to come back here and do your duty. I know that you always will. And when you have time to sneak away and make omelets in the kitchen with your own regal hands, I'm your man."

To his astonishment, her eyes welled up. Then actually spilled over, tracking tears down her face. "I think I will take you up on that," Mila whispered.

And he found himself smiling, wide and bright. And real. All of this was *real*.

No wonder the joy of it hurt.

She took a breath. "I don't know what you've been doing for the past few weeks—"

"I've been getting myself right," he said. And he took a step closer. "To claim you, Mila. To claim my wife in whatever way she will have me."

And the way she smiled at him made his chest feel as if it was bursting wide open.

"I'm happy to hear that," she said. "Because I intend to claim you, too. And not as some secret affair who has to sneak in and out of tunnels to see me. I'm not doing that again." She leaned in, sliding her hands up his chest and around his neck. "Do you remember when you asked me to marry you?"

"Of course I do. We were muddy and sore and it's one of the best memories of my life."

She was still smiling up at him. "I always expected that I would marry one day, but it was never going to be like that. I was never going to get a surprise proposal, a man suddenly on his knee out of nowhere. It was never going to be based on love, emotion, sex. Any proposal that I could expect to receive would involve half the palace. A vetting committee. There would be many discussions and signatures. So you have already given me the most romantic gift that I could receive."

"I think you need more gifts, My Majesty," he murmured.

"I would like to return that gift."

Mila's damp eyes were fixed to his, and even though he could see the tears on her cheeks, he could also see that core of iron in her. Every inch the Queen.

But also *his*.

She didn't go down on one knee. She held his gaze steadily. "Caius Candriano, would you do me the honor of becoming my king?"

"I accept," he said at once.

"I wasn't finished," Mila told him reprovingly. "Will you be King Caius, my chosen consort? My liege man and protector as long as we may live? Will you help me do my duty, both in and out of the marital bed?"

"Your Majesty," he said, lifting one of her hands to his lips so he could kiss her knuckles, a courtly gesture from another age that seemed to fit this—and them—to perfection. "It would be my very great pleasure."

"And will you promise that you will always find me?" she asked softly. "Because I fear that it's possible that I might get lost again."

"I will always find you," he promised, without hesitation.

"And I will always love you," she told him in return. "Caius, I hope you know, I always have."

And then the Queen Las Sosegadas sank down onto her knees, tipped her head back so she could smile at him in the wicked way he loved most, and proved it.

CHAPTER TWELVE

QUEEN EMILIA OF LAS SOSEGADAS was perfect. Everyone
agreed. And Caius surprised everyone—especially himself—by becoming an excellent King Consort.

If he said so himself.

But he was not required to say so himself, because everyone else said so, too.

Eventually.

There was an initial period of uncertainty, but he
passed that test the way he had every other test in his
life. And this time, he didn't do it by assuming that same
old character. He did it as himself.

He stepped away from his life in Hollywood, because
he didn't need it. Not when he had Mila. Besides, it turned
out that he was far better at setting a scene and creating a
publicity narrative than anyone on any of her crisis teams.
He could do that job in his sleep. He did.

The best part was that all of the narratives they crafted
were true.

In essence.

They divorced in secret so that they could remarry
in style. It was the most lavish affair either one of them
had ever taken part in, and they loved every moment of
it. The bells rang for days. Holidays were called, view-

ing parties were gathered. There were celebrations in the streets, and his mother was not allowed in the country.

"I will accept nothing less," Caius told her.

"I will see to it you don't have to," she replied.

And as the years passed, that was exactly what they did. He piously applied himself to their most important duty and made certain that there was not only an heir, but a great passel of them.

And better yet, he gave his children gifts that he had never had. A sense of place. A sense of purpose.

Because Mila had set him free. And he, in turn, understood that he was her true home.

Together, they made certain the children would grow up balanced between the two. Aware of the duties attendant upon them as members of their family, but still free to make their own choices.

In his spare time, Caius worked on his passion project— a charity that created free cinema opportunities for children all over the world, to help them imagine something better than what they had. To help them wonder. To allow them a little joy when that might have been in short supply.

It took him much longer to win over his mother-in-law, but Caius was a very patient man.

"I always knew that you would adore me, Queen Alondra," he said as they danced at his eldest's wedding. "I've been waiting."

"You are a questionable man," the Queen Mother said with a sniff. But then she smiled, because being a grandmother had mellowed her. Even she and Carliz had found a sweeter side to their relationship. "But you make a good king. Far more important, you're an excellent husband to my daughter. She needs both."

And much later that night, he crawled into bed with his queen, his wife, his love. He told her of his triumph, then pulled her close the way he did as often as possible, because there was nothing better than this.

The bright fire between them. The light that never went out.

The love that only grew with each passing day.

And at least once a season, they went to the September House, just the two of them, to make sure that they were still *them*. To get back to *them* if they'd drifted a little. To see the truth of who they were in each other's eyes.

Some years, that took a minute. Some years, there were conversations to be had, misunderstandings to clear up.

But sooner or later, they ended up on that same rug before that same fire, watching the flames dance and flicker.

And they found their way back to the real beat of their hearts that felt like one heart shared, one kiss at a time.

* * * * *

If you couldn't get enough of
Forbidden Royal Vows
then be sure to check out these other
pulse-racing stories by Caitlin Crews!

A Billion-Dollar Heir for Christmas
Wedding Night in the King's Bed
A Tycoon Too Wild to Wed
Her Venetian Secret
Pregnant Princess Bride

Available now!

COMING SOON!

We really hope you enjoyed reading this book.
If you're looking for more romance
be sure to head to the shops when
new books are available on

Thursday 26th September

To see which titles are coming soon, please visit
millsandboon.co.uk/nextmonth

MILLS & BOON

MILLS & BOON®

Coming next month

ITALIAN BABY SHOCK
Jackie Ashenden

'I'm so sorry,' Lark said quickly as the phone vibrated again. 'But I really need to get this. It's my daughter's nanny.' She bent to pick the phone up off the table, turning as she looked down at it.

He could see the screen over her shoulder. On it was a photo of a baby, a little girl dressed in pink. She had a cloud of soft, rose-gold curls and blue, blue eyes.

It was a singular colour that rose-gold, as was the intense blue of her eyes. He'd never met anyone else who'd had hair that hue apart from his mother. And as for that blue...

That was Donati blue. Two hundred years ago the Donatis had been patrons of a painter who'd created a paint colour in their honor. And that's what he'd called it.

Cesare went very still as everything in him slowed down. Everything except his brain, which was now working overtime. Going back over that night. Going over everything.

Because if there was one thing he knew, it was that the baby in that photo was his daughter.

Continue reading
ITALIAN BABY SHOCK
Jackie Ashenden

Available next month
millsandboon.co.uk

FOUR BRAND NEW STORIES FROM
MILLS & BOON MODERN

The same great stories you love,
a stylish new look!

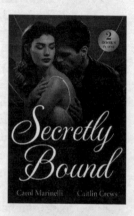

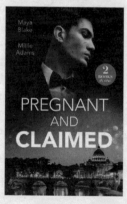

OUT NOW

MILLS & BOON

LET'S TALK
Romance

For exclusive extracts, competitions and special offers, find us online:

f MillsandBoon

X @MillsandBoon

◉ @MillsandBoonUK

♪ @MillsandBoonUK

Get in touch on 01413 063 232

Afterglow Books is a trend-led, trope-filled list of books with diverse, authentic and relatable characters, a wide array of voices and representations, plus real world trials and tribulations. Featuring all the tropes you could possibly want (think small-town settings, fake relationships, grumpy vs sunshine, enemies to lovers) and all with a generous dose of spice in every story.

♪ @millsandboonuk

⊙ @millsandboonuk

afterglowbooks.co.uk

#AfterglowBooks

For all the latest book news, exclusive content and giveaways scan the QR code below to sign up to the Afterglow newsletter:

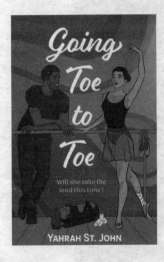

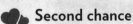
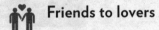
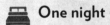

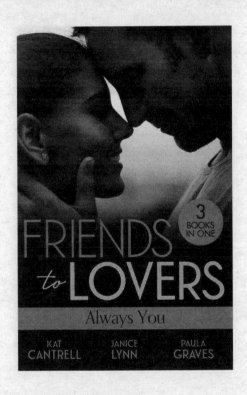